# THE MASK OF APOLLO

# THE
# MASK OF
# APOLLO

## MARY RENAULT

PANTHEON BOOKS

*A Division of Random House*

NEW YORK

δάκρυα μὲν Ἑκάβῃ τε καὶ Ἰλιάδεσσι γυναιξὶ
  Μοῖραι ἐπέκλωσαν δὴ τότε γεινομέναις,
σοὶ δέ, Δίων, ῥέξαντι καλῶν ἐπινίκιον ἔργων
  δαίμονες εὐροίας ἐλπίδας ἐξέχεαν.
κεῖσαι δ' εὐρυχώρῳ ἐν πατρίδι τίμιος ἀστοῖς,
  ὦ ἐμὸν ἐκμήνας θυμὸν ἔρωτι Δίων.


Tears were for Hekabê, friend, and for Ilion's women,
Spun into the dark Web on the day of their birth,
But for you our hopes were great, and great the triumph,
Cancelled alike by the gods at the point of glory.
Now you lie in your own land, now all men honor you—

But I loved you, O Diôn!

PLATO

(Translation by Dudley Fitts)

# THE MASK OF APOLLO

# I

NOT MANY PEOPLE REMEMBER LAMPRIAS NOW IN Athens. But his company is still talked about in the Peloponnese. Ask in Corinth or Epidauros, no one will have heard of him; but down in the Argolid they will go on about his Mad Herakles, or his Agamemnon, as if it were yesterday. I don't know who is working his circuit now.

At all events, he was in Athens when my father died, and owed him more money than anyone else did; but as usual he was nearly broke, and trying to fit a tour out on a handful of beans. So he offered to take me on as an extra; it was the best he could do.

As I suppose everyone knows, my father Artemidoros was an actor before me; the service of Dionysos runs in our blood. Indeed, you could call him a sacrifice to the god. He died of a chill he caught here in Athens, playing second roles in the *Bacchae* of Euripides, which was that year's classical revival. It was one of those bright spring days you get at the Dionysia, warm in the sun but with a cutting wind. He came on first as

King Pentheus, wearing a heavy sleeved costume, red cloth with thick embroidery, also some padding in the chest and shoulders, since like me he was a slender man. I don't know what possessed him to put on under all this his maenad dress for Queen Agave. There is plenty of time after Pentheus' exit; but he was always proud of changing quickly. Of course he sweated; when he changed masks and came on again in this damp thin robe, the sun went in and he got chilled to the bone. One would never have known it. I was on as a Maenad, and thought he was at his best. He was famous for his women's roles, especially the crazy ones, like Agave and Cassandra, or tear-wringers like Niobe.

He had no luck that day, for the leading man, who had played the god, got the actors' prize and gave a party. My father did not like to leave early, in case it was misunderstood, so he stayed drinking till past midnight. The cold went to his chest with a high fever, and on the third night he died.

Though I was nineteen at the time, it was the first death in our own house since I was born. I felt half-dazed, and confused with the noise of the rites, the house all upside down, my father on his bier, feet to the door, my mother and grandmother and sister flinging their arms across him wailing, the small room full of neighbors and actors edging and shouldering in and out to pay respects and hang on the door their black-ribboned locks of hair. I can still feel the pull on my scalp as I stood in a dark corner, hacking at mine with my mother's scissors. It was short already, like every actor's; being fair and fine it seemed to go to nothing, however close I cut. I tugged and hurt myself, my eyes running with the pain, and with grief, and from fear I should not have enough to show up in the grave-wreath.

From time to time the wailing broke off as some new caller spoke his lines. The neighbors left soon—outsiders don't know what to say about an actor—but his fellow artists hung about, for he was always a well-liked man. So indeed they kept saying —how good he was to work with, and always ready to help a friend. (My mother, I thought, would sooner have had the news that he had saved a little.) He never dried, they said, he

] 4 [

could keep going through anything; and they told some tales that made me stare, not having learned yet that anything can happen on tour. What talent he had, they said, poor Artemidoros! A disgrace he was passed over at the Lenaia; no one remembers seeing Polyxena done with more feeling; but the lot fell on some poor judges this year.

I put down my scissors and ran inside, my hair half-shorn like a felon's, leaving my clippings on the towel. As though everyone would not have approved my weeping, I hid like a dog, gulping and choking on my bed. It was not the mourners I was hiding from, but my father on his bier, as silent as an extra, masked in his dead face, waiting for his exit.

I'm not sure how long I had known I had more talent than he had. Two years—no, three; I was sixteen when I saw him as the young Achilles in *The Sacrifice at Aulis*, and I doubt if it came new to me even then. He always moved well, and his hands could say anything. I never heard his voice more charming. He made Achilles a delightful youth, spirited, sincere, with an arrogance too boyish to offend. They could have eaten him up; they hardly noticed his Agamemnon, waiting for him to come back as Achilles. Yes; but the shadow of all that darkness, of that black grief beside the shore, the dreadful war yell whose rage and pain scared all the horses, it is close ahead, his goddess mother knows already. One ought to feel it breathe. It crept in my hair, where he speaks of his slighted honor; I shivered down my backbone. And I heard another player, hardly yet knowing whom.

If he had been self-satisfied, jealous or hard to work with, I should have learned to justify myself. But he had all an artist needs, except the spark from the god. No one knew better than I did what he was like backstage. I had been on with him almost since I could stand alone.

At three, I was Medea's younger son, though I can't remember it; I don't suppose I knew I was on a stage. My father told me later how he had brought home his Medea mask beforehand, in case it frightened me; but I only stuck my fingers through its mouth. It is hard to make actors' children take masks seriously, even the most dreadful; they see them too soon, too near. My mother used to say that at two weeks old, to keep me from the draft, she tucked me inside an old Gorgon, and found me sucking the snakes.

I do remember, though, quite clearly, playing Astyanax to his Andromache. I was turned six by then, for Astyanax has to work. The play was Euripides' *The Women of Troy*. My father told me the plot, and promised I should not really be thrown off the walls, in spite of all the talk about it. We were always acting out such tales as a bedtime game, with mime, or our own words. I loved him dearly. I fought for years to go on thinking him great.

"Don't look at the Herald," he said to me at rehearsal. "You're not supposed to know what he means, though any child would that was right in the head. Take all your cues from me."

He sent me out in front, to see the masks as the audience saw them. Climbing up high, above the seats of honor, I was surprised to find how human they looked, and sad. While I was there he did his part as Cassandra, god-mad with two torches. I knew it by heart, from hearing him practice. It was his best role, everyone agrees. After that he changed masks, ready for Andromache. This is the play where they bring her in from the sacked city on a cart piled up with loot, her child in her arms, just two more pieces of plunder. A wonderful bit of theater. It never fails.

I was still small enough to be used to women's arms; it was odd to feel, under the pleated dress I grasped at, the hard chest of a man, holding each breath and playing it out with the phrases, the rib cage vibrant like the box of a lyre. If one thinks, I suppose most men's sons would die of shame to hear their fathers weep and lament in the voice of a woman. But as he never missed his exercises, I must have heard them from the first day I drew breath: old men, young men, queens and booming tyrants, heroes, maidens and kings. To me it was the right of a man to have seven voices; only women made do with one.

When the day came, I was still aggrieved there was no mask for me, though I had been told again and again children did

THE MASK OF APOLLO

not use them. "Never mind," said my father, "the time will come." Then he pulled his own mask down, the smiling face going into the solemn one. He was in the prologue as Athene.

Outside the parodos the cart was waiting, drawn by four oxen, with the gilded spoils of Troy. At last came the call boy, and my father in the pale mask of the shorn-haired widow. He clambered up, someone hoisted me after, he settled me on his knee, and the oxen started.

Out beyond the tall gateway was the great curve of the theater. I was used to the empty tiers. Now, filled with faces, it seemed vast and unknown, murmuring and dangerous as the sea. My father's voice whispered, "Don't look at the audience. You're scared of strangers. Think how they chopped up your poor old granddad. Lean on me."

This is not how I myself would direct Astyanax. He is Hector's son; I like him alert and bold, thinking no evil till the time. But my father knew his business too. Even the men were sighing as we came slowly on into the orchestra; I could hear the little coos and cries of the women, floating on this deep bass. Suddenly it took hold of me. My father and I, by ourselves, were doing this with fifteen thousand people. We could carry them all to Troy with us, make them see us just as we chose to be. I can taste it still, that first sip of power.

Then I felt their will reach out to me. It was like the lover's touch, which says, Be what I desire. All power has its price. I clung to Andromache my mother and leaned upon her breast; but the hands I answered to were Artemidoros the actor's. As they molded me like wax and sculptured us into one, I knew the many-headed lover had caught him too; I felt it through both our skins. Yet I felt him innocent. He did not sell, but gave freely, love for love.

The Herald came, with the news that I must die. I remembered I was not supposed to heed him; but I thought I should look sorry for my mother's grief, so I reached up and touched the mask's dead hair. At this I heard sighing and sobbing rise like a wave. It was coming from the block where the hetairas sit; they love a good cry more than figs. But it was a few years yet before I knew enough to look for them.

When the Herald bore me off to die, I thought everyone backstage would be there to pay me compliments; but only the wardrobe master's assistant came in a hurry, to strip me naked and paint on my bloody wounds. My father, who had exited soon after me, ran over to pat my bare belly as I lay, and say, "Good boy!" Then he was off; it's a quick change from Andromache to Helen, what with the jewels and so on. It is always a splendid costume, meant to show up against the other captives'. The mask was most delicately painted, and had gold-wreathed hair. He went on, and I heard his new voice, bland and beguiling, answering angry Menelaos.

Soon after came my cue to be brought on, dead. They stretched me out on the shield, and a couple of extras lifted it. The day was warm, but the breeze tickled my skin, and I gave my mind to lying limp as I had been told. The chorus called out the dreadful news to my grannie Hecuba; lying, eyes shut, while the Herald made a long speech about my death, I prayed Dionysos not to let me sneeze. There was a pause which, because I could not see, seemed to last forever. The whole theater had become dead silent, holding its breath. Then a terrible low voice said just beside me:

*"Lay down the circled shield of Hector on the ground."*

I had been well rehearsed for this scene, but not with Hecuba. I had nothing to do but keep still; and this was Kroisos, the leading man. He was then at the peak of his powers, and, fairly enough, did not expect to tutor children. I had seen the mask, and that was all.

I had already heard him, of course, lamenting with Andromache; but that is her scene, and I had my own part to think of. Now, the voice seemed to go all through me, making my backbone creep with cold. I forgot it was I who was being mourned for. Indeed, it was more than I.

No sweetness here, but old pride brought naked to despair, still new to it, a wandering stranger. At the bottom of the pit a new pit opens, and still the mind can feel. Cold hands touched my head. So silent were the tiers above us, I heard clearly, from the pines outside, the murmur of a dove.

I was not seven years old. I think I remember; but no doubt

I have mixed in scraps from all sorts of later renderings, by Theodoros or Philemon or Thettalos; even from my own. I dreamed of it, though, for years, and it is from this I remember certain trifles—such as the embroidery on his robe, which had a border of keys and roses—glimpsed between my eyelids. When I think of these dreams it all comes back to me. Was it Troy I grieved for, or man's mortality; or for my father, in the stillness that was like a wreath of victory on Kroisos' brow? All I remember for certain is my swelling throat, and the horror that came over me when I knew I was going to cry.

My eyes were burning. Terror was added to my grief. I was going to wreck the play. The sponsor would lose the prize; Kroisos, the crown; my father would never get a part again; we would be in the streets begging our bread. And after the play, I would have to face terrible Hecuba without a mask. Tears burst from my shut eyes; my nose was running. I hoped I might die, that the earth would open or the skene catch fire before I sobbed aloud.

The hands that had traced my painted wounds lifted me gently. I was gathered into the arms of Hecuba; the wrinkled mask with its down-turned mouth bent close above. The flute, which had been moaning softly through the speech, getting a cue, wailed louder. Under its sound, Queen Hecuba whispered in my ear, "Be quiet, you little bastard. You're dead."

I felt better at once. All I had been taught came back to me. We had work to do. I slid back limp as his hands released me; neatly, while he washed and shrouded me, he wiped my nose. The scene went through to the end.

> *In vain*
> *we sacrificed. And yet had not the very hand*
> *of God gripped and crushed this city deep in the ground*
> *we should have disappeared in darkness, and not given*
> *a theme for music, and the songs of men to come.*

As the extras carried me off in my royal grave-clothes, I thought to myself, surprised, "*We* are the men to come." As well as everything else, I had been responsible to Astyanax. His shade had been watching from the underworld, hoping I would not make him mean. What burdens I had borne! I felt I had aged a lifetime.

My father, who had been standing behind the prompt-side revolve and seen it all, ran up as they slid me off the shield, asking what had come over me. If it had been my mother, I daresay I should have raised a howl. But I said at once, "Father, I didn't make a noise."

Kroisos came off soon after, pushing up his mask. He was a thin man, all profile, like a god on a coin except that he was bald. When he turned our way I hid behind my father's skirts; but he came towards us, and fished me out by the hair. I came squirming, a disgusting sight, as you may suppose, all smeared with blood-paint and snot. He grinned with big yellow teeth. I saw, amazed, that he was not angry. "By the dog!" he said, "I thought we were finished then." He grimaced like a comedian's slave-mask. "Artemidoros, this boy has feeling, but he also knows what he's about. And what's your name?"

"Niko," I answered. My father said, "Nikeratos." I had seldom heard this used, and felt somehow changed by it. "A good omen," said Kroisos. "Well, who knows?"

Now, while the women wailed over the bier, a dozen such scenes from my childhood up came back to me. My father always got me in as an extra when he could.

Outside came a lull; Phantias the mask-maker had come to condole, bringing a grave-pot painted to order with two masks and Achilles mourning by a tomb. The women, who were getting tired, broke off to talk awhile. I was master of the house, I ought to go out and greet him. I could hear his voice, recalling my father as Polyxena, and turned over again, biting the pillow. I wept because the god we both served had made me choose, and my heart had forsaken him for the god. Yet I had fought the god for him. "What a house today," I would say. "They must have heard the applause at the Kerameikos. That business with the urn would have melted stone. Do you know I saw General Iphikrates crying?" There was always something one could say, and something true. But the great things every artist hopes for, the harsh god closed my mouth upon, and pushed them back down my throat. He missed them; I know he missed them; I saw it sometimes in his eyes. Why not have said them, and left the god to make the best of it? The gods have so much, and men have so little. Gods live forever, too.

I could not lie there like a child. I got up and wiped my face, greeted Phantias, finished cutting my hair for the grave-wreath, and stood at the door to receive people. I was there when Lamprias called.

When he made his offer, my mother, without asking me what I thought, thanked him with tears. Lamprias coughed, and looked at me with apology, knowing what I knew. His great black eyebrows worked up and down, and he glanced away at my father. I too, as I accepted, half looked to see him sit up on his bier and say, "Are you mad, boy?" But he said nothing; what indeed could he have said? I knew I should have to take it. I would do no better, now.

At nineteen, one is good for nothing in the theater but extra work. To get into a company, even as third actor, one must have the range that will let one play not only youths and women but warriors, tyrants and old men. No lad of that age can do it; whereas a good man, who has kept his voice in training and his body supple, can wear juvenile masks till he is fifty, and do everything else as well.

So long as my father lived, I always got work, singing in choruses, carrying a spear, or doing silent stand-ins, when two roles played by one actor overlap, needing an extra to wear the mask and robe for one of them. Lately I had even gotten odd lines here and there, in modern plays where the rule of three is not so strictly kept, and the extra sometimes speaks. Though I knew little else, I knew the theater; and I was not fool enough to think that any more of this would come my way. Any actor good enough to appear in Athens has a son, or a nephew, or a boy friend training for the stage. From now on, I would be like the little orphan in *The Iliad*, who gets no table scraps. "Outside!" say the other boys. "*Your* father is not dining here."

I reckoned I would need three years to make my way, at

the very best, before I got parts in good productions; and even for three months my mother could not keep me idling. We had been left really poor; she would have to sell her weaving, my sister would have to earn her own dower or else marry beneath her. Somehow I must pick up a living at the only trade I knew.

Lamprias was pleased I agreed at once and said nothing to embarrass him. He would be getting something for money he owed outright, when cash down was what we needed. "Good boy, good boy," he said, patting me on the back. "The choice of a real professional, and your father's son. The range will come, we all know that; meantime, you've a head start over most lads I could get. You've lived backstage since you could stand, you know something of everything, from lyre-playing to working the crane. A tour like this will be the making of you. No artist knows himself till he's done a tour."

I did not tell him I had toured only last year, with my father, playing Samos and Miletos as extra in a first-class company, berthing aft and eating with the captain. I would make what was coming no better by putting on airs and being resented. It might have been worse. Boys left like me have had to choose between selling their favors to some actor in return for work, or going right to the bottom: the village fit-ups where, if they don't like you, you can make your supper off the fruit and greenstuff they throw. At least Lamprias' company played in theaters, though only in the little ones.

At sunset they buried my father. There was a very good turnout; it would have pleased him. Philotimos himself showed up, with a tale of some scrape my father had got him out of when he was young and wild. When it was over we went home and lit the lamps, straightened the room, and looked about as people do, not wanting to think what next.

I would be leaving within the month. I went out and walked about; everything looked strange. On my way I passed the door of an old hetaira I had had a night with when I was seventeen, because I was ashamed never to have tried a woman. I could hear her now inside, humming to her lyre. She was always kind to boys. But I owed my father more respect; and all I had really wanted was a little mothering. My first real love affair was still fresh in my heart, though it was three years since. An actor visiting from Syracuse had come for a month, and stayed another for love of me. We had had a beautiful parting, quoting from *The Myrmidons;* a whole year after, he had written to me from Rhodes.

Before we started rehearsals, I was asked to sup at Lamprias' house and meet the company. We lived at Piraeus near the theater; he had lodgings on the waterfront. I walked there anxiously, picking my way over fishy nets and around kegs and bales.

"The scourge of a third-rate tour," my father used to say, "is the second actor. He's the failed one. As a rule he makes everyone pay."

This time he was wrong. Old Demochares had had his taste of honey, and it had kept him sweet. More than once he had worn the victor's ivy crown; he had come down through serving Dionysos all too well in a crown of vine. When I got there he was pretty drunk already; and in the end, to keep him from falling in the harbor, I helped carry him home. He was as jolly in his cups as Pappasilenos, except when we were putting him to bed; then he clasped my hand and cried a little, and quoted *O fair young face, sorrow and death pass by you,* in a voice that still showed some beauty through the fog. As we walked back after, Lamprias coughed, referred to his past triumphs, and gave me to know I would be expected, along with my other duties, to share the common task of getting him on stage sober.

The third actor, Meidias, had gone home already in a pet, if you will believe it, because I, rather than he, had had compliments from an old drunk who could not see straight to walk. My father had been half right; here was the failed man; not six and twenty, yet he had outlived his hopes. Some mocking god had given him a handsome face, the one beauty an actor can do without; it had brought him some success offstage, to which he owed his start, and made him think the world was at his feet. Now he was learning that feet are to stand upon, but did not want to know it. We had barely filled the first cups when he began telling me what splendid roles had been offered him if he had cared to sell his honor. He was as free with great names as some old madam showing the girls her jewels. Though young-looking for my age, I knew enough to guess he had gone through whatever his honor would fetch before he signed on with Lamprias. I fear he saw this in my eye.

Next day we started rehearsals. We had a repertory of two or three modern plays, without chorus, and a couple of classics in case some sponsor hired us for a festival.

Of course we were bypassing Corinth. Corinthians know what is due to them, and throw things if they don't get it. We were opening at Eleusis, then on through Megara and south around the Argolid. When Lamprias went on, as he did every day for both our good, about the fine experience I would be getting, what he meant was that we would hardly see a bit of modern equipment from first to last, or, probably, a sponsor; we would cart along our own costumes, masks and props (stuff bought secondhand after the Dionysia, when richer companies had had their pick), fix up the skene with whatever we found when we got there, and practice making do. Though I never thought I would live to say so, one can make worse beginnings.

It seemed a pity that in the last week of rehearsals I had to knock Meidias down. Even though he took against me from the first, I had tried to get along with him for the sake of peace; but that day he thought fit to quote me a piece of envious bitchery about my father, from one of his fancy-friends. He was bigger than I, but had not troubled, as my father had made me do, to go to a good gymnasium where one learns how to stand and move. One also learns some throw-holds. We had been rehearsing in the Piraeus theater and were walking up the steps between the benches when I hit him and tipped his knee; so he did not fall very soft, and rolled a good way down. Some little boys, who had perched at the top like sparrows to watch us act, were glad to get so much for nothing, and cheered the scene. Luckily he broke no bones, and his face was no one else's business. So Lamprias said nothing. I knew I should be made to pay; but that could not be helped. Little I guessed, though, how far along my life that blow would cast its shadow.

The day of departure came. My mother saw me off by dawn and lamplight, shed a few tears, and warned me against temptations, which she did not name, guessing no doubt that I could have instructed her. I kissed her, shouldered my bundle, and went whistling down the twilit streets where half-wakened birds replied. The shouts of the night-fishers, bringing in their catch, rang far over the gray water. At the meeting-place I found that Lamprias, to show we were a troupe of standing, had hired a handyman for the baggage-cart, asses and mules. This cheered me; I had thought I might have to do that too.

It was a chancy year for touring, he said as we moved off. It was—like most other years. Lately the Thebans had amazed the world by throwing the Spartans first out of their citadel and then out of their city. They had run them clear of Boeotia; we Athenians had beaten them at sea; all over Hellas men stretched, and breathed more deeply. However, with all this, troops were forever marching about the Isthmus; Lamprias said he would be glad to leave it behind. No doubt Megara would be quiet; they are apt there to mind their own business; but in the Peloponnese the cities were working like a pan of yeast, throwing off the dekarchies the Spartans had set over them. We might run into anything.

People are always saying what fine free lives we actors lead, able to cross frontiers and go anywhere. This is true, if it means that hired troops have nothing against us, and others respect the sacred edicts. You are likely enough to get where you are going with a whole skin, and can count there on roof and food at least from your choregos, always provided this sponsor is alive, and not exiled overnight. But for a company working its own way, to arrive is hardly enough, if you find that the men have taken to the hills, the women have battened themselves inside the houses, while a squadron of cavalry has hitched its horses in the orchestra and is chopping up the skene for cook-fires.

However, it was a fine morning. The straits of Salamis glittered against the purple island; remembering my Aischylos, I peopled the water with grinding oars and crashing prows, and rammed galleys spilling gold-turbaned Persians into the sea. Eleusis was just ahead; we would be playing there tomorrow, setting the skene today. I rode my donkey, getting the cart when I could between me and Meidias. Lamprias led on his riding mule; Demochares liked to start the day on the cart, where he could have out his sleep on the bundles and favor his morning head. I looked at him hopefully, planning to ask him if he had ever met Euripides. He looked old enough.

There is nothing really worth telling about the first part of the tour. A hundred artists could tell it for me. I had the hardest bed at the inn with the oldest straw, ran everyone's errands, mended the costumes, put laces in the boots, combed the masks' hair and beards, and daubed on paint when some old skene needed freshening. I did not mind, except when Meidias told people it was what I had been hired for.

He was the gall under my harness—not the fleas in the straw, nor the hard work, nor looking after Demochares. I loved the old soak, even when he drove me mad, and soon learned to manage him. In his heyday, as he let me know, he had been a great amorist; it was some while, I think, since he had taken to a youth whom he trusted not to mock him. Being the ruins of a gentleman, he was never disgusting, even in his drink; more like some old dancer who, hearing the flute, steps through his paces where the neighbors will not see. Self-respect kept him in bounds when sober; after the play, when he started drinking, he had no time for lesser interests. All it came to was that he taught me a great deal, which has been of use to me ever since, and recited me some beautiful epigrams composed by Agathon and Sophokles for youths they courted, with the name changed to mine wherever it would scan.

It was only in the morning, before the play, that he gave me any real trouble. Then he would slip off for a cup to warm him up, and, if I did not watch out, go on and finish the jar. I would run to the wineshop for him, mix in the water on the way, and keep him talking to spin it out. With luck I would have him dressed in time to get my own work done.

"The theater is in your bones," he used to say to me. "You have the open face. Not like that oaf Meidias, who is in love with the mask he happened to be born with, and soon won't have even that, since his fatuous conceit is already marking it. The artist flows into the mask the poet offers him; only so will the god possess him. I have seen you, my dear, when you have not seen yourself. I know."

He spoke to comfort me. No one was kinder, when he could be kind sitting down. I never hoped of him that he would stay sober to fight my battles. He was near sixty, which seemed very old to me; but he still moved like a man who knows he looks distinguished, and behind a mask it was surprising how young he could sound, on a good day. I bore him no grudge for Meidias, who would snigger to strangers in taverns about the old man's darling.

So things were jogging on, till the day we put on Philokles' *Hector*. It calls for Homeric battle dress, showing one's legs to the thigh. Meidias was thin-shanked, had to wear padded tights, and still had knock-knees. He was cast as Paris.

We were playing at a little market town between Corinth and Mykenai. Such places always have the local wit who gives his own performance. Paris exits saying, "What do I care, while Helen shares my bed?" This man yelled out, "She must have got thin, to fit between those knees." It stopped the play for some time, and worse was to come. Meidias was playing the Greek herald too, and Paris, who must be on to hear his challenge, is a stand-in bit. Backstage, Meidias gave me his kilted corselet and his mask as if he wished they were steeped in poison. Sure enough, when I came on this joker cheered, and set the whole house off.

After this they had Paris in a long robe for *Hector*, writing in a line about his unwarlike dress; and Meidias, from plaguing me in spare time, became a serious enemy.

Let us omit the daily chronicle of his devices. Sit down in any wineshop by any theater, and you will hear some actor pour out the ancient tale as if he were the first man it had happened to; but at least the listener has been bought a drink. We will pass by, then, the thorn in the boot, the sewn-up sleeve, the broken mask-string, and so forth. One morning I found a dark sticky splash and a broken wine jar by the seat where Demochares had taken the air. The wine had been neat, and I guessed who had sent it; but that time he reckoned wrong. Demochares might be too easy with himself; but he was not easy enough to let a Meidias make use of him. I think at this time he warned Lamprias we should have trouble. But Lamprias wanted to hear of no more troubles than he had; and he knew about Meidias all that signified, namely, that there was no chance till the tour was over of getting anyone else.

We had an engagement at Phigeleia, a small town near Olympia. This was an important date, because the city had hired us. They were celebrating, on the feast of their founding hero, their liberation too.

This was one of the towns which the Spartans, after they won the Great War against Athens, gave into the power of their oligarchs to keep the people quiet. Here as usual they had chosen their Council of Ten from the worst of the old landowners, who had been exiled by the democrats and had most to gain from holding them down. These Dekarchs had paid off old scores tenfold—done as they chose, helped themselves to any pretty young wife or handsome boy they fancied, or any man's best bit of land. If anyone complained, the Spartans would send a troop there, and when they had done with him he thought he had been well off before. Then came the Theban rising; Pelopidas and the other patriots there had shown the world that Spartans are made of the same stuff as other men; and while the Sons of Herakles were rubbing their heads and running about to see what hit them, the subject cities seized their chance. The Phigeleians had been prompt in this; but as they had begun by rushing with one accord to tear in pieces the most hated Dekarch, the others with their faction had got away to the hills.

The City Council had sent us word of this beforehand, and

asked for a play to suit the feast, no expense spared; some of the Dekarchs' gold had been saved from looting. Lamprias had found just the thing for them—a *Kadmos* by Sophokles the Younger, glorifying Thebes. It was a new, middling piece, which no one has thought worth reviving; Kadmos, punished for killing the War God's dragon, is redeemed from bondage, made king, married to Harmonia, and so on to the finale with wedding procession. For good measure Demochares, who doctored scripts well when his head was clear, had written in some prophecies for Apollo, somehow dragging in Phigeleia. The Council was delighted. We had a week rehearsing with our chorus, who were about as good as you would expect when leading democrats' sons had been chosen first and voices afterwards.

I looked forward myself to this production, because it gave me more to do than usual. I had a few lines as an extra (one of Kadmos' earth-born warriors) and for the whole finale I was standing in for Apollo, since Meidias, who played him, was doing Harmonia as well.

This was the first time I had worn the mask of the god.

Meidias, who sneered at all our costumes to show what he was used to, despised more than anything this Apollo mask. He said it must be all of fifty years old; and in this I found he was right. It was heavy, being carved from olive wood, but no hardship to wear, for it was finished as smooth inside as out, a real craftsman's job. No one makes them to last, nowadays.

I remember the first time I unpacked the hampers, at Eleusis, and saw it looking up at. It gave me a start. It was a face, I thought, more for a temple than a stage. I know I sat back on my heels, among all the litter, looking and looking. Meidias was right in calling it old-fashioned, one must allow him that. No one would say, as they do before a modern Apollo, "Delightful! What a nice young man!"

Demochares, whom I asked about it, said it had been left to Lamprias by some old actor who had thought it brought him luck. It was supposed to have been made for the first revival of Aischylos' *Eumenides,* where the god has a central role. That would be in the great days of Alkibiades and Nikias, when sponsors were sponsors, Demochares said.

Our overnight stop, before Phigeleia, had been at Olympia; I had never been there, and could not stare enough. In fact the place was stone-dead, it not being a Games year; but youth is easily pleased, and I set out with Demochares to see the sights. Like an old horse to its stable, he plodded to his favorite tavern near the river, and, seeing in my eye that I was going to move him on, said in his ripest voice, "Dear boy, you were asking me about the mask of Apollo. It has just come back to me whose workshop it came from, as I was told. Go along to the Temple of Zeus, and you will see. Let me think . . . yes, the west gable."

I gave in, not sorry to get on quicker. Heat filled the wooded valley, for spring comes like summer there. Already the river was shallow in its pebbly bed; the dust was hot to the foot, the painted statues glowed. A tender Hermes, dangling grapes before the baby god he carried, made one want to stroke his russet flesh. Further on were the penalty statues, given as fines by athletes caught cheating; shoddy hack-work done cheap. The giltwork dazzled on the roofs, the white marble glared. The great altar of Zeus, uncleaned since the morning sacrifice, stank and buzzed with flies. But there are always sightseers for the temple. The porch and colonnades were noisy with guides and cheapjacks; peddlers sold copies of Zeus's image in painted clay; quacks cried their cures; kids and rams bleated, on sale for sacrifice; a rusty-voiced rhetor declaimed *The Odyssey* while his boy passed round the plate. I went in from the hot sun to the soft, cool shadows, and gaped with the rest at the great statue inside, the gold and ivory, the throne as big as my room at home, till my eye, traveling upward, met the face of power which says, "O man, make peace with your mortality, for this too is God."

Going out, I had to shake off a low fellow who seemed to think a free supper would be my price, and nearly forgot to look at the west gable. But a guide was herding a gaggle of rich women with their children, nurses, and big straw hats:

I saw him pointing, and talking of the sculptor Pheidias. My eye followed his finger.

The triangle of the gable end was full of the battle between the Greeks and Kentaurs. Theseus and Pirithoos and their men were battling to save the boys and women: men against half-men, wrestling, bashing, trampling, swinging axes; and in the midst, tall and alone, his right arm stretched above the melee, was the Apollo of the mask.

You could not mistake it. But here the mouth was closed, and the face had eyes. I walked back to see better, so lost that I bumped a lady, who scolded me. I scarcely heard. My flesh shivered with delight and awe. Even now sometimes, at Olympia, that shudder will come back to me.

He stands above the battle, needing only to be, not do. The world is still green and raw. He alone knows it is for him the Greeks are fighting; yet some light from him shines back in young Theseus' face. The Greeks must win, because they are nearer his likeness; his prophetic eyes look far beyond. He has no favorites. He is stern, radiant, gracious and without pity. A perfect chord is the friend of him whose strings are tuned to it. Can it pity the kitharist who fumbles?

I walked back doing a speech for him, boyish nonsense in the hack verse any actor can think in. There was no time to finish it, for Demochares had drunk himself silly, and had to be got back while he could still stand. He greeted me as his lovely Hylas, making the other drinkers laugh and cheer; but I was used to that. "Hylas?" I said. "You know what happened to *him.* Herakles let him go sightseeing on his own, and the local nymphs took and drowned him. And Herakles lost his passage in the *Argo.* Heave-ho, shipmate. Come back on board, before the skipper casts off."

But when I unpacked the hampers at Phigeleia, and hung the mask of Apollo on its peg, I plucked a bay-sprig to stick above it, and poured a few drops of wine on the floor below. As I went with my flickering lamp out of the old wooden skeneroom, I half thought as I turned that there were eyes in the eyeholes, watching me off.

] 21 [

On the morning of the performance, long before sunup the audience was pouring in. Every soul who could walk must have been there; indeed, I saw one old granddad carried from his donkey to his seat.

I made sure Demochares took his breakfast watered, buckled him into the panoply of Ares, laid out everyone's things, and tuned my lyre, which I should have to play for the bridal song. Then I got dressed as the Theban Warrior.

Everything went quite smoothly, as far as I remember, until about two-thirds through. Lamprias and Demochares were on stage as Kadmos and Telephassa. Meidias had exited as Harmonia, to do his change for Apollo; presently he would appear and prophesy, on the god-walk above the skene. I was still on as a warrior, with nothing to do but hold a spear.

Standing upstage center by the royal door, I was looking out beyond the theater at the hillside it was carved from. Suddenly I noticed a crowd of men coming down towards it. My first thought was that the citizens of some neighbor town had come to see the play, and got here late. When I saw they all had spears and shields I still did not think much of it, supposing they were going to do a war dance at the festival. Looking back, I find this simplicity hard to credit; but when you work in Athens, you get to thinking the world stops still for a play.

Lamprias went on with his speech; the men got nearer, till suddenly, down in the orchestra, one of the chorus gave a yell and pointed upward. The audience stared, first at him, then where he was pointing. Then chaos began.

The troop above gave the paean, and charged downhill. The Phigeleians, all weaponless, started tearing up the wooden benches and their struts, or running away. The women, who had been sitting in their best on the other side, began to huddle, scramble and scream. One young man, a quick thinker, jumped up on stage from the chorus and snatched my spear from my hand. I hope he got some good from it; it was a property one with a wooden blade. I offered him my shield, which he would need still more, but he was off, with his bearded mask pushed back on top of his head.

I don't know what I would have thought of doing next. But, booming away close by, I heard the voice of Lamprias, still speaking his lines.

Those people who did not say that actors are mostly mad, said afterwards that a god possessed us. But in fact there is more sense in going on at such times than you would suppose. At least everyone knows who and what you are; we would have stood a far better chance of being speared or trampled on if we had bolted than we did by staying on stage. Man's nature asks a reason, say the philosophers, so there I offer one. I doubt if I thought of it at the time. Theater, to me, was still the Dionysia at Athens. I was used to ceremony, respect for the sacred precinct, priests and statesmen and generals in the seats of honor, everything done decently, and the death penalty for violence. This brawling outraged me. We had rehearsed the play especially for this one festival, and I had not done my stand-in as Apollo yet.

The turmoil was getting worse. Here and there men in the audience had jumped up, paused in two minds, and run round outside to join the oligarchs. Some women had clambered over to the men's side to grab their kin and keep them out of it. Now men who had run away at first, not in fear but to fetch their weapons, were coming back armed. But Demochares had come in on cue, and was fluting gravely as Telephassa. He even had an audience—one ancient priest in front, who had noticed nothing amiss, and some children, who it seemed were used to faction fights but had never seen a play.

I had just noticed, startled, that blood was flowing out in front—the first I had ever seen shed in war—when Lamprias ad-libbed something, beckoned me near, and said out of the side of his mask, "Get Apollo on."

I made an exit and ran behind. Before I reached the skene-room I knew what I would find, which of course was nothing. I even looked in the hampers. He must have run off still costumed as Harmonia. His own clothes were there.

The robe and mask of Apollo were where I had put them out. I stripped and scrambled into them, picked up my lyre, and went out to the back. The skeneroom was just a flat-topped shed, with a crazy ladder to the god-walk on its roof. Meidias, but not I, had rehearsed getting up there, holding on with one hand and managing with the other both lyre and skirts. As I floundered up, tearing my sleeve on a nail, I cursed the oligarchs of Phigeleia who had got so rich without spending a drachma on this wretched theater. Down with them, I thought; up with the democrats. Apollo blesses their cause.

As I waited under the entrance ramp for my cue, I ran over all I knew of Apollo's speech from hearing Meidias plowing through it. It was just the thing for the Phigeleians, if anybody listened. I touched the mask for luck, saying, "Help me through this, Apollo, and I'll give you something"; there was no time to think what. Then I swept up the ramp, striking my lyre.

From on top, I could see a proper battle. About half the citizens were now armed, if only with knives or cleavers. There were spears and swords too, serious business. To stand up here, mouthing away unheard, seemed stupid in an actor, and undignified in a god. I raised my arm, in the pose of the Pheidias Apollo, and cried out, "Victory!"

Some women exclaimed and pointed. A few men started to cheer. At once the speech of prophecy went clean out of my head. For a moment I felt like dying. Then—how sent, I leave you to decide as your nature prompts you—there came back to me my own childish voice, declaiming the Messenger from Salamis, in Aischylos' *The Persians*. It was the first long speech my father had made me learn. I slammed a loud chord on the lyre, stepped to the god-walk's edge, and threw it out for all I was worth.

> *Onward, sons of the Greeks! Set free the land of your*
> *    fathers!*
> *Rescue your sons, your wives, and your holy places,*
> *Shrines of ancestral gods, and tombs of those who begot*
> *    you!*
> *To battle! Winner takes all!*

The theater at Phigeleia was short of everything else, but at least it had good acoustics. The cheers came back from right up the hill. Later, I was assured that some of the women thought it really was Apollo; from what I have seen on country tours, it would not much surprise me. The men, if less simple than this, still thought it a lucky omen, believing it was in the play. I heard them calling on the god, as they pushed the oligarchs backward.

The rest of the speech would take the Greek sons to sea, which I feared might spoil it. But I was sure it would disgust my father to think I had dried because of a slight mischance on tour; besides, down below, on stage, Demochares was blowing kisses and saying, "Go on! Go on!" So I took it all as it came, bronze beaks, rammed sterns, shattered cars, corpse-strewn beaches, wallowing keels, wailing upon the waters. I broke off now and then and played Dorian marches, to spin it out.

I forget how far I got before the oligarchs fell back out of sight beyond the hill-ridge. (They ran till they got to Sparta, where they stayed, and got just what they deserved.) So I lost most of my audience, the citizens going in pursuit. Since the play seemed over, I tagged it off from Euripides this time:

> *In vain man's expectation;*
> *God brings the unthought to be,*
> *As here we see.*

Then I came down, and tore my sleeve on the nail again.

The evening's party went on all over Phigeleia. They had a great krater in the Agora the size of a well-head, full of free wine. I left Demochares to enjoy Dionysos' bounty—he had earned it—and wandered off. People kept asking me who had enacted Apollo; a man of towering stature, they mostly said, who had appeared as if from heaven. I had been meant to wear lifted boots, but had not had time to lace them on. It is a fact that you can make an audience see nearly anything, if you yourself believe in it.

I missed Lamprias for some hours, and wondered where he had got to. Later I learned he had spent all that time in the skeneroom, sitting on a hamper-top as patient as the Fates, waiting for Meidias to come back for his clothes.

He had a story ready, how he had seen some citizen being

set upon and rushed to help. This ungrateful fellow never came forward; and Harmonia's wedding dress was ruined, all over muck from a nearby pig-house, where there had not been room to stand.

The City Council begged us to do *Kadmos* again next day, to celebrate the victory. We did so, with much acclaim. When it came time to pay, they said they could not give more than half-fee for the first performance, since we had not finished it. I still laugh when I think of Lamprias' face. For myself, I had no complaints, being cast this time as Apollo and Harmonia, while Meidias stood in for me.

As I was saying, anything can happen on tour. At all events, that is how I got my first chance as third actor.

# I I

BY THE TIME I WAS TWENTY-SIX, I WAS NOT QUITE
unknown in Athens. I had played first roles at Piraeus, and at
the City Theater done second in some winning plays. But they
had had big male roles for the protagonist, and my best ones
had all been women's. It would be easy to get typed, being
my father's son; while anyone casting a great female part
would think first of Theodoros. It was a time which comes to
many artists, when one must break away.

It would take more than applause at Piraeus to get my
name on the City Theater list of leading men. Competition
was deadly; the books were full of old victors who could
hardly count their crowns. But there were still contests in
other cities; it was now I should try to bring home a wreath
or two.

My mother was dead. I had dowered my sister decently and
got her settled; nothing held me in Athens; and I am footloose
by nature, like most men of my calling. For all these reasons,

I went into partnership with Anaxis.

It is a good while now since he took up politics full time. His voice and gestures are much acclaimed; and every rival orator, who wants a stone to throw at him, accuses him of having been an actor. Well, he chose his company, and is welcome to it. But though he might not thank me now for saying so, at the time I am speaking of he was very promising; and I have always thought he gave up too easily.

He was older than I, past thirty, and had a name for touchiness; but one could get on with him if one did not tread on his corns. His family had been rich, but lost everything in the Great War; they never got back their land, and his father worked as a steward. So Anaxis, though he had talent, only wanted to be an artist with half his mind; with the other he wanted to be a gentleman. Any fellow artist will understand me.

He was the only actor I've known to wear a beard. How he bore it under masks I can't think, but even in summer he only trimmed it. He valued the dignity it gave him, and he certainly had presence. But he was growing no younger, and had not got on the list; so he was getting anxious.

Under our contract, we would take turns as directing protagonist. He was fond of the stately parts, like Agamemnon, which meant that even when the choice was his, he would be handing me some first-class acting roles. Always the man of breeding; on other hand, he did live up to it. He might be pompous, but was never sordid or mean, which is worth something, on tour.

We had a booking at Corinth in a brand-new play, Theodektes' *Amazons*. Anaxis, who had the choice of lead, took Theseus, leaving me Hippolyta, which to my mind was the better role. Herakles was done by our third actor, Krantor. He was the best we could afford to hire, a steady old trouper, long past ambition but not gone sour, who stayed in theater because he could have borne no other life. For extra we had a youth called Anthemion, who was Anaxis' boy friend. Anaxis likened him to a statue by Praxiteles. This was true at least of his head, which was solid marble; for the rest he was harmless,

and would do as he was told. I could have improved on this
choice, but had known Anaxis would never stir without him,
so kept quiet rather than have words right at the start.

The Corinth theater is one of the best in Greece. It has
seating for eighteen thousand, and in the top row they can
hear you sigh. The revolves turn smoothly; the reveal runs out
on oiled wheels; you won't find Clytemnestra, brought forth
in the final tableau of the *Agamemnon,* come jerking and
tottering with a couple of bouncing corpses at her feet. The
crane swings you up over the god-walk as if you were really
flying, and puts you down like a feather right on the mark;
it will take a chariot with two life-sized winged horses and
two actors, without a creak.

Our sponsor, who like all Corinthians was so rich that gold
ran out of his ears, had hand-picked a chorus of the loveliest
boys in town to do the Amazons. I spent all my free time with
one of them, a splendid creature, half-Macedonian, gray-eyed
and with dark red hair.

Anaxis was very happy there. In Corinth actors are asked
to the very best houses. So are charioteers and wrestlers,
though I knew better than to point this out to him. What a
pleasure, he used to say, to be among gentlemen, away from
theater talk with its narrow jealousies. Still, theater men do
know what one is doing and what it is worth; even their
jealousy is a kind of praise. For me, I would rather sit drinking with a paid-off soldier from Egypt or Ionia, telling his
tales, or swap advice on inns with some ribbon-seller who
knows the road, than share a supper couch with some rich
fool who thinks that because he owns three chariots his notice
must delight you, who does not know good from bad till the
judges tell him what to think, but who has you in his supper
room like the Persian tapestry and the talking jackdaw and
the Libyan monkey, because you are that year's fashion, and
tells you without fail that he feels it in him to write a tragedy,
if his affairs would only give him time. All you can say for
such a host is that he does hire the best hetairas. I can live
very well without women, on the whole; but any sensible talk
you get at such a party, you get from them. They really know

the tragedies, starting with the texts. One soon learns, at Corinth, where their block is in the theater; everyone plays the subtleties to them.

*The Amazons* is one of Theodektes' better plays, and won the poets' prize. He had ridden over from Athens, and was so pleased with us that he never said a word about the places where I had sharpened up his lines. Our sponsor put on a victory feast, truly Corinthian; it took us all next day to get over it, and I lazed with my gray-eyed Macedonian, in a rocky pine-shaded cove near Perachora. An actor's life is full of meeting and parting; one can't tear one's heart out every time; but I was touched when he gave me a necklet of blue beads to ward off the evil eye. I have it still.

Our next engagement was at Delphi.

Anaxis was full of this prospect. With every year as his hopes in the theater fell, he went further into politics, scouting out the land; and he had got wind of this booking from afar. The reason for a play being put on outside the festivals was to entertain the delegates at a peace conference, a very big affair.

Peace of some sort was overdue; for some years artists had had trouble in getting about at all, what with Spartans marching on Thebes, then Thebans marching on Sparta. Everyone was for Thebes in the early days. But since all her victories, the old neighborly jealousy had waked up in Athens; and we had an alliance with Sparta now. I suppose this was expedient, but it disgusted me; it is things like this which make a man like me leave politics to the demagogues. The one good thing was that those dour-faced bullies needing to ask our help proved they were down to third roles for good and would never play lead again. They had been thought invincible, only because they were in war training from the cradle to the grave; but the Great War went on so long that other Greeks too got this professional experience, though against their will. By the end of it a good many had borne arms since they were boys, and barely knew another calling. So, like actors short of work, they went on tour. There were still nearly as many wars going on as drama festivals, and all of them needed extras.

No sooner had the Spartans been put down than the Arcadians, who had been content till now with fighting here and there for hire, thought to try ruling the roost on their own account. So the Peloponnese was full of smoke and soldiers, just when it had looked like a good season with clear roads.

Most other cities, however, had had enough. Hence this peace conference at Delphi. Anaxis assured me, too, that backstage promoting it were powerful states outside of Hellas altogether. They had learned the worth of good Greek mercenaries, were grieved to see them wasted fighting for their own homes, and wanted them back in the open market.

Anaxis was full of lore about intrigues. I tried to attend, but found it hard. We had come by sea to Itea; now on hired mules we were hauling up the twisted track through the Pleistos valley, following the river in the shade of the olive groves which wind up through the gorge. Sometimes the trees would open wide, and one could glimpse Delphi high above, tiny against the huge flank of Parnassos, shining like a jewel.

It was warm in the olive fields; the sunlight came dappled, and one was never far from the sound of water as the river lapsed towards the sea. Now and again the boughs would stir, and a different air blow from the mountain, cold, bright and pure. It made my nape shiver, as a dog's nose twitches before he knows why. But Anaxis had been as busy as a squirrel in Corinth, getting informed, and did not like to see my eye wandering. Pharaoh of Egypt, he said, and the Great King, would be sending agents for certain.

"Good luck to them," I said. "At least, in peacetime, Greeks can choose whether to fight or stop at home."

Anaxis cleared his throat and looked about; a needless bit of business, since only the mules were in earshot. Anthemion had grown bored, and fallen back to bore Krantor. "They say, too, there will be an envoy—unofficial, of course—from Dionysios of Syracuse."

I slapped my knee, startling my mount, which nearly threw me. These words had waked me up. "By the dog of Egypt! Only envoys? Are you sure? Perhaps he'll come himself; we might even set eyes on him."

Anaxis frowned and clicked his tongue, hearing levity in my voice. We were talking, after all, of the most famous sponsor in the world.

"Of course he will not come. He never leaves home except for war, when he takes his army with him. Thus they cannot be corrupted; and are at hand if treason springs up behind his back in Syracuse. He would not have held power for forty years, in Sicily, if he were not one of the shrewdest men alive. On the other hand, the envoy he sends may well be someone high-ranking at his court, who has been told to look out for talent."

I had read this in his eye before he brought it out. His solemnity tempted me. "Leave me out," I said. "He might want to read us one of his odes, as he did to Philoxenos the poet. He was asked for his opinion, gave it, and got a week in the quarries to mend his taste. Then he was forgiven and asked to supper. When he saw the scrolls coming out again, he clapped his hands for the guard and said, 'Back to the quarry!' "

I must own to have heard this story at my father's knee. Philoxenos had been dining out on it for twenty years, improving it all the time, and I daresay had made it up on the way home, after hailing his host as a second Pindar. But it was too good to waste. "And then," I said, "there was that sophist who keeps that school, the man Dionysios' young kinsman fell in love with and brought to Syracuse, hoping, poor lad, to change the tyrant into a second Solon—how touching young love is! When the poor professor opened his mouth too wide, wasn't he not only chased out of Syracuse, but put on a ship for Aigina when they'd just passed sentence of slavery on any Athenian landing there? And his learned friends had to bid for him at market. I forget his name."

"Plato," said Anaxis, breathing slowly to keep his temper. "Everyone agrees he is a stiff-necked man, who missed his chance for fear of being called a sycophant. He was asked to a party, but wouldn't wear fancy dress; he wouldn't dance—"

"Can he?"

"Nor, when he discoursed, would he avoid political theory—"

"What was he asked to discourse on?"

"Virtue, I suppose. What does it matter? All I am asking is that you keep your eyes open at Delphi, and look what you are doing. Opportunity only knocks once."

"Well," I said, "if Dionysios is as rich as people say, no doubt he can stand his envoy a theater seat. It only costs two obols."

"Niko, dear boy, you know I think the world of you." He was trying hard. "You have a gift; audiences like you; but never think you can't end where *he* is now"—he looked back at Krantor, who had slid off his mule to piss—"if you take no trouble to get known by people of influence. That boy in Corinth! A charming creature for a night, but to spend your days with him! And that party you said you were too tired to go to—do you know Chrysippos owns the biggest racing stables in the Isthmus? Everyone was there. Yet you were not too tired to go round the wineshops with Krantor."

"Krantor knows the best. Everyone was there; why didn't you come too?"

"In a city like Corinth, an artist of your standing should not be seen drinking with a third-part actor. I assure you, such things are not understood at all."

"Thanks for the compliment, my dear. But if I'm too good for that, then by Apollo I'm too good to play in third-rate fustian, even if the Tyrant of Syracuse writes it and puts it on. Let him hire Theophanes, and put him in purple boots; they deserve each other."

I could see Anaxis holding himself in, remembering, as I ought to have been doing, how quarrels ruin a tour. Men can't get away from each other long enough to cool off; I have known it to end in blood.

"Very well, Niko. But an artist should know whether it is art he is talking about, or politics. In this case, I doubt you do."

"Look!" I said, pointing upward. "That must be the Temple of Apollo." I had had politics enough.

"Of course. The theater is just behind it. Tell me, Niko, have you yourself seen one of Dionysios' plays performed?"

"Not I. I've never set foot in Syracuse."

"His *Ajax* won second prize at the Dionysia, in Athens, some years ago."

"*Ajax?* Was that his?" It had been put on of course by an Athenian choregos, acting for him, and one gets wrapped up in one's own play. I had forgotten, if I had known, and own that the news surprised me.

"Yes, it was his. Athenians don't sit through trash without complaining, still less see it crowned. Let us keep things in their places. Dionysios, the ruler, is a despot and the friend of despots. He governs with spies. He plunders temples. He has sold Greek cities to the Carthaginians. He is allied with oligarchs everywhere. He lends troops to the Spartans. To hate him, therefore, is the password of a democrat. In a speech to the Assembly, of course one must say his verse is bathetic and limps in every foot. If one said it is passable, do you think they would debate its structure? They would merely accuse you of wanting the Thirty Tyrants back. But we, after all, are artists and grown men; and nobody is listening."

"Well, that's fair. But would you really act for him, even so? I shouldn't care to play to an audience an orator had been at first, like that one at Olympia."

"My dear Niko! One can see you have been in theater since you were born. That was more than four Olympiads ago. How old were you?"

"About seven—but it seems like yesterday." I had been there when friends of my father's, who had seen it, called with the news. Dionysios had entered some choral odes at the music contest. Not content with hiring first-class talent, he had not known where to stop, but had dressed them as richly as Persian satraps, adding a marquee for the show, of purple rigged with gold cords. It came, I suppose, from his never leaving Sicily. Cultivated people laughed, and all the rest cried "Hubris!" Visiting the Games was Lysias the orator, then an old man but still impressive, who had been at war with oligarchs all his life—not without cause, seeing his brother had been murdered by the Thirty, and he himself barely got away. Seizing his chance, he made a fiery speech against Dionysios and urged the crowd to show what Hellas thought of him. They duly booed off the artists, pulled the pavilion down, and looted it of everything they could carry. At this point of the tale, I drew attention to myself by squealing out with laughter. My father, who never passed a mistake until next time, had fixed the thing in my mind forever by the taking-down he gave me. Olympia, he said, was a sacred festival; if it was unlawful for Lysias to use violence there himself, he should not have done it through other men. And at an art contest, nothing should be judged but art. How would I like to be one of the artists pelted while giving their best work? He hoped I might never find out for myself. After this I had crept away. Even now, I shrank from telling Anaxis.

"He was provincial in those days," Anaxis said. "He is just a clerk's son, after all. But he has bought good advice since then; and he always was a worker."

"I'll read his plays," I said, to keep him quiet. We were getting up towards the shoulder Delphi stands on. The groves were thinning. A pure bright air blew from the peaks. The place smelled of bliss, danger and gods.

"In any case," Anaxis was saying, "one must remember he is a Sicilian ruling Sicilians. The old stock of Corinth has run pretty thin there. Fighting back the Carthaginians all these years, they've learned their ways, and bred with them. It's said Dionysios has a touch of it. The best they could hope for, as they are, would be to change a bad tyrant for a good one."

For a moment the dark-browed face of my boyhood's lover came into my mind, and I wondered if he would still delight me. Then we came out from the trees, and stood upon the shoulder.

Ask some poet to describe the awe of Delphi, and some philosopher to explain it. I work with the words of other men. I looked back down the valley, the olives winding and falling mile on mile to a rock-clipped blink of sea. Beyond a vast gulf of air were the highlands of Mount Korax, cloud-patched with sun and gloom; westward the iron cliffs of Kirphis; above us reared Parnassos, more felt than seen. Its head was hidden by its knees, the rock-towers of the Phaidriades, which themselves seemed to gore the sky. Truly, Apollo is the greatest of all chorus-masters. The town, with his temple in the midst, is tiny as a toy in all this vastness; yet all those titan heads stand around that and look towards it. They are the chorus round his altar; if he raised his arm they would sing a dithyramb. I don't know any other deity who could bring off such a show. At Delphi, you don't ask how they know it is the center of the earth.

I looked up the great steeps of the Phaidriades, which stand behind the theater like a skene reaching to heaven. "Look!" I said. "Eagles!"

"My dear Niko, they are as common here as doves. Do let us get to the inn while they have something left to eat. If this is your first visit, you need not tell the world."

Next morning we looked over the theater. We were pleased to find not a bit of obsolete equipment anywhere; after the big earthquake of five years back, they had had to refit completely. There was still scaffolding round the temple, and the roof a makeshift of pinepoles and thatch; Apollo and the Earth Snake kept up their ancient war. We shouldered back through the town under the tall proud statues, past the treasure houses for the cities' offerings, Anaxis waiting patiently while I tipped the guardians and gaped at all the gold. He squeezed past sightseers and guides and pilgrims, soldiers and priests and slaves, temple-sweepers with brooms and whores with fans; stalls selling lamps, ribbons, raisins, books of oracles, and sacred bayleaves for lucky dreams. Looking up and about, I thought it was like dwarfs playing on a stage designed for titans. I suppose it was still a small, solemn place when Xerxes' army came to lift the gold, and they asked Apollo what to do. "Get out," he said, "I can take care of my own." They still show the rock-peak he hurled down on the Persians, blazing aloft the Phaidriades and yelling through the thunder. I bought, for keepsake, a little gilded bronze of the god drawing his bow. A pretty thing. The old statue in the temple, that is an Apollo to shoot straight. But the shops don't copy it now; they say it is crude, and art must move with the times.

Presently came a slave to meet us, bidding us take wine with our choregos.

We were led to a fine painted house beside the Stadium, and saw at once that our sponsor was a syndicate. Three were Delphians; but by watching whom everyone looked at first, we guessed it was the fourth who was putting up the money. He was one Philiskos, an Asian Greek from Abydos. What with his clothes and his ivory fly-whisk, and Delphi being as full of gossip as a winter hive of bees, we added two and two. This was King Artaxerxes' agent, playing host to the conference with Persian gold.

While sweets and civilities went round, we discussed the play. The citizens of Delphi weren't mentioned from first to last; it was the delegates who must be pleased. It was my turn to direct and choose a role, and I had proposed *Hippolytos with the Garland*. It was as good as settled, when some little man, who I'll swear only wanted to go home saying he had spoken, said it might give offense to the Athenians, by showing King Theseus in the wrong. We both assured them it was revived in Athens about one year in five, and was the surest hit in repertory. Too late; the damage was done, the panic started. At a peace conference, it went without saying that everyone would be looking for slights and insults. *Helen in Egypt* might affront the Pharaoh; *Medea*, the Corinthians; *Alkestis*, the Thessalians. Once or twice I stole a glance at Anaxis, meaning, "Let's leave them at it; before they miss us we'll be in Thebes." But he had set his heart and hopes on this production. When I whispered, under cover of all the dickering, "Try offering them *The Persians!*" he looked down his nose and would not laugh.

From mere boredom I started dreaming, and dreams bring memories. Next time they paused to scratch their heads, I said, "Why not *The Myrmidons?*"

How often, if ever, you have seen this play depends upon where you live. It is a favorite in Thebes and well liked in Macedon. In Athens it is hardly ever revived; no sponsor likes to take the risk. Ever since Aischylos' own day, some people have always disapproved; and you never know when they will get on the judges' board. Demagogues have proclaimed that the love of man for youth is a relic of aristocracy (a politician will say anything, if it strikes where he wants to hit), and the last thing they want to hear is that the play is noble. They would rather those great avowals did not ring on so in the heart.

Today, however, it turned out to be just the thing. Having looked at it backwards, sideways and upside down, they could not find a single slur on anyone's ancestors, gods or city.

We went our way, stuffed full of Persian sweets and almonds, cursing the waste of time but satisfied with the outcome. Anaxis was content with his roles. I, being protagonist, would do Achilles; but Patroklos has some lovely lines, and so has Briseis later. Krantor would do Odysseus and the other odd parts. "And," said Anaxis, "I suppose Apollo in the prologue?"

Walking as we talked, we had come out on top of the theater seats, and were gazing over the temple roof at the mountains. I said, "No, I'll take Apollo myself."

Anaxis raised his brows. "Do you want to? It's a very quick change. Don't forget Apollo is flown on; you'll have the harness to get rid of."

"I've a fancy for it. One's not in Delphi every day. Call it my service to the god."

That evening we were summoned back to meet the chorus-master, the flute-player and the skene-painter. The painter, Hagnon, was an old friend from Athens. Between rehearsals, I stayed to chat with him while he painted trophies-of-arms on the reveal and Greek tents on the flats. From time to time he would shout for his man to bring him ladder or paint, or shift his scaffolding, complaining that the fellow was never at call. He was lanky and spindle-shanked, with a straggling yellow beard; once I caught him staring at me, and it stirred some memory I could not place; but it was clear he would stare at anything rather than work, and I thought no more of it. Hagnon had had to take him on at Delphi, having come to

do murals in a private house and getting this contract afterwards.

Rehearsals went smoothly. The chorus of Myrmidons were
fine well-built men and could sing as well. I found a saddler
to make me a flying-harness. The crane-man weighed me for
the counterweight; finding him skillful, I only did my fly-in
once with him, and rehearsed the prologue from the god-walk.

I enjoyed working on *The Myrmidons*. I had steeped my
soul in it when young, and it still moved me. I have heard
Patroklos better done—Anaxis had technique enough to
sound young, but fell short of charm—still he did bring out
the character's goodness, without which nothing makes sense.

Delphi was filling up every day. Delegates were arriving,
and, as Anaxis told me, all kinds of agents to watch the delegates, sent by the opposition in their various cities, their secret
allies in rival cities, the interested kings and tyrants, and I
don't know whom. I was more amused by the high-priced
hetairas who had come in from other towns and set up house
to the rage of the Delphi girls; they would make a better
audience than all these peace-traders. Leaving Anaxis to
smell about, I went walking on the thymy hillsides or through
the olive groves, hearing for chorus the cicadas and mountain
birds, while I ran over this speech or that. One day Anaxis
came bustling up to say that the envoy of Dionysios had come
at last, and bettered our hopes by being some great personage
and the tyrant's kin. My mind was on the placing of a breath-
pause, and the name went straight out of my head.

At my request, Hagnon was painting the masks for the
principals; the local mask-maker was fit only for chorus work,
but Hagnon worked wonders with his carving, as a good
painter can. He had done me a fine Achilles, and was working
on Patroklos. The Apollo was not yet carved.

Ever since Lamprias died and his widow sold up his things,
I had kept the mask of Pheidias hanging, in a box like a little
shrine, on the wall of my room in Athens. Remembering
Phigeleia, before every contest I would wreathe it and make
some offering. There was no good reason why I should have
brought it with me—one can always find a friend to mind

one's things when touring—yet some reason had seemed good, and it was on the table at my lodging. That evening, when the lamp was lit and the shadows moved with the flame, it seemed to look straight at me with eyes inside its eyeholes, as if to say, "Nikeratos, you have brought me home. Dionysos' winter reign at Delphi is past and gone. Have you not heard my music on Parnassos? I should like to smell skene-paint again."

It gave me a start. I sat down at the pinewood table, chin in hand, as my father had taught me to do before a mask, when one wants to think oneself into it.

"Glorious Apollo," I said presently, "are you sure? Wouldn't you like your face to be more in fashion? You could have anything—a solid-gold wreath, jeweled earrings—it's nothing to the backers here. And they'll be at the dress rehearsal."

A night breeze blew in from the heights of Korax; the lamp flame quivered; Apollo looked at me with dark lidless eyes. "At Phigeleia," he said, "you promised to give me something. Have I asked for anything before?"

In the morning, I took it to the light. The paint was dull and worn, but the carving perfect. Hagnon was in the theater, touching up; I opened the box, and asked him what he thought.

He looked long in silence, frowning and biting his lips. I waited for him to say the usual things: stiff, harsh, primitive. But he looked up as if some pain had griped him, and said, "Oh, God, what was it like when men had certainty like that?"

"God knows, " I said. "I'll wear it and see what comes to me. Can you repaint it?"

"Oh, yes, of course. I can touch it up and tone it down, till from in front you'd hardly tell it from a modern one. Listen, Niko. I'll buy you a new one and paint it free. Just give me this and we're square."

"No, I meant can you do it as it was?"

He lifted it out, turning it in his hand and scratching the paint with his finger. "I can try," he said. "God help me. Leave it with me."

He put it by, and hauled his ladder along the skene. I gave

him a hand, asking where his man had got to. "I turned him out, and good riddance. It's quicker to work alone. Bone-idle, sullen, and drunk half the time. Niko, did you ever hire him?"

"Not I, by the dog."

"When I paid him off, he said he supposed it was your doing."

"Mine? What could he mean? It's true, there was some look about him . . . What is his name?"

"Meidias . . . You do know him, then?"

I told the story. I daresay in those days it would have pleased me to see him now; you would think he had been a seedy, shiftless day-laborer all his life. Maybe I might still have known him without a beard; but I think it was his legs had jogged my memory. Who else would have believed that after all these years, having got where I was, I would stoop to rob him of his wretched pittance? I suppose it was what he would have done himself.

"Well," I thought, "I've looked my last on him now." Which indeed was true.

Next day Hagnon did not come to the theater. Someone said he was shut in his room and would not open; he did not sound sick; he must have company in bed. At evening, he met me in the wineshop. "The paint's not set," he said, "but come and see."

He had propped the mask on a table with a lamp before it. I gazed in silence, while the eyes of Apollo Longsight, full of unplumbed darkness, stared out beyond us. We had served his turn. He had come back to his mountain lair, like a snake in springtime, to have his youth renewed.

My long quiet made Hagnon uneasy. "The room's too small. I should have shown it you in the theater."

I said, "Did you do this, or did he do it himself?"

"I'll tell you what I did. I found it was a day for the oracle; so I sacrificed, and took this with me, and went down to the cave."

I stared. He looked rather shamefaced. "It was just to get the feel. But one must ask something, so I asked which at-

tributes the god's face should show; and the Pythia answered
—quite clearly, I could hear it without the priest interpreting
—'Pythian Apollo.' So I went home and started work."

"Apollo Loxias," I said. Before, rubbed down almost to bare
wood, it had seemed to show only the Olympian, balanced and
clear. But poring in the faded lines of mouth and eye and
nostril, Hagnon had found lost curves and shadows. A shiver
ran down my neck. Here was the double-tongued, whose words
move to their meaning like a serpent in a reed-bed, coil and
countercoil; how can a man tell all his mind to children, or a
god to men?

Presently I asked Hagnon what the Pythia had been like.
He answered, "Like weathered rocks. She had lost her teeth,
and under the drug she dribbled. But the fact is, I didn't look
at her long. In the back of the cave, behind the tripod, is a
crack running into the darkness; and in its mouth is a seven-
foot Apollo cast in gold, with eyes of lapis and agate. It must
go back beyond the Persian Wars; it has that secret smile. I
couldn't take my eyes from it. But I heard what she said."

I sent out for some wine, and tried to make him take the
price of his time; but he said it would be bad luck. Before
we drank, we both tipped our cups before the mask.

I asked him why, if these old forms moved him so, he still
worked in the current style. "Just put me back," he said, "in
the glorious age of Perikles, and dose me with Lethe water,
to unknow what I know. Once men deserved such gods. And
where are they now? They bled to death on battlefields, black
with flies; or starved in the siege, being too good to rob their
neighbors. Or they sailed off to Sicily singing paeans, and left
their bones there in sunken ships, or in the fever swamps or
the slave-quarries. If they got home alive, the Thirty Tyrants
murdered them. Or if they survived all that, they grew old
in dusty corners, mocked by their grandsons, when to speak
of greatness was to be a voice from the dead. They're all gone
now; and here are you and I, who know just what became
of them. What will you do with that mask, Niko, when you
have it on?"

"Well may you ask. At least I'll play in Aischylos, which is what it was made for. Perhaps it will teach me something."

The lamp smoked, and Hagnon trimmed it. As he pricked up the wick, there was a flicker on the face of Loxias, and it seemed that the dark side smiled.

At dress rehearsal, just as I had foreseen, the sponsors asked Hagnon why he had fobbed them off with old stuff repainted. When he showed that he had not charged for it, they said, amazed, that they had ordered everything of the best. This mask lacked grace and charm; it was too severe. Sponsors are sponsors, so I did not ask them what Apollo needs charm for, coming to tell of doom in words like beaten bronze. Instead we said the god had chosen this mask expressly, through the oracle, for his Pythian likeness. That kept them quiet.

When these fools had gone, Gyllis the Theban courtesan—getting on now, but still famous for her verse-readings—came round to kiss us all. She had been in front, and vowed we should make a hit. Mikon the mechanic, who loved his work, asked if I found the crane run smoothly. "I like an artist to feel secure, or he can't do himself justice. Here in Delphi, we never make an old rope do. Twice for a man, once for a chariot, that's my rule. The last play was *Medea*, so you get a new one." I assured him I had not felt safer in my mother's arms; and he scrambled back into his wooden turret with his oil flask and his crock of grease.

That evening it rained, which damped our spirits; but day broke cool and blue, with barely a breeze. When we got to the theater, the upper tiers were full, and the sponsors' servants were fussing about the seats of honor with rugs and cushions. Through the cracks in the skene, it looked like a real occasion. I stripped for my flying-harness, and belted over it Apollo's white, gold-bordered tunic, while my dresser worked the harness ring through the slit.

On my table stood the mask in its open box. From the mask-maker I had bought it a new, fair wig. It was young, strong hair, such as the peasant girls sell when they have to cut it for mourning. The life of the face flowed into it; I pictured it streaming from the head of the furious god, while his arrows clattered at his back with his angry strides, as he came down the crags like nightfall to the plain of Troy. That is the Apollo of *The Myrmidons*—straight from Homer.

I lifted my hands palm upward, asking his favor, and then put on the mask. As the dresser arranged the hair, the flutes and kithara began, and Mikon from his turret signaled "Ready."

I ran out, waving on my way to Anaxis, who was kissing Anthemion for luck, and to Krantor strapping on the corselet of Odysseus. Behind the back of the skeneroom was the hidden platform, with Mikon's boy waiting there to hitch me on the crane-hook. The music rose, to cover the creak of the machine; the rope at my back went taut. I grasped my silver bow, and leaned on the harness in the arc of flight.

Up I soared, out above the skene; the crane-jib, with its traveling screen of painted clouds, lifted and turned upon its pivot. The sea-sound of voices hushed; the play had started. Above the Phaidriades an eagle wheeled and cried, balanced like me upon the air. The jib slewed up and outward, and the music stopped for my speech. It was then I felt, quite close above me, a twang in the rope, and a slight sag down. A strand had parted.

At first I thought it must be just a jolt of the pulley. Mikon was trustworthy and the rope brand-new. I resolved to think no more of it. I was about one-third through, when I felt something go again. No doubt this time. I felt it strain and part; I sagged down a good inch.

> . . . *Zeus' battle-shattering aegis* . . .

I could hear myself going on; while quick as a heartbeat the thought ran through me, "A notched rope—Meidias. Thirty feet down, on stone."

> *When the tawny eagle with his stallion crest*
> *Swoops down, safety is hard to find* . . .

Wise words. It was still coming out of the mask, one line prompting the next. Two strands gone, how many left? The

] 44 [

last taking all my weight could not last long. If I called out
now, they might just get me back in time.

> For I am Phoibos, zenith-cleaving, sun-shafted archer,
> Unforsworn tongue of truth . . .

Brave words. I could hear myself as I spoke them, breaking
off to yell, "Help! Help! Let me down!" and the theater echoing with a belly-laugh that would sound in my ears if I lived
to threescore and ten. And it might be still too late. What a
way to end, bawling like a scared child on a swing; what a
line to be remembered by. The eagle circling the crags gave
a long shrill "Yah!"

I thought of the mask I wore. I had sat so long before it, I
knew its face like my own. I thought of that human bleat
coming out of it. And I thought, "My father would have gone
on."

This had passed in moments. My voice still spoke the lines;
now I put my will to them. The words, the light, the rock-
peaks seen through the mask-holes; the smell of the mask, old
and woody, mixed with new paint; the scoop of the hillside
filled with eyes, struck on my senses clear and brilliant, as
each moment passed which might be the last of my life. A
kind of ecstasy, such as I have heard men can feel in battle,
flowed all through me.

Suddenly the audience had grown restless. There was a
buzz; then someone shouted aloud, "Watch out! The rope!"

It had started in the side seats where they could see behind
the screen. I wished they would keep quiet. I might be dead
before the end of this speech; they could at least attend, not
interrupt with stale news. I lifted my hand palm out, Apollo
commanding stillness, and threw in the first tag I thought of:
"Lord of all gods is Fate!" Then I picked up the speech again.

Dead silence now. Each word dropped into a breathing
stillness. In the harness straps I felt a tremor and strain from
the rope above. The third strand was parting.

It went. The fourth must be the last, I thought; it was giving
already; I was sinking down. Then as the audience groaned
with relief (or else with disappointment) it came to me what

was happening. Mikon had been warned; he was paying out softly, letting me down on stage.

One moment, it seemed, I was dangling from death's forefinger; the next my feet touched ground. It was over. The silence broke then. Here I was right downstage, with nobody to unhitch me, and they expected me to stand there taking bows. I got my hand back and slipped the ring, and made some kind of exit. My last line was about flying back to high Olympos. I had just enough sense left to cut it. With a keyed-up audience, it would have been the very thing for a laugh.

By now it seemed I had been up there by myself for days. It was quite strange to have everyone grabbing me backstage and asking me how I felt. "Later," I said. "Just let me change."

Anaxis rushed up to me, his boyish Patroklos mask shoved back, his beard and eyebrows staring; he had gone quite pale. He pushed a wine cup at me, but after one swallow I put it by; I was afraid of throwing up. "Can you go on?" he asked. "Would you like Anthemion to stand in for you?" I pulled my face straight just in time. "No, thank you. In the name of the gods, get out on stage; nobody's there."

My dresser unharnessed me, and strapped on my panoply for Achilles, clucking and chattering. Mikon came running, the frayed rope in his hands, waving it about. "Later," I said.

Achilles has a good while to sit sulking before he consents to speak, which would give me a rest; but when he does break silence, he has to be worth hearing. My blood was still stirred up, I felt ready for anything; I remember thinking, "This is just how one feels when acting badly." However, when I got to the lines where he chooses glory before length of days, suddenly a burst of applause broke out and stopped the play. I had never thought of that; I think it was the nearest I got to losing my lines.

At last it was over. The noise seemed to last forever. Even after I went to change, I could have taken another call; but of a sudden I felt hollow as an emptied wineskin, sick, and deathly tired. Even the applause seemed empty; it would have been the same for some juggler who had jumped through a ring of knives. I thought with loathing of my performance, which I was sure had been ham all through. Stupidly I stood while my dresser stripped me, trying to be civil to the people who had come behind. Presently Mikon brought his rope again, and showed it round.

"I checked it overnight, every foot." He pushed it under the noses of two sponsors, who had come behind to complain. "Look here, at the cunning of it. The strands were opened, and a hot iron laid inside. With filing it would have frayed, and I'd have seen it as I ran it out. This was done in the night. That drunken loafer, the painter's man—I'm told that he was seen here."

Hagnon said, "I saw him, round about midnight. I thought nothing but that he'd picked up some odd job. Well, I hope they find him. The young men were off on the mountain trails; they reckoned he might have gone up there, to watch it work."

"Maybe." I could not feel concerned. Nearby was the bier of the dead Patroklos; I pushed off the dummy corpse, glad of something to sit on.

Krantor said, "Where's that wine jar?" He poured, and held out a cup to me. I would have swallowed anything; but the rich Samian fragrance told me this must be the best in Delphi. It ran through me like new warm blood.

Anthemion tittered. "It's a gift from some admirer in the audience. It came round before the end of the last chorus; the message just said, 'To honor the protagonist.' But you'll be hearing his name, I'm sure."

I put it down. "You fool! Someone's just tried to break my neck; and now you give me wine from you don't know who." I wondered if I ought to take an emetic. It seemed less trouble to die.

"No, no, Niko." Old Krantor patted my shoulder. "Drink it up, my boy, I saw the slave who brought it. Groomed like a blood-horse; born and bred in good service, that one. It must come from a sponsor." He looked at the two who had come behind; but they coughed and looked elsewhere.

He filled my cup again. The wine, though neat, was so smooth it went down like milk. On an empty stomach—I can never eat before I play—I pretty soon felt the difference. I started floating on air, needing no crane. Everything was golden, everyone kind and good and beautiful. I turned, the cup in my hand, and saw on my table the mask of Apollo, propped in its box. My dresser had plaited the hair and bound it, as I had shown him, in the style of Perikles' day. As the wine lighted me up, it seemed about to utter prophecies. I swayed to my feet before it. It was never I who had made that speech; the mask had spoken, I thought, while I hung like a doll in Apollo's hand. I tilted the cup, and poured him a libation.

"You do well," said a new voice. "Truly, the god must love you."

I turned. The skeneroom crowd had parted, just like extras for a big upstage entrance.

A man stood there who might have stepped straight off a statue plinth in the Street of Victors. Six feet and a hand-breadth tall; dark curly hair, the temples graying, but the face still young; a face of the gravest beauty, austere even to melancholy, yet keen with life. Surely a face of those days Hagnon had talked about, when men deserved their gods. His eyes were dark, and fixed on me.

I don't know, with so much having come between, what I felt then. Only that he had come, as if sent, when I poured the offering.

All this, and the wine, had slowed me down. My answer halted; and Anaxis rushed in, all talk and civilities. The sponsors had come back and were edging up. I saw this was someone to everyone, not just to me.

While Anaxis talked, I had time to look. He was dressed very quietly for a feast day, with the severity almost of a philosopher: a long robe, no tunic under it, the left shoulder bare. There was a great battle scar running half the length of his upper arm. His robe was simple, barely an inch of border. But the wool was fine-combed Milesian; his sandals, stamped Carthage work with gold clasps. This was the plainness of a man who only knows one shop, the best in town.

He spoke upper-class Attic, yet with a touch of Doric somewhere, and some other accent mixed with that, which I had no chance to define; for his answer to Anaxis was so short and formal that the compliments all dried up. Then, with his face still set in this sternness, he looked back at me, and swallowed. I don't know what cleared my eyes; I expect it was the truth of the grape; but I thought at once, "Why, he is shy. But too proud to own it."

I had gazed on him with awe; he seemed from another world. Now, discerning an infirmity which proved him mortal, I began to love him.

I got up from the bier, keeping one hand on it to steady me. I was not much put-out at being drunk; after all, he had sent the wine. He was here in friendship, never, as any fool could see, having set foot backstage before. He must feel all at sea; and I was his host.

"Thank you," I said. "The best drink I ever had, just when I most wanted it. You saved my life, next after Apollo, who stood by me like the gentleman he is. I'll give him a goat tomorrow. And I owe a grave-offering to my father, Artemidoros. Did you ever see him as Cassandra?"

He half-smiled, looking easier, and saying, "Yes, let me think." He put his word to nothing lightly, that was clear. "Yes! It was in *The Troiades,* was it not—not the *Agamemnon?* I was a very young man then, visiting friends at the Academy; but I have never seen it rendered so movingly. If I remember, Hecuba was done by Kroisos."

"Kroisos!" I said. "Then you saw me too. I was the child Astyanax."

He gazed at me intently, and said after a pause, "Then you have always been an actor? All your life?" He seemed surprised; yet it was clear he meant no discourtesy. I told him yes. "Why then," he said, "there are some true words in Euripides, about the many faces of the gods. How does it go?"

I said:

> *The gods wear many faces,*
> *And many fates fulfill*
> *To work their will . . .*

"Was it that you meant?"

He smiled, without stiffness this time, but like a serious boy. "Yes, and now I can complete it:

> *In vain man's expectation;*
> *God brings the unthought to be,*
> *As here we see.*

"Words of good omen, this time."

He paused, and looked about the skeneroom crowd, all breathing down our necks. His smile faded; he said formally, "We must talk more of all this. You will be needing rest now; but won't you sup with me this evening? Come about sunset, or a little before."

"Delighted," I said, more happy than surprised, for I knew we were ordained to meet. "But whose place shall I ask for?"

I could hear the two sponsors cluck and suck their teeth; Anaxis gasped, and started making signs again. But I saw the man was not displeased. It is never bad to be liked for one-self, by anyone.

"I will send my servant for you," he said quietly. "I have rented a house on the bluff at present. My name is Dion, a citizen of Syracuse."

# III

BY EVENING, WHEN IT WAS TIME TO DRESS AND go, I would just as soon have got out of it. I had slept off the shock and the wine, and for what seemed hours had listened cold sober to Anaxis, telling me what to say and still more what not to. For of course my host was the envoy of Dionysios. Perhaps, Anaxis said, he would ask me to give a recital.

"Don't count on it," I said. "He didn't look the man to make a guest sing for his supper." A citizen he had called himself, like any Athenian gentleman. Syracuse, one knew, still kept the ancient forms, but he could as well have said a prince, for it came to that. Such a man, if he is curious and has nothing else to do, may give supper to a touring actor, and will treat him with the breeding he owes himself; but that would be the end of it, as any fool could see. Very likely the place would be full of delegates and politicians, who, when they remembered I was there, would condescend with silly questions. In my heart, I cherished this meeting, sudden and strange like an act of fate; rather than spoil it with banalities, I would sooner we never met again.

It would have been something to dress in peace, without Anaxis fussing like a bride's mother. He even brought a barber to curl my hair. I nearly lost my temper, and asked what kind of monkey he meant to make of me, when my host had seen it that morning, straight as rain. Luckily the barber walked out, saying it was too short to work on. I had trouble to escape from wearing Anthemion's party robe, red with embroidered borders, a love-gift from Anaxis. Like many actors who wear finery enough on stage, I like a rest from it. My spare robe was quite clean, a plain dark blue; one can't keep white fresh on tour. Having got my own way I felt kindly to Anaxis. He would have given his ears for my chance, feared I would wreck all our fortunes with my careless tongue, and yet had not got spiteful. As the time drew near, I would gladly have changed places. Gyllis of Thebes was giving a party in her room, and I was the only one not going.

Presently came the slave and led me to Dion's house, which stood beyond the town, on the spur above the Pleistos valley. The sun was sinking, and Delphi had on its tragic robes. A blood-red light dyed the pale steeps of the Phaidriades, and filled the gorges with cinnabar and purple. From somewhere high up I heard hallooing, as if the maenads were running there. But it was long past time; it must be the young men, still hunting Meidias. They would have some light, for the moon was rising. I thought, "He must be in Thebes by now. Poor wretch, let him go." If he had really lurked somewhere to watch his triumph, I reckoned my score was paid.

The square white house faced outward; its terrace hugged the edge of the bluff; beyond was space and the red sky. It was half dusk; on the terrace a torch in a gilded sconce burned with an upright flame. There were urns of trailing flowers, sweet-scented shrubs between the flagstones, a trellis with a vine. A young boy was singing somewhere to a kithara. The music ceased; my host rose from the shadows and came to meet me, his tall head brushing the vine above.

"Welcome, Nikeratos." On his own ground, not stared at,

he seemed ten years younger. The faded light showed him smiling; he touched my arm to lead me in. "I am glad to see you. We are out here to catch the last of the day. But we will go in when the cold begins." It was a mild evening; I remembered he came from Sicily.

The terrace was paved with colored marbles. The low rush couches had cushions of white linen, whose embroidery looked like Egypt. There was no sign of a party; it was a good thing I had turned down Anthemion's robe. Only one other guest was there, a man of about sixty, gray-bearded, with a heavy brow and deep-set eyes. He was squarely built, but not fleshy with it, in good hard shape for his years, like an old athlete from those days of the gentleman amateur they talk about. There were white battle-scars on his left arm. Hoplites with shields don't get wounded there; he must have been a knight. Indeed, even standing by Dion he still looked quite distinguished. Not a Sicilian—Athens was written all over him. Not a politician—he looked too honest, and was too graceful when Dion presented me. But by accident both spoke at once, so I missed his name, and did not like to ask.

"We saw the play together," Dion said. "Do you know that neither of us had ever seen it performed before? But we had read it . . . of course."

He looked across, smiling. One could not miss it. I suppose *The Myrmidons* is least acted and most read of all great plays. Lovers meet at it, as if it were a shrine like that tomb in Thebes. However long ago that had been, something of it hung about them still.

"Indeed, we have," said the other. I understood this must be a thing the whole world knew about them; there is a certain air which tells one so; but it seemed to me, too, that it had surprised him to see Dion so unbend. As if to hide this, he added, "And then the mind hears an ideal rendering, which reality seldom equals. But you, on the contrary, enriched the play for me. I shall be many times your debtor."

We walked over to the terrace balustrade. The sunset was rusting away, but Delphi seemed still to glow from the light it had drunk before.

"I have been making Dion envious," he went on, "by telling him how I saw you as Alkestis, last year at the Piraeus. The death scene was very fine. Her steadfastness, her loneliness . . . a voice receding, it seemed, with every line, as if already on her journey—that was memorable, far beyond the pathos most actors aim at."

I was pleased, yet for some reason answered, "Who wouldn't be lonely, dying for a wet stick like Admetos? I'm always glad to change masks for Herakles and the drunk scene, even though I do have to play it on three-inch lifts." He made me nervous. I don't think he meant to; some men are used to distance. It had not stopped him from giving me, once, a certain glance which said that if I had been five years younger it might have been a serious matter. I don't think he meant to do that either. He had the nature he was born with, though he might never slip its leash.

I could tell my answer had disappointed him. But Dion smiled. One seldom saw him laugh aloud; but he had a certain smile, with the head thrown back a little, which was a laugh for him. There are men hard to be at ease with, whose walls one breaks by some stroke of chance; this was my good fortune here. And it comes, I thought, through a man who tried to kill me. Somewhere a god is working.

After more talk about the play, we went in to eat. The food was excellent, but simply cooked, and two courses only, not at all the Sicilian banquet of the proverbs. The flowers came in, small yellow roses, and the wine, the same he had sent me at the theater. He had given his best. He was always all or nothing.

A splendid lamp-cluster hung from the ceiling, Etruscan work, a sunburst with outward-soaring nymphs whose arms held up the lampbowls. You don't get such things in a hired house unless you bring them with you. There was nothing in the room which did not serve some use, but what there was, was royal. I found it hard to take my eyes off him long enough for manners. Reclining wreathed on the supper couch, cup in hand, he could have modeled for a vase-painter drawing a feast of gods. His bare arm and shoulder were like fine bronze; he could not make an awkward gesture; the dignity actors train for was bred into his bones. And his face passed the test of motion. Often beauty grows dull or common when speech breaks the mask; but here each change, like a change of light, brought out new quality.

Presently he sent out the slave, saying we would serve our-selves; the krater was set in the middle, the dipper laid on a clean cloth, our couches pulled up nearer. "Now tell us, Nikeratos," he said, "about your escape this morning; and if I am intruding on your mystery, forgive me; for I am a soldier among other things, and I never saw such coolness in the face of death. Were you inspired? Or do you prepare for such things in training?"

He spoke as if to a guest of honor. I paused to think. "Well, no," I said. "After all, a theater is a sacred precinct. It's a crime to strike a man there, let alone shed blood. We don't train for such things, though we do reckon not to be put out easily; I've known a man who fell off the god-walk to change masks and play on with a broken arm. But today, I think . . . You saw the mask of Apollo. It's not a face one would care to make a fool of."

He threw a quick look at his friend, as if to say, "I was right," then turned with his grave eager smile. "Not without cause, then, these words were in my mind: *Do you think I have less divination than the swans? For they, when they know that they must die, having sung all their lives sing louder then than ever, for joy at going home to the god they serve. Men, who themselves fear death, have taken it for lamenta-tion, forgetting no bird sings in hunger, or cold, or pain. But being Apollo's they share his gift of prophecy, and foresee the joys of another world . . .*" He broke off, and said to his friend, "I speak without the book."

"Near enough," he answered, smiling.

"No. I forgot the hoopoe."

I had been listening with all my ears, and could hardly wait to exclaim, "What marvelous lines! Who wrote them? What is the play?"

They looked at each other. I seemed to have made them happy. Dion said, "There is the poet. They are from Plato's dialogue *Phaedo*."

The name amazed me. These were the people whose story I myself had told Anaxis! All those years ago—near twenty it must be—and here they were still meeting. But I had thought this Plato was some kind of sophist.

"The words are mine," he was saying. "The thought was a better man's."

"But the words!" They were still sounding in my head. "Sir, have you more like that? Haven't you ever thought of writing for the theater?"

He raised his brows, as if my little compliment had startled him. At last, however, he said half-smiling, "Not lately."

"Plato!" said Dion. "What is this?"

"Strange to say, in my youth it was my first ambition. I was full of images and fantasies; they had only to knock and I would open; only to ask, and I would feed and clothe them . . . oh, yes, Dion, surely I told you that?" I noticed again his expressive voice, like a low-pitched aulos played by a master. But no volume with it. With that chest of his, he could have overcome it in a month, if I had had the training of him. Forcing would make it thin; it seemed he had learned that and no more. "I assure you it is so," he said. "I once wrote a whole tragedy, and brought it as far as the Theater Bureau, to enter it for the Dionysia. From what I saw at the contest, it might have been considered; I cannot tell. But by chance, as men say who are content with ignorance, I met Sokrates in the porch—the friend, Nikeratos, who brought me to philosophy—who asked to see it, and put some questions, all too much to the purpose. I saw I had a lifetime's work before me, to find the answers I had given so glibly. Everything was there but truth."

"Well, sir," I said, "even Euripides was a beginner once. Truth to nature can't all be learned in the study; it comes half the time from getting out in front to listen. The actors will soon show you if a line speaks badly. From what I've just heard, I should think you've let your friends put you off too easily. Believe me, the theater is crying out for good new tragedies; just look at all these revivals. Why not get it out and go over it, and this time get it read by someone in the business? Would you care to let me see it, and tell you what I think?"

"Why not?" said Dion. "Then I can read it, too."

"I burned it," he said, "as soon as I got home." Seeing my face he smiled—he could be a real charmer when he chose— and said, "My friend, Apollo does not ask us all for the same offering."

Dion filled my cup. The bottom was painted with an Eros playing the lyre, pretty, flowing work, heightened with white, in the style of Italy. "Well, Nikeratos, if Plato has no play to give you, some other friend must step in as best he can. I intended asking you, but was diverted by the pleasure of our talk—"

He broke off short. We all started bolt upright. From the sky, as it seemed, outside, had sounded a scream that stopped my breath. In all my life, I don't think I ever heard a sound so dreadful. As a meteor plunges trailing light, so plunged from some great height above us this shriek of terror, then ceased as if cut with a knife. I put down my cup, which was spilling in my hand. It was Dion who, calling the slave in, said, "What was that?"

The man beamed, like a good-news-bringer sure of his welcome. "Why, sir, that must be the godless fellow they've been hunting since this morning, who tried to pollute the precinct with this gentleman's blood. The young men were saying, before they went up after him, that if they caught him they'd throw him off Aesop's Rock."

The wine went cold in my belly. Dion said, "Aesop's Rock?"

"It's called, sir, they tell me, after some old blasphemer who was sent off from there. It's above those great white cliffs, the Phaidriades. They go all the way down."

"Thank you," said Dion. "You may go." He turned to me. "They have done justice, and avenged you . . . What is it? You look pale."

He is a soldier, I thought. Does he think I should have been up there, lending a hand?

"I was avenged already," I said. "He was an artist once."

I thought of the long hunt, the quarry stumbling and thirsty like a wolf run down; and then they must have dragged him a long way to the place, knowing what he went to.

Both of them were staring. They did not look scornful; but then I was a guest. Dion said, "He tried to take your life; yet you would have spared him?"

"I would have spared him that. After all, here I am, alive and feasting. Do you think me poor-spirited?"

His eyes opened. I have never seen such dark eyes so light a face. "You are surely joking. Poor-spirited, after what we saw today? By Zeus, no! It is greatness of soul that spares the enemy in the dust. Better than vengeance is not to share the evil." He leaned forward glowing like a man in love. I did not fool myself; honor was his darling. My head was not fooled, at least.

"It is an old bad proverb," he said, "that one should outdo one's friends in kindness, and one's enemies in cruelty. No; I have seen . . ." He paused, and turned to Plato: ". . . too much."

Well, I thought, Sicily must be the place for that. How does such a man come out of it?

"Believe me, Nikeratos, as much as for your courage I honor you for taking no joy in vengeance." Being shaken and sick, I could have wept at his kindness; but that he would not have honored. I said something or other, about having enough, in my work, of other men's revenges. I saw Plato stir at this; but after all he kept silent.

"Surely," Dion went on, "to crave revenge is to fall down before one's enemy and eat dust at his feet. What worse can we let him do to us? In hatred as in love, we grow like the thing we brood upon. What we loathe, we graft into our very soul. The man has more profit who beggars himself for a whore. The mind neglected; the soul starved of its true food; condemned at last to some base rebirth, if, as I am persuaded, Pythagoras taught us truly. Who in his senses would give that triumph to the man who wronged him?"

These words impressed me. I had never thought of any of it, and said so, adding, in apology, "I was thinking about this wretched Meidias. All his life he wanted to be somebody, but without having to pay for it, which is always death to an artist. Now this. I couldn't have done it to a dog. But of course you are right about the soul. You have shown me the riches of philosophy."

"Borrowed riches," he said, smiling and catching Plato's eye. "It is the fate of the teacher to hear his words come limping back from the pupil's mouth."

"The pupil," said Plato in that low light voice of his, "who lives what he learned, is a teacher too. A city of such pupils could teach the world." Then, as if he had lapsed from courtesy by speaking of some private thing, he turned to me, saying, "You are clean of this death, having neither willed nor welcomed it. Remember, the man suffered it for sacrilege. It was the god's honor they avenged."

I drank some wine, which I could do with, and held my peace. But I was saying within me, "Is that what you think, wise man? If I had called for help up there, squeaking with fright through Apollo's mouth so that they all laughed and despised me, they would have beaten the cover round the precinct, from duty, and then gone home. But I pleased them; they took trouble for me; this is my wreath of victory. So wise, and you can't see it." They were quoting Pythagoras to each other. I looked at their fine faces full of mind, and thought, "I'm only an actor; the best I do will be gone like smoke when the last graybeard dies who heard it; these are great men whose fame will very likely live forever. But for all they know, they don't know a crowd."

"Your cup is empty," Dion said, dipping into the mixer. "We cannot have you melancholy. Did Achilles grieve for Hector? And here's only a Thersites dead. Which brings me back, Nikeratos, to what I had to say. Would you like to play Achilles again, in another tragedy, at the next Lenaia?"

So it's come, I thought. For a moment I saw Anaxis with

the barber. But in Athens? "I am happy that you thought of me; but I'm not yet on the roll of leading men; and besides, the sponsors draw for them." I had forgotten he was a foreigner. So near, so far.

"Apply again," he said, smiling. "I think friends of mine can manage that. As for the draw, if we miss first turn we may still have the luck to get you, while your name is new on the list."

I saw he knew what he was about. Past victors get chosen first; the draw exists, indeed, to give sponsors a fair chance at them. He was telling me that even if his choregos drew first turn, he would still choose me. The door I had knocked on for years was opening at his finger-touch. I thanked him as best I could. Even now, though, I had been too long in the business not to ask, "What is the play?"

I guessed the answer before I got it. I saw him swallow.

"The title is *Hector's Ransom,* a work by my kinsman Dionysios, the Archon of Syracuse." He would rather not have looked at me, so he gave me a soldier's stare. "As you will know, his work has been presented at Athens in the past, and won the lesser prizes; but, like every poet, he sets his heart on the first." He clapped his hands, and said to his slave, "Mago, bring me the book from my bedside table."

We talked while waiting, I forget of what. I was thinking he had done it well; he knew how to ask like a gentleman. The man being his kin and ruler, he could scarcely beg my pardon. And no one could say he offered a mean reward.

The book came. He said, "Would you like my secretary to come and read it? He is a Tarentine, and reads quite well."

"Thank you," I said, "but it's best to hear oneself. The torch still burns on the terrace; may I go out there?"

He hoped civilly that I would not be cold. I went into the cool garden, fresh with dew, and full of the sounds of a mountain night, trees rustling, a bell-like bird call, goat-clappers tinkling across the gorges. Rivers of moonlight washed the Phaidriades as pure as crystal. The dark foam of the olives flowed to the sea. Vine-shadows crossed the veins of the marble pavement. The torch was burning low, but I hardly needed its light.

I sat down on a couch with the book closed in my hand. In the dappled shadows of the oleander I seemed to see a waiting face. I untied the ribbon from the roll, then paused again. "Loxias," I said, "if there's good here it comes from you. Then I'll play in it, and people can say what they choose. But if it's pretentious bombast, it's not yours, and I won't touch it, not if I have to wait till I'm forty for another chance like this, besides losing the friendship of a man who makes one believe in men. I promise, Loxias. A man hasn't much to give a god in thanks for saving his life; it's the best I have."

I unrolled the book, and read.

To Zeus on the god-walk, enter Thetis grieving for Achilles her doomed mortal son. It sounded quite well, Thetis especially. Nothing much developed, but it would pass in production well enough. Exeunt gods, enter boys' chorus (captive women), the men's chorus (Greeks). Center doors open, Achilles within, discovered mourning, brought out on the reveal. So far, so-so.

Scene for Achilles, lifted from Homer with a touch of Sophokles. If one is going to borrow, by all means use the best. One could do something with it; there was no bathos, at least. I read on; the plot was not badly contrived and had touches of originality, as far as it is possible with such a theme. After a scene for Phoenix and Automedon, chorus, while the actors change masks; then enter Hermes, forerunning Priam. Not a bad speech for third actor. Now for Priam, a chariot entry through the parodos, which always goes well. The chariot stops center, and Priam speaks.

I had been skimming, to get the shape of the play. Now suddenly I was held, and started reading aloud. The old man speaks of his dead son whose corpse he has come to ransom from the victor: first as the hero-king he will never be, then as the child he was. The father recalls his scrapes as a daring lad, and how he beat him. It was a marvelous transition; even I, trained to read with my head, was near to tears. There was an entry for Agamemnon: nonrecognition, cross-talk, irony, the usual thing. The play was just respectable, except for

Priam. Then it breathed, and you could not fault it. The scene with Achilles would have melted bronze.

I was surprised, having heard from everywhere that Dionysios thought pretty poorly of his own son and heir. Here it was, at all events—a part one couldn't miss with.

I went back to the supper room. They broke off their talk; Plato's cool eye told me, in case I had not known, that I had paused in the doorway to make an entrance. "I like this play. It should act well. Did I understand you to have offered me the lead?"

"Certainly," Dion said. "How not?"

"The lead is Priam. Achilles only feeds him."

"Any part you choose, of course." He looked amazed. I might have known the Achilles in his own soul would hide the rest from him. But Plato, whom I had forgotten, said, "He is quite right, Dion. The Priam has some freshness; the Achilles is everywhere derived. I did not tell you so; I doubted I could be just."

In that moment I was as sure as if I had seen it that the tale was true about the slave market at Aigina. Aristophanes, I thought, could have done something good with that. While we discussed the play, I trifled with this thought; but one thought leads to another. This was a proud man if I ever saw one. How he must have loved Dion, if he could love him still. It quenched my laughter.

Presently Dion said, "You will want a good supporting actor. I thought of Hermippos, whom I have never seen give a bad performance."

I ought to have foreseen this. I thought of Anaxis with his fancy cloak and his barber, fussing and nagging, simply because he trusted me not to be making what I could for myself alone—by no means a thing one can take for granted in the theater. Well, I thought, I may not be much in this company, but I'll keep honest at my trade. "I know Hermippos. A sound artist. But my partner is Anaxis, whom you saw today." Our contract was only for the tour; but with laymen one has to simplify.

He looked rather put out. I suppose most people think

theater men live hand to mouth, taking what they can get. "Forgive me," I said, "but we servants of the god have our honor too."

"Say no more," he replied at once. "Your partner is welcome." It was Plato who had looked the more surprised.

But Dion had now started talking about plays, and I saw before long that here was a man who could teach me something. Nothing, as a rule, is more tedious than an amateur ignorant of technique and full of theories; and he was ignorant enough. But what he talked of, he knew. Most of tragedy is concerned with kingship, and the choices it compels men to; and what he said that evening has been of use to me all my life. The theater, after all, can only teach one how; men as they live must show one why.

He knew war and command, what soldiers trust in a leader, how one must be strong before one dares be merciful. His favorite poet, he said, was Sophokles, who wrote about responsibility and moral choice—Antigone and Neoptolemos weighing their own decency and honor, which they knew first-hand, against causes they were asked to take on trust. "A city," he said, "is only a crowd of citizens. If each of them has renounced his private virtue, how can they build a public good?"

"And Euripides?" I asked. "We've said nothing yet of him."

He said at once, "I only like *The Troiades*, which teaches mercy to the conquered, though no one shows it in the play. For the rest, his men and women are the sport of gods who behave worse than human barbarians. What can one learn from that?"

His heat surprised me. "I suppose he shows how things are, and that men have to bear them. He lived in hard times, from all one hears. Hecubas ten a drachma."

Plato said, "He was dead before the worst." It gave me a start, as always when one meets a man who lived it through; to me it was childhood tales. "As it happens," he said, "I know what he wished to teach, though he died when I was still a boy. Sokrates told me. Euripides used to show him his work before he sent it in, because their purpose was the same.

Sokrates told him he would never come at it by the means he used, but he said he was an artist, not a philosopher. They had this in common, that it disgusted both to see the gods debased by crude peasant folk-tales which made them out worse than the worst of men. Sokrates called it blasphemy. For this fools killed him; but they could not kill his truth, because he did not destroy without offering something better. Not so Euripides, a maker of phantoms as all poets are. The truth is one, illusion manifold, and diversity makes a play. He believed it was enough to show these gods of the field and agora as the legends make them—capricious, lustful, lying, outrageous in revenge, careless of honor—and leave the audience to its thoughts. His cure for a leaky roof was to knock the house down. Sokrates taught that since it is inconceivable the gods should be evil, they must be good. But Euripides sent home his audience—and still does—saying, 'If those are the gods, then the gods are not.'"

I thought this over; I could see what he meant. "It's true," I answered, "that if we leave out *The Bacchae*, which is something by itself, he is not so successful with the gods as with humankind. You, sir, will know best whether he meant it so, or couldn't help it. But you will allow, I think, his skill in the second. He was the first to show men and women as they really are."

"Say, rather, he was the first to say they can be satisfied with what they are, and need try to be no better. 'I know,' says his Medea, 'what wickedness I am about to do, but passion is stronger than good counsel.' 'I am helpless,' says Phaedra, before she deceives a just king into killing his innocent son. Men are seldom helpless against their own evil wishes, and in their souls they know it. But common men love flattery not less than tyrants, if anyone will sell it them. If they are told that the struggle for the good is all illusion, that no one need be ashamed to drop his shield and run, that the coward is the natural man, the hero a fable, many will be grateful. But will the city, or mankind, be better?"

Not being a sophist, trained to bring out answers pat, I

could only say, "But it's such marvelous theater."

Plato raised his brows; then he looked down into his wine cup. An audience of twenty thousand, sitting on its hands, could not have produced such an echoing silence. I went hot right up into my hair.

Dion leaned over, and laid his hand on my shoulder. "Plato, I won't have even you scold Nikeratos. Haven't we seen him risk his life only today, rather than that a god should speak unworthily? He was a pattern for us all."

Plato replied at once with something graceful, making amends. I think he even meant it. Though he was certainly not drunk, I daresay the strength of his own thoughts had carried him away. So, though it was time to go, I stayed a little longer to show there was no offense.

When I took my leave, Dion filled my cup to drink to the Good Goddess; then, when I had done so, dried it and put it in my hand. "Please keep this," he said, "to remember the evening by, and in thanks for a performance I shall not soon forget. I wish there had been time to get one painted with Apollo or Achilles, especially for you."

I went out into the sinking moonlight. Fathomless shadows filled the gorges. In the bowl of the wine cup, Eros crowned with white flowers played his lyre. Behind me in the house I heard the voice of Dion, telling his friend whatever could not be said with strangers there. As for me, I knew I had met a man I would gladly die for.

# IV

THE DELPHI PEACE CONFERENCE WAS A PLAY THAT
failed to hit, and won no prizes. Dion put this down to the
delegates not having prayed or sacrificed beforehand. One
would think that being in Delphi they might at least have
consulted the oracle; but I suppose each of them was afraid
of finding himself at the losing end.

"Some of our guests," Dion said when he sent for me to
confirm our contract, "who had seats of honor at the theater,
should have gone to school there. If men with weightier business had shown half your piety, they might have prospered
better." I saw he meant this well; so I did not ask whether a
jobbing treaty, meant to last till everyone goes home and
thinks again, is weightier business than Aischylos, who has
been with us a hundred years and looks good for another
hundred.

Anaxis was in ecstasies, and had scarcely stopped talking
since he got the news. Of course I never told him it was Hermippos whom Dion had wanted. Some actors never miss such

chances; but they hadn't lived with my father. One pays for it later, too; and it's always at the bad time that the bill comes in. He was delighted I had chosen to take Priam; Achilles was just the sort of part in which he saw himself. He was like a cat in a cream bowl.

"No year could be better," he said. "There was never less public feeling against Dionysios in Athens than there is today. If you remember, when he lent us troops in the Theban War he was given the freedom of the city. With any luck, the judges will vote upon the play and not against the author. Have you thought, Niko, that if it wins he is sure to want it put on in Syracuse with the original cast?"

"Spit!" I said. "It's bad luck to price the unborn calf." On this he went through every rite of aversion he could think of. I was afraid of his working himself into such a fever he would forget to act. Poor Anaxis, I could read his mind. He dreamed of getting his father's land back, and setting up as a gentleman.

I would be glad to make money myself. I had enough saved to eat in a bad time, if it didn't last too long, but not the money that lets one hold out for good roles. What took my mind much more, however, was the thought of getting launched in Athens—that, and something beyond. I knew what Anaxis guessed, that if the play won it would go on in Syracuse. Dion had told me. It would mean my seeing him again.

If you ask me what kind of love this was, I asked myself the same. I had known from the first he was unattainable as a god. I was too old for the love of a boy who reveres a man; nor, like a boy, did I wish to emulate. My calling was in my blood. Yet some need in my soul had known him for what it sought.

I walked out alone, the last night I was in Delphi, trying to reason with myself. It was late; the streets were empty; the votive statues looked at me in the moonlight, the bronzes showing the whites of their agate eyes, the painted marbles with a calm, blue gaze. "What do you want, Niko?" they seemed to ask. "Can you even say?"

I had found my way to the theater, and was walking uphill beside it. The crane, that engine of the gods, poked up like a finger against a pale glimmering sky. I climbed higher, and came to a victor's chariot-trophy done in bronze, a car and horses with a tall lad holding the reins, not in action as a sculptor would do it now, all straining muscles and flying drapes, but just quietly standing there in his long robe, waiting for the start. "Here we are," he seemed to say, "I and my horses, trained and ready. We have made ourselves all we can be, but we are mortal. Now it is with the gods."

I thought, Were you real, young hero, or just a sculptor's dream? But it works too the other way. The artist conceives the perfect athlete, the youth creates him. You were real; those big-boned hands and feet persuade me. You brought someone's dream to pass. Homer's? Pindar's? Plato called the poets "makers of phantoms." Yes, but sometimes they take on flesh and come back to say, "Hail, Father." Well, here's one the parent need not blush for. It makes one think.

I thought of Dion. He had caught a dream from Plato, and willed himself to be. A proud creation. Yet I too had dreamed, and many more. How not? When the springs are brack, everyone's mind is on clear water. Look what Athens, and most of Hellas, has seen in our fathers' time and ours. First war; then weakness, tyranny, revolution; then the breaking of the tyranny, and at last the good life could begin. But men's fires burned low; fighting the base with base weapons had shrunk their souls; before one can make the good life, one must remember what it is. There's always one more war to win, or one more election, before the good life; meantime, they wrangle about the good, those who still believe in it. So we dream. Of what? Some man sent by the gods, first to make us believe in something, if only in him, and then to lead us. That is it. We have dreamed a king.

I thought of the delight I had felt while he talked of kingship and its choices over the wine, of justice, mercy and command. I had thought it was because I was learning how kings and heroes should be played. Not so. When I had played kings and heroes, I had been making a likeness of what I wished for, like sailors whistling for a wind; it had been a conjuration. And that which I called had come.

Now I knew my own heart, I felt at peace. It made sense that I should love him just for being; there was nothing he need do for me but be real. Beyond that, I would only ask the gods for a word with him now and then, to prove he still lived and walked the earth. In return I would do for him, if I could, whatever he needed done, like getting a prize for his kinsman's play.

I turned home, lifting my hand in salute to the horse-boy in the chariot. He had worked for it, and so must I.

We left Delphi next day, to go on with our tour. None of the sponsors stood us as much as a drink. They did not care two straws about the theater, but would as soon have provided flute-girls if it pleased the delegates; in fact they did that too, so Gyllis of Thebes told me. However, we were paid in full, which one can't always count on, so they were welcome to keep their wine.

It was a good thing I had told Anaxis that Dion liked his work, for he never got asked up to the house. Of course Dion should have done so if he wanted to get the best from him; I had to cover it with some lie or other. It had been his bad luck to be sober in the skeneroom when I was drunk; he had taken too much trouble, and Dion had written it down as sycophancy. There were people he was helpless with; rather than own it, he took refuge in his rank as in some high acropolis, out of their reach. All his life it made him enemies, and I suppose he must have known it; but he preferred this to showing weakness. That was the man.

When we got home, we put both our names down again for the protagonists' list at Athens. Before long, I heard that my name was on. Anaxis heard nothing, but he had very good roles, and if the play won would stand a better chance next year.

We had done well for money on our tour, between Delphi, Corinth, Thebes and Megalopolis. I could live quite well till winter, when rehearsals for the Lenaia would begin. I went about, treating old friends who had treated me, buying plays for my library, taking exercise at the gymnasium, and so on.

I went most often to the one at the Academy gardens, though
it was a good way from my lodging, just in case Dion, instead
of sailing straight home, might be staying with Plato first.
Though he never appeared, I did not give up hope of him,
knowing he was not a man who liked to be stared at in the
streets.

Plato's school was not far from the gymnasium, behind a
grove of plane trees. One saw his young men, freshly bathed,
oiled and dressed, going off that way after exercise, talking
and laughing, but no horseplay. Sometimes two would stop
by the Eros statue in the grove and offer a handful of flowers
plucked on their way, touching hands, which I found charming. Once or twice when there was laughter I walked near to
learn the joke; but I could never make head or tail of it.

They mostly dressed very well, some richly, though without
ostentation. Those who were plainly dressed wore their clothes
with an air, so one could not say if it was from poverty or
choice.

Among the second sort was a youth I saw often in the garden, though not in the gymnasium. His looks always caught
my eye; he had a boy's smooth chin, but a fine clear profile,
too serious for his age. Meeting him one day in the path, I
took the chance to ask if Dion was a guest there.

"Not now." He had a low pleasing voice, without the rough-
ness of his years. "You've missed him by a month or two. He
left with Plato, for Delphi, and went on home to Syracuse.
Have you come to see him?"

I passed this off, and to cover it asked some questions about
the school. The boy had seemed shy, but this unlocked his
tongue. "It's not a school at all, in the sense you mean. We
meet to work, and think, and discuss, and experiment; and the
younger learn from the elder. From Plato, everyone learns;
but anyone can disagree, if he can make it good. Join us! It
will change your life. It did mine."

Plainly, he took me for a man of leisure. Before one has
become known, one can hang one's mask up and go anywhere,
free as air; nobody knows one's face. Even now I sometimes
miss it.

I said, "I don't suppose I could raise the fee. How much a year?" If he was not too high-born and rich, I was hoping to see more of him.

"Why, nothing. I've never paid one drachma. As Plato says, Sokrates never charged; he said he liked to choose whom he conversed with."

I looked at the painted colonnades, flowers, and well-kept lawns. "But didn't he spend all day in the streets and Agora? One can do that for nothing."

"True. Plato isn't rich, though he has more than Sokrates had; but the school does accept endowments. Only from Academy men; he won't be beholden to outsiders. Dion gave us the new library. But no one, ever, is accepted for what he owns—except *here.*" He tapped his brow. He had gray eyes, with an inner ring as dark as smoke. "Thank you for the pleasure of your conversation; I must go, or I shan't get a good place for Plato's lecture. This is his great one. He only gives it once every few years."

"Well, we may meet again here. What is the lecture?"

"On the Nature of the One," he said, as if surprised at my asking.

When he had gone, I loitered on in the shade of the plane trees. All the young men from the school had gone in; the palaestra gave out a different noise, louder but hollower. The gardens and lawns were empty. I walked nearer. A dolphin fountain murmured softly; the buildings, though newish, seemed to be at home like an old olive tree. There was an open door, with men's backs filling it. It seemed to me that one more would scarcely be noticed, and if Plato charged no fee one could not be defrauding him. I might learn what had made Dion the man he was.

As I got closer, I could hear a voice I recognized. Great God, I thought, these amateurs. Why does he throw it all off the top of his mouth? A beautiful voice, half-wasted. The chest is there; he should be able to fill a theater; even now, if a good professional took him in hand . . . Nobody noticed me in the doorway. I could hear quite well; they could not have kept quieter for Theodoros in *Antigone*. Well, I listened for as long as it takes to sing an opening chorus, and for all I could make out of it, he might as well have been speaking Scythian.

I slipped away, stopping for a last look at the house. There were words carved over the portico, and filled in with gold. But when I went up, all they said was NO ENTRY WITHOUT MATHEMATICS.

The cobbler to his last, I thought. A wasted morning, except for those gray eyes. I went home to my exercises, and *Hector's Ransom,* and took the air nearer home thereafter. It would have been different if the lad had ever shown himself in the gymnasium; but, clearly, he was all for the mind and the Nature of the One. It could only end in grief.

However, one fine autumn day some weeks later, friends called me to come walking, and we found ourselves there. As we crossed the park, one of them nudged me, saying, "Niko, you dog, you said you would go anywhere, but you took care to steer us here. Where do you find such beauties? Don't pretend you don't see him looking. It would serve you right if we didn't go away."

I got rid of them, before he saw what they were laughing at, and went to meet him. He greeted me, and said at once, "I know you now. I remembered as soon as you had gone last time. You are Nikeratos, the tragic actor."

I said yes, feeling pleased, as who would not, that he should have remembered my face from those few moments at the theater when one takes one's bow.

"I saw you," he said, "as Alkestis, at the Piraeus. I've seen the play twice before, but the other two were sniveling and self-pitiful, compared with you. You made the whole transit of the Styx, lying there all alone with the mourners round you. I wept, but as one should, with the soul and not the belly."

There was not a hair on his face; he could hardly be more than fifteen then; his poise and assurance startled me. I said, "Then it's not all mathematics here?"

"Of course not. Why didn't you join us, as I said?"

"My dear boy, though one doesn't pay, one still has to eat. But we can meet again, I hope?"

"You could come and study when you're not working."

" 'No entry without mathematics.' I'd be a white crow in the flock, you know. Will you sup with me this evening?"

"Is it because you are an actor? Plato is not conventional. He paused in thought. "I believe he would even take a woman, if he thought her fit."

"You believe more than I can, then."

"So everyone told me. Yet here I am."

I opened my mouth to speak, and kept it open to gasp. Sure enough one could see under the man's tunic, once one was looking, the shallow curve of breasts.

"I am Axiothea from Phlios. At the Academy, everyone knows. I don't dress like this as a disguise."

I could only stand blinking. If I had known from the first, no doubt I would have disapproved; as it was, I simply felt winded.

"I could see," she said, "it was becoming unkind not to tell you. I hope you are not angry." Her smile, and her frankness, won me over. I could not be cross, perceiving she was the same sort of woman as I was a man. "Friends are friends," I said. "May I take a friend's privilege and ask your age?"

"Nineteen. You thought me precocious." We laughed, and I asked how she had begun all this. She said that when she was fifteen, she had won the girls' race at Olympia. Plato had been there; she had seen him, and heard the Academy spoken of. "But," she said, "I thought of it as one might of driving in the chariot race—splendid, but out of reach. I did the only thing I could—bought his books and read them. So I lived in my father's house, a white crow in the flock, as you said just now, and suitors avoided me, which angered my father." She had been through hard times; he had beaten her, and burned her books when he found them; those that were left, she had had to hide in the rocks and read by stealth. No one had spoken for her except her mother's brother, a man who had studied at Phaedo's school in Elis. But her mother was dead, so no one heeded him. Then suddenly her father died, and this man became her guardian. "Everyone, and I myself, was sure my father had disinherited me. But he had put it off, or changed his mind; and when this became known, suitors sprang up all round, like the Sown Warriors. My uncle, the best of men, not only understood my disgust but shared it. So we talked, and he granted me my wish. He would rather I'd gone to Phaedo; he said Plato was a man of dreams; but, he said, Plato was the likelier one to take me."

She had cropped her hair and worn men's clothes to go to him, because she wanted her mind tested for what it was worth in itself, not as something remarkable in a woman. "But," she said, "having put them on I found they fitted my soul. You, I expect, will understand."

"Yes," I said. "The theater can give one that."

"So I came before him, as it seemed, in my true likeness, which I expect was why he was deceived, if you can call it so; at all events he questioned me, and said I should be welcome. But by then I felt such respect for him, I would no more have lied to him than to a god, so I told him everything. Truly, Nikeratos, he is a great-souled man. He might well have been angry, and thought I had meant to make a fool of him. But he said I had proved his thesis, that women can be taught philosophy if they are given to it by nature, and that I was welcome more than ever. As for my clothes, he said one must be true to the mind before the body."

"And he has really kept to it? He gives you equality with the rest?"

She made a gesture so fierce and eloquent that I noted it in my mind to use at work. "Equality! I hope I need never sink so low. That poppy syrup! Does the soldier ask to be equal with every other? No, to prove himself. The philosopher? No, to know himself. I had rather be least of Plato's school, knowing the good and taking my own measure by it, than run back to Phlios, where I could command what praise I chose. Equality! No, indeed, Plato doesn't so insult me. People whom such things concern you'll find at the schools of rhetoric. They don't come here."

"I'm sorry," I said. "An artist ought to have known better." We sat down on a bank under an olive tree. Once one got used to her, I found her easier to talk to even than easygoing

Gyllis of Thebes. The one could have furnished a regiment
from her lovers; the other had virgin written all over her, but
she was used to men's companionship, friendly without bra-
zenness and self-respecting without defiance. It seemed Plato
had known his business.

After we had talked a while longer, I told her I had met
Dion at Delphi. Her face lit up, and she said, "He is our hope
for all the world!"

I had expected praise of him, but this was a good deal more.
"You look surprised," she said. "Have you read nothing of
Plato's, then, not even *The Republic?*" I confessed that this
was so. "You will find it all," she said. "in Books Four and
Five, where he says mankind will never be free of evil till
some great state comes under the control of a philosopher
trained to kingship. Someone has to begin, before people will
believe it works. He says most polities today are like ships
being steered by a half-blind master. The crew know he's off
course, and plan to mutiny; but if they manage to seize the
helm it will be no better, for none of them can navigate;
they've not learned that such a science exists. If a real pilot
came by and said, 'Steer by Arcturus,' they'd mock him for a
star-struck zany. The philosopher is the pilot. He knows where
the harbor is, and the reef; he knows the constant stars. But
men still pursue illusions. Their prejudice will not be broken
till such a man takes the helm and shows them. Once he has
saved them from the rocks, that will be the end of guesswork.
No man will drown if he sees the remedy, will he?"

She paused for a feed-line, as philosophers do—just like
comic actors, though one must not say so. I answered, "Surely
not."

"So, then, when Dion gets his ship, a new age will begin."

"What?" I said startled. "Is Dion planning revolt then?"

"No, how could you think such a thing? He is a friend of
Plato's. Plato has always taught that violence and treachery
can beget nothing better than themselves. This was also the
teaching of Pythagoras, the wisest of men."

"Then what does he hope for? It's true, he is like a man the
gods made for kingship. But Dionysios has an heir."

"One he despises."

"Blood is blood, when the last push comes."

"Sometimes pride talks louder. Dionysios didn't build up the Syracusan power to bequeath it to the Carthaginians at his death."

"Is that what he thinks of his son?"

"So everyone says. He has scared him since his childhood; now he despises him for a coward."

"Is he really one?"

"Maybe. Maybe he just wants to keep alive the best way he can. Old Dionysios is brave enough in war; but he sees an assassin behind every chair. Did you know that even his own family can't come in to see him till they've been searched down to the skin? Almost since his childhood, young Dionysios, the son, has lived in dread that his father may suspect him of some usurping plot, and decide to make away with him. He can't be made to touch any sort of public business; he'll scarcely offer a sacrifice at the Games, or dedicate a fountain house."

"Well, you can't kill the cow and milk it too. What did his father expect?"

"Who knows what an untrained mind will think? One thing is certain; he trusts Dion further than any other man alive. He is even let off the searching, because the tyrant knows him for what he is—incapable of treachery. He is kin by marriage, not by blood; he comes of the old nobility, while Dionysios is a nobody; he is an envoy other states respect and will do business with, when they'd not trust Dionysios across the street; a soldier proved in battle, whom his men would follow anywhere. He has not always even carried out his orders; where he was sent to strike terror and make examples, he has done justice and won respect. Yet the heir is searched, while he is not."

"I can believe all that. But only a philosopher, surely, would pass his own blood over and choose an heir for virtue."

"Oh, yes. We don't expect it. But Dionysios has two sons by his other wife, Dion's sister. They're young yet, but he has helped bring them up; the elder thinks the world of him.

Dionysios might decide to name him heir; and then Dion would have the chance he needs. It's not the show and pride of power he wants—only to change a city ruled by men to one ruled by laws." I could tell, by the way she spoke these last words, that she was quoting, I suppose from Plato.

"Which laws?" I asked. "Athenian?"

"Oh, Nikeratos, how can we talk till you've read *The Republic*? Listen. Wait here. I'll see if it's free in the library. You'll take good care of it? If it gets lost, I couldn't afford to pay a copyist; I'd have to do it from the wax myself, and it would take a year."

"Is it so long?" I asked, alarmed. But then I thought of Dion and said, "Yes, I'll keep it safe."

She was gone some time; at last I saw her hurrying through the trees, the dark curls ruffled on her brow. Certainly she had made her confession none too soon; I wondered if Plato had felt the same.

"I am sorry," she said, "it's out. And then Speusippos, Plato's nephew, kept me talking. But I've brought you this. It's quite short, and of course you will like it better. I should have thought of it at first."

There was only one roll, not thick. I thanked her, perhaps too gratefully. "Is this about law too?"

"No; love."

"I shall surely like it. Tomorrow I'll meet you here to return it, at about this time."

"I will be here. Do you know, you are the first man to be my friend who has not been a philosopher? The rest have thought me a monster."

"That would come ill from an actor. When I put on a woman's mask I am a woman; I could do nothing if I were not. There are two natures in most of us who serve the god."

"You will like this book. I'm glad I chose it."

"And I that we met." And there was more in this than civility.

I had meant to meet friends that evening; but it being too early, I untied the book and looked into it. It was called *The Drinking Party*, a cheerful start at least; and my interest quickened when I found it was supposed to take place at the house of Agathon the Tragedian after his first winning play. I had acted in his *Antaeus,* a charming piece, and the beginning of modern theater, for he got rid of the chorus from the action and enabled us to have plots which don't assume the presence of fifty onlookers. Though to my disappointment there was no account of the production, the dialogue held me, and I kept reading. Presently they started a party game, a round of speeches in praise of love. The next thing I knew, it was getting too dark to see. I lit the lamp, and went back to the book, and did not move till it was done.

As one finds later, the early speeches are only supposed to show the bottom of love's ascent. But it was the dream of my boyhood, the knightly bond of Aristogeiton and Harmodios, Achilles and Patroklos, Pylades and Orestes. I remembered how I had lived it with my first lover, the Syracusan actor. He had worn the hero's mask for me, not in deceit, but, as I had long since understood, at my demand. Poor man, he would far sooner have had a listener for his little troubles—the rival who topped his lines or spoiled his big scene with bits of business, the tour that went broke in the wilds of Thessaly. I looked back at his kindness gratefully; he had been tender with my illusions; I had been lucky, as it mostly goes today. I had long since ceased to believe that the reality existed. Now I knew that it did, though not for me.

Plato and Dion had known it. I had seen proof. Twenty years after that torch was kindled, with all the heat burned out of it, it still gave light. It was bitter to me, though I had hoped nothing for myself; such is man's nature. However, words and their sound being in my blood, I could not cease to read. I was like someone who, hearing a lyre upon the mountain, must follow it over rocks and thorns. The man wrote like a god. Now he is dead, people begin to say his mother conceived by Apollo. Well, he was mortal. I met him; I know. But I can understand the story.

Aside from all this, it was splendid theater. One itched to put it on a stage. Alkibiades was a bravura role I would have given my ears for. Sokrates seemed to fall between tragedy and comedy (the modern writers are just starting to explore this ground), but the character arrested me, since I knew him mostly from the lampoon in *The Clouds*. If he was really such a man as Plato makes him, then his death was murder, and Aristophanes' hands are far from clean. This set me thinking that it was not wonderful if Plato had no time for dramatists, nor much for actors.

When I gave the book back to Axiothea I asked her if this was so. Though it was long before her time, she had heard the tradition of the school: that at Sokrates' trial Plato had got up to speak for the defense, which, considering the temper of the court and of the government, must have put him in great danger. He had opened with, "Gentlemen, though I am the youngest who ever stood up before you—" planning to say he spoke for the young men Sokrates was accused of having corrupted. But the dikasts all bawled out, "Sit down!" and, being an amateur, he could not make himself heard. I suppose it was hardly surprising that he never got over this; but, as I told Axiothea, it was a real loss to the theater. There was no doubt he had it in him.

I met her often in the park, because I liked her company, and for the sake of what she could tell me about Dion. Not having lost hope of bringing me to philosophy, she introduced me to her friends, one of whom was Speusippos, Plato's nephew. He was an elegant young man, spare and wiry, with a face like a handsome monkey's, who usually looked as if he had been up late, sometimes at his books, but sometimes not. In spite of this he missed nothing; Axiothea said he was one of their most brilliant men. He certainly had charming manners, and, though he knew every play worth hearing, always asked my opinion first.

On the other hand there was Xenokrates, a lean fellow with an untrimmed beard and dirty nails, who never moved any of his face but his mouth to talk, so that I often felt like telling him he could buy a better mask for ten drachmas. As coolly as if I had been a deaf post, he maintained to the company that it was casting nets for the wind to try and philosophize an actor, a man, he said, who lent himself to every passion, not to learn the mastery of pain and pleasure, but rather

to display their worst excesses for the applause of the ignorant. As well expound chastity in a brothel. No one rebuked
him for his rudeness; it was their custom that any proposi-
tion must be debated before it was condemned. Perceiving
this, I kept my temper; the discussion lasted some time, but
Speusippos took my side, and was agreed to have won the day.

They often talked about Dion without any prompting from
me. They believed (getting it from Sokrates) that a memory
of justice is born in man; and Dion was their favorite illus-
tration.

His father, Hipparinos, had come of the highest blood in
Syracuse, and had always spent like a king. What with race
horses, palace-building and banquets, he was nearly broke
when he backed Dionysios' rise to power, and got his stake
back fivefold. Dionysios must have liked the man as well as
valuing him, for he bound their families as close as law allowed, marrying Hipparinos' sister, Dion's aunt, and, when she
bore a daughter, betrothing the girl to Dion, whom he treated
almost as a son.

Sicily, however, is not Greece, whatever the Greeks there
tell you. Dionysios, a king in all but name, indulged a king's
whim and took two wives. Aristomache, the sister of Dion's
father, was for friendship and support at home, Doris of Lokri
for foreign policy. It might have set the kindred at each other's
throats if he had not been a resourceful man. He avoided dis-
putes about precedence by marrying them both the same day;
what's more, he lay with them both that night, and no one
was allowed to see which door he entered first.

It was Doris of Lokri who first bore a son; this was not, it
would seem, what he had hoped, for after some time, Aristomache still not conceiving, he had Doris's mother put to death
for casting a barren spell on her. (As I was saying, Hellas
stops at the straits.) Doris' son was a growing lad when Aristomache's first son was born.

Meantime, young Dion was growing up, all the gods' darling: as free of the Archon's house as of his own; so rich he
need never ask what anything cost; ranking like a king's
nephew, or rather higher; and with the looks of some youth

on a frieze by Pheidias. Courted both for his favor and his person, in that most dissolute of cities, he managed to keep his honor. It left its mark on him; though not vain, he learned aloofness in self-defense, and people called him proud. At sixteen he escaped, with relief, to war. The gods had stinted him of nothing; he was brave as well. Campaigning in Italy, he found time to study with the Pythagoreans. At twenty, with his brilliant youth dawning into a manhood not less splendid, he received news that Plato was their guest. He dashed at once across the straits to offer homage.

By now I had read one or two of Plato's dialogues, written some time before this happened. There is nearly always, somewhere, a glorious youth, Lysis or Alkibiades or Charmides, as athletic in mind as body, who neglects his jostling suitors to alight by Sokrates, asks all the right questions, modest but keen, and goes off all radiant from the play of minds, sure to return. Here was the dream come true. I could imagine how Plato felt.

Before long they were in Sicily, climbing Mount Etna to view the craters. The pure form of the distant mountain, floating in ether, white as foam; the climb above the orchards among fierce shapes of black lava; the snows bathed in light sighing out dragon's breath; the fire-fuming stithy plunging unfathomed from the skies to the core of earth—nothing less, I daresay, seemed worthy of the elements released within them.

Meantime, Dion had sent word to Syracuse; and Dionysios, who loved to think his court a Helikon of muses, sent the expected summons.

Young Dion was enraptured. Love and philosophy had opened his eyes; he saw all was not well in Syracuse where things had gone so well for him. But he had learned too that man only sins from ignorance. He must love the good, once seen. And—how not?—everyone must love Plato.

As I heard this tale in the Academy olive grove, I must say I felt for the man. He had been brought up to politics; lived, in forty years, through the bitter end of war and three kinds of misgovernment at home; had seen his own kinsmen, earnest reformers, turn to ruthless despots once they had seized power; had had to beg Sokrates' life from them; then, having cut himself off from half his family and given up his career, he had been forced to watch, helpless, while his friend who had defied the tyranny with unflinching courage was murdered by the democrats under form of law. Now here was the beloved youth, who believed in him like a god, inviting him to bring the good life to Syracuse. What could he do?

I was told in full, by my friends at the Academy, what Plato and Dionysios said to each other. Even philosophers are human, and I never knew a man, repeating a set-to he had had with anyone, who did not improve it here and there; however, I believe most of it. Plato's manners were superb and he must have begun with courtesy. But having lived under the Thirty, he could not miss the smell of tyranny where it sweated from the very walls. Meantime, he was made much of. In due course he was asked to do his act, and speak on the Good Life.

I don't know if Dionysios expected to be used as an exemplar; in Sicily it would not surprise me. It turned out that Plato's good life was that of just men in a just city, whose governors were chosen for merit without regard to rank, and trained up in temperance and virtue. He had been by now to one or two Sicilian banquets, where guests stuffed with food and soaked in drink finish up with an orgy on the supper couches; this, he made pretty clear, was how not to make life good. He quoted Pythagoras upon Circe's swine.

Dionysios was not broken-in to free Athenian speech. He lost his head and his temper. Plato was as used to respect as Dionysios was to flattery; there were high words. Dionysios was furious; perhaps he was jealous, too, of Dion's new allegiance. He lost the argument, but planned to have the last word.

Plato, of course, would leave at once; he only needed a ship, and this Dion had found him. It sailed with sealed orders from the Archon. It must have looked like a choice revenge to have Plato betrayed into slavery by the man to whom Dion had entrusted him. When later he learned that Plato had never doubted Dion for a moment, I daresay he was astounded.

The well-off philosopher who bought Plato would not take back a drachma; he said it had been a privilege. Plato went home and kept quiet from pride; when it got about, he testified to Dion's innocence. Old Dionysios, who cared what people thought of him, became uneasy; he wrote trying to patch things up, and saying he hoped Plato was not speaking ill of him. Plato replied that he had been too busy to recall the matter.

What Dion thought, when he heard the news, is not recorded. But his life was changed. When he was free to travel, he was already so much a man of the Academy that he seemed rather to have returned there than arrived. He was temperate as Pythagoras; he studied, he met philosophers; but in Sicily, any mission he was trusted with—war, embassy, judgment—was faultlessly discharged. If he departed from his orders for justice's sake, it was always in the open. No conspirator would have thought of sounding Dion's loyalty. It was as if, because Plato had not been allowed to stay in Syracuse to defend his own honor, Dion had made his whole life bear witness for his friend. As Axiothea had said, treachery was not in him— nor in Plato, who thought no cause greater than truth, and had lived through revolutions enough in Athens, each sowing hate, perfidy and revenge like dragons' teeth, to beget the next, each changing one sort of injustice for another. They had all failed, for the simple reason that men had got no better. Hate, he had found, destroys; only love creates; a state can be redeemed only by good men spreading goodness round them, till the lump is leavened, and there are enough just men to govern. All this they told me at the Academy; and I saw sense in it, if it could be got started. If anybody could do it, Dion could.

Soon, however, it was time to forgo these pleasures. They would be casting for the Lenaia, and then rehearsals would begin.

"You must win," said Axiothea, when I told her this. "It will draw Dionysios towards Athens and away from Sparta. That can't but be good."

"Can't it?" I said. "From what I've seen of politics, anything you can think of can go bad; it only needs bad will. I leave all that to the experts. Artists in politics are like the whore's child at the wedding; we remember things out of season, and get the stick."

"Take care, Niko, how you shrug off public business. One day it may concern you whether you choose or not."

"So may the black plague or the marsh fever. Meantime I'll stick to what I know. The more time Dionysios spends writing plays, the less he'll have for his tyranny; a day's no longer for him than any other man. Besides, an artist has to know himself, which can't do anyone harm. Can it?" I added, remembering the method.

"No, indeed."

# V

*HECTOR'S RANSOM* WAS PASSED BY THE SELECTORS and booked for the Lenaia, a rich Syracusan resident standing choregos. Everything went as planned, except for one hitch over the casting. Leontis, our sponsor, had drawn third turn to choose his protagonist; and the man before chose me. He said he had seen my work at Delphi. There was a hasty conference, and the other sponsor changed his mind. I don't know what he got for it, but there was no cheese-paring in that production. When we heard who were doing the masks and costumes, painting the skene and training the chorus, and for how much, even the Persian-backed play at Delphi looked like a fit-up.

Phileas was a chorus-master who, if he had had to stand the chorus upside down, would still have achieved faultless grouping and each syllable crystal clear. I used to sit in front often just for the pleasure of watching him work. You may ask how I felt, playing lead and directing where Aischylos once did it; where Sophokles danced as a chorus boy and, later, had only to walk on as an extra in one of his own plays to bring the audience up standing. Well, the place was my second home. I could not remember a time before I had known it. It was like being the son of a great house, who has come of age. I don't know when I have been happier.

I had lived with the play by now; I knew what the verse would give the actor, and where it would need heightening or throwing away. Just as I'd feared, Anaxis had got overkeyed and was ranting terribly as Achilles. "My dear," I said at length, "you were splendid today, but you showed up the lines a little, if you understand me. We must cover for the old man here and there. Don't forget that to get us to Syracuse, it's the play that has to win."

He took this pretty well, but complained that the third actor, Hermippos, was always trying to upset him, which was only too true. This was the man Dion had wanted instead of him. I had agreed he was a sound artist; and so I did not like to object, when Dion put him forward, that it might not answer to have a well-known second man playing third. The fee was big; there was also the golden lure of Syracuse; Hermippos had sunk his pride and accepted, but needed to show us he was somebody in case it was forgotten. This he did not by being pompous, which was not his style, but by playing the fool. He was one of the few actors to do well in both tragedy and comedy, and it was the latter which seemed to have shaped his face, which was round, with a big mouth and a button nose. On stage he behaved perfectly; but he was one of those men who, once having learned their lines, can do anything they like up to the moment when they go on. He would crack jokes with the mechanics, lay bets on races, clown about in masks from other plays, to let us all know he thought as well of himself as ever. For myself, my father taught me to think what I was about, but not to be put off by trifles. I had met Hermippos' sort before. But Anaxis, who thought it proper never to put his mask on till he had brooded before it like an actor carved on a gravestone, was driven mad and had not the sense to hide it. This was all Hermippos needed to egg him on. It was tiresome having to keep peace, when I wanted my mind on Priam.

Sometimes I got anxious about the role. I had turned down Achilles because it was too easy; I could have got the effects in my sleep. Perhaps I ought to have taken it, and proposed for Priam some good old actor who had done the role in this or that play more times than he could count and could get the effects in his sleep, too. That would have been the safer thing. I had wanted the part because it was something new for me; it was testing; I had thoughts about it; in a word, I had pleased myself. If I was not to break faith with Dion, and throw my own chance away, I had better be good.

I have never been the sort of actor who blusters about while rehearsing Herakles, smolders for Medea, and so on. But this time I swear my bones would ache when it rained, and when I got out of a chair I leaned upon the arms. I read the *Iliad* through and through, coming back to the passage where Priam tries to keep Hector from the death-fight. You are our last defense, he says; when you are gone, I shall see our house in ruins, Troy sacked, the women ravished, the children dashed on the stones, before I am cut down to lie where I am thrown until my own dogs eat me. *A young man fallen on the field, rent with sharp bronze, looks seemly even in his blood; death can lay nothing bare that is not beautiful. But an old man's corpse flung down, his gray hair and his beard and privates torn by curs, ah, that is the most wretched sight in all mortality.* These lines always came into my mind, when I played the scene with Achilles.

Then came the day for the Presentation of the Poets, which always makes the contest seem very near. We went to the Odeion in our festival robes and garlands, to make our bow while the subjects of the plays were given out. Our poet being in Syracuse, some sweet-voiced orator deputized, no doubt a good exchange. I was anxious lest our robes might be overdone—it is, after all, a ceremony, not a performance; one appears as oneself, without a mask, and should dress without hubris. But we were fitted out with sumptuous elegance; if our sponsor did not have good taste, he knew where to buy it.

As Anaxis had foretold, the name of Dionysios got no boo-ing; but Hermippos was greeted with a few laughs, because he had last been seen in comedy. A comedian, in the nature of things, gets more typed and known by sight than a trage-dian; and if audiences remember you waving a string of sau-sages, with a great stuffed phallos bouncing about, it takes more than a gilt wreath to make them forget it. If Hermippos was displeased he did not let it show, but bowed as if to a tribute. He was a stout-hearted man; even when he was tire-some, I could not keep from liking him. I said to Anaxis, later, that it was a good thing he had been there to keep the public sweet.

"That clown! Let me forget him while I can. Dionysios took second prizes here while he was much more disliked than now. I can't think why you should be so anxious."

I was about to deny it, but had a better thought and said, "My dear, you must bear with me; the truth is, I'm strung up like a lyre with this trouble between you and Hermippos. It's amazing you put up with him so well. But the fear of your being put off on the day, with so much depending on it, keeps me awake at night."

"My dear Niko!" he said at once. "I trust it would take more then Hermippos to do that to *me*. We are in the hands of the god. It may start to snow, the Chief Archon's wife may go into labor in the seats of honor, or the Thebans cross the frontier. These are real evils, which we may pray Iakchos to avert. But as for Hermippos, let us keep our minds on serious things."

At dress rehearsal, therefore, he was all graciousness; and Hermippos, like the good artist he was at heart, found no time for foolery. "It's going too well," I thought. "The bad luck will come on the day." Then at my chariot entry after Hermes, one of the horses stretched its neck, picked up Hermippos' mask by the wig, which I suppose it took for straw, and plucked it clean off his head. We laughed ourselves sick and felt better.

Now came the fateful draw for playing order. It was rain-ing that day, but we joined the crowd of artists and sponsors waiting in the theater colonnade to see the lists go up.

The first days would not concern us; comedy is king at the Lenaia, and always opens. After that there were trilogies with satyr-farce finales, one day for each. Then came the single plays. The list went up, the word went around. Leaving out the comic closure, we were on last.

Now if this happens at the Dionysia, it is plain good news. But at a winter festival like the Lenaia, you can't tell if you are blessed or cursed till the very day. If it is showery, or there is a bitter wind, the older people, and the sickly, and those with thin cloaks, start going home. The rest get restless, going off to stretch their legs or relieve themselves; their minds are half on hot soup at home; they are getting sulky and fidgety and hard to please. On the other hand, if it turns out fine you have the best of the billing and of the day as well. The mildness and sweetness of the theater on such afternoons is an artists' proverb. No wonder Zeus, and Dionysos, and Apollo Helios do so well for offerings beforehand.

On the eve of the festival, I lay listening to the noise of the midnight rites—the cries of the women trying, as they ran about the streets, to sound like maenads on a mountain, playing at danger in safety, as they do at the Lenaia, and garlanding King Vinestock to placate him for being pruned. Their hymns, and their squeals of "Iakchos!" and the red light of torches sliding across my ceiling, would wake me whenever my eyes had closed. Towards morning, I heard a huddle of them go by with their torches out, shivering and grumbling, and complaining of the rain.

Next day opened cloudy—not the rank bad weather that gets the show put off, but gray and threatening. During the first of the comedies it looked so black that people stayed at home, and the theater was half empty; if the cast had been less discouraged, I think the play might have won. Later it cleared a little; the theater filled; a play no better was well received, and got the prize.

On the day when the contest of tragedies started, the wind got up. The audience came muffled to the eyes, their cloaks pulled over their heads, and with two cloaks if they had them. The wind snatched at the robes of the cast and chorus; the flute-player, who had to use both hands to play, had his skirts flung up till they showed his naked backside. This did not help the protagonist, playing Bellerophon and doing a solemn bit of recitative. In the next part of the trilogy he had to be flown in riding Pegasos. My heart bled for him as he swung to and fro, with the audience squealing or laughing. Of course the play was sliced in half; but it was middling work, which I doubt stood a chance in any case.

Next day started even windier. The chorus of women had trailing scarves, a stupid thing at the Lenaia; during a choral dance they got tangled up together and had to unwind. They were quite young boys, and started giggling; I don't suppose they sat down for a week, after the trainer got his hands on them. The play was uneven, the poet having put into the first part all he had to say, but being resolved upon a trilogy. During the last part the wind dropped and the sun came palely out; but by then the audience was bored, and waiting to see the slapstick.

The following day was ours.

I could not sleep. I thought of taking poppy syrup; but it leaves one dull, and one would do better tired. Just as I was going off, a wedding procession passed, singing and shouting; there is one nearly every night in that month of marriages. I tossed and turned, and put out my hand at the window, and felt the air still, but very cold. Dim light from the sky showed me Apollo in his wooden frame. Since I was up, I lit a small clay lamp and stood it before the mask. The flame moved faintly in the air from the window; the eyeholes looked at me; they seemed searching, but calm. I went back to bed with the lamp still burning, and lay in thought. Suddenly I awoke to daybreak. The lamp had burned out; birds were chirping. The sky was clear.

I jumped up and looked out. A mild white frost furred the edges of the oleander leaves and the black fingers of the court-yard vine. My breath lay unstirring on the air.

I threw my blanket round me, and did my practice at the

window. My voice sounded true and flexible. A ruffled-up bird in the vine whistled so like a flute that I did a bit of recitative as well. I blew up the embers in the hearth and mulled some wine, breaking some eggs into it and adding white meal and honey—an old-fashioned posset which suits my stomach at these times. I sopped some bread in, knowing I would eat nothing later. Then, having scattered the crumbs outside as my flute-player's fee, I said an invocation before Apollo's mask and poured him an offering.

By the time I went out I felt warmed and brisk. My landlord and his wife, who seldom noticed me except of an evening to see whom I brought home, called out to wish me luck, which I took for a good omen. The sky was getting quite blue. My feet and fingers tingled still, but I could feel the cold grow less.

I stopped at the barber's, and found Hermippos being finished. As soon as he could talk, he offered me a bawdy tale about two girls he had met last night returning from the rites. I was in a mood for quiet, but could see that under it all he was on edge, and this was his notion of keeping up both our spirits. So I gave him his laughs, and in return got his company all the way, since he waited till I was done.

When we got to the theater, the public benches were full of people bundled up in all they had, with hats pulled down on their ears. In the side seats, where actors sit to hear what they can of other plays, Anaxis had kept us places. Beside us sat the cast of the second play; they would have to leave halfway through the first. A little way below were the cast of the satyr-farce which would end the day, *Silenos and the Gorgons*. They greeted Hermippos as a lost brother, and asked when he would come back to comedy. Above us, right to the top, were the chorus men and boys, gossiping among themselves or swapping boasts and jokes.

Down below, in the seats of honor, ambassadors and archons, priests and choregoi and their guests were coming in, their slaves all laden with rugs and cushions to make them snug. Then came the greater priests and priestesses: the High Priestess of Demeter, the High Priests of Zeus and Apollo and

Poseidon and Athene. Presently drums and cymbals sounded; the image of Dionysos was carried in and set down facing the orchestra, where he could see his servants play; his High Priest took the central throne; the trumpet sounded, and ceased. The theater hushed. Out of sight, beyond the parodos, were heard the first notes of the flute playing in the chorus. Whether you are behind or out in front, there is nothing quite like this moment.

The first tragedy was an *Amphytrion* by a poet whose name escapes me, a new writer, who was never heard of again. He must have written himself out with this one, for it was far from bad. He had had his ear to the ground, and not missed one new effect, or bit of business, which had hit last year. It was polished like a racing chariot. Though everything had been lifted from something else, you felt the poet had hardly noticed this, it was done with so much confidence. The choral interludes were very striking, with Lydian obbligatos for the flute—what, in those days when it was newer, we used to call belly-music. Even today, it puts me in mind of the wailing for Adonis. The flute-player was not quite up to such a tricky score, but I doubt if the audience noticed it. It was a brisk, sharp, neat piece, and was going down like hot spiced wine. Hermippos, I saw, was quite out of laughter. I said to Anaxis, "This is a hit."

He nodded, more calmly than I expected, and said, "The judges are an elderly lot this year."

I craned over to look at the tribes' ten representatives. A man has to be of sober years to get onto the ballot, and this year, true enough, there were some solid granddads. They did not look the men to relish that sobbing flute; and some were sure to take the wrong notes for modern music. I could picture the poet biting his nails each time.

However, the play had taken; the audience shouted, stamped, waved hats and shawls. The judges kept their own counsel. I was somewhat dismayed to meet such a challenge from this first play; it had been the second one I had had fears of. Anaxandrides, the author, was a prizewinner from the Greater Dionysia; such poets seldom trouble to enter at the Lenaia at all. Perhaps he had something sharp to say; people prefer hearing the City criticized when winter has closed the roads and seaways, keeping foreigners out of earshot. In any case, he would be a strong contender; and besides, his sponsor, winning first draw, had got Eupolis, who had been getting actors' prizes for twenty years.

The opening chorus had some fine lines, yet was patchy, and not in Anaxandrides' latest style. I began to suspect this was some old discarded play worked over, which he had not cared to risk at the greater festival. But he still had Eupolis, who now came on as Telemachos, son of Odysseus, moving beautifully, as he always did. I thought, "What crazy hopes have I been feeding? We shan't even be placed."

Hermippos leaned over to me. "I thought he had more sense. He should have cast himself as Penelope."

I raised my brows. Eupolis was famous for his juveniles; he was not much over forty-five, and graceful as a boy. Then he started to speak. I was amazed. He sounded twenty years older than he had last summer.

"Has he been sick?" I whispered.

"No; he's had three teeth pulled. He's been in torment with them half the year; at last his doctor warned him they'd be his death if he kept them longer. Hadn't you heard? But to think of his trying Telemachos!"

I have much to thank my father for, not least that he had strong teeth which gave him no trouble all his life, and passed on the same to me. Each actor, I am sure, who heard Eupolis that day shivered as if he had seen an owl in sunlight. It might happen to any of us next year. Once an artist is finished as an all-round man, he is mostly done for. It is rarely you get a play like *The Troiades*, where the lead is old and need never change to a younger mask.

Our chance now looked better. But I could not rejoice, when I heard a fine player sing his swan song, and the whole theater knowing it. When Anaxis nudged me and said we should be going, I knew it was too soon. But I got up; I had not the heart to stay and listen.

Down in the skeneroom there was the usual quiet scramble.

I had known it since I was so small that I came and went like a mouse in a busy kitchen, scarcely seen if I troubled no one. After that I had been a chorus boy, one chirping bird in the flock, giggling and gossiping and showing off and mocking each other's suitors; then carrying a spear, delighted to get some bit of business; then standing in for some real actor, sitting in front at rehearsal to study how he moved; at last, third man, the foothill one scales in triumph, to see from there the real mountain all to climb. Then second lead, where one may live and die unless one gets the chance and can take it. Now, for the first time, I came here as protagonist; here in the First Men's dressing room was my table, the dresser waiting, my costumes on the wall pegs, my masks and props laid out.

I put on the robe of Zeus for the prologue, a lovely thing, purple worked with golden oak leaves. The dresser rubbed up the great mirror of smoothed bronze. It showed me at my back the other end of the room, with Eupolis' table. In the quiet, I heard clearly his voice on stage, and the audience coughing. From the sound of the lines, he would soon be due for his last exit. I picked up my scepter, pushed back the mask on my head by its august beard, and said to the dresser, who was fidgeting with my girdle, that I would be back shortly. I expect he thought my bowels were griping, which is a common trouble with actors just going on; he did not keep me, and I got away in time. Eupolis had nowhere else to go between his exit and his bow, and in his place I would have liked the room to myself.

I don't know where I went to wait; the next thing I remember is sitting enthroned down center on the god-walk, eagle on left fist, scepter in right hand, Anaxis in the mask of Thetis coming on towards me, and all the eyes of Athens skinning me to the bone.

As I sat, right foot advanced upon my footstool, in the pose of Olympian Zeus, it was as though I had sleepwalked here, and only just found out where I was. Suddenly I was gripped by terror. My first five lines sounded in my head, turning round on themselves, leading nowhere. When I was through them I was going to dry. You can't be prompted up there without the whole theater hearing it. With a god it always gets a laugh. If this happens, I thought, I'll be a wreck all through the play. I thought of Dion; I was going to fail him; of Anaxis, whose hopes I would destroy. Here he came. In an instant I had lived an hour of fright. *Daughter of Ocean*, I thought, *Daughter of Ocean* . . . My hands felt icy cold. I thought, My father would die of shame. He never dried. He was twice the artist I am.

At once my lines came back to me. I started my speech, taking care of the little things about which he was exacting. I could scarcely believe he was not in front. Soon I got into the part; and when I came on as Priam I felt no more fear than at rehearsal. But all through till the end I was aware of him, as if he had never been away.

# VI

I DON'T REMEMBER THE VICTORY FEAST VERY
clearly. Gyllis of Thebes, who was in Athens for the festival,
said she never saw a man drink so much and keep so sober. I
am no great drinking man, but I daresay I drank whatever was
put into my hand. My happiness must have burned it out.

The party was given by the Syracusan consul, and was the
most lavish seen for years. In his speech on behalf of the
author, he invited us straight away to Syracuse to play before
our poet. He had bespoken our passage on the first good ship.

Anaxis and Hermippos sang a skolion together, their arms
round each others' necks. Hermippos had forgotten he ever
was in comedy, recalling only his tragic roles; each story ended
with a laugh, though. We were all like brothers; I don't recall
any prize party with so little bitchery. Anaxis had given a
much sounder Achilles than ever at rehearsal, simply, I think,
because he played down to give me a better chance, only protagonists being in the running for the actors' prize. I had
worked like a dog to get the award for the play, but could

scarcely believe I had been crowned as well. I kept putting up my hand to the ivy garland, as if to straighten it, but really to convince myself that it was true.

There was only one misadventure. Axiothea, though too discreet to enter a wineshop or pass the gymnasium door, took a fancy to attend the party. Speusippos, as he told me later, knowing more than she did, tried to dissuade her; but she said she would not think of staying; to congratulate me would only take a moment and a friend could do no less. He agreed to escort her, if she would not leave his side. I was amazed to see her enter; and, feeling in love with all the world, went straight over and took her in my arms. The poor girl, cold sober, looked quite startled; some fool, who supposed she was Speusippos' boy friend, called out a joke which made people look; her blush made her still handsomer, and the joker declared he would cut us both out. Speusippos, who I was surprised to find had a blazing temper, would have set about him, and it would have ended God knows how; luckily I managed to keep the peace and pass it off. When I begged her pardon, she said I had only welcomed her like a friend. I think she was more put out than she pretended; but she was a generous girl, and would not spoil my victory.

Though the Lenaia prize was founded when money was worth more than now, it is still a pleasant sum, and with our expectations I saw no harm in spending it. I knew enough about Sicily to understand we must make some show off stage as well as on; so, since I hate tawdry stuff, I went to Kallinos. He made me a robe of fine-combed Milesian wool, cream-white, the borders embroidered in fine stitching with a deep band of crimson stars, edged above with pointed rays in blue picked out with gold. Unlike stage costumes, it looked good across the room but much better close up. I did not mean to come before Dionysios of Syracuse looking as if I owned nothing but what he chose to give me. There was Athens' credit to think of, besides my own.

Anaxis and Hermippos felt this still more. Anaxis' robe was embroidered nearly all over; he could have played King Midas in it. Hermippos even had his dipped in purple, having heard that in Syracuse it was common wear. I guessed this must have left him without a month's rent in hand; my ingrained caution, settled since childhood from hearing of artists' ups and downs, nearly made me say, "Take it back"; but I feared he might think that I was jealous.

We waited some days for a ship, the consul being anxious we should arrive in style, and not be risked in storms on a small craft in the bad season. We set out, however, in very good weather for the time of year, and had a smooth run across from Korkyra to Tarentum. At Sybaris we put in to unload a consignment of painted vases, which were packed and handled like eggs, being no doubt as costly as everything else in that city. Hermippos, who visited a brothel there, said it was like a noble's house, with murals in every room, the most instructive he had ever seen, put there, he supposed, lest thinking of the price should make the patrons impotent. He was now flat broke, but made nothing of it since we were so near Sicily.

There was nothing on at the theater; but we saw a fit-up in the Agora, a mumming show in the Italian style. As we all know, bawdry in comedy pleases the god, and I don't think I am prudish; but in Athens, we do keep inside the bounds of blasphemy. Dionysos, being master of the revel, is fair game; but with Zeus Almighty no one jests, and even in a satyr play Apollo is done straight. Here he was being chased with a club by Herakles, and scolding from the roof of his shrine like a treed cat; tempted with cake, he leaned down, got walloped, and fell into a water tub. Worse still, we had Zeus, with a big nose and phallos, scrambling up a ladder to debauch Alkmena; Hermes peeped in at the window after him and told the audience all about it. Even Hermippos, after laughing at the gags at first, finished quite shocked.

But this, disgusting as it was, did not so turn my stomach as a show put on by some Etruscans from up north. They are brown, sloe-eyed men, good dancers and flute-players, whose forebears came, it is said, from Lydia. I don't know what story they were enacting; the Italians seemed to follow their jargon. All I can tell you is that their faces were quite bare; they were using them to act with.

It is hard to describe how this display affected me. Some barbarian peoples are ashamed to show their bodies, while civilized men take pride in making theirs fit to be seen. But to strip one's own face to the crowd, as if it were all happening to oneself instead of to Oidipos or Priam—one would need a front of brass to bear it. One knows, as one plays, that behind the mask one's face is speaking, as it must if one feels at all; but that's one's own secret, and the god's. Anaxis, outraged as a gentleman not less than as an artist, said one would feel like a whore.

Two days later we rounded Cape Herakles, and saw the cloud-white breast of Etna float high above the sea. Standing astern, to get windward of the rowers' stink which a springlike sun made ranker, we saw the loom of the land appear. The shipmaster, a friend by now, clapped our shoulders and said we should be made men once we got to Syracuse. Apart from Dionysios' own gifts, which were sure to be magnificent, we could play all the Greek cities along the coast, which had splendid theaters, and pretty well name our terms. This trip should set us up for life.

When he had gone, Anaxis said, "This is his regular run; he must know what he is talking about. As I may have told you, before the war my family had a small estate near Marathon. A very good piece of land—the olives were sold by name in Athens. The man who owns it now lives in town, and farms it with a factor. One never knows; he might sell."

"What I should like," said Hermippos, "would be to form my own company and do first-class tours. Three actors, two extras, a good flute-player who can train a chorus. One year, say, Corinth, Epidauros, Delphi, and north to Pella; another, Delos and Ionia. One hears great things of Pergamon. Samos I know; Ephesos—ah, there's a city! As for Sicily, while we're here I shall look about. Think of those top-rank companies, like Diphilos'; what really marks them out from ours? Only trimmings—costumes, masks, a good traveling turn-out, fancy-marked mules and some gilding on the cart. Once set up, one can stay there. I'd buy a little house in Corinth, in Theater Street, to come back to between tours. I know just the girl to keep it warm. She'd jump at it; she's kept now by a paunchy spavined old banker who . . ." And so on. After a while he said, "And you, Niko? Why so quiet?"

I laughed, saying, "Don't price the unborn calf." I was as full of myself as the others, just more superstitious. My father bred it into me. We used to walk tiptoe before a festival, in case we should speak ill-omened words, or frighten the house-snake, or tell an unlucky dream. But nothing was so bad as counting on a win beforehand. I learned that for good the first time, he was so angry. Someone else won, too, and I blamed myself for years.

The wind favored us so well that the rowers shipped oars. At sunup we sighted Syracuse.

As we sailed into the Great Harbor, Anaxis said, "So this is the place that made me an actor." I knew what he meant. His family had been ruined in the Great War, and here Athens had lost it. We must just about be crossing where the boom had trapped our fleet. Over there—good drained land now—were the swampy flats where they had camped, and got the marsh fever, which I'm told was unknown in Greece when our grand-fathers were young. It was all flattish country; even the famous Heights of Epipolai one would call a ridge in Attica. But none of the actors in that old tragedy would have recognized the skene. The upper town was now armored like a dragon, all walls and gatehouses; and it had a dragon's head. At the end of its neck of causeway, scaly with towers, the island fortress of Ortygia thrust out into the sea, bristling with war engines, and with walls like cliffs. All this was the work of Dionysios. The cost hardly bore thinking of; but then his rapacity was famous all over Greece; it was said, and I started now to be-lieve it, that he taxed his subjects' incomes as high as twenty percent. I asked the captain how they bore it.

"You would soon know how," he said, "or rather why, if you'd been, as I have once, into a town the Carthaginians had just been sacking. I thought I'd seen evil, before that day. It's better, I tell you, not to know that men can do such things. Nothing here makes sense, without the Carthaginians. It was for fear of them, not of the tyrant, that free men worked on these walls like slaves; and the old man has kept power all these years for the same reason he got it: because they'd still sooner have him than the Carthaginians. Remember that when you go ashore, and watch your tongues."

Presently the theater came in sight, on the footslopes of Epipolai. We craned and stared, and Anaxis said, "We may need extra rehearsals. It has that sound cave." I agreed, this being well known. It was a theater where the low rake spoiled the acoustics and they had had to put in amplifiers. Some theaters use hollow bronze to throw up the sound, others wooden screens; but here they had worked on a natural cave hard by. The echo chamber had the shape of a pointed ear; some wit had named it Dionysios' Ear, referring to the ass-ears of King Midas, and it was so known by artists everywhere. I had been warned one needed to practice with it.

Some kind of bustle had started on deck; the sails were down, but the rowers sat idle. Instead of taking us in, the captain was up in the prow with the pilot, shading his brows. When I came up he said, "Are your eyes good, Niko?"

"What's to see?" I asked.

"Not enough by half. Too quiet; too few people about, and their heads together. No crowd to watch the ship in. Something's amiss on shore."

I could see this too. If an odd man came from the upper town, people were stopping him for news; it looks the same anywhere. Then they would huddle in talk again. There was hardly any of the working noise and shouting one expects in a busy port.

The other two looked at me. I said, "Whatever it is, it will take a good deal to stop Dionysios from seeing his play." Some Sicilian passengers were starting to look uneasy. I said to the captain, "What do you think it is? The plague?"

"No; there would be smoke from the pyres. And in war they would all be busy. This is something political. If we stand well out, someone will come—a merchant for his cargo, or someone wanting a passage. Then we shall know." A knot of Syracusans came up to him, demanding to disembark, while others argued against it.

"By the dog!" said Hermippos. "Always some scare or other before a big performance. Well, whatever it is, they'll have had time to get over it before the end of rehearsals with the chorus."

We dropped anchor where we were. The sun grew hot, the sights grew tedious. Some of the passengers chaffered with a fishing boat to take them off, and we saw them on the water-front, asking for news. It made us fidgety, and we said to each other that we would take the next boat ourselves. Soon we saw one. There was no need to hail it, it was heading for the ship.

Two men scrambled on board, the first clearly a merchant—Greek clothes, Greek barbering, brown skin and hooked nose from some Sikel or Carthaginian strain; Sicily has always been a meeting-place of races. In good Greek, he asked the captain after a consignment of lapis from Ephesos. The captain sent to the hold for it, and asked what news. You may suppose they could hardly breathe for eavesdroppers.

"No news since yesterday," said the Syracusan. "No one's been let through the posterns, and the guards won't open their mouths. The doctors have been in there three days, and even their own wives can't get word to them."

The captain said, "My friend, you're starting the race at the turn-post. What's wrong with whom?"

"What, you know nothing?" He looked as if it should have been written on the air.

"Only what I could see. You're our first news-bringer."

The man looked about him as if from habit; then, though there were a dozen of us breathing down his neck, "It's Dionysios. Dying, they say."

I could feel my mouth open, like the jaws of a landed fish. There was a gasp from Hermippos. Anaxis stood like stone. For longer than any one of us had lived, Dionysios had ruled in Syracuse. I had thought of pretty well every stroke of fate, except this.

Someone asked how long he had been sick. Six days, the merchant said, with fever; then his eyes went past us to the wharfside, where some stir was going on. He ran to the rail, waving at someone. The man on shore lifted his hand, and dropped it palm down. There was no need of an interpreter.

Someone, however, always explains. "The news is out," said the merchant. "Dead."

A babble broke out all over the ship, in three or four languages: bleating, barking, clucking; it was like a farm at feeding time. Actors are said to be talkative, but I think we were the only ones dead quiet. Nobody dared speak first. Not that there was anything to say. We put off our hopes in silence, like gorgeous costumes and masks from a failed play; we would not be needing them again. After a while I said, "Well, my dears. That's the theater."

Someone moved sharply. It was the merchant, who had turned to stare. He was waiting for his goods, while the other man from the boat talked with the captain. He had a bundle with him, and seemed to want a passage. Breaking in on this, the merchant pointed at us like one who complains that the cargo stinks. "Are those men actors?"

Reminded of our troubles, the captain said we were distinguished artists from Athens, who had been sent to play at Court, but had lost our luck. At this, I saw the other man sidle away, trying to get the captain between him and us. It made me notice him; there was something I half remembered. But the merchant had not done. "Are they," he said, still pointing, "the actors from the Archon's play?"

I had had enough before and found this too much. "Where do you think you are?" I asked. "Pricing goats at market? Ask civilly, if you want to know."

He neither took this up nor begged our pardon; he was too full of his feelings to waste the time. "Well, then, if you care for your own good you'd turn straight round with the ship. How it will end what god can say, this day's work you did for our city, you and your fellow there?" He jerked his thumb, as it seemed, at the other man. "I'm no politician, no sophist"— he was working right up into the next register—"all I ask is to live in peace. Say what you choose about the Archon, but he built these walls, yes, hitched up his own gown and carried a hod, and made the quality do their stint, too. He built them, and kept them manned, and saw the shipping got through. And now whom are we left with? What now?" He spun round at the second man, who had been creeping off, and gazed back like a snared rabbit. "You! You bad-luck piece, you cadging Athenian mummer with your moneybag up your shirt! May you never get fat on it! I hope it buys you a rope!"

We could make nothing of these Delphic ravings, but the captain, sharp as a nail, said, "What? What's this man done? Was it murder then? You, there—get off my ship before you're put overside. Do you think I want the war fleet out after me? Look alive—off!"

The man ran forward, gabbling. With one hand he grasped the hem of the captain's tunic, with the other the breast of his own, where I suppose he had his money. Invoking every god from Zeus to Serapis, he vowed he had done nothing, nothing, contrary to any law of gods or men. A babe unweaned was not more guiltless. I could not believe, with all this grabbing and swallowing, he could be any sort of actor; and yet something said theater in my mind.

Next moment Hermippos caught my arm. "Niko! I know him now. He was in the chorus; the first line of the antistrophes. That fellow who used to come in half a beat early. Don't you remember?"

He was right; it had happened as late as the dress rehearsal. "But," I said, "how in the name of Hekate did he get out here?"

"Let us ask him," said Anaxis. We all moved forward. The chorus man clutched his brows and shook his head about, like Orestes beset by Furies. But there is a time and place for everything. So I stepped up sharply, and suddenly letting out my Angry Achilles voice, said, "Enough! Tell us the truth."

Wringing his hands till I thought they would come off, he gasped out, "Oh, Nikeratos! I appeal to you, sir, I ask you, how could I have foreseen it? On my life, by all that's holy, I meant no harm to anyone. Somebody had to bring Dionysios the news, and get the good-tidings gift; why some hired courier, why not me? I rode up to Corinth, and got a ship through the gulf from there, and saved two days. Who could have thought of its harming artists like yourselves, who were sure of all the honors? Who could have known? Am I a soothsayer? A god?"

"No," I said. "Not by the look of you. So you shipped ahead of us with the news. What then?"

He showed the whites of his eyes, like a beaten dog. I would have shaken it out of him, but the merchant said, "I can tell you quicker. When the Archon got the news, he paid Wing-foot Hermes here the price of it, and a good price too. Then he began the victory feast. It went on two days and I daresay they would still be at it, but that he took a turn in the gardens to get cool. He wasn't young; he'd had the marsh fever more than once, and it clings then to one's bones. He went sick within two hours."

The chorus man gazed from one to the other of us, his silence giving assent. Hermippos caught Anaxis' eye, and jerked his head at the water. They rolled back their gowns from their arms.

It was hard to blame them. I had half a mind to it, too. But the wretched man had only done what anyone else might who thought of it; and the sponsor's courier, no doubt, would still have got here before us with the same effect. Even when I had talked them out of it, they were all for putting him back on shore, saying he carried bad luck enough to sink a squadron. The only man more superstitious than an actor is a sailor, and I saw the captain listening. The chorus man—whose name I can't recall, though I thought it graven on my mind forever—fell down and clasped my knees. I have seen it done better. Weeping, he cried that his sole hope of life was to get away before the Syracusans started to blame him for the death; otherwise he would be crucified on the walls, and his ghost would haunt us.

It was a good long speech, so I had time to think. I had been pretty late about it. Still, what need of time? A man who gets omens at the hour of fate should not turn back at the door and call it chance.

"Stop grizzling," I said. "No one can hear himself speak." He choked it down, and I went on, "Very well, you meant no harm. But you did it. You've still come off with your profit, which I'm sure was a good one; while these artists here have

lost the chance of their lives. As I see it, the least you can do is
to stand them their fares to Athens. In that case, we will ask the
captain to let you sail."

He could not offer fast enough. Anaxis said, "Of course that
includes Nikeratos, though he was too much the gentleman to
mention it. As protagonist, he has borne the greatest loss."

"Thank you, my dear," I said. "But there's no need, I shan't
be sailing. I've a fancy to see Sicily."

This line, as I had feared it might, stopped the show. Then
the big scene started. Even the captain joined in. Had I lost my
wits, they asked. What would be doing in the theater? Civil
war was the likeliest thing, and then maybe the Carthaginians
moving in while the walls were weakly manned. Even for a
man tired of life, said the captain, there are ways and ways of
losing it. To all this I replied that I could look out for myself,
and had always wanted to see Syracuse. After a while Hermippos and the captain gave me up; but Anaxis drew me aside.

"Niko, my dear friend." He grabbed my shoulders, a thing I
had never known him do. I saw, surprised, that he really liked
me. "Don't, I beseech you, rush off like a boy into a battle,
looking for the one he loves without helm or shield. I said
nothing before the others, out of respect for your feelings; but
it needed no oracle at Delphi to tell me how things were with
you. Think! You have no head for affairs; you know it; you'll
find nothing but trouble; and the man whose fortunes you want
to follow, excellent as no doubt he is, won't be at leisure now
to remember that such a man as Nikeratos walks upon the
earth. You have no notion what can happen in a city when a
tyranny changes hands. Once faction fights begin, and throats
are cut in the streets, men don't wait to ask if you are a stranger
in those parts. Come, sail home with us now, and come back
later when everything is settled."

"Don't fret so, dear boy," I said. "I toured with Lamprias at
nineteen, on the second-class circuit, and came out of that alive.
I daresay I can shift in Sicily."

"How will you even eat?"

"I've some prize-money still in hand. Look, the boatman's

shoving off; I must catch him now." If I had to wait for another, I should have all this two or three times over.

When I had packed my things, I brought Anaxis the mask-box of Apollo. "Keep this for me, my dear. Set it up somewhere, and give it a pinch of incense now and then—the god is used to it—and ask him to keep me in mind till I come home."

He promised, shaking his head over me as if it had been the boat of Charon I was boarding to cross the Styx. He and Hermippos both embraced me. They watched me all the way to shore. Further along the rail stood the man from the chorus, staring after me as if at a man bereft of his senses running into a house on fire. It stuck in my mind, as I set foot on the wharf of Syracuse.

# VII

I DECIDED TO DO THE NATURAL THING AND MAKE for the theater. It would be a starting point; something would come to me there. I found my own way, seeing nobody I felt like asking.

Syracuse is a splendid city, taking after Corinth, which founded it. But it was warmer, greener, dustier, stank more, and already smelled of spring. There seemed more of everything—more gilding, more marble, more shops, more people. They had traits of every nation under heaven: fair Hellenes and dark Hellenes, brown hawk-faced Numidians, black thick-faced Libyans; reddish little black-haired Sikels, and every kind of cross-breed these could produce. All they had in common was their Greek dress, and fear. The place was like a kicked anthill, before they start putting it to rights. Only they did not look to me like doing it, but as if they were waiting to see what would be done to them. There was a kind of meanness with it too, as if each watched his neighbor lest he might find a foothold quicker in this slippery time, and manage to make something out of it.

The theater was empty. Even the caretaker and cleaners had gone off, leaving it unlocked. The streets had been full of people in their working clothes. I went in, and felt better for it, more myself. As I had expected, there was too much of the best of everything—colored marble, gilding, painting, over-decorated statues—a place designed to make one think, "I am playing at Syracuse," rather than, "I am playing in Sophokles." I had never seen such machinery as there was backstage and under it. Dionysios must have turned his war engineers loose there when they had nothing else on hand. One huge device of wheels and levers left me quite at a loss; later I found it was to raise the stage or lower it by pumping water in or out of chambers below.

However, as I had guessed I would, from here I knew where to go next. I went down into the street and found the theater tavern.

One could tell it at a glance, as one always can: a barber's stand in one corner; a set of the tragic masks on one wall; on another a scene from the *Agamemnon*, with actors' names written in. Though the theater had been empty, this was cram-full; the noise came out to meet me, the sort which, in cities all over Hellas, makes an artist feel at home. No muttering and whispering, as in the streets. An actor always knows that if one city gets too hot, there are others.

The barber's chair was free, so, having shaved that morning, I asked to be pumiced, a good long talkative job. News buys news.

The barber was a Corinthian, as every barber in Syracuse is, or claims to be. When he asked me whence I came, and so on, I told him everything, except that I knew Dion; there seemed no sense in hiding the rest. While he spread his towels he passed on the news over his shoulder; presently, to save him trouble, people got up and sat around. Some of them offered me wine. It was as unlike as possible to the city outside. Here one could feel one's footing. Actors understand actors, as dogs do other dogs.

No one was surprised that, having come so far for nothing, I should stay to see the city before going home. The barber, who owned the tavern, introduced me to the leading actors who were there, and to some old ones who I expect sat there all day. Then he remembered that Dionysios' chorus-trainer, who would have worked on *Hector's Ransom*, lived nearby, and sent someone to fetch him. Meantime, everyone told me about Dionysios' fatal party, some adding that by habit he was a sober man, and might have lived if he had been better seasoned to it. They talked of the plays he had put on; there was a good deal of smooth backbiting among the leading men, far more than at Athens, which came, I should say, from their having had to compete for the tyrant's favor. The man I took to most was a second-role tragedian called Menekrates. As he seemed talkative, and I had learned nothing useful yet, I asked him whether young Dionysios would be as good a patron as his father.

For a moment everyone glanced round in search of eaves-droppers; even here one was still in Syracuse. But they seemed satisfied. Menekrates smiled, flashing his white teeth; he was dark almost to blackness, with a high-bridged Numidian nose. "My dear Nikeratos, that is the riddle of the Sphinx. No one knows anything, about theater or anything else. If you want my opinion, the man who would most like to know what young Dionysios is like is the man himself. Since he left off playing with his toys, he's not dared to be anything that a man of rank could take seriously. He won't even laugh at a comedy till every one round him has laughed first. He cries more easily. I made him cry once. That's as much as anyone knows. He may be sitting at this moment, like an actor without a mask, waiting for someone to write him a part."

"Or," said a man with a flute-player's flat-topped fingers, "he may be taking off the mask he's been playing in all this time, to make his bow and show his face."

Just then the chorus-master came in, a little bouncing man who knew artists all over Greece and demanded news of them, and I had to talk theater. After all, it was the center of these men's lives, and it was only chance that was making me any different.

What next? I was no nearer knowing than when I landed. If I had been anyone else, I could just have walked to Dion's house and asked how I could be of service. But what kind of entrance could I make which would not seem to say, "Here I am, stranded without work after coming all this way. You hired me; now look after me."

The barber had done, and it was noon. But Menekrates would not let me order food, and shared with me a good fish stew. Then, when we had eaten, he said that since I had come to see the sights, he would be happy to show me Syracuse, and to offer me the spare bed at his lodging.

Here was an omen at the crossroads. I had taken to the man; he liked gossip, too, and might have some useful knowledge. All over Hellas, a web of guest-friendship binds the artists of Dionysos; it went without saying that when next he came to Athens I would return his hospitality. So I could accept it without loss of pride—a great piece of luck, with my passage home to think about.

"It will have been worth your visit," he said, "just to see the funeral. There is always a big show for an important man; but this should be the sight of a generation."

"Of two," said the chorus-master. "Dionysios has ruled for two, by the common reckoning."

I asked who would arrange the rites. "Why, the heir," he answered. "Young Dionysios." Plainly no one doubted who the heir was. I wondered what was going on in the island stronghold. There was not much chance of my ever knowing.

After this Menekrates took me to the small street where he lodged, in a good clean room with whitewashed walls opening to a courtyard. He showed me my bed, lay down upon his own and slept at once, as everyone does there at that hour. Even so early in the year, it was getting warm. Not being used to it, I lay thinking, looking out through the window at the court with its green shade of palms and gourds.

When the shadows started lengthening, he woke up. As we

splashed well-water on our faces, he said, "Let us go and see if my cousin Theoros has got home yet. He should have been purified from the death chamber by this time. We shall learn something at first hand from him."

As we slipped along a crooked alley where two could not walk abreast, I asked who this Theoros was. He answered, "Oh, he is the great man of our family. He works for Leontis the physician, puts on his poultices and so on. For three days now he and his master and the other leading doctor, Iatrokles, have been locked up in Ortygia. My cousin (he is really my cousin's husband) has been at her wits' end, poor girl. She said if the Archon died they would all be executed. I told her not to fret; there was no one the old man's life was as precious to as it was to him."

Apollo, I thought, you have not forsaken your servant.

"He does not approve of me," said Menekrates. "He thinks I should have had foreknowledge of so dignified a person marrying into the family, and chosen another calling. But we'll hear something from him; he is too self-important to keep it in."

Some children playing in the street told us he was back. We went on, and found a small room fast filling up with kindred and acquaintance. The women had hidden inside, but the door-curtain bulged with them; two little boys ran about underfoot like chickens. There was no room to sit down. Theoros, a weighty fellow with a long combed beard and a manner copied from his master, held forth beside the hearthstone. He received me civilly, but condescended to Menekrates. I saw that all the family, except for him, was quite fair and Greek. This often happens in Sicily.

I will cut Theoros' opening narration, which followed Dionysios' sickness from the first shiver through rigors, vomitings, sweatings, purgings, and so on, with all the treatment. He described how every time Leontis sent him outside for anything, before being let back into the sickroom he was searched to the skin by the guards. "A foolishness, when so many means of healing can be means of death, misused. But they had their rule and no one dared change it; when Iatrokles, our colleague, complained of the delay, the captain related how a guard was once put to death for handing a javelin to the Archon's own brother, when all he wanted was to draw a siege plan in the dust for Dionysios to see. He would not have a razor near him, even to shave himself, but singed his beard with glowing charcoal. So now, as you can understand, they feared he might yet recover and make them answer for it. When he began to sink, and they heard us say it was only a matter of time, they stopped searching young Dionysios; but you could see it made them anxious. If it had been Dion, that would have been different; the rule had always been waived for him."

There was a buzz in the room. Someone said, "Dion was not there?"

Theoros coughed, and stroked his beard. "It was difficult. A very delicate matter. On the one hand, the patient was exhausted, and just the man, as his son had no need to remind us, to overtax what strength was left. On the other, he was the Archon still. Yet to obey a sick man without discretion may be to make oneself his murderer."

The company weighed this in a respectful pause. My question was burning my tongue, but the manners one is bred with stick. It was a white-haired old granddad, sure of his standing, who piped up, "What? What? Did Dionysios ask for Dion?"

"That again, Glaukos, is a thing more easily asked than answered." He nodded approval of himself, till I thought I should go mad. "In the earlier phase, when the patient was full master of his faculties, he was occupied, as often happens, with trivialities, the gods having sent him no foreknowledge. He discussed his play, sent for Timaios the skene-painter, and talked a full hour with him against our advice, sending out more than once to learn if the actors had come from Athens." Then he remembered, bowed, and said, "Ours is the privilege denied him." I bowed back. Menekrates caught my eye and winked.

"Dion of course visited his kinsman, but found him full of these affairs. Calling us to the anteroom, he charged us to inform him at once if our prognosis altered. 'I have seen these fevers in the field; they change quickly, either way. If he worsens, tell me directly, without fail.' You know his manner. My principal said, afterwards, that a general he might be, but we were not his men though he seemed to think so."

My heart sank. From the man one may infer the master, and I could see the scene.

"He was given the civil answer due to his rank. It went without saying that the heir must hear first of any change. And *he* said at once, 'My uncle has never known how to spare himself. Nor has my father. It will be his death if we let them meet.' When Dion returned, therefore, he was told the patient must have quiet. Indeed, with the fever's evening rise he grew restless, wandering in his thoughts, giving and canceling orders, then demanding something to make him sleep. In the course of these ramblings it is likely that, as you, Glaukos, were asking, Dion's name came up. Had we obeyed them all, we should have had the sickroom full of mercenary captains, engineers, envoys, tax-collectors, masters of horse and actors—a chaos, as our new Archon put it. He himself behaved with great propriety. As for Dion, I believe he did come back once or twice, and latterly brought his sister's sons; and once Dionysios called out to him to come in if he wanted anything, not stand talking with the guard. But at once the patient had rambled off again, cursing us for calling ourselves doctors when we could not so much as dispense a draught of poppy. His son, who was there, begged us not to refuse this comfort, so likely to be the last. We therefore complied, and the end was peaceful."

Peaceful for the doctors, too, I thought. If you can't save your patient, it's next best to know when you can stop fearing him, and start fearing his heir. They were better off than the guards.

After this everyone started telling stories of Dionysios. It seemed even those who hated him were powerless to look beyond him; how not, when no man under fifty could remember the days before he ruled? But before Menekrates and I slipped off, I overheard Theoros impart to some favored friends the last sensible words of the old tyrant. When he had had the draught, he beckoned his son and said, "If these fools let me die, even a fool like you should be able to keep hold on Syracuse. I leave you a city bound with chains of adamant." These words he repeated, like a craftsman speaking of a good job done, and closed his eyes.

As we walked away, I thought, Whatever part did I think to play here? This is not Kreon's Thebes, but the modern age, the hundred and third Olympiad. Well, I would stay on with Menekrates to see the funeral. It would give me a glimpse of Dion, since I could not think now of calling on him; he had trouble enough, without being touted by resting actors. I would just stand in the crowd, and see him pass.

Perhaps, I thought, he would spend more time in Athens now. I asked Menekrates his opinion. "Rather less, I should think," he said, "unless young Dionysios is an even worse fool than his father thought. He never apprenticed him to his trade, for fear he'd want to own the business; he will need Dion at his elbow for years to come, to run the state at all. If that man is human, he must be waiting for his chance. Thank God I've no family of my own. I think I shall go on tour."

"If you mean," I said, "that Dion might seize power, I don't think it likely. He doesn't hold with revolutions, or civil war. I met him once." He might hear this any day from some actor lately in Greece; it would look strange to have said nothing, unfriendly too. I told him the story, dwelling only on the theater part.

"Don't dream," he said, "of leaving before the funeral. No one will dare give parties, but we'll pass the time. Not with my father's kindred, whom I'm sure you have seen enough of. I don't mix much with them; there was a family quarrel over my birth. As you see, I'm dark; my father's sister, the fat frog, put it about I'd been got by our Libyan slave. Do I look like a Libyan? My father believed my mother, but the scandal soured him; he never had much use for me. When I was a man I searched the records. The Numidian strain's from their side, and I told them so, for which they liked me no better. Well, I vowed I'd turn out the best of them, and so I have. Theoros is a servant for all his airs. Last year, when my brother stabbed a man and they had to find the blood-price, whom did they come to? Me. He's as fair as you to look at; but inside, Numidian to the bone, savage as a desert wildcat. I am all Hellene; but they don't look below the skin. However, it's all one in the theater, under the mask."

Rather than I should lack entertainment, he offered to take me to the best boy brothel in Syracuse, which he assured me would keep open. I thanked him and excused myself; I like Eros with unclipped wings, and the smiles of a slave, who might spit in one's face if he did not fear the whip, have no power to warm me. So instead, that evening we went back to the theater tavern, finding it fuller than at noon; there Menekrates told everyone about Delphi and the crane, so that I was forced to relate the story. Then Stratokles, the chorus-master, said he had never seen the full text of *Hector's Ransom,* having been given only the choral parts, and everyone demanded a recital. In no time they had me up on the barber's stand, with an audience packed to the doors; some court gentlemen had come in who had no diversion that night, on account of the mourning, and were eager to hear the play which, as they said, Dionysios had died of.

"The verse is not bad," said one of them. "Not quite Sophokles—except where it *is* Sophokles—but not bad at all. There was an oracle, you know, that the Archon wouldn't die till he had won a victory over his betters. He's let the Carthaginians off lightly more than once, when he could have pushed them into the sea." Everyone started looking about in terror. The youth who had been speaking said, "He's dead." The green shoot bends quickest to the changing wind. "They made it worth his while, and he needed them now and then, to keep the city needing *him.* But this was the destined victory, after all. Two-tongued Apollo laughs last."

"I don't think so," I said. "I heard the other plays and I thought the judging fair. It usually is, in Athens." My mind went back to Theoros' story of the old tyrant shouting for his sleeping draught, with Dion at the door. Yes, he had beaten his better at the end.

Next morning Menekrates woke me early, to go sightseeing in the cool. We were crossing the Agora, when we heard a crier calling all the citizens to the Assembly. I was surprised that under a tyranny such a thing existed, but Menekrates assured me all these forms had been kept on. "Come and watch," he said, smiling sourly, "and you will understand. My friend Demetrios, the coppersmith, will let you stand on his roof."

The Assembly place was down on the flats. On the way we passed the quarries where they put the Athenian prisoners in the Great War, and where so many died; they are not far from the theater. Menekrates told me Dionysios had had them carved out twice the size and there was no knowing who might be in them. "Well," he said, "things may change, who knows? Let's go and see."

The Assembly field had been cleared overnight of stalls, sheep pens, cockpits and so forth. A tall rostrum in the center was hung with white, instead of purple. Menekrates had joined the citizens; from the roof of the smith I heard trumpets sound and the clank of armor. In marched about half a regiment, lining the middle of the square two or three deep. The Syracusans seemed to think nothing of it. They waited, chattering and shouldering, as women do for some spectacle others have prepared for them. I understood Menekrates' smile.

Through a lane of soldiers the new Archon rode to the rostrum, and mounted the steps without grace. My eyes strayed to Dion, who had gone up with royal dignity behind him, and stood there with a few other men of the family. Him I would have known anywhere by his bearing and his height. As for young Dionysios, the soldiers had raised a dust, and it was too far to see faces well. But as one knows in the theater, the whole body speaks. He was thinnish, and held himself like a man with a stoop who had never before pulled back his shoulders. Sometimes he forgot, and let his neck poke forward. You could have told at a mile that he had neither looks nor charm.

He started speaking, coughing now and again from the dust. His voice matched his deportment: forced, anxious, and striving for effect, which only brought out its faults. His speech seemed empty and formal stuff, probably written by someone else. From what I could hear of it, he praised the departed, deplored his own loss and the city's, and asked for the people's loyalty. There was some acclamation, such as you might expect with all those soldiers standing about. I missed a good deal, since the smith had had no notion of leaving his slaves to idle while he was gone, and the bursts of clattering from the workshop often killed all other sound. It seemed no great loss.

After one such din, I found he was speaking of his father's obsequies, which were to be worthy of Syracuse's greatest man. The people brightened at news of a show, and there was some real applause. At this the young man picked up a little life, like a nervous actor with a good house. He stopped peeping at his notes, without which he would not have gone far till now, and, with a sudden burst of eloquence, spoke of his father's poetic talents, the fruit of nights with the lamp while other men were reveling. (I am told this was quite true.) The hammers began again downstairs, after which I caught something about the gifted artist who should have painted the skene being at work upon a funeral pyre of no less splendor. You could tell, from the jerks and pauses, that he was now speaking extempore. After some more hammering, the loudest yet, I pulled my fingers out of my ears in time to hear ". . . will be spoken by the protagonist."

*Protagonist?* I thought. What's this?

Dion had been standing up there like a statue all this while. Now, even at this distance, I saw him start and look about. I knew then I had heard right.

I suppose the speech finished somehow. Menekrates met me at the door. He had been quite near the rostrum and heard everything. I was to speak the funeral oration.

"My dear," I said, "we must both be dreaming. It should be Dionysios himself."

"Of course it should. He can't be such a fool as he looks. He couldn't do it, as we've seen; he's a stick; he loses his lines, he fluffs; he barely got through. At a state funeral, people expect something. The whole audience would have walked home saying, 'Now Dion would have been worth hearing.'"

"You must be right," I answered. "Nothing else makes sense."

"If he'd hired an orator—and Demodoros must be spitting blood—everyone would know why. But this is a tribute to the old man's last achievement. You could call it clever. He was gagging, you know. It came to him on stage; he was playing to the audience. By the dog, Niko, your guardian god looks after you."

"He sent me a friend," I answered. Indeed, I was lucky in Menekrates. He was generous by nature; not a rival, being still a second-roles actor; happy enough as my host to share the event and spread the news. Some artists would have been so jealous, especially of a foreigner, that I should have had to move out.

We returned to the lodging, so that I could be found. Just after siesta-time, when the sun was leaving the courtyard, the palace messenger arrived with my summons to Ortygia. I was to go next morning.

At the hour, therefore, when the market opens, I put on a plain white robe, since I was going to a house of mourning, and walked in the cool sunrise towards the sea. Menekrates saw me halfway. He said it was against nature, for a Syracusan, to linger before Ortygia.

There was a thick-walled fort to pass through, before one even set foot upon the causeway. The swarthy Iberian mercenaries who manned it looked at my summons, and opened the triple gates. Any one of them would have done by itself for a small town. I came out on a cobbled square by the Little Harbor, with the causeway still to cross.

I never saw at one time so many ships of war. Here I had my first sight of a quinquereme, as high as a two-floored house. Strange engines were mounted on the decks, for flinging fire, or stones, or dropping weights from mast-height to sink the enemy. Their beaks glared with huge painted eyes. There was an eye on the pennants, too; it was Dionysios' house flag. The barracks of the galley slaves, with their walls and guards, seemed to stretch for miles.

A thirty-foot gate tower closed the landward end of the causeway. Its roof was manned by Nubian archers, polished black men with ox-hide cuirasses and thick horn bows. In front of the gate below, fair as the men above were dark, stood eight towering Gauls.

They wore Greek armor, for show, because they were on guard. I had heard a good deal about these troops, mainly from

soldiers who had run away from them. It was old Dionysios'
rule that his mercenaries should fight in the panoplies of their
homelands, which they felt at ease with; and the Gauls, as
these men assured me, used to go into combat stark naked,
singing paeans like the yowling of cat-a-mountains, tossing and
catching their swords as they came on. They charged with
wide, fixed blue eyes, seemingly insensible to pain and strange
to the name of fear. A Gaul under six feet was reckoned a runt;
altogether, one man told me, it was like facing a battle line of
insane gods. Afterwards they would cut off the heads of the
dead for trophies. Some said they ate the brains.

Now here they were, just as described: shaved chins and
long mustaches, braided ropes of yellow hair down to their
waists and bound with scarlet, long swords with curiously
wrought hilts, neck and arm rings of plaited gold. I had not
much time to stare; the captain shouted to me, without leaving
his place by the gate, and asked my business. Just getting the
drift of his vile Greek, I went up and told him. He must have
topped me by a head, and I am not short. I showed him my
letter; he waved it off, as if it were my fault he could not read,
and in their lilting tongue ordered a man inside to ask. At last
the portcullis went up. A new Gaul beckoned me. We crossed
the causeway, passing between the great catapults I had seen
from afar and their piles of throwing-stones. At the far end was
another gateway, more Nubians on top, more Gauls below. My
Gaul gave a password. This gate opened at once. I was inside
Ortygia.

I had not entered a fort, but a hidden city. In fact, this had
been the first Syracuse, the colonists from Corinth having perceived its strength at sight. They had held it against assault
both from sea and land, till the city had burst its bounds and
overflowed across to the rise upon the mainland. Dionysios had
enclosed all of that in his defense walls; then for his own benefit he had cleared Ortygia of all its ordinary citizens. Each man
in this teeming town was in the Archon's personal service. It
was self-sufficient; all trades needed to maintain it in peace or
war were established here. I saw a street of armorers; a great
clattering forge; a tannery, with a leather works as big as a

small market; potters' and fullers' shops; and as for timber-
yards, I passed three, not counting the shipwrights'.

The ground rose; going up steep cobbled streets and steps,
we came to the barrack quarter. It was more like a soldiers'
town, with a street for each race: Greeks, Gauls, Campanians,
Iberians, Nubians, Egyptians. We went through that of the
Spartans, whose officers would not let them mix with their
fellow Greeks for fear they should be corrupted. They stared
from their doorways, haughty and stupid, and looking quite
little beside the Gaul, which made me laugh. Now we were
higher, I could make out the towers of a huge castle, jutting
into the sea at the island's toe. I asked the Gaul if that was
Dionysios' house: but he said it was the grain store. It was
clear that this place could hold out forever, if it had ships to
command the sea.

At last we came into a much wider street, all one side of
which was a great high wall studded with watchtowers. The
Gaul knocked at a postern and spoke into a grille. The oak door
opened. Sun sifted through green shade; there was bird song;
water plashed and tinkled. We were in a garden. I don't know
what I had expected—anything but this. It had seemed the
core of Ortygia must be solid iron.

It was really a royal park; scattered among the lawns and
groves were handsome houses, belonging to people of rank and
office. There were a good many statues, modern ones, fluent
and suave; the old man must have gone on collecting to the
last. It was hard to believe in the Ortygia outside. At a fountain under a marble porch, women were drawing water in polished jars. Then I began to hear the shrilling of professional
mourners, and knew we must be near the palace.

A tall portico, gilded and painted, was flanked with seated
lions of red Samian marble. A guard of Gauls stood outside; but
otherwise it was a palace, not a fort. So at least it seemed; but
as I went through (the Gaul had passed me to a Greek chamberlain) I saw there was an inner wall fully six feet thick, before one got to the royal rooms. Outside its door of gilded
bronze stood eight Gauls, the tallest yet. When they let me
through, I was led into a place for all the world like the chang-

ing-room in an expensive bathhouse. There were clothes stands, shoe racks, all full—even a mirror. Two of the guards had come in with me. Up from a chair got a fat Egyptian eunuch, bowed, and started without a word to undo my girdle. I was just about to hit him over the ear, when I remembered. This little ceremony had quite slipped my mind.

The eunuch stripped me, shook out my clothes, looked at both sides of my sandals, and hung them up. Then he fitted me out from head to foot from the stands beside him. Some of the robes here were quite splendid; the one I got, second or third class I suppose, was better than my own. While he dressed me, the guards never took their eyes off him. Being used to putting on what I am given to wear, I suppose I minded less than most people.

When I was ready, the chamberlain scratched at the further door, listened, threw it open, and announced, "My lord: Nikeratos, the Athenian actor."

I entered the presence chamber.

But, after all this, there was nothing royal about it. It was just a rich man's room, and new-rich at that, overfilled with valuables, statues, murals, enamel inlays from Egypt, an easel with a Zeuxis on it. The excess, though vulgar, had yet a certain air of sincerity; this was not bought taste; good and gaudy were one man's choice. By the window was the best piece in the room, a massive green marble table standing on gilded Sphinxes, Corinthian of the best period. I remember admiring it, before I really noticed who was sitting at it.

Perhaps old Dionysios was still loitering about somewhere; he can't have been one to let go easily. At all events, the young man at his desk seemed like some clerk who would get up and ask me to wait. Luckily I have been taught how to come through doors, so these thoughts did not betray themselves. I bowed.

I can't remember how he greeted me, or told me what I was wanted for. He was not, as you will have understood, a man of memorable words. One's mind was inclined to wander. I reflected that this was no doubt the desk at which his father had written *Hector's Ransom*, and that he himself was ill at ease here, having some homely lair of his own where he would rather be. When I looked at the room, it seemed natural he should keep me standing; when I looked at him, I remembered I was a prize protagonist of Athens, and thought I should have had a chair. I said what was proper—that I was honored, and so on—adding something about his father's work and the loss to the theater.

"Well," he answered, fidgeting with a scroll before him, "his last wish, almost, was to hear you in his play, so I hope it may please him to hear you speak his eulogy—at least, if the dead know anything, which we cannot tell." He said this last like a man who liked to sound up-to-date. "Here it is; may I hear you read some?"

What's this, I thought, an audition? But I suppose he thinks it due to him.

As I was unrolling it, he said, "I hope you can read my writing. I worked late, and there has been no time to get it copied."

It was quite clear, and I said I wished my theater scripts were always as good. His face brightened like a child's. I asked which passage he wanted.

"Let me see," he said, and fumbled through it head down, like a dog in long grass. He was nearsighted. "This part," he said.

I read a paragraph about the building of the walls of Syracuse. To my surprise the prose was excellent—an Attic style, restrained yet forceful, with beautiful speaking cadences. It almost spoke itself. Looking up, I saw him eyeing me anxiously under a front of judicial calm. Of course, I thought, I should have guessed; he did not want to test me but to hear how his own work sounded. I had met such authors before. So when I came to a passage which was muddled and fidgety and without much shape, I gave it a pleasing contour, as one can if one learns the knack.

A very good piece came next, but he held up his hand and said, "Thank you, Nikeratos. That was excellent. Do bring up that chair there; then we can talk."

He could not wait while I did it, but ran on, "I had heard you were in Syracuse. Among all my concerns—my father's death, my own accession—it must have stuck in my mind. For while I was addressing the Assembly, having prepared nothing at all upon the matter, it came to me as if sent by a god. I just spoke as my thoughts formed themselves. Is not that strange?"

I said nobody would have guessed it; and that is strange, if you like. I have never liked fawners, and can't imagine that I would have flattered his father so. But in the presence of this gangling youth (for with his awkward rawness he seemed no more)—lank-haired, his mourning crop showing his pink scalp here and there, sitting fidgeting with a writing tablet, digging his nail into the wax, picking out bits and rolling them like a schoolboy, clutching at dignity, while his eyes begged like a dog's for notice—with him it seemed trivial to stand upon one's status rather than help him out. So I soothed him as well as I could without being familiar, since it was clear he must dread being taken lightly. In the end, he called for some sweets, which I hate at such an hour, but which he himself ate greedily, and started talking theater, bringing out truisms about the classic tragedies as if no one had thought of them before. He dug down among the stuffed dates and candied rose-leaves, holding forth about the comedy element in *Alkestis;* and all the while my mind's eye retraced my steps that morning: the fort, the Iberians, the drawbridge and portcullis, the Nubians, the Gauls, the causeway with the catapults; the quinqueremes and triremes and pentekonters; the armament shops, the barracks, the walls, the grilles, the searching room. Here we sat talking banalities about Euripides, while around us the greatest power machine in Hellas—or the world—idled along by its own momentum, beside its dead engineer, its quivering levers awaiting the new master's hand, this damp pale hand with bitten nails, rolling wax along the table.

Presently he said I would no doubt wish to pay my respects in the death chamber before I left, and clapped his hands for the chamberlain. When I had changed into my own clothes, I was led towards the wailing. Old Dionysios was lying in the banquet hall, on a catafalque hung with black and purple, in a chest lined with lead. They had packed him round with ice from Etna, to keep him fresh for the funeral. As it melted it ran into a tank below; there was a steady come and go of slaves, bringing fresh ice and emptying the tank with buckets. It had kept him from stinking; I saw his square fighting face, his black stubbly chin, his short pug nose. The hired mourners had got into the swing of it, howling and pummeling their breasts in a drugged rhythm. But at the head of the bier were others who were clearly kindred. One, who had a square face like the dead man's, and the same dark brows, I thought must be his daughter, maybe the one who was Dion's wife.

I took the shears on the offering table, and cut off a lock of my hair and laid it on the pile, which was big enough to stuff a mattress. I was on my way out with the chamberlain when, in the outer courtyard, a man who looked like an upper servant came up and said, "If this gentleman is Nikeratos, the tragedian of Athens, my master would like to see him about the rites."

I followed him into the park, past the fountain, and down to a grassy terrace. Beyond was a house, not very large but perfectly proportioned, with a herm in front of it that looked like a Praxiteles. I had expected the lodging of some official; but even before I was inside, I knew. Everything spoke—the good lines, the plainness, the splendor of the few adornments.

The servant brought me to a white-walled study lined with shelves of scrolls. At a table of polished pine, by the open window, Dion was sitting. I stepped forward. "Good day," he said, as if to a stranger. I was shocked stupid, and just stood there. I'm not sure I even replied. He dismissed the servant; then at once his whole face changed.

"My dear Nikeratos." He got up and grasped my hand. "Forgive me that cold greeting. One moment." He flung open the door, but the passage was empty. "I have had my man ten years; but doubtful times, doubtful men, as they say. Sit down, and let us have some wine; I have been busy since dawn, and you too, I daresay."

He went over to a side table, where a mixer stood in a big krater packed with snow. Having poured for us both, he offered me fresh bread to dip. Nothing could have surpassed the dignity with which he did these simple services. It had a charm too, like that of a well-bred boy looking after his father's guests.

We sat down near the table. On a trellis above the window was an old knotty vine just budding; its sharp shadows fell on the soft waxy shine of the wood, and his brown soldier's hand which rested there.

"The other actors, I hear, went back," he said. "You, Nikeratos, faced the change of fate with your usual courage. And it would have prospered as you deserve. Your speaking of the Eulogy would certainly bring you offers, not only hereabouts but in many other cities. I tell you this in fairness. When one comes to a man for help, one should let him know what it will cost him."

He paused. I could find nothing to say. I feared I must be dreaming this. Had he really asked help of me?

"As for the mere money," he said, "of course I shall cover that. But a rising artist, still young, looks first for reputation. Don't think me ignorant of this. I know what I ask. You must judge if the cause deserves it."

I said I would do anything. I could feel myself blushing like a boy, which seldom happened in my boyhood.

"You are a man I trust," he said, not making a speech of it. "When I heard you had been sent for here, it seemed like the hand of God. We have the business of the rites, and no one need know of any other."

He took from a writing box a letter folded small and sealed.

"To you, Nikeratos, who have heard us share our thoughts, I can say more than just, 'Get this out of Sicily to Plato.' In the first place, you won't fear its being seditious; you know our views on violence. No, the enterprise I urge him to is one of honor to us both. It can bring good beyond reckoning to our young Archon, to this city, even to the world. But of necessity I had to write with frankness, which might give offense and spoil our hopes. Perhaps you understand me?"

I said I thought so.

"If Plato comes, as I have urged him here to do, the thought must seem to Dionysios to be his own, or he will resent it. This is natural in a young man new to power, following such a father. But Plato's welcome depends on this, and on his welcome, everything. As you too may have heard him say, philosophy is not a tool which can be passed about like a mason's rule; it is a fire struck from the glow of minds in search of truth. Without that fire, it is nothing."

His voice, his face, took me straight back to that room at Delphi. The noble folly, the mad beauty of it struck me dumb. Twenty years, or thereabouts, since the golden lad in love brought his friend to Syracuse, to change the old tyrant with philosophy. (I thought of the square pug face in its bed of ice, the jaw clenched like a fist in death, the shrewd wary lines round the closed eyes.) And after everything—after that legendary clash of disparate prides, after the tricked parting, the slave market at Aigina, all these years of half-stolen meetings —now in this man of forty, a diplomat, a soldier, the flame revived when the coals were blown on; he was ready to try again.

I must have been a long time answering. He said, "Yes, speak, Nikeratos. There are few here I can share my mind with. You have met Dionysios. What do you think?"

After thinking how best to put it, I said, "Plato won't stoop to flattery. Do you think it will matter less this time?"

He smiled, and paused. Then he said, "I see you have the funeral speech there in your hand. Have you had time yet to run it over?"

Since he preferred to change the subject, I answered, "Not much of it. Dionysios took me through a little."

"What do you think of it?"

"Most of it is very good; he must have some of his father's talent. There are one or two awkward passages; do you think he would notice a cut or two? This, for instance, adds nothing to the sense, and it doesn't speak well."

"Where?" he asked. I showed him the place. He said, "I think you had better read that just as it stands. He put that in himself."

Our eyes met. I could not believe I had been such a fool as

] *127* [

to need telling. When one thought, his signature was all over it.

"And yet," he said, "when you read this to him, didn't you improve it as best you could?"

"I daresay. He is only young; and he looked so anxious."

"You see, Nikeratos? You are not a servile man; you look for achievement, not for favor. Yet you flattered him. I am not servile either, yet I have done the same. As you see, he copied out the speech himself; by now he thinks he wrote it, but for a few hints here and there. Well, if you and I can feel for his untried hand and his unformed mind, don't you think Plato will? If you had heard him teach, you would know his gentleness with a beginner feeling his way. The will to learn is all he asks. And he knows how to waken that."

I said I was sure of it. What else could I say?

"You yourself have seen Dionysios' hunger to excel. So far, the appearance is enough for him; we may blame his education, or rather lack of it. But as Plato always says, this is the beginning from which young men come to love excellence itself. Sokrates, he says, stamped these words on the souls of all who came to him: *Be what you want to seem.*"

"That's good advice," I said. But I thought to myself, Of course it is. But like the long race, it needs staying power. In theater too, one picks out the stayers early on. If I were choosing a company, I doubt I would hire young Dionysios. However, fate did the casting; I suppose they can only direct him and hope for the best.

Dion, who had been sitting in thought, said, "His father, in what concerned his own affairs, was a judge of men. He knew a son with his own qualities would have been his rival. He feared such a son, yet wished for one. Neither wish nor fear was realized. He admitted no regrets. Whether he felt them, whether the son guessed them, who can say?"

I thought of *Hector's Ransom.* Much was now explained.

"One thing is beyond doubt; the young man wants to be something in himself. As yet, he cannot tell what. So it is now Plato must come. He must, Nikeratos." He looked dog tired. I doubt if he had slept all night. I don't suppose he would have talked like this to me at any other time. "He has a gift from the gods of catching souls. No god has given it me. I hope I do my duty to my city, to my kin, to heaven. Plato made me love honor, and I can say I have not betrayed it. But I cannot light fires in other men. It has been a grief to me."

"That is not true," I said.

I could not help myself. I could have bitten out my tongue next moment. Not for having said it—it would have done well enough as a courtesy—but for saying it with my heart.

He had been looking at a golden lion he used to hold down his papers. Now he looked at me. He swallowed; I could see him thinking what one could say. I have made it sound like a painful moment; yet it was not, for through it all I saw him glad, not I daresay for the sake of the man who said it, but that someone should.

He lifted the lion from its place, set it down, and with the soldier's firmness he always turned to when he was shy, said, "Well, though I did not share your danger at Delphi, I was there to offer the honors of the field. That gives a bond, as it does in war." He was a great gentleman. It rescued us both.

He stood, and turned to a wall niche at the far end of the room. There was a bronze Apollo in it: a calm searching face, the two hands held out, in one the bow of death, in the other the cup of healing. "Surely," he said, "the god you kept faith with then, whom Plato all his life has served, whom proportion pleases in men and cities—surely he led you here in the day of need."

"I won't fail him," I said. "Or you. Let him be witness."

A good exit line, but of course there was still the business of the rites, which took another hour. It was just as well; it made things easy between us.

Before I left he paid me an advance on my fee for speaking the eulogy, more than I had expected for the whole. So, knowing I ought, I picked up my courage and took Menekrates to dinner at the theater tavern. At first the actors who were drinking there looked away, but I had known that would have to be faced. I went up to Stratokles and his friends, saying I should never forget I had them to thank for my good fortune; if they had not entertained me here, Dionysios would never have known I was in Syracuse, and I hoped they would give me the pleasure of standing them all some wine. A few still looked sour, but no one left. In the end they all came round, and we spent a pleasant evening. I was glad to have done it; it seemed to me that Dion would have thought I should.

All next day I was rehearsing for the funeral, which would take place the following evening. The shop of the royal robe-maker had been at work two days and a night upon my tragic robe. It was of black dipped in purple, with foot-deep borders crusted in bullion, amethyst, agate and pearl.

The procession set forth at sunset, down from the palace through the fivefold gates of Ortygia, on through the old town and the new, then between lines of torches down into the plain again, where Timaios the skene-painter had prepared the pyre.

First walked a men's chorus, singing the Lament for Hector from the dead man's play, to the music of double flutes; singers and flute-players wore dead-black robes, and cypress garlands. After these came a troop of soldiers, dragging their spears, their helmets under their left arms. Then a car shaped like a war-ship, draped in black, with an effigy of the Spirit of Syracuse, in a pose of mourning, twice life size. Then fifty boys, singing the Women's Chorus for Hector's wake. After these, the priests of Dionysos, the dead man's name-god, with their sacred emblems. Then torch-bearers, their torches made up with precious incense, for the kindling of the pyre. After that, walking before the corpse, came the male kindred, young Dionysios, and his half-brothers by Aristomache, Dion's aunt, and Dion himself.

The funeral car stood fifteen feet high, and was drawn by an elephant, taken from the Carthaginians in war. They are most fearful beasts, left over as it seems from the Titans' age, as high as two men, gray, hairless, wrinkled, with a tail at both ends, the bigger before; one can tell the head by the great ears. It pulled patiently, guided by a man upon its neck. On a bier draped with black and purple, Dionysios lay clothed in white and wreathed with gold. In spite of the ice, he was starting to go off by this time; I got the whiff of him all the way. I walked just behind, in my tragic robe and a wreath of gilded laurel, carrying his prize vase from Athens. It was of course the usual kind, painted with a chorus and the god; against the other grave-goods it looked as simple as a kitchen pot. But it had arrived before he lost his senses; and till his eyes closed for good he never let it out of his sight.

After me came the women of the household, keening; then a great catafalque with his arms and ensigns and trophies of war. His war horse, and the other victims to be sacrificed before the pyre, were led by Gaulish warriors. Here was a glimpse of the chains of adamant; but the murmuring never got very loud. I suppose it was true that even the poor, whose children scratched in the middens while he ate off gold, preferred a hungry lifetime within his walls to one night of sack by the Carthaginians. I had heard things, by now, which made me understand it.

It was now nearly dark, with just a deep red glow where the sun had set under the sea; but the space around the pyre was lit with cressets whose flames rose six feet high, making it almost as bright as noon.

I should like to have seen Timaios' designs for *Hector's Ransom*. They must have been worth looking at. However, he had spent himself on the pyre instead, and they talk of it to this day. It was so high, the onlookers' necks were cricked from watching the dead man hoisted. The gilded bier-stand would have served to throne a Pharaoh, the offerings to equip a banquet hall; the sides of the pyre, which sloped inward like a pyramid's, were boarded flat and painted all over with pictures of Dionysios' victories. Sicilians love paint. They cover their houses with it, their chariots, even their carts. These battle scenes were framed in every kind of scroll and flourish, touched up with gold. To an Athenian it looked gaudy beyond words, but the Syracusans were squealing and groaning with admiration, and it has found its way into the histories as a major work of art. It was certainly remarkable, and I should think would have kept the poor of the whole city in bread and oil for a year. At all events, they settled the old man up there among the pitch and terebinth and scented oil and tinder. There he lay, waiting to hear my piece before they sent him off to meet

Judge Rhadamanthos. I mounted the rostrum before the pyre. I had been rather nervous; but now the silence was so unlike grief, so like the theater, that I felt quite at home.

While he lived, you would not have found me speaking praise of a man like Dionysios, whoever wrote it. But at a funeral it is proper to remember only the good, or one offends the gods below, and calls the angry ghost to vengeance. Dion's lines were quite honest, as far as they went. He gave him credit as a soldier and defender of the city, and used most of the speech on that. He said also that, though entrusted with supreme power by the Syracusans (as he really had been, in the beginning), he had outraged no household in the city through incontinence or vice. People assured me afterwards that this was no more than the truth, and was probably the secret of his long reign. As Hipparchos found in Athens, wronged kin and lovers are far more dangerous than demagogues; they will kill at the cost of their lives. The old man had learned from history; besides, he had been a demagogue himself.

I had worked hard over his son's little pieces in the epitaph to make them sound like something beside Dion's fine prose. The young man had to be kept sweet, to send for Plato.

At the close, I heard the deep murmur which is applause on such occasions. Then the victims were sacrificed; more offerings were flung; the kindred took their torches and kindled the pyre. At once huge rushing flames leaped up and hid the body, driving the crowd back with their heat. I stood with a scorched face, sweating in my tragic robe, watching Timaios' pretty pictures curl and blacken. Then everyone went home. I remembered my father's poor simple burial, and how we had sat round afterwards thinking, What next?

In due course I was paid, very handsomely. Dion had booked me a passage on a ship sailing next day. I had said goodbye to all my friends, except Menekrates, who was coming to see me off. I felt as good as gone, when a palace messenger came, saying that Dionysios wished to see me.

This time all the gates opened for me easily; but, once inside the palace, I was led by a different way. Presently we came to a door without pretensions, the office of some functionary, I supposed. My usher knocked, and opened. There was a pleasant smell of wood and paint, like a carpenter's shop. Which is just what it was—and at the bench sat Dionysios the Younger, with a toy chariot before him, and a tiny brush in his hand, painting on scroll work. This time he had really done me honor. He had let me into his sanctuary.

"I was very pleased, Nikeratos," he said, "with your speaking of the Epitaph. I have sent to Timaios' workshop for a copy of his Siege of Motya, one of his paintings for the pyre. You may have it, in memory of the day."

He waved his brush at it. It was on an easel against the wall, more garish than ever, seen close to, and too large to ship home without a great deal of trouble. I thanked him as if he had fulfilled my dearest wish. Dion had been quite right. It was like giving sweets to an eager child.

He invited me to go up and inspect the brushwork, which I did. But the table beside it drew my eye; I could not keep from looking. It was full of small toys—chariots and horses, carts and asses and mules, a war galley fully rigged—all painted up Sicilian style, and perfect as real things shrunk by magic. One longed to touch. All these years, when his father had been watching him like a mousing cat for some twitch of dangerous capacity, he had indulged himself with doing one thing well.

Since he would hardly have asked me here if he did not want it noticed, I praised the fineness of the work. I was curious to hear what he would say. I got more than I bargained for. He jumped up and came over to the table. He must have talked for at least an hour. He told me what woods he used, and how, and why; he showed me his gouges, chisels and glue, and his lava dust for smoothing; he pointed out the racing chariots, and the processional. His face grew lively, firm and keen; he looked a different man. Suddenly I pictured him in some nice clean shop in a good street, advising a client about the design of a chair or bed-head, successful, esteemed, content, a happy craftsman, doing the one thing he had in him.

Neither of us, I thought, is perfect casting for a philosophic king. I'm the lucky one; I need not try.

He asked me which of the models I liked best. It was hard to choose, but I pointed out a state chariot with gilded wreaths, which must have cost him most trouble. "Take it," he said. "It's yours. Not many people notice the finer points. I gave one not unlike it to my son, but he broke it within the day; small children don't feel for fragile things." The news that he was a father gave me such a start, I nearly dropped the chariot. Of course he was quite old enough, but it seemed absurd.

"I shall have less leisure for pastimes now," he said, the sureness in his face changing to a weak conceit. "Come back, Nikeratos, when the time of mourning is over, and give us a taste of your art. Then you can sample the pleasures Syracuse affords. Our girls deserve their reputation." The greed in his eye showed something new and none too pleasing. I remembered stories in the wineshops.

Soon after, I left, with the chariot in my hands. The last I saw of him, he was back at his workbench, peering with his weak eyes at his little tools.

# VIII

THE FOLLOWING DAY I SET SAIL FOR HOME, BY
way of Tarentum. Dion sent for me again before I left, to
give me a letter for Archytas, the chief man of the city, and
leader of the Pythagoreans there. It was to urge him, Dion
said, to join in persuading Plato, his guest-friend of long
standing. I undertook to deliver it without fail. Something in
Dion's face assured me it was a forceful letter, and told me,
too, that there lived on within the statesman, general and
scholar a beautiful lordly boy who was not used to hearing
"no."

I had been lucky with weather on the outward journey. The
homeward trip looked like being just as good. I hate even
now to talk of it. Whenever I cross a gangplank it comes back
to me. I have turned down good engagements, time and
again, because it meant a crossing in the bad season.

Not to give you at length my shipwreck story, we capsized
outside Tarentum, in a gale that blew down off the hills. Before this happened, I had felt so sick I thought I would wel-

come death; however, I found myself swimming. I was almost spent when some men, who had found the ship's boat floating free, hauled me on board it. In the harbor mouth, that capsized too. I half-remember coming to on the wharf, feeling worse than dead, cold all through to the core, tilted head-down to let the water run out. I don't know who did that for me. I went off again, and woke in a bed, with a young man sitting by me. After saying I was among friends, he went out to fetch a graybeard. There were heated stones wrapped in cloth warming the bed, and sweet herbs boiling somewhere. It turned out, when I was able to understand, that I was being tended by these same Pythagoreans whose leader I had come to see. It is their rule to succor the distressed, as an offering to Zeus the Merciful.

I had a bad chest, and fever, and nearly went my father's way. I remember little of it, except some of the dreams. They played soft music to restore my body's harmony, and dosed me with sweet hot syrup. The alembic's blue steam danced all day before my eyes like a snake to the charmer's flute. I sweated, or shivered, and they raised me on high pillows to let me breathe. Once I woke from a dream to see my own body propped in the bed, myself looking down upon it. A priest stood praying that I might be reborn as a philosopher. Then I dreamed I was beside some tomb or grave, holding a skull in my hand. It was clean, and I knew this was a play. Some flashes still come back to me: I was the son of a murdered king whose shade had cried me to avenge him; yet I was not Orestes. It would be nonsense, I suppose, like most dreams, if I could recall the whole.

When first I came to myself, the young man who was nursing me showed me my money belt with my gold; I was lucky it had not drowned me. I had only lost my silver, about a tenth of the whole. I asked at once after my letters; he said they were safe, but had had to be dried. They fed me on broths and pottages, meat being forbidden them; they will not kill, saying one should be as just to sensible beasts as to men. But my strength returned on their food. When next I asked for my letter bag, the young man begged my pardon. I had had no

such thing when I was saved; but he had feared to distress
me and bring my fever back again. I thanked him for his
kindness and said he had done right. Presently he asked me
why I was weeping. What precious thing had I lost? It was
not that, I answered; but now I would have to do the letters'
work myself, and I was too tired.

When I could sit up by myself, and felt a little more like
a man, I asked to see Archytas. They said his work and his
meditations took up most of his day, but they would ask him.
He came within the hour: a man of about fifty, with deep-set
eyes, lean, wiry and active. He was a man much trusted by
the Tarentines; though no one was supposed to hold supreme
command for two years running, they had kept voting him in
for seven, never doubting his good faith. I could believe it;
he had a calm that filled the room.

He sat by me, heard me out, and thanked me with great
courtesy, saying we would talk when I was stronger. I slept
well that night, feeling half my burden lifted.

When I could walk with the help of the young man's shoulder (I scarcely noticed he was handsome, which shows you
how weak I was), they brought me to Archytas' house. He
was in his study, a large white room, all shelves and tables,
with books, and dried plants, and geometers' figures—cubes,
prisms, cones and so on—carved in wood. There were pieces of
complex tackle with ropes and levers; he was a great inventor,
and some improved hoist he had devised was used all over Tarentum. There were also lyres and flutes and tuning rods, and a
noble Apollo playing the kithara in a long straight robe.

Having asked how I was, he questioned me closely about
affairs in Syracuse. Dionysios, he said, had often made war
in southern Italy, but through Dion's good offices had never
attacked Tarentum. What kind of man was his son? I told him
all I had seen myself, then repeated, as near as I could remember after all this, what Dion had said to me, and why he
wanted Plato there.

At the end he said, "You have caught the very tone and
pitch of Dion's voice. You must have heard him with great
attention."

"I did, sir. But also I am an actor; one falls into it without thinking."

"Indeed?" he said, looking at me with curiosity. "Your ear must be very true." He picked up his lyre, and struck some notes for me to sound; but soon said I looked tired and should be in bed. "Rest," he said, "and fear nothing. I will give you a letter for Plato, recommending you as a man who has my confidence. I daresay, too, he will remember you himself. He seldom forgets a face."

"And you'll ask him," I said, "to go to Sicily?" He smiled. I expect I sounded, as Homer says, like a child who drags at her mother's skirt and whines to be carried.

"Indeed I shall. You have been Dion's living letter; paper and ink could not have pleaded with such power. No doubt you and he have been linked in your former lives, in love, or kinship; or he gave you true teaching, or your life, or some great benefit for which your soul is still grateful. These ties can be many times renewed, in many births. You are both souls, no doubt, in the series of Apollo. Eat well of pure food; hear the proper music to wake and sleep; take your physic; pray to Apollo and Asklepios. The future is only with the god. Rest in his hand."

All this I did. My strength increased, and in the mirror I saw my face less gaunt. I had dreaded the voyage home, but now was content to let what would be, be. Archytas, who was weather-wise from much observing the heavens, kept me back from the first ship I would have taken; when I sailed, the passage was as good as summer.

Whereas the first part of the voyage had nearly killed me, the second did me good. Nonetheless, when I got to Athens, having been kept up half the night with my friends calling to learn what had become of me, I could not face the long walk to the Academy, but hired a riding ass.

Plato's private rooms looked out upon scythed grass and rose-trees. An old decent slave woman opened; I did not trouble her with my name, but said I came from Archytas. She came back and led me in.

The study was light and sparely furnished, with few but

perfect ornaments. Like Dion's, I thought; then saw it must be the other way about. In the window was a great table full of a scholar's litter: cubes, cylinders and spheres, a model of the planets' courses, music rolls, books, compasses, and a writing board with a scroll taped out across it, before which Plato sat, copying in ink from a wax tablet.

As the slave left, he got up, and, gazing at my face with his deep overhung eyes, said slowly, "You are the actor, the tragedian of Delphi. Nikeratos. It was you whom Dion meant." These last words puzzled me. "You look ill," he said. "Be seated." I told him my business, and what had delayed me in it, and gave him Archytas' letter. He took it in his hands, seemed about to open it, then called the old housekeeper instead and told her to make me a posset to warm me, since the wind was cold. Still he did not break the seal, but asked me about the shipwreck, and my health. Then, like a man making up his mind to something, he excused himself, and read.

When he had done, he said, "Archytas tells me here that Dion saw you in Syracuse, and told you the substance of his letter. Now all is clear to me. I have heard from him since, you understand—a formal letter, supporting an invitation from his kinsman Dionysios. The postscript said, 'I recommend to you Nikeratos, who as you may know is back in Athens. He has done good work here.' I had seen no one of the name, and could not tell what he meant."

Nowadays, when well-known artists are sent openly upon state embassies, this would seem slow in a man of Plato's position. But at that time, the practice was just starting, coming about almost by chance, since actors must travel, and meet all classes, and no one thinks anything of it. It was all undercover business at first, like this of mine. I had never supposed I would be Plato's notion of an envoy.

"Sir," I said, "I won't trouble you with Dion's words. You know him and how he speaks. This was the substance. In the letter I carried, as in the formal one, he urged you to come to Syracuse. But he added that it should be soon, while young Dionysios' mind is still pliable. As Dion told me, his private message was his estimate of this young man. And he wanted me to tell you I had audience twice at Ortygia, if you would like to hear about it. He seemed to think it would confirm what he had written."

Just then the housekeeper scratched on the door, bringing my posset. He assured me it would do me good; he had had the recipe from a priest in Egypt, who had nursed him through a fever there. It tasted odd, and rather nasty; but it was warming and I sipped it up. While I took it, he went back to the letter. Once, while I was looking out of the window as I drank and thinking my own thoughts, I felt him looking at me, and turned. I had been prepared, I suppose, because it was important business, to find him making sure of me, weighing me up. But he was thinking—thinking through me, you might say. He looked away, from courtesy; but for a moment I had felt him, as it seemed, going right through to whatever appeared to him the causes of my being, as if I were a cube or a star. Not for my sake, but for something beyond. He was suffering, and perplexed in mind, and had to break the surface somewhere. I happened to be there, opposite. All that I knew in an instant; it is only finding words that's slow. I finished my drink, and thanked him.

Suddenly he smiled, the same smile, I daresay, which had conquered Axiothea. "Well," he said, "I can interpret Dion's postscript now: 'Trust Nikeratos, as I do.' Tell me then, about your meeting with him, how he was looking, and all he said. We shall agree, I think, in giving him precedence over Dionysios."

Once or twice he interrupted me, to ask if Dion seemed in good health, and what his house was like. Of course he had never been back to Sicily in all these years, but it seemed odd to be telling him. In due course I came to Dionysios, the Eulogy and the toy chariots. He questioned me closely, and often beyond what I knew. What had Dionysios read, did he study geometry or music? I said I did not know, but Dion considered he had had no education. It had seemed to me that he longed to be valued, but was not much concerned whether it was fairly earned or not.

"So many begin with that."

I looked at his face, and this time it held no enigma. I found in it something I could understand myself. It was just the face of a good professional, measuring a piece of work and feeling the call of the god.

I went on talking; ad-libbing, really, till he felt ready to speak. While I talked of Dion, and his feelings were engaged, his face had been a courteous mask; now, as I have said, it was open to a man like me. He was tempted. It was a great role, worth taking; but he was an old hand who had played, so to speak, Sophokles in Boeotia, and been hit with half an onion. He could remember the Athens the old men talk of: war, defeat, despair; tyranny, rebellion; revenge, injustice, hope gone sick. As I spoke and he sank into himself, I could see the weights going into the balance, this side and that.

He looked at the table, with its tablets and open scroll, just as I have seen a man look at a favorite dog he had to leave behind. Then he said, trying to throw it away, "Well, Nikeratos, you have endured a good deal, but not for nothing. I daresay I shall go to Sicily."

It was plain he wanted no speeches, so I just said it would be happy news for Dion, who had set great hopes on it.

He said rather drily, "Too many are doing that. My art, unlike yours, does better without spectators." He paused and added, "But one does not want to end by finding one has been only a thing of words."

As it happened, I was not long ignorant of his meaning. I had scarcely left his garden-close after taking leave of him, when Axiothea and two young men ran out from the olive trees where they had clearly been waiting. After the briefest greeting she said, "You have seen him? Did he say anything? Will he go?"

My surprise at their knowing seemed to amaze them. Nothing else, they said, was talked of here. Didn't I know the invitation had been public? In short, Dionysios had not just sent letters by an envoy, but—as I suppose I might have expected—a kind of embassy to the Academy. All was now clear: Plato's calm, his lack of eagerness for Archytas' letter. I had supposed I brought him news. All this time, he had had a crowd of philosophers, students of law and civics, sophists and geometers and historians, his young men and no doubt many of their fathers, all breathing down his neck, to learn if he would go and prove his theories by demonstration. I suppose most of what I had told him of Dionysios, too, he had picked up already here and there. I admired his courtesy. Maybe I had shed some new glimmer of light upon the work ahead; but mostly I had just loaded on him the Tarentine philosophers, pushing like all the rest.

Certainly, I thought, Dion means to have his way. But I suppose that's what makes a king.

# IX

AFTER THIS, I WAS BUSY FOR SOME TIME WITH my own affairs. When the choregoi drew for protagonists at the Dionysia, I was picked quite early, and cast as Orpheus in a play of that name by Eucharmos. It was a good acting role, very pathetic; my music was done off stage by a concert kitharist, but I sang myself. The play was well received; I was told later, on good authority, that I was in the running for the crown and did not lose by many votes. It went to Aristodemos, who had done a big bravura part as Ajax, perhaps a little florid, but, I don't deny, sound on the whole.

If I do not dwell on this time, it's not from pique at having missed the crown; I was lucky to get so near it. But I started a little love affair, of the sort that is well enough if you don't let it take hold. If he had been anyone else's choice, I should have known just what to advise. But getting deep in, I started to deceive myself, finding all that I wished to see, and calling the rest youthful heedlessness. So, when my Alkibiades of the Agora left me for a well-off fool with a racehorse and a house in the Kerameikos, I could not sweeten it with the thought that I had lost my peace for something worth my pains. I had known well enough, but would not know, for the sake of his laughing eyebrows and golden bloom.

Even so, once I could have taken it lightly. I could not now. I was at war with myself. All the while, when I was wasting hours in guessing where he was, planning the next supper, which had always some bitterness in the cup, brooding on a word or look—in a word, fishing for moonshine—the mask of Apollo looked at me with empty eyes. Once he gives you knowledge, you can't unknow it; if you try, he makes you suffer. I was haunted by those scornful eyeholes, and by a youth whom only my mind's eye had seen, climbing the slopes of Etna with the snow-light on his upturned face. He had stolen my joy in my old contentments, by showing me what men can be.

With such thoughts, I took a walk one day to the Academy in the warm green of spring. I did not seek Axiothea; she might have heard things, and would not understand. But I happened to notice in the garden the dour-faced Xenokrates, who I knew would neither question nor detain me; so I asked when Plato intended going to Syracuse. He raised his brows. Plato had been gone, he said, above a month.

Had all that time slipped by? Since the Dionysia, I thought, every day wasted. Suddenly I felt the need to shake it all off, as a wet dog shakes off water. Here in Athens, I would be meeting at every turn the youth, or his new lover, or friends who had seen my folly. The very air felt stale.

Next day, therefore, I did a round of the foreign consulates, to learn what cities were planning plays. It was not an Isthmian or Pythian year, and too early for Olympia. I hoped I had finished with small-town theaters, and was therefore passing by the Megarian proxenos' office, when I met Eupolis coming out. I greeted him and said I was thinking of a tour. But he was already not the man he had been before he lost his teeth and spoiled his voice. He had been drinking though it was not mid-morning; and, without taking the trouble to wrap it in civility, said he wondered I did not try Sicily again, if I had had such a success there as I claimed.

"As for that," I said, "I don't claim even to have trodden a stage in Sicily. All I did was speak Dionysios' epitaph. But since you ask, it's true I've been thinking of going back there. I daresay that's what I shall do."

I walked on, amazed at myself, thinking, "Now I shall have to go, or he'll put it all over Athens. I, who swore never to set foot in a ship again. What fate made him cross my path? And why did I speak to him? He would have passed me by." Then I went home, to think. The mask hung on the wall, straight-faced in the bright light of noon. But when I turned my back, I felt it smiling.

At least, by now, it was sailing weather. The Sicilian consul greeted me warmly, offered me wine, and said he had been expecting my inquiry. "Not," he said, "that I have any special commission. But with youth at the helm, as the saying is, the crew will all be singing. Syracuse today is a gay city, very gay. I don't think it would be possible for an artist like your-self to lose by going just now. I shall announce you by letter, mentioning your success as Orpheus. Such poetry, such pathos —we were all in tears." I thanked him, but could have done without it; I knew I had overworked the pathos, feeling sorry for myself just then. At all events, I left committed; he was writing by a ship which left that day. It had all been as if a hand in my back were shoving me.

All the same, remembering young Dionysios' fitfulness, I did not mean to put all my eggs under one hen, but called on the consuls of Leontini, Akragas, Gela and Tauromenion, tell-ing them of my visit, and anything else it would do me good for them to know.

The question was whether to try and form a company. But Anaxis had joined a tour going to Ionia; Hermippos was back in comedy; and I was short of capital, having spent too many of those beautiful gold staters they mint in Syracuse, on hu-man gold as lovely and as quick to slip away. I thought I would chance Menekrates' being free, and willing. Though I had never seen his work, he had seemed well thought of; and one can learn much from an artist's way of talking.

Some nights later, when all was done but my goodbyes, at the time of lamplighting came a knock upon my door. There he stood, sure of his welcome, in all the insolence of his beauty and my past surrenders, waiting to see me reel with joy. He had quarreled, he said, with the new friend; after all there was no one like me. I suppose he had asked too much; rich men get the measure of that sooner than poor ones. For a moment Eupolis, the consuls, the westbound passage, seemed never to have been. It would do next year. Then, when I thought I had eyes only for him, I felt other eyes upon me. In the lamplight which flickered in the draft from the open door, the mask was watching.

Beside those eyes of shadow, the blue ones looked shallow as glass. I found my voice. He should have told me, I said, that he was coming; I had promised to dine out with friends. He stayed awhile, not believing that I meant it, then made to go, certain I would call him back. In the street outside I heard his feet pause, and go away.

I had a perfect passage to Syracuse. Halcyons could have nested on the sea. At Tarentum I called on my kind hosts with some gifts to show my gratitude, then on Archytas, in case he wanted any letters taken to Plato. When I went in he did not know me, properly dressed and with something on my bones under the skin. I had put on my soberest robe; but an actor going to Sicily is bound to look frivolous in the study of a Pythagorean, and he gazed doubtfully at first. Presently, finding me the same man still, he talked more freely. He would be glad, he said, to write to Plato, from whom they had heard quite lately. The letter had been brought by a court courier, to whom he could have entrusted nothing private, but he had seemed cheerful and hopeful. He had asked for some of Pythagoras' treatises on geometry, and some of Archytas' own works, for plane and solid figures, and instruments. All these had already been sent. He spoke too of Dionysios' eagerness to improve his mind, with which he had infected his whole court; this was why Plato's own equipment was not enough to go round. "If the gods please," he had ended, "this is the beginning of new things for Syracuse."

"Plato knows how to be discreet," Archytas said, "but is incapable of falsehood. You can picture, therefore, our rejoicing. One must be happy to see Zeus' work done anywhere on earth. But our city lives in the shadow of Ortygia's sails; the health of Syracuse is ours."

He added that this good news had followed hard on bad, for not long before, rumors had been pouring across the straits about young Dionysios' dissipations and debaucheries. Archytas, a veteran of many wars and not one to call three cups of wine an orgy, sounded quite impressed.

The young man had sobered up, however, in time to give Plato a state welcome. A gilded chariot had been sent down to the harbor for him. But this had been as nothing, it was said, to the effect of Plato's presence. Archytas added that if on my way home I would report to him how matters stood, I could expect his gratitude; and, as he hinted civilly, some solid token of it.

When I asked if he had any word for Dion, he said at once that he was anxious to get a letter to him by someone of discretion. This was state business, a serious matter, and I showed him I understood it. Now I was sure of seeing Dion, I would have put to sea in another Tarentine gale, if nothing else would get me there.

In fact, however, we had a good passage and sailed straight into harbor. As I made for Menekrates' lodging, I saw Syracuse was itself again. The streets were loud and jostling; the shops had everything a ship can bring from the shores of ocean; in the gutters bony children scuffled like rats for bits of garbage, while the painted mule-carriages threw dust on them, and the carriage folk held flowers to their noses against the smell. When a Gaulish or Iberian or Nubian mercenary came in sight, the stall-holders would hide their choicest things before he passed.

The sun was just declining. Menekrates, still drowsy from his siesta, was shaving when I arrived. He jumped and cut himself; we had to clamber about finding cobweb to stop the blood. I felt I had never been away.

It was a thousand pities, he said, that I had missed these last few months, especially to get shipwrecked instead. I told him that at Tarentum I had heard wild stories; but no doubt they had gained in the passing-on.

"Not possible," he said. "Lost, more likely. Well, at least there was work for artists."

"I never thought young Dionysios had it in him."

"My dear Niko, even he would hardly ask flute-girls and rope-dancers to his father's funeral. He did observe the month of mourning decently. I suppose it took him as long as that to believe the old man was really dead. Even then, it looked for a while as if Dion would step smoothly in and become another father." Then he seemed to catch himself up, and changed the subject. When, however, I asked him for news of Dion, he answered that he was well, and, lest the Carthaginians should grow too bold with the news of old Dionysios' death, he had made the city a gift of thirty triremes.

"*Thirty!*" I exclaimed. "The richest man in Athens would cry murder if he were tax-assessed at more than one."

"Well, he gave thirty. Our rich men are very rich, believe me. Didn't you sail past the patrol?" He pushed it off too briskly; again I felt words unsaid.

"What is it?" I asked. "You have heard something. I wish you would tell me, and not beat about."

"Didn't you stop at the barber's tavern on your way?"

"No; it was calm enough to shave on board. What news would I have heard there?"

"Why," he answered, making a business of giving me a drink, sweetmeats, and so on, "the story of young Dionysios. To put first things first, it began when Philistos was recalled." This name meant nothing to me. He said, "He's still a great name here, though I was a lad when he was banished. Captain of Ortygia, he was before, as rich as King Midas; gave parties that made history. So did his love affairs. Old Dionysios' mother was one of his mistresses, but the Archon was only just in power, and turned a blind eye because he was too big to quarrel with. Later on, though, he married into Dionysios' family without his leave, and that was another story. That looked ambitious. He was whisked straight off into a trireme bound for Italy, to honeymoon in exile. There he stayed till this year, when we had the amnesty."

"So," I said, "there have been reforms, then?"

"Oh, yes. As I was saying, Dion did wonders in the first couple of months, getting people out of the quarries who had been in for years, or recalling exiles. When Philistos applied, I suppose he advised consent as a matter of principle. It can hardly have been Dionysios' doing; he was too young to have known the man. At all events, he came. They say he's spent his leisure writing history, as all these broke generals do, so no doubt he's kept himself informed. He's still very game for his age; he'd hardly set his house in order before he gave a party, quite up to the former ones, so people say who remember. Dion left early. But young Dionysios stayed. The party broke up two mornings later."

"And that was the beginning?"

"Well, he always stole a little entertainment behind his father's back. No, I think it first came home to him then that he was the Archon and could do just what he liked."

My mind returned to my second audience at Ortygia, and his face when he spoke of the pleasures of Syracuse. As Menekrates said, it was the mourning that had kept me from taking notice.

"It might have been worse," he went on. "It might have been blood he had a taste for. But while living like a mouse in his father's wainscot, he hadn't much chance of making enemies. He called for no heads but maidenheads. All he fancied was a party that would last forever, without his father roaring in to demand quiet for his writing, and pack everyone home. So the next banquet was at the palace. I heard a good deal about it from a girl I know who dances with a snake. Remarkable what she has taught it; you must see her act. But she left on the third day of the party; by then they were looking for something fresh. When the host wants novelty, and can pay, with the place so full too of hetairas and acrobats and so on, one thing leads to another. After a week or so, there was no tale coming out of Ortygia so farfetched that someone couldn't cap it. There has always been a back-door traffic between the citadel and Carthage; the old man used it when he chose; Philistos knew of it.

Now instead of secret treaties, the exchange or death of hostages, and so on, it came in useful for summoning jugglers, fire-swallowers, knife-dancers, or experts in never-mind-what.

"From time to time the party would come out for fresh air, first into the streets of Ortygia, later, sometimes, through all the gates into the town. Pretty soon, when the torches were seen weaving along, wives and sons and daughters were bundled behind locked doors; the revelers seemed to think they conferred a favor on anyone they ravished; no one was expected to pull a long face and spoil the fun. Anyone on business was shown the door at once. Soldiers and ephors ran the city; the bribery rate doubled overnight, when they knew no one was watching them."

I asked, "What did Dion do?"

"Looked in at the party, so my friend told me, to try and get sense out of someone. Of course Dionysios refused to delegate, and only tried to make him drink. That was while she was there; next time he came, I expect everyone was dead-out on the floor, or busy on the couches. So he bided his time, and waited for his philosopher friend from Athens; and not in vain . . . Well, at least no artist starved. Between parties, a play nearly every week; we don't keep them for the high feasts as you do in Athens. I can live half a year on what I've made. A good thing, for the grasshoppers' summer is over." He gave me a glance under his brows, as if in hope he had said enough.

"All summers end," I answered. "I'd not heard of this when I set out; I was only hoping for something at the festivals."

He stood silent, biting his lip, his dark brows pulled together. There was now no mistaking it; he looked bitter. I was getting on edge, and told him sharply to come out with it, whatever it was.

"I wish," he said, "you'd stopped at the tavern and heard it there." He walked past me into the high-walled courtyard. It was green now with vine-shade, and the gourd dangled great yellow flowers. It gave his face the tint of bronze that has lain under the sea. He came back in again and I thought, "Now it is coming."

"Who wants to bring a friend bad news? The truth is, Niko,

your Dion and his Sophist want to make an end of the theater. Finish it, root it up. That's all."

I said, "What? Impossible," while feeling the shock that only truth can give. "But the festivals are sacred."

"So sacred that the theater is unworthy of them. Or so the word goes round." The hot dark anger of Sicily set his face in a frowning mask; then he overcame it, and put his hand on my shoulder. "I'm sorry, Niko. One would think I was blaming you for it. Maybe one shouldn't believe all one hears. This I do know, though. Artists were everywhere in Ortygia, giving recitals, asked to supper, paid in gold. Now, overnight as it were, since this Plato came, nobody, no matter how distinguished. And what's more, for thirty years at least, there's been a play on the Archon's name day. One of his own, if he had one ready, but always something. This month, the new Archon's day came round. Nothing, not even a party. Just sacrifices and hymns."

The shadows had lengthened in the courtyard. Its green light had become cold-looking, like light before rain. I thought of Delphi, of the painted wine cup with Eros in it, the talk by lamplight. I could remember thinking what a high-class supper I had been asked to, all conversation instead of jugglers and flute-girls, a real gentlemen's symposion. I had no more expected this to come of it, than at a fencing class one expects to be run through.

"Don't you think," I said, "that Dionysios is just lying up with a crapula? Has your cousin Theoros heard anything? After a debauch like that, there must be some palace stomachs needing physic."

"I saw him yesterday in the street. He waited, so I walked away. If Theoros wants to give me news, I can guess what kind it will be. No, Niko, no crapula lasts so long. It's this philosophy. Everyone says so."

We were looking at each other with faces of disaster, when I remembered what this meant. Dion had won the victory he, and the Academy, had been praying for. I ought to have been rejoicing.

Trying to bring all this to terms, I said, "But surely, then, he must have given the city proper laws, and called a free Assembly? Even if the theater stops for a time, and artists have to tour, you are citizens too, so wouldn't the good outweigh the bad?"

"If that happened, it might. There were rumors at first, when we had the amnesty. But nothing came of them. I tell you, Niko, I don't mean to sit here eating up my savings. I must get upon the road, as soon as I find a man to tour with. I could make up a company of nobodies tomorrow and play lead, but I'd far rather do second to a good protagonist. More credit, more pleasure, and the money about the same."

"I'm ashamed to ask," I said, "whether I would be good enough."

He flashed his white teeth and grasped my hand, saying, "I hadn't the face to ask outright." I told him I had come here in the hope of it; we laughed, and at once found all our prospects looking brighter.

"I tell you what," I said. "Tomorrow I'll present myself to Dionysios. He told me to, next time I came, so I'll take him at his word. I'll learn what I can, and while I'm there I'll try to see Dion too. If I do, I'll ask him straight out about the theater. Then at least we'll know where we stand." In spite of everything, I was wondering whether he might have some business for me.

We then turned to planning out our tour, on the usual terms. I would put up two-thirds of the expenses, including the hire of the third actor and extra (which I could afford, now I had not their fares to pay from Athens) and split the profits the same way. Then we went to drink to it at the barber's tavern. It was half-empty; the few men there were drinking almost in silence, or getting quarrelsome. We walked home still pretty well sober. He was in better spirits than I; the tour was fixed up, and he was a man for living from day to day. It was I who lay awake. I felt both my heart and mind being torn in two.

Next day I set out early, knowing how long it took to get through all the gates. This time I had no pass; besides, I might find the guards all drunk or dicing. But discipline still seemed fairly good. The assets of a mercenary captain, and his future, are in his men, and he will do his best not to let them spoil.

The guards had been changed at the causeway gatehouse. Instead of the Gauls there were some Italians, who spoke a dialect strange to me: dark, curly-haired men in polished armor, with straight-sided shields and heavy six-foot throwing spears. Their drill was much smarter than the Gauls' and their Greek less barbarous. They looked as proud as the Spartans but more at home; Spartans hate crossing water. These troops seemed as tough, and more professional. They asked my business (I had hoped for someone who knew my face) and then for tokens of my errand. Since Archytas' letter to Dion was confidential, I showed the one to Plato, which I thought should serve my turn, seeing he was the Archon's guest.

The captain read the name; at once his black brows knitted above his haughty nose, and his nostrils curled as if the paper stank. "Plato!" he said for his men to hear. There was a general growl, and a clank as they shook their iron-shod javelins. The captain handed the letter back as a housewife picks up a dead rat. "Well, Greekling, if you get a quiet word with Plato, just tell him this from the Roman cohort." He drew the edge of his hand across his throat. His men supplied the sound.

They let me through. But the news that I was going to Plato was passed on along with me, and from each lot of guards I got, allowing for race and custom, much the same message. Even a Greek, who conducted me through the royal gardens, said, "If you've come from his precious school to fetch him home, you can drink your way through every guardhouse from here to the Euryalos. Only let me know."

He was a big hairy Boeotian, but I felt more at home with him than with the foreigners; so I asked what Plato had been up to, to be so much hated. At home, I added, he had the name of a quiet man.

"Let him keep quiet at home, then, or someone will quiet him for good. He was brought here to corrupt the Archon and make him fit for nothing; and you can guess who hopes to gain from *that*. Disband the hired troops—oh, yes, that's Plato's counsel—and the city left as a gift for his friend Dion. I wish the old man were back. He'd have nailed his head and his four quarters to the gatehouses long before this."

I made no answer. The long night had brought no peace to the war within me. We were getting near the palace. The Boeotian stopped, to have his say. "Have you seen these Syracusans on Assembly Day? They've not shifted for themselves these forty years. How long do you see them keeping off the Carthaginians, without us trained men?" He spat into the grass, saying, "Tell Plato that from me."

We went through the outer court, and a columned porch, to a court within. "Wait here," he said.

I waited just inside the porch, and looked about. It was a green shady place, with flowering creepers trained above, and a big square fountain pool in the center, maybe fifty feet wide. This had been drained, and the tiles scattered with clean sand. On the marble edge, a number of well-dressed men were sitting, and seemed, at first glance, to be fishing in the sand. Then I saw that the rods they held were really pointers; they were drawing geometric figures, with letters and numbers beside them. A slave was going about with a rake, to clean off finished work, and sand, to start again on.

When I had got over the oddness of this spectacle, I noticed something else; one side of the court was much busier than the other. I soon saw the cause. The fountain made a little island, a bronze palm trunk twined with a snake upon a base of serpentine; and on the slab sat Plato and Dionysios. It was the courtiers at my end, behind their backs, who were taking it easy. I saw two of them do a lewd drawing and quickly sweep it over.

Plato was turned a little my way. He was talking, sitting with his massive brow and heavy shoulders leaned rather forward, as if with their own weight; I remembered the pose. His hands were on his knees; sometimes he would lift one in a gesture so spare, but clear, that an actor could not have bettered it. Dionysios came further round, so that I partly saw his face. His lips were parted, and his countenance changed like a field of barley in a breeze, to show he was following every word.

My guard walked about looking for a chamberlain, passing on his way a couple of Gauls at the further door. The sight of them reminded me what a change this was. Nobody had searched me.

Dionysios beckoned my escort, who told his errand and presently came to fetch me. I scrambled across the balustrade, picked my way over the sand, side-stepped a diagram (Plato's I suppose) they had been discussing, and made my bow.

Dionysios had changed greatly. Of course, last time he had been in mourning, unshaven and with cropped hair; but it was more than that. His skin looked clearer, he fidgeted less; he seemed better-favored, like a plain girl pleased with her marriage. Plato was watching him, not as I had once seen him look at Dion, close and proud; still, there was a kind of affection in his face, like a mother's when her child is learning to walk.

"Well, Nikeratos," Dionysios began, but then at once turned round. "Here, Plato, is a man you know, though without, I daresay, knowing his face. This is Nikeratos, the tragedian of Athens, who was protagonist in my father's play."

Plato greeted me with courtesy, but as a stranger. It did not offend me; I guessed the cause, and replied suitably. He complimented my performance, and congratulated me on my crown. He did, at least, seem to hear and see me; Dionysios, from first to last, talked through me at Plato, not slightingly, but as if nobody else were real to him.

"And what brings you to Syracuse?" he asked me.

Good, I thought; now we shall see. "Just the business of my calling, sir. I have come to work."

He looked pleased with this answer. "Well, Nikeratos," he said, going back to his opening line, "so you have lately been in Athens at the Dionysia; and I suppose, after your success at the Lenaia, you were given a leading role?"

I told him yes; he inquired the name of the poet, the theme of the play, how it had been received—things that anyone might ask. But as he went on, I began to recognize that special tone I had observed at the Academy, when they played the game of questions, leading someone on till they scored a point. Being new and half-baked at it, he sounded rather silly. With the side of my eye I glanced at Plato. He was a man who would not have fidgeted if he had sat down on an anthill; but his patience was starting to show.

"So you enacted Orpheus. Did the play treat of his descent into the underworld to ransom his wife, or of his death at the hands of the maenads?"

"The second," I said. "Though he relates the first in a soliloquy."

He brightened. I must have given him the right feed-line.

"Orpheus was the son of Apollo, as we are told. Is it possible that being god-begotten he should have failed to calm the maenads with his song, inspired as he was by the divinity?"

"I don't know," I said. "But some audiences don't want the best, and let you know it."

"Tut," he said, brushing this off. "How will men think of the gods, if their sons are shown in error, or defeated?"

"Perhaps, sir, that they took after their mothers' side."

Plato's eye flickered, like an old war-horse's when he hears the trumpet. But he kept quiet, and left it to the colt, who as I saw was looking put out. I should have held my tongue, as Anaxis would have told me.

"In any case," he said, "you imitated the passions of Orpheus in his desires and fears, hopes and despair; and the audience was pleased with you?"

"I think so. They gave the usual signs."

"And I expect you are also skilled in imitating women, whether old and in sorrow, or young and in love?"

"Yes, I can do that." I wondered how long he could keep this up, in any hope of making me look more foolish than himself. I recalled the quick smooth give-and-take at the Academy, and the humor, of the sort you get when people are really serious. So did Plato, I suppose.

"And you can imitate, too, brawling drunkards, scolding wives or thieving slaves?"

"A comedian would do it better."

"Then you think such parts unworthy of you?"

"No, my skill is different."

"You mean," he said, his nose pointing like a game-dog's, "that you find no kind of person too base to imitate?"

] 156 [

"That depends on how the author uses baseness."

I could see I had cut his cue, whatever that should have been, and it had annoyed him. He came pretty close to asking me how I dared to argue, but then remembered the principles of debate. He peeped round at Plato, partly for approval, but partly in hope that the champion would ride into the battle, and spear me through.

Plato did not notice this appeal, and I saw why. A man was coming along the colonnade which ran round the empty pool. He seemed about Plato's age, and held himself like one who has been somebody all his life. His red weathered soldier's face was getting pouchy with good living, but his light blue eyes were still bright and hard; they had an air of having seen everything worth notice, and knowing what to think. He was well dressed for Sicily, meaning very florid by our standards, but within the bounds of breeding there, covered with clasps of malachite and heavy gold, even to his sandals. He came along by the balustrade, limping a little, from a stiff joint or some old wound, eyeing each man and acknowledging greetings, sometimes warmly, sometimes not; one felt none of it was without meaning.

Plato had noticed him, Dionysios not yet. When he passed two men drawing in the sand, he said something, straight-faced, which made them grin, and followed it with a mock reproof. Plato, clearly, was meant to see. Then he swept along till he was level with Dionysios, to whom he bowed deeply.

The young man said, "Good day, Philistos," and their eyes met. Philistos paused a moment. His face was that of a man who sees his superior, a nice inexperienced boy, making a fool of himself, but blames rather the man who should know better, yet leads him on. The glance was eloquent of respect, discretion, and quiet irony, with a touch of patronage to make it sting.

Dionysios looked in two minds whether to call him over. He refrained however. There was a moment when Philistos seemed to ask himself whether anything he could say would open his poor friend's eyes; then, as if deciding the time was not yet ripe, he gravely withdrew. He remained, though, at the far end of the court, watching the geometrists.

Dionysios looked after him, then back to me. He had been put off, and was now stuck. I would have given him his line, if only I had known what it was.

"But," said Plato, "we were talking, I think, about the nature of the actor's skill."

He was not joining the debate, just making himself felt, like a protagonist who enters upstage and, though silent, at once commands the scene. That was his quality; it cut down Philistos at once to a rich old gentleman, rather overdressed and overfed, who is getting set in his ways and sniffs at everything beyond him. Dionysios revived. He was ready now to dash on and finish the scene.

"Well, Nikeratos, in spite of all your varied skills, I would rather hear from you always that dignity and seemliness with which you spoke the Eulogy. Shall I tell you why?" I saw Plato stir, but his pupil was off by now, showing his paces. "All things here below are only imitations of the pure forms God knows: good if they approach the likeness, bad if they fail. So, when you enact men and their qualities, you are imitating an imitation, isn't that so?"

"So it would seem," I said. I was anxious to keep him going, and get it over.

"Then, if you imitate the worse rather than the good in men, however well you do it, you are giving, really, the worst imitation, the least like the true model. Doesn't that follow?"

I had not met Axiothea and her friends for nothing; one must keep the rules. "Yes," I said. "It would follow on the first."

"But, Dionysios, are we not forgetting how recently Nikeratos joined us?" Plato's clear voice came in like a silver knife slicing an apple. "You and I have come step by step to the concept of divine originals; but he in his courtesy conceded the premise without demonstration. There is a saying that one should not press a generous man too far. At present we may thank him for the pleasure his art has given us; later, when he has followed all the argument, we may win him to our conclusions."

Dionysios looked dashed, as well he might. He took it, though, as pupil from master. The lord of the fleet of Syracuse, of the gates and the catapults and the quarried prison, sulked like a chidden boy. He shot me a look. I saw not the anger of a tyrant put down before a traveling actor, but just a pique, because Plato had not taken his side.

I was trying to think of some civility which would get me off, when at the end of the colonnade I saw Dion enter.

I can't tell how I felt. It was wind against tide. There he stood, the same man as always, without a mean thought in his soul, a man who, if he had pledged protection to a suppliant, would have stood to it till death, though it were for a thrall on a peasant farm. Yet this same man wanted to take away not just the bread out of my mouth, not just the reputation I had worked for all my life, but, as it seemed to me, the soul out of my body.

As he came on, he passed Philistos. I saw it was a greeting of open enemies. They measured one another, like men who do it daily as the fortunes of conflict shift. A child could have picked the better man. Philistos went out sneering; Dion did not look back. I saw a glow on him of victory and hope. He saluted Dionysios. But before that, his eyes had sought Plato's from far off, and the young man had not missed it.

When he noticed me, Dion did not show surprise. He must have known I was coming. His greeting was formal, but I knew he wanted to see me afterwards. When, therefore, I was dismissed from the presence, I made my way to his house. Waiting in the anteroom, I had a good while to think, but found no answer. It needs a sophist, I thought, for that.

At last he came. Keeping his distance before the servant, he went in, then sent for me; but, once we were alone, he greeted me even more kindly than before. He shone with happiness. I had thought he would be ill at ease before me, but no. Among his great affairs, he had not even remembered.

I gave him his own letter, and the one for Plato. He put down my constraint, I think, to bad news I brought, for he read Archytas' letter standing; then, reassured, he offered me wine. The cup was Italian, the painting touched up with white, like his gift at Delphi. Memories crowded me: the crane, Meidias' death cry, the battle at Phigeleia, my father as Cassandra, the great theater at Syracuse where Aischylos put on *The Persians*, Menekrates saying, "It's all one under the mask." The cup shook in my hand. As one learns to do, I steadied it. He had been putting back the jug, and had noticed nothing.

Raising his cup, he said, "To the fortunes of Syracuse. A glorious dawn, Zeus prosper it."

I held myself in, and answered slowly, "Shall we offer the prayer of Hippolytos, *Grant me to end life's race as I began?*"

"Choose," he said, smiling, "some prayer of better omen, for, as I remember, that one the gods rejected."

"I see you know your Euripides. Well then, a toast to purified Syracuse. Down with all riffraff—hired troops, spies, gluttons and drunkards, whores, and artists." I lifted the cup, and threw it down on the marble floor.

I had not known I would do this. The wine made a great red star, and spattered both our robes. A piece of the cup lay at my feet, a crowned goddess, in the Italian style.

He stood stock-still, amazed, then angry. Sicilians of his rank don't know such things can happen to them. Well, I thought, he is talking to an Athenian now, and must make the best of it.

"Nikeratos," he said, "I am sorry to see you so forget yourself."

"Forget?" I answered. "No, by Apollo, I have remembered what I am. I am a citizen of no rank; I don't understand philosophy; when you were studying, I was playing stand-ins and extras, picking up my trade which you want to take away. But whatever I am, or you choose to call me, one thing I know: I am a servant of the god, and though I honor you and love you, I will obey the god, rather than you."

He had listened unmoving; but at these words he started, as if he knew them. I waited, but he did not speak.

"You have been godlike to me." If I had let myself, I could have wept. "But beside the god you are just a man. Farewell. I daresay we shan't meet again." I paused at the door, but there was nothing to stay for, so I only said, "I am sorry I broke the wine cup."

"Nikeratos. Come back . . . I beg of you." The words came

out stiffly. His tongue was strange to them. It was that made me turn.

"Come, sit down," he said. We sat by his desk. It was covered with letters and petitions such as are sent to men in power. There were sheets too of geometric figures and a diagram of the stars.

"My friend," he said, "Archytas tells me that you almost lost your life upon my business. I have grieved you, which I cannot help; but I did it thoughtlessly, and for that I ask your pardon."

"If the thing is true," I answered, "does it matter how you say it? Is it true, or not?"

"This is hard," he said, and leaned his brow on his open hand. "Plato could say this better than I; but it rightly falls on me, the man who you feel betrays you . . . What did you mean, Nikeratos, when you said you served the god? Not just that you perform the sacrifices to Dionysos and Apollo, and respect their precinct, but something more?"

"Surely," I said, "you don't need to be an artist yourself to understand me. It means not setting oneself above one's poet, nor being false to the truth one knows of men. When one can see that the audience wants the easy thing, or the thing just in fashion, and even the judges can't be trusted not to want it too, for whom does one stay honest? Only for the god."

"You hear him speak, and obey him. But could you have heard so clearly, if you had not learned your art from boyhood?"

"No, I think not. Or not so soon."

"Suppose you had been badly trained, and always heard bad work praised above good."

"A great misfortune. But if an artist is anything, sooner or later he thinks for himself."

"But others, not? Bad teaching spoils them past remedy?"

"Yes, but they are men the theater can do without."

"You mean they can take up some other calling. So they can. But, Nikeratos, all men have to live, either well or badly, as they are taught. If enough are taught badly, the bad will get rid of the good. And you, whether you choose or not, are a teacher.

Young boys, and simple men, don't go to the theater to judge
of verse; they go to see gods and kings and heroes, to enter the
world you make, to steep their minds and souls in it. Can you
deny this?"

"But," I said, "one plays for men of sense."

"You keep faith with your art, Nikeratos. You will not offend
the god with anything unworthy, even though men would reward you for it. But your power stops there. You cannot rewrite
your play, though the poet may be doing the very thing you
would scorn to do."

"That is his business. I am an actor."

"But you both serve the god. Can his god say one thing, and
yours another?"

"I am an actor. He and I must each judge for ourselves."

"Truly? Yet you have to enter his mind. Have you never once
felt you were entering a false world, or an evil one?"

I could not lie to him, and replied, "Yes, once or twice. Even
with Euripides, in his *Orestes*. Orestes has been wronged, but
nothing can excuse his wickedness. Yet one is supposed to play
him for sympathy."

"Did you do so?"

"I was third actor then. I should have to try, I suppose, if I
were drawn for it."

"Because that is the law of the theater?"

"Yes."

"But, my dear Nikeratos, that is why we want to change it."

"I understood," I said, "that you wanted to destroy it."

"No, not so." He looked at me with kindness, as if I were a
decent soldier he had beaten in war. "Plato believes, as I do,
that an artist such as you, who can portray nobility, has his
place in the good city. In some such way as this: that the parts
of base, or passionate, or unstable men should be related in
narration, while only the good man, who is a fit example, or the
gods speaking true doctrine, should be honored by the actor's
imitation. In such a way, nothing evil would strike deep into
the hearers' minds."

I gazed at him, solemn as an owl. If, having begun to laugh,
I could not stop, which seemed likely, he would despise me for

instability. I told myself this, to sober up. Not that I feared his displeasure now; as I had said, he was just a man. But the man was dear to me.

"You mean," I said, "that in the *Hippolytos*, for instance, where Phaedra reveals her guilty love, and where Theseus curses his son in ignorance, all that would be narrated? Only Hippolytos would speak?"

"Yes, just so. And we could not admit of evil being caused by Aphrodite, who is a god, to a just man."

"No, I suppose not. And Achilles must not weep for Patroklos nor tear his clothes, because that is a failure in self-command?"

"No, indeed."

"But do you think," I asked at length, "that *any* of it would strike deep into the hearers' minds? You don't think it might be dull?"

He looked at me, patient, not angry. "As wholesome food is, after those Sicilian banquets that have made us the scorn of Hellas. Believe me, our Syracusan cooks are artists too, in their way. Yet you would not lose your figure, health and looks to please one of them, would you, even if he were a friend? And is not the soul worth more?"

"Of course it is. But . . ." It was no use, I thought, against a trained wrestler of the Academy. I had learned my art by asking how, rather than why.

"Only look, Nikeratos," he said, his fine face lit with eagerness, "at the world around us. Look what men as they are have brought it to. War, tyranny, revenge, anarchy, injustice everywhere. Somewhere, somewhere one must begin."

At these words, my feet seemed to feel firm ground. I said, "That is true. Then why, seeing Dionysios is eating out of Plato's hand, doesn't he seize his chance, and get the Syracusans a proper constitution? Soon it will be too late; even I can see that. Why is the city as full of mercenaries as ever? The tyranny goes on, while you all scratch circles in the sand—" His face reminded me, if my own sense had not, that I was speaking to the first minister. I said, "I go too far. But we were talking about justice."

"We were," he said after a pause, "so I will tell you why. You have been very sick this year. When the fever had left you, could you get up at once, and go about your business? Or did you need an arm to lean on? Well, Syracuse has been sick for almost forty years. A whole generation, reared in sickness . . . even to the highest."

"And so," I said, "you must begin with the child at nurse, with the schoolboy at the theater. And Dionysios—he must begin with mathematics."

He clenched his hand on the desk, as if begging the gods for patience. "Nikeratos, don't make me angry. Don't treat me like a child, and Plato like a fool. He was learning politics at first hand before I was born; and so was I, before you were. If you think you know your own business best, give us some credit for knowing ours."

I was ashamed, and begged his pardon. He only put up with me out of gratitude, and because I had shown him my heart.

"Try to see you are not in Athens now. This is Sicily. Beyond the River Halys are the lands of Carthage. The enemy stands with his foot in the door, pushing as soon as our shoulder slackens. What use is it to pay off the mercenaries, and pull down the walls of Ortygia, and set the people by the ears with a new regime, before we have made a man to lead them? They are better off as they are than as slaves in Africa, or nailed on crosses, or spitted over fires, and they have always known it. Dionysios has no root of greatness"—he had forgotten in his deep earnestness even to drop his voice—"he cannot lead men nor make them love him. But he can still save Syracuse, if he can only be taught to think."

"Yes," I said. "All this is true, if you had time. How long do you think you have?"

He began to answer, then asked sharply what I meant.

"Only what you have surely seen yourself—that Dionysios is working at his geometry not because he likes it, but because he is in love."

"In love?" He frowned to himself, looking for a joke. Like many good men, he had not much sense of humor. Plato had far more.

"You are not serious," he said. "Plato could be his father."

"True indeed. He should know himself better. He is in love all the same. Youth worships the mask of love; that is his Eros, a powerful god. Didn't you once know him?"

"No. Our play was real."

"How the gods loved you. Do you think all men have such fortune? That poor little man in the palace has had to be his own poet. His father wrote plays, he lives them. He has got right into his part, too; don't you see what it is? A young aristocrat, brilliant, dissolute, charming, reckless, called to the good life by a philosophic lover?"

For once he laughed aloud. "Alkibiades! Come, this is a serious matter."

"It is to him. He is rather short of beauty and charm, but, as he sees it, he can still improve upon his model, that bright falling star. He will be true to Sokrates' teaching, and deserve his love."

"You cannot mean this. Plato's conduct has been in every way correct."

"How not? Yet the young man's devotion touches him, and he is kind. After all, Sokrates mastered his desires; do you think Dionysios wants to know the difference? All he wants is to be the beloved disciple, to know that he comes first. If something seems to stand in his way, will he prefer to blame Plato's coldness, or an old rival who won't stand out of the light?"

"My dear Nikeratos! This is not one of your tragedies." He was brisk, yet not quite at ease.

"Maybe not," I said, "but it's theater all the same. I don't know much of politics, as people are always telling me; but at least an actor knows jealousy when he sees it. You should watch his eyes."

He paused, biting his lip. "That is nothing new. I was proving myself among men, fighting battles, leading embassies, while his father kept him shut up like a woman." He did not add, though he must have known it, that it was he who had Alkibiades' lifelong beauty. "Envy is natural."

"Well, this is one thing more. You can load so much on a

donkey, then he won't go. How long do you count on? A generation? From what I saw today, I'd not lay two obols on it to last a year."

He gazed at me, only half his mind on the matter. He was wondering, as I could tell, how it had come to pass that I could take such liberties. A just man, he blamed himself and would not punish me. Maybe he still liked me a little; it was time to go, while this held good. But there was something I had forgotten to mention.

"I think," I said, "that it would be as well if Plato's friends warned him not to walk alone about Ortygia. The soldiers want to cut his throat."

"What? Who told you this?"

"They did. I heard it at every gatehouse. They all say he's working to get them turned off."

Aroused at last, he struck the desk with his hand and cursed as if he were in the field. "The young fool! He will talk—like a barber, a bawd, a midwife. He leaks like a cracked water jar. He cannot be kept from talking."

No need to ask whom he meant. "Then Plato didn't advise it?"

"Plato has fought in war! Of course he counsels it, but as the goal, not the means. When the new laws are established; when the citizens are trained in public business, content, and loyal; when the ruined cities, which the Carthaginians wasted, are resettled and could fight beside us. Who but a madman would strip the city now?"

"Now I understand. Dionysios proclaimed his good intentions? He's always wanting to be crowned before the race."

"You may as well know, Nikeratos, what it seems has become known all over Ortygia. Not long ago was his name day, and the usual sacrifices were offered. The priest made the accustomed prayer, composed in his father's lifetime, to the appropriate gods that they might preserve the Archon in his power. In the middle of the prayer, he flung up his hand and cried, 'No! Don't invoke a curse on us!' Then he looked at Plato, expecting praise."

I forget what I said. Anything would do, except what I was

THE MASK OF APOLLO

thinking: Why, in the name of every god, do you keep this mountebank playing lead, instead of taking the role yourself?

I might not, as he had told me, know much about affairs. But I was not such a fool as to suppose that if I said this aloud, I could enter his door again. If I could think of it, so could he; there must have been times when he could think of nothing else but that, and his honor; and as fiercely as he had thrust aside temptation, so he would thrust me. So I covered my thought; but it burned within like a banked-down fire. From these unspoken words till I took my leave, there is no more of our talk that I remember.

# X

I ENJOYED MY TOUR WITH MENEKRATES. WE
worked well together, though I had been warned of him, behind his back, as a man who would not give. Theater in Syracuse is full of malice. Maybe he did not like being put upon,
having had plenty of that at home, but as I never tried it I
cannot say. After running through a few scenes with him I
knew that he was sound, so chose plays with strong second
roles, and never had to regret it.

It was at his suggestion that we put into our repertoire a
modern comedy by Alexis. He is such an innovator, tragedians
might as well play him as old-style comedians. Not only has he
got away from all the topical satire and scolding which stale
as quickly as cheap wine; he has even dared to put away that
poor old prop the phallos, too tired these many years to pleasure the goddess Thalia much. Alexis has real men and women
in real scrapes, natural masks for the juveniles and the sym-
pathetic characters, and, between the jokes, much kindness for
mankind. Menekrates said he liked to think, when he took off

his mask, that maybe someone in front had gone home less ready to beat his children. This was about as near as he got to talking about his boyhood. It was a pity, I thought, that he and Dion would never understand each other.

We had both started young and poor and slept hungry in old straw; we laughed over it together, sharing our pleasure in good food at clean inns. Often we improved even on this, for Sicilians are theater-mad, and lords with land to the horizon would not only ask us to supper, but put us up. The backstage gossip of Athens or Corinth was all they asked; if one felt like giving an excerpt from some success not yet on tour, then nothing was too good for one. As for the peasants, they would walk all night to see a play, when the grind of their lives would let them. At Leontini, Tauromenion, Akragas and Gela, even in the little towns, the audiences were splendid and took all the finer points. The skies were blue, the fruit trees blossomed, thyme and sage scented the hills; and we had, as Menekrates had foretold, no competition. The leading men of Syracuse feared to lose status by doing local tours, and were holding out in the city for better times and then, when they did not come, going off to Italy. Our own third actor and extra were much better men than we would have had when things were easy. We made good money, and lingered in the pleasant places.

No one we met believed for a moment that theater could stop in Syracuse. People laughed or shrugged, saying young Dionysios had run through a dozen crackpot whims already; we should get back to find him learning the kithara. Hadn't we seen for ourselves that all Sicilians had theater in their blood? At this the company would all cheer up, and I myself along with them; then I would think of Dion, trying to shift from its foundations a forty-year load of tyranny, and would be at odds with myself, not knowing what to feel.

We were playing Heloros, which is about twenty miles south of Syracuse, when we heard of bandits in the hills. By now we were carrying a good deal of silver, from smaller towns which could not give us bankers' letters. I showed the company the accounts; it was agreed I should go over to the city and get the surplus takings safely banked.

] *169* [

I did this business without trouble, and went to look about me. The theater tavern I avoided; by now it would be a desert of old men and embittered failures. I chose a wineshop where the gentlemen resorted; it had a cool shady courtyard with a vine. I had hardly sat down and given my order, when a voice cried, "Niko! What are you doing here?" It was Speusippos, Plato's nephew.

He came over to my table, as usual well dressed and barbered; yet I thought at once that he was not as young as I had supposed, the wrong side of thirty. Lines showed in his face, and his mouth looked drawn.

I offered him a drink—which he refused, saying he had just been drinking with some Syracusans—and asked how long he had been in Syracuse. He said he had come out shortly after Plato, who was in need of help with his work and correspondence from someone he could trust.

I had always liked Speusippos. In spite of his hot temper, he was not the man to pick a quarrel, or drag it on. Though he was agreed to have one of the best minds at the Academy, and was an expert on the growth and properties of plants, he also studied girls and horses and the theater, and found no trouble in talking with common men. I would have been pleased to see him, but for his look of having had bad news.

He asked about the tour; I told him, since Plato had better know, how rooted the theater was in Sicily. He nodded, but I saw this was the least of his troubles. So I asked outright whether Dionysios was making good progress.

He ran his hands through his dark hair, upsetting the barber's curls. "Progress! You met him, I believe. The progress a boy makes with his book, while someone is showing him a cockfight."

I looked round; I had been in Sicily long enough for that. But he was no fool; the near tables were empty. "Philistos?" I asked.

"You know the man?" He had sharpened, as if eager for any scrap of knowledge about a dangerous enemy. I said I had barely seen him, but had heard things before I left.

"You'll hear more now. And mostly praise. Can you believe

it, Niko? That venal, greedy old lecher, who did as much as anyone to set up the tyranny! Now they call him a sound states-man because he wants the city kept in chains, and a good fel-low because he wants to make the man whose slaves they are the slave of his own appetites."

"Well," I said, as one Athenian to another, "they were bred up without justice, like bats without light. It must hurt their eyes."

"We all come from the light, Niko. The soul can remember, or forget." For all his easy manners, he was Academy through and through.

"How much," I asked, "does Dionysios' soul remember?"

He gave a short laugh, then answered seriously, "Enough to open his eyes. If that were all."

"He won't work for it," I said, "and wants to blame someone else?"

"You must know him well."

"No, I've known actors like him. Yet Plato is still in favor?"

"He won't hear of his leaving. Of course all Greece would know, and say the son had followed the father. But I don't think it's only that."

"Nor I. So he loves him still?"

He looked down his high-bred nose. As a youth he must have been striking. Perhaps he had had some share in Plato's love.

"You may call it that; or you can say he would like to be Plato's best student, without working. Of course he would like to be Philistos' best student, too. He has rolled by this time in enough logic for some to stick; he knows when two propositions exclude each other, but . . ."

"But he feels," I said, "right down in his soul, that logic should make an exception just for him."

He propped his chin in his palm and looked at me. "You are mocking us," he said.

"What am I, to do that? A phantom in a mask, a voice of illu-sion."

"You too, Niko, even you."

A harsh Sicilian sunbeam stabbed down through the vine, picking out the lines of thought and pleasure in his face, deepened by weariness. He had meant it; in his trouble even I had power to cast him down.

"Forgive me," I said. " 'He who mocks sorrow shall weep alone.' But if you think me sour, talk to some Syracusan actors, and I'll seem like honey."

"It is your life," he said wearily. "I know it. But somewhere the surgeon's knife must cut, or the patient dies."

"Artists are few among many; that I understand. But bear this in mind, Speusippos: while you, sitting in front, are watching our illusion, we are looking at reality. While you see four men, we see fifteen thousand. Twenty years I've played to them. One learns a little."

He said harshly, "What do you mean? That they won't forego the theater? Or something more?"

"Well, both. What is it you Academics say of Plato? Like his master Sokrates, he won't sell his teaching, he'll choose his audience. Does he think he can do that here? He must make do with what comes, just like an actor."

"Plato was born among great affairs, and has lived with them ever since."

Here's another, I thought, who loves him still. I said, "Once at the Dionysia, someone in the skeneroom fell down deathly sick, and they fetched a doctor. The good man came running, took the wrong door in his haste, and found himself upstage center, standing next to Medea. Hasn't Plato seen yet where he is?"

He fetched a deep sigh. "Oh, Niko. I think I will have that drink you offered me."

I called the boy. When we were alone again, he said, "What do you think I was doing here before you came? I'm about the city all day, scraping acquaintance, joining hetairas' evening parties, talking to bathmen and barbers, to learn the temper of the people. It's the best I can do for Plato; that, and staying away from the Palace. The Archon thought we were too close; he was getting to hate me nearly as much as Dion."

"Hate!" I said, shocked. "Has it come to that?"

"Hush," he said, as the boy came with the wine. Then, "On your life, Niko, keep that quiet. Every day that doesn't bring it

out in daylight is something gained. So far it's only slights, coldness and pinpricks. If it comes into the open, what can Plato
do? Honor, truth, the pieties of friendship, are his very soul. To
put it as low as you can, he is a gentleman. He can't be neutral.
It would be the end of this whole great mission."

"Nearly two months ago," I said, "I tried to tell Dion this."

"It is hard," he said slowly, "for a lover of truth, who lives in
a corrupted polis, not to become rather unbending. He has seen
too much base compromise; any accommodation scratches his
integrity. With his looks, he must have come young to that."
He frowned into his cup, and drained it. I lifted the flask from
its bed of snow, and poured again.

"At the Academy," he said, "we think that truth, being man's
highest good, should be sought like joy, not endured as children
take a purge. From that faith comes all philosophy . . . Don't
look so anxious, Niko, I won't engage you in elenchos. I mean
it's no shame to make persuasion pleasing. If you want clear
water, don't tease the squid. Plato is forever saying that to
Xenokrates—a kind man, if he would own it to himself—who
charmed you so by likening actors to whores. 'Sacrifice to the
Graces,' Plato says; I told him once I'd build them an altar in
the garden. Well, not long ago I heard him say it again; but to
someone else."

"You mean Dion?" The blood stirred round my heart. I
slammed my cup down on the table. "*He* need not sacrifice. He
has the graces of a king. Why should he use a courtier's? Do
you know what I think, Speusippos? If it comes to an open
break, so much the better. Then he will be free to take his
rights."

Speusippos' face changed. He laid his hand over mine; it
looked affectionate, but his nails dented my flesh. I took their
message and was silent. He leaned forward and dropped his
voice discreetly, but not quite enough. "Of course, my dear, if
they quarrel you shall be the first to know. That is, if you really
want to court this boy? But I warn you, he's spoiled, as mercenary as he's pretty, and tells more lies than a Cretan."

I had heard, while he spoke, the benches scrape close by, and
thanked him with my eyes. "You're jealous," I said, "because he

went home with me after the party. A charming lad. I can't
think why you call him mercenary. When he asked me for my
ring, it was only as a keepsake."

When I returned from the city to our inn at Heloros, the
company crowded round me, asking the news from Syracuse.
I told them I could not see much change. All their faces fell. I
asked myself why I was hiding news which would have made
them happy. They were fellow artists, and friends. The third
actor, Philanthos, a promising young man who should have
been playing second in better times, had stopped at every
shrine of Dionysos along the road, and made some little offering.

I had affronted Dion to his face—with such difference of
rank one can scarcely speak of quarreling—yet had been ready
almost to fly at Speusippos for his sake. If Menekrates and the
others, elated by my news, went drinking to his speedy down-
fall, no doubt I would also fly at them, which they did not deserve.

Trying to understand myself, I thought how often I had sat
before the mask of some hero king—say, Theseus in *Oidipos
at Kolonos*—to feel my way into his greatness. As Plato said
(from what I could make out of it), before there can be imitation, the original must exist. Can one hate the Form whose essence one has tried to enter? But having found the nature of
my problem, I was no nearer solving it.

We played one or two more engagements, and a return visit
to Leontini. Having seen us in Alexis' comedy, they now offered
us a chorus, to put on *Hippolytos* at a public festival. I played,
as the protagonist always does, Phaedra and Theseus; Menekrates was a good Hippolytos, moving in the death scene; and
we had an excellent house. The party which followed went on
till dawn; the hotter it gets in Sicily, the more they turn night
into day. We were all offered hospitality, my own host being a
retired captain of Dionysios' mercenaries, one Rupilius, a Roman, but quite civilized in his manners; he had been given
some land here, by way of pension.

It was past noon the day after the party, and I was still in
bed, playing with a breakfast of melon chilled in snow and pale

cold wine from the slopes of Etna, when my host scratched at
the door. Begging my pardon for waking me so early, he held
out a letter. It had come from Syracuse by fast courier; the man
had changed horses, and was waiting for my answer.

I put down my cup on the marble side table, and took the
letter. It was sealed with a crest which I could not make out,
the shutters having been closed against the noonday glare; but
I could think of only one. He needs me, I thought; in some
trouble he has turned to me. He trusts me still.

If my host had been Greek, he would have been dawdling
by me, in hope of learning all about the letter; but Romans are
too proud to show curiosity, which they think undignified, and
he had withdrawn. I jumped out of bed in the dim room,
opened the shutters, and stood naked in the sun to read. The
strong light dazzled me; it had been a real Sicilian party. I
blinked and tried again.

"Dionysios son of Dionysios, to Nikeratos of Athens. Joy to
you. When you spoke our late father's epitaph, we expressed
the wish to see you in classic tragedy, when the mourning time
had passed. Cares of state, and our course of studies, caused us
to defer it. These studies being now complete and ourselves
at leisure, the City Theater will present, on the ninth day of
Karneios, the *Bacchae* of Euripides, with yourself as protagonist. You may choose your own supporting actors. A not unworthy chorus is already training. Philistos is choregos. Farewell."

I read it twice. Something stirred in the courtyard; it was the
courier's fresh horse, waiting to take my answer back.

I closed the shutters, and threw myself on the tumbled bed.
The room smelled of melon rind and wine and sweat. The flask
was still three-parts full; I reached for it, but put it back. It
would not help me think.

Syracusans use the Dorian calendar; I tried to think which
month Karneios was. It must be the coming one, our Metageit-
nion. The ninth was fifteen days ahead, barely time for rehearsals.

Why, I thought, did I ever come back to Sicily? I had my
work, my friends, my life at home; I knew where I was, there.

Out of a thousand actors minding their own business, why must it fall on me to be grasped by both hands and pulled in half? When did I speak the bad-luck word? What god have I offended?

Not Dionysos; here he was, through his mortal namesake, inviting me to play himself in one of the greatest bravura roles of classic tragedy; no deity of the machine, but the kingpin of the action. I thought of young Philanthos, lingering by all those altars with his pinch of incense or bunch of grapes. Who says the gods don't regard men's offerings? After a command performance, he could step into second roles at once. As for Menekrates, he would do a first-rate King Pentheus—his Hippolytos had shown me that—and be made for life. His family would offer him the chair of honor, and Theoros stand up for him.

Dionysos blesses his faithful servants. So much for Dionysos.

I lay a long time, while the flies buzzed round the melon rind, my arms behind my head, watching a gekko on a beam. At last I got up, and opened the mask-box on the table. This time I had brought it with me.

I propped the mask upright on the pillow, and lay before it, naked in the oven-hot Sicilian afternoon, my chin cupped in my hands. It gazed back at me, not empty-eyed as in those months at Athens, but secret, Delphic, dark. It answered nothing, only asked. "Are you not Nikeratos, son of Artemidoros, who said to a man he loved and honored, 'I will choose the god, rather than you?' Choose me then, if you can find me. The courier is waiting, and so am I."

"Phoibos," I answered, "they call you Longsight. You can see what this means. This is Philistos' triumph-song. Dion is out of power. Standing before your image I said I would not fail him. Must I sing for Philistos now?"

The mask looked formal and holy, as in a temple. "Truly, friendship is sacred. Guest-friendship above all."

"You mean Menekrates. My lord, I know. I am bound to both. What shall I do?"

"Most men count the cost."

"To my fortunes? Little either way. If I play, I shall have a fine role with a handsome fee, and my company will love me. If not, I can go back to Athens and say I refused the tyrant. Everyone will admire me, and someone will give me an important lead, to reward my constancy, and because a well-liked protagonist helps a play to win. Someone else will pay: Dion, or Menekrates, as the case may be."

"Which loses most?"

"Each loses something dear."

"Are you a god, to measure loss with loss?"

"Apollo," I said, "we are starting to talk in stichomythia. This is not a play."

"You say truly. Well? Are you asking me to help you choose between your friends? You said you would choose me."

He had stared me out. I laid my face on my folded arms, but not to weep. I could do that later. The courier was still waiting. At last I said, "It is my turn to ask you if I am a god."

He answered in the voice of Speusippos, "We all come from the light, Niko. The soul can remember, or forget."

"Dion remembers, or so he and Plato claim. Justice, and the good life."

"They remember their share." A sun-glint through the shutters struck the pillow near him; the reflected light changed his face; he seemed to smile. "And you? What do you remember?"

There came before my eyes, seen through those very eyeholes, the theater at Phigeleia. I felt on my head the hot gold wig, smelling of Meidias, the lyre in my hand, my youth beating like wings in me, and words sounding out across the empty battlefield. I said aloud:

*The gods wear many faces,*
*And many fates fulfill*
*To work their will . . .*

Far off in the mountains a shepherd's pipe was sounding. Now Phigeleia was gone; I heard Athenian flutes receding, the singers dying away beyond the parodos, the stillness left in the heart.

"Well?" said the god impatiently. "So you remember the tag of *The Bacchae*. I should suppose as much. No more?"

He was going to tell me, so I waited. "It seems to me, Nikeratos, that when last you sat in front to see this play, you said something to the youth beside you. He was not attending, since it was not for his knowledge of Euripides that you had sought him out; but I, as it happened, overheard. Don't you remember? 'To my mind, Phrynon, one cannot go everywhere with Euripides. He is sometimes impassioned over dead things, the war, the oligarchs and demagogues of his day, or that old scandal when the Spartans bribed the Pythia; then he gets angry himself, instead of leaving justice to the nature of things, which after all is tragedy. The old scores are settled, the scar on the play remains, like the mark of an old rotted goat-tether on a living tree. With *The Troiades* he rose above it; but with *The Bacchae* he digs down far below, to some deep rift in the soul where our griefs begin. Take that play anywhere, even to men unborn who worship other gods or none, and it will teach them to know themselves.' "

There was a silence. He waited a little longer, then said in a voice as cool as water, "Do you deny those words?"

I answered, "No, my lord."

"Goodbye, Nikeratos," said the mask, making its eyeholes blank. "The oracle is over."

# XI

I CALLED ON PHILISTOS AS SOON AS I GOT BACK. He was genial, brisk and businesslike, had clearly done choregos countless times, and knew what he was about. The secret of my work for Dion must have been well kept, for it was a sponsor's interview like any other. He was very correct, knowing what was due to his rank and to my standing; he would not nag or fuss, or try to teach me my work. If he had been a stranger in a strange city, I should have gone home well satisfied. As it was, I thought how easy he must have found it to undermine Dion with this one weapon the other lacked—the knack of pleasing useful men for whom he did not care two straws.

The company was treating me like the eldest son's wife who at last has borne a boy. While I was thinking the matter over at Heloros, the news of the courier had got to all of them. Menekrates told me the other two had almost gone on their knees to him to intercede with me, but knowing me best he had more sense. When I told them I would play, they looked like men reprieved from the quarries. I had to go drinking with them, or we should never have been at ease again.

One thing rode my mind, that I must get to Dion—not to excuse myself, for I had broken no pledge to him, indeed had declared I would do this very thing I was doing, but to say I was sorry to cross him even for the god I served, and was still at his service in any other way. But I had never used his name to get through the gates; if he had private work for me, it was the last thing I ought to do. I could have gone on there from Philistos, who also lived in Ortygia, but he gave me the feeling that spies surrounded him, and I feared he might have me followed.

I was wretched over this matter for two nights and a day; then I was summoned to go and see Dionysios.

This, as before, might serve my turn. I must own that I was full of curiosity, too. He was a man who could put on three masks in a day, believing each to be his face, and I longed to know the latest one.

The gatehouse guards all seemed to be in better humor. The Roman officer remembered me and asked if I had come looking for Plato, not angrily, but as a man jokes with a boy. When I showed him Dionysios' letter, he became very correct. Once more I noticed how his men's obedience was without servility, how well they kept their panoplies, and the air they had, as if they not only thought themselves the best, but expected the world to know it.

I was led in through the searching room, where I was well gone over. The eunuch even ran his fat fingers through my crotch. But the robe he gave me was handsomer than before; I had gone up a class, it seemed.

The room of state had been altered. From the quick look I had time for, I should think nearly everything good of the old man's had been bundled out, and the places filled (for the room seemed fuller than ever) with modern art. The Zeuxis had gone; the statues were all gesturing like orators, or, if female, wrapping their arms round their privates. One Aphrodite looked as shy as if she had just been through the searching room. Luckily, before I started to laugh I saw Dionysios waiting.

He was sitting at the marble desk (it would need a crane to shift that) in an ivory chair which, this time, he had quite succeeded in filling. He was dressed up to the height of Syracusan fashion, and a bit beyond. His hair had been camomiled, curled, and dusted with powdered gold; his robe, which seemed all border, was bordered with purple embroidery. I wondered if I could get at his chamber-groom and offer for his castoffs; you could have played Rhadamanthos in this one. Close up it almost knocked you down; so did his scent, which was drenched on like an old hetaira's. He had painted his face with Athlete's Tan and carmine, and touched up his eyes with kohl. I was surprised to find he wore all this stuff as if he were used to it, till I remembered Menekrates' stories. Of course, it had been put away when Plato came. I daresay I was the only man in Syracuse whom it could still surprise.

He was cordial, but had nothing much to say to me; it seemed he was just giving me an audience by way of favor. Presently, as he talked about past productions in the city, praising this artist or that, I saw why I was there: to spread the news that the theater ban was over.

I wondered how Plato had been chased out of Syracuse this time, and pictured the dejection at the Academy. I must bring home some gift for Axiothea, to cheer her up.

"Only today," said Dionysios, digging in the sweet-bowl that stood between us, "Plato was telling me how you were shipwrecked going home last time. I had not known of it."

I related the tale, my mind busy elsewhere. So Plato still cast his spell. What? I thought. Will the bird he's whistled to his hand neither sing for him nor fly away? Else why this naughty costume? But then, all the world knows how Alkibiades used to slip the leash, and come coaxing back to Sokrates, showing his radiant grace for password.

"And I suppose," he said, "you lost that painting I gave you, of the Siege of Motya?"

"Alas, sir, yes." He looked as downcast as a child, so to please him I said, "A loss to me and Athens. But I grieved even more for the model chariot, not just for the giver's sake, but because I never saw, in that line of work, craftsmanship to equal it."

I hoped to see his face light up as it had before; but he just looked gracious, and sent to summon his steward. The man came with his keys; he said, "Go to that old workroom of mine and fetch a model chariot." When it came, he turned it over once or twice in his hands (I saw he still bit his nails) and said, "Well, here is one loss I can make good to you. State business gives me no time for toys." There was dust on it. I am ashamed to confess such folly, but I felt near weeping.

No one troubled with me when I left, so I made for Dion's house, thinking, as I went, what Dionysios had said about his state business. He had sounded full of consequence. Having met Philistos, I could see him flattering the young man, as an expert charioteer coaching a rich young blood will let him think he is driving. Dionysios was the very one for it. I don't suppose Dion had ever stooped to such pretenses. It was not in him.

His house, when I got there, was well kept as ever, nothing shabby or run-down. Yet I felt a change, a loss of life and movement in the air around. As I reached the door, I saw this was more than idle fancy. Before, it had stood open. Now it was shut.

I knocked, and sent in my name. While I stood waiting, a young boy of seven or eight, a handsome child, slipped round the corner of the house for a peep at me. One saw the likeness at once. He was curious, I suppose, having heard my name, but dodged back when he was seen. Soon came the servant to say his master was at his studies and could see no one. No word of my coming some other time.

I walked through Ortygia, sick at heart. I had thought he would forgive me; he himself had done what he thought right, sorry it hurt me, but never turning back. This was the same. I would never have shut my door to him. But to me, man's life is a tree with twisted roots. To a political philosopher, it must be like a diagram of Pythagoras.

Soon after, I met Speusippos in the street. I hardly dared greet him; but he crossed over, and invited me to drink with him. I took courage, therefore, to ask if Dion was very angry with me.

"Angry?" he said. "Not that I know of. Why should you think so?"

When I told him, he said the play had not been announced yet; I could see that it was news to him, and news of no great importance. He spoke kindly, however. "Don't lose your sleep over it. If Dion knows of it, which I doubt, he can see you must work to eat. Give him credit for being just. You know, I take it, that Dionysios stopped the plays of his own accord? Neither Plato nor Dion urged it; *they* are here to get law instead of tyranny. But Dionysios found it in *The Republic*—a thing he could do at once, without trouble. You know him, like a child with new clothes."

"Still," I said, "Plato wrote it."

"Yes . . . You know, Niko, at the Academy we aim to provide the world with statesmen. Already now cities are coming to us to draw up their constitutions. But like shoemakers, we cut to measure. *The Republic* is, shall I say, a discussion of principles, not a working code. Between you and me, I think the purpose of those passages was to startle our poets into responsibility. Half of them today have the souls of whores: give me my drachma, never mind who gets my pox. Plato is a man who would not add a grain to the weight of the world's evil for a golden crown. When no more like him are left, men will devour each other and perish from the earth. That's why Dion defended him to you, just as I do."

"Well then," I said, "if it's not on account of the play, why does Dion shut his door to me?"

"I doubt you were singled out. He has refused himself to a good many people lately. He found if he tried to advance anyone's interests, just the opposite happened. That was Dionysios' way of making himself felt, without an open quarrel. He won't, if he can help it, force Plato into taking sides; he might learn what he has no wish to know. So he pricks in ways like these. Dion found he did his friends no good by taking notice of them. That's why he shuts his door."

"I am sorry for it. But with me, I'm afraid he must be really angry. If not, knowing I would think so he would have sent a letter."

Speusippos drew his black brows together, and shook his head. "No, Niko. You think so, because it is what you would do yourself. Dion is proud. Till you know that, you do not know him."

I remembered his desk, piled with petitions and state papers. How should a man like him beg pardon of a man like me, for being no longer even a trusted servant? The thought freed me from bitterness.

Since the year of my father's death, when I had come on as an extra, I had never been in *The Bacchae*. While a second actor, I had once been offered my father's roles but had turned them down, more, I suppose, from superstition than from piety, for no doubt he would have thought me foolish. Now, as pro- tagonist, I would play the god, with one short double as Tiresias the Prophet. Menekrates, as Pentheus and Queen Agave, was keen and shaping well.

It is a play about a mystery, and a mystery in itself. Ask any actor what he thinks Euripides meant by it, and he will tell you something different. Myself, I have played in it now some seven times, and still don't claim to know more than what one man makes of it, on one day. It is even possible, I suppose, that it was written to show that the gods are not. If so, some- one crept up behind the poet, and breathed down his neck when he wasn't looking. One thing I take it we may agree upon: the god of *The Bacchae* is not supposed to be like men.

There are first-class mask-makers in Syracuse, and of course we had the best. The Dionysos was most beautiful, a delicate blond face, almost feminine, as the play describes him, but with slant eyes, darkly drawn round like a leopard's. It seemed to me just right. Menekrates was very pleased with the Agave, and Pentheus was nearly finished.

Philistos gave no trouble. He looked in now and again at re- hearsals, sat quietly in front, would come behind to say it was going well and ask if we were satisfied with the machines, for there are a good many effects, with the earthquake and so on. Of course such things are better done at Syracuse than anywhere in the world, but he seemed anxious to be cordial, and even asked the cast to a drinking party. The others went, which I did not hold against them. I begged off with the excuse that I had had a feverish flux on tour (a common complaint in Sicily, where there is much bad water) and the doctor had me under orders. He could hardly press me, if he wanted the play to go on, so I was left in peace. I was doing this role to serve the god, not as Philistos' sycophant.

During the half-month of rehearsals, I made it my business to visit small wineshops in poor streets and find out what the people were saying. I reckoned in this way to cover ground Speusippos would miss; for he could never look like anything but a gentleman, while I, if I choose, can look like a soldier or an artisan, not by dressing up but just in small ways of sitting and standing and slicking down my hair. As a rule I said I was a skene-painter from Corinth. The accent is very easy.

From being so much in Ortygia among the soldiers and servants of the Archon, I had begun to think Dion had not a friend left in the city. I now learned otherwise. The working folk, with one accord, had blamed the theater ban on Plato, a foreign sophist of whom they only knew he was Dionysios' latest fad, which in itself was enough to damn him. Dion, they were all sure, would do nothing so impious or so odd. Dion was a great gentleman. When the old Archon died, and he had got the young cub at heel, it had been an age of gold while it lasted. People could bring their wrongs to judgment, even against the rich; taxes had been fairly levied, and the worst extortioners had gone to the quarries. The mercenaries had been made to behave themselves in the town, instead of acting like conquerors. And so on. Everyone, they said, had had hopes of his doing great things for the city; but it seemed, when it came to the push, he was too much the gentleman.

I could not make out just what it was they thought he would do, without help from them. Subvert the mercenaries, I suppose, and form a conspiracy and seize Ortygia; but nobody seemed to have a notion how such things are really done. Used as I was at home to being told I was a fool at politics, here any Athenian, even I, seemed as expert as a man among children.

However careless we may be, there are some things we take for granted grown men will do for themselves. All this they had forgotten.

They talked of Dion as of a god, whose mind they did not expect to know. But even the gods have oracles, and priests who will take them messages from common folk. Dion had no such thing. I suppose, in Sicily, it was to be expected.

I sought out Speusippos with my findings. He was glad of the information, saying he had had most success himself with the middle-class citizens, with whom, he said, the friends of Philistos were daily making headway. They did not attack Dion directly, knowing how he was respected; it was through Plato they slipped their poison in. "In the time of our fathers," they were saying, "the Athenians sent out two armies and a battle fleet to conquer Syracuse. None got home alive but a few wretched fugitives from the mountain brush, or slaves on the run. But now, Athens sends just one sophist with a silken tongue, and look what *he* has achieved. He has wound up the Archon in his web; soon he will suck him dry and hand over the power to Dion, who, as all the world knows, has been his fancy boy."

Speusippos said that the men of culture, who had read Plato for themselves or spoken with those who had, were not so easily led; but even they were starting to believe what they were always being told, that the reforms would be hurried breakneck in, and cause civil chaos. Dion's most solid support, he said, lay among men whom I had seen nothing of and he not much—the ancient aristocracy of Syracuse, whose fathers had fought the older tyrant. Their rising had been brief but savage; Dionysios' revenge no less so; they, or their widows, had passed on the blood-feud to their sons, and it smoldered still.

All this he told me, and much more that I forget, for I was now in *The Bacchae* up to my neck. I recall, though, his saying there was talk of a Carthaginian embassy coming about a peace treaty. In the old Archon's day, Speusippos said, their envoys had always been seen by Dion; they trusted his word, and his manners were such as they admire—commanding, spare of words, and stern, for he knew their ways. Now he was getting anxious lest Dionysios should try to handle it himself. He would be no match for them; at best they would get the profit of the bargain, at worst he might lose his head and provoke them into war; they might be all too ready once they had seen his quality. Dion was doing his best, therefore, to keep their chief men ignorant of his fall from power.

I said I hoped he would succeed, wondering in my heart whether he would come to see me act, and whether, if I did well enough, it would change his heart to me and open his door again. I feared this was not his play; he might only see it as one more folk-tale of Olympians behaving worse than men. But one cannot take this deity with the head; that, I suppose, is what the play is about. I must do it as I felt it, and leave the rest to the god.

Stratokles, old Dionysios' chorus-trainer, had stayed on in the city to put on dithyrambs, so was here at need. He was good at his work, and not above taking some direction from the protagonist, which is important in this play. Everything went so well that, lest some god should be getting jealous, we were almost relieved when the mask-maker told Menekrates his Pentheus mask had been spoiled by some apprentice spilling paint on it, and would not be ready till the day.

"At the worst," he said, "I can wear the second mask from the Hippolytos." (There are three: the happy, the angry and the dying.) "Pentheus is an angry young man all through; it will do well enough in a pinch, and we can say that the luck-god has had his sacrifice."

"Amen," I said.

Plays start at dawn in Sicily, for the heat of the day comes soon. The theater of Syracuse faces southwest, built into the slopes of Achradina. Behind these the sun comes up; one begins in the dusk of their shadow, till presently the long sun shafts strike the stage.

That day there was a glowing sky, with great wings of flame from the hidden east almost to the zenith. But when we opened, the wings were folded still; we had a subtle and somber glow, dusky-red, bronze and purple. Seeing this light, spellbound and lowering, which Euripides himself might have written in, Menekrates and I looked at each other, neither daring to say, "A lucky omen!"

They doused the cressets which had lit the audience to their seats. I pulled down my mask as the flutes began.

Dionysos opens alone. I have a bit of business I always use when the play starts early in half-light. I cross to Semele's altar, where, as the dramatist directs, the fire is sinking; then, picking up a torch which lies there, I kindle it, lift it, and gaze around. I do the whole opening speech like this, walking here and there, looking at the royal house I shall destroy. The god must not seem like a mortal man plotting malice. He is curious, smelling out the ground, a stalking panther from the upland forests who snuffs at the walls of men, softly prowling, innocent of what he is.

I like this quiet start. Then when I raise my voice to call on the Phrygian Maenads, everyone jumps, which is good. In they come dancing, with their pipes and drums and cymbals, shattering the hush and stealth. There were young satyrs with them, doing a torch dance.

Coming off, I found Menekrates dressed, with the Hippolytos mask pushed up; his new one had not come. I said it was hard, the masks being so good, that only he should have an old one. "I'd rather, now," he said. "I'm played-in with this. I was only afraid the other would come by a panting messenger while I was lacing my boots. I know these eminent artists; one daren't offend them, the choregos always takes their side because he'll need them again. I should have had to wear it, with barely a glance in the mirror. One can't do oneself justice." Grateful he took it so well, I went to do my change for the seer Tiresias.

When I went on, I found the sky growing blue. The highlands were in sun, and the dewy chill was lifting. This is right, when mortals take the place of gods.

One can work up Tiresias if one likes; some leading men do; but I had rather give this scene to King Kadmos, that old trimmer who will dance on the hills with god or mountebank, no questions asked, if it gives him status. I just did straight man for his laughs. It helps the play; for bigoted and stiff-necked as Pentheus is, one must point up his integrity. That is the tragedy's core.

Tiresias has a blind-man mask; one sees through slits between the eyelids. Turning my empty gaze upon the house, I perceived the play had taken.

Menekrates started his shouting off, denouncing the Bacchae and their rites. Just at his entrance-cue, the first sunbeams struck the stage, one falling on the very door, all ready. I thought, Some god loves us today.

Into the light stepped Menekrates, a big upstage entrance with supporting extras. The bullion and gilt jewels of his costume flashed, the crimson glowed. And he had on his new mask. It must have come at the very last, while I did my change. Enough to unsettle any artist; but he was sound and would keep his head.

Then I started to hear the audience. There was a pause, a buzzing, an angry mutter, a laugh. Good masks get their best effects with distance. I peered through my blind-man slits, which are less good than proper eyeholes, trying to see what was amiss, while Menekrates came on in the mask of Pentheus. A good character mask: a harsh proud face for an enemy of laughter and the joyous god. What, then, was wrong with it? Then I saw.

It was a portrait mask, such as they use in comedy, only less crude; a caricature, but a subtle one, toned down to the tragic style. It was the face of Dion.

I stood rooted, wooden as a post, while Menekrates went into his long entrance speech. I recalled the delays, the mask maker's excuses, then its coming at the very last, after I was on stage and would not see. And just as a man will stare at a spear in his flesh, as if asking what it is, till suddenly the pain begins, so it broke upon me that Dion must be out in front there, in the seats of honor, getting this full in the face. What could he suppose, but that I knew?

He had thought the worse of me, no doubt, only for playing; and now, how much would he think Philistos and his master had paid me to make this worth my while? A nothing in a mask, a seller of illusions, a poets' whore, whose life is spent in the public show of those passions the philosopher lives to master; a stroller from town to town, without a household; such men are easily bought.

My stomach heaved. For a moment I thought I would throw up on stage. By now Menekrates was halfway through his speech.

> *They tell me that a stranger out of Lydia*
> *Has come to Thebes . . .*

Dionysos, in whose mask I would soon be entering. I thought of that opening speech by torchlight, promising vengeance on the man who forbade my worship. Dionysos, god of the theater. A perfect buildup—for this.

As when I was a naked child on a Trojan shield, I longed for an earthquake to swallow up the skene. But that came later. I was a god, I would be giving the cue for it. I could have sat down, at that, and laughed until I cried.

> *Just let me get him here within my walls;*
> *He'll swing his thyrsos no longer, nor toss his head . . .*

Menekrates came forward, gesturing threats. Poison was everywhere. I thought, What does *he* know?

The mask came late. But one always finds time to stand back and look. Perhaps he had not; did not want to confuse his interpretation, and would rather just clap it on. But, I thought, what is Dion to him, to offend a powerful sponsor for, except that he is my friend? If he saw, he'll never own it; who would? He lives in Syracuse; what free Athenian dare reproach him? So there will be this between us.

> *Ha, this is* your *work, Tiresias . . .*

He had crossed down towards me. At the end of this tirade came my cue, for a speech about twice as long. I could not remember a line of it.

> *You are greedy for burnt-offerings, you scent*
> *New fees for divination . . .*

I should be reacting to all this. Already he felt my numbness and was losing force. I was giving him nothing. My hand came up for the affronted seer, and tapped my staff on the stage.

Well might Tiresias be angry. I thought of that vain young fool in Ortygia, sitting like a clerk at his great, wicked father's desk; of jolly Philistos with his gentlemanly manners, the fat old spider shaking his web; and of Dion out in front, keeping a philosopher's straight face (the good man bears pleasure and pain with an equal mind) in the hour of fallen fortune, bitten even by the stray he had fed from his own dish. There had been no time till now for anger.

One is finished if one loses one's temper on stage; so it was lucky I had learned young to master it. If, at nineteen, you have had to keep going when you find the inside of your mask has been smeared with turd, you never really forget it. Poor Meidias had never, right till the end of the tour, given up such attempts to make me lose my lines. So, now, I grasped the weapon that had served me when I had no other. I was here to honor the god, in the precinct where if a man meets face to face his own father's murderer, still he must hold his hand. One seldom thinks of these sacred laws; one seldom needs to; but they are bone of one's bone. I could only fight within them. These people had tried to take the play from me, and turn it into a third-rate satire. If it cost my last breath, I would take it back.

I went into my speech on cue, living from line to line; once I saw Menekrates' eyes blinking within his eyeholes, and wondered how much I had just cut. Luckily, it's the dullest speech in the play. I shook my staff, or rather held up my hand, which was shaking of itself; but Tiresias is very old, and angry. It was a ham performance; at all events it warmed Menekrates up again, and I did get his cue line right.

When I exited with young Philanthos, who was doing Kadmos, we were hardly off before he lifted his mask and gaped at me, so full of words they jammed his mouth. I raised my hand, saying, "No. We will get through this performance first. And nothing to Menekrates either."

In my dressing room I had just started to strip when Mene-krates came straight in from his exit. "What happened, Niko? What was the matter with the audience? Do you know you cut twenty lines, and ad-libbed half the rest? This mask has wretched eyeholes, too."

I did not say, "You need not act to me, my friend." It might well be the truth. Even with good eyeholes, one can't see much more than straight forward; to see sideways one must turn one's head. Anything might have happened, for all he knew, beyond his sight-line, to cause the stir.

"My dear," I said, "leave it till after. It's politics; but let's keep to our own business while we are doing it. If you do find out, don't be upset; the play's the thing. When I'm dressed, I shall sit with my mask awhile."

Some actors swear by this rite, and it is much beloved by wall-painters and sculptors. For myself, I get my masks home beforehand (or I make trouble) and consider them there in quiet, with no witness but the god. Yet it is a good tradition of the theater that an artist who sits before his mask should be left in peace. It gives one the chance to compose oneself, if anything has put one out. I could hear my dresser at the door, turning people away in whispers. The voices of the chorus boys rose and fell down in the orchestra as the dance brought them near or far. Chin on fist I sat, looking at the leopard eyes of bland fair Dionysos, thinking about the im-mortal hunter and his prey.

My call came; I was led by the guards before angry vir-tuous Pentheus. The god is disguised as a human youth; but all have felt divinity somewhere about him, except the King, to whom he gives soft answers, speaking truth darkly, smiling.

The audience had quieted now; but I could feel them on edge, rustling like mice in the wainscot. I must get hold of them now or never, for this passage is the axis of the play.

Pentheus denounces the god as a juggling charlatan, crops his long hair (the wig is a trick one), then orders him to give up his thyrsos. He, however, stands still. "Take it yourself," he says quietly. "This belongs to Dionysos."

] *192* [

This line I spoke with its meaning; and Menekrates, who was a sensitive actor, played back to me, holding off a moment and pausing, before he snatched angrily at the wand. I turned to the maenad chorus, and made the gesture which says, "It is accomplished." There was a hush, fraught, as I meant, with fear.

The thyrsos is the madness of the god, which the man must choose for himself. Thus each fulfills his nature.

The god came kindly at first to Thebes, saying, "Bring me all that wildness in your hearts; I understand it, it is my kingdom. My gift is the lesser madness which will rest your souls and save you from the greater. Know yourselves, as my brother Apollo tells you. You have need of me." The Theban women answered, "How dare you? Would you make wild beasts of us? We have laws and live in the city. You insult us; go away." That's why they have the madness of the god without his blessing, and run on the mountains tearing wolves with their nails.

Then comes Pentheus, saying, "You dirty foreigner, debaucher of decent ladies, don't try your tricks on *me*. I am master of myself; don't deny it, or I shall be angry. I am pure; I can't rest for thinking of those women's lecheries in the woods. To prison with you, out of my sight. Let me hear no more of you."

It is from the man's own soul that the god with the smiling mask will draw his power, enchanting Pentheus with the hubris in his own secret heart. Once drunk on this sweet poison, he will know himself the one sane, righteous man in a wicked world. He has refused the little madness, to choose the great.

Yet the god warns him, as gods do before they strike. One can play it mockingly; indeed, I had rehearsed it so. But suddenly, now, it seemed to me the mortal veil should be lifted here, for the man to see if he would. The line, *You know not your own life, nor what you are,* I spoke softly, pitching it at the echo chamber. It was a lucky try. I nearly frightened myself.

Menekrates played back, recoiling. I had asked a good deal

of him, changing the tone like this, but he had caught it. Well, I thought, when one sits with one's mask, one calls the god. I must take what he sends.

When we went off, the audience shouted and stamped, as people do after tension—another gift of Dionysos, I daresay. There was no such release for me. I did not lift my mask, though the sweat was pouring down my face. Menekrates put his hand on my shoulder, saying, "Niko, this is a great interpretation. This is truly Euripides, I am sure."

He has found out, I thought, if he didn't know before. I loved him for his kindness, but could do with nobody just then. I said, "We shall do, my dear," and went away.

The chorus were lamenting their gracious leader in his chains. In my dressing room I could not rest, but paced about. The sun was well up now; on stage the mask helped shade one's eyes, but one felt the heat. I wondered where Dion was sitting. The one thing I dreaded like death was that someone might come and tell me.

It was time to command the earthquake. I was so wrought-up, I felt a shiver, like a sailor when someone whistles at sea. Well, let it come, I thought, as I ran backstage to the sounding board and made a noise like doom. The effects were tremendous; they can do anything at Syracuse—thunder far and near, whole columns falling, lightning that nearly blinds you.

Out steps the god, delicately, from his broken prison, a human youth again, chaffing the maenads for their fright, while the fire effects smoke up behind him. Pentheus comes on enraged, his captive free, his roof on fire, his herdsmen in flight from the mountain maenads. He has learned nothing. He curses the smiling god, and orders his army to fetch the women. Even then Dionysos gives him one more warning. "Don't fight the gods; it would be better to offer sacrifice. If you ask it of me, I will bring the women home in peace." But Pentheus knows best; no smooth-tongued Lydian shall trick him. He calls for his armor. He is like the mouse that runs about before the crouching cat. And now the paw comes down.

Pentheus has had his run. Now the god will play with him.

Yet it is not Dionysos who by himself has devised the game like a cruel child. It takes two to play. The god is that which is. If we will not know him, it is we who make the ironies the Immortals laugh at.

When the scene was done, we stood listening to that great chorus which stops one's breath each time—the beauty before the horror. Menekrates said, "Niko—we don't do this next scene for laughs?"

"No," I said. "But someone will laugh in any case. They have to. Never mind it." I had played myself in, and knew where I was going.

We were coming to the scene where the god leads forth King Pentheus in a woman's robe. Softly his wits have been charmed away; now, obedient as the bird to the swaying snake, he goes to spy, as he thinks, upon the maenads who will tear him piecemeal. Dionysos walks around him like a tiring-maid, patting his hair and dress, stealing even dignity from his dreadful death; while the insensate man giggles at the joke, or boasts that his strength can uproot the mountains.

Euripides wrote this play in Macedon, where, if this did not get some laughs, it would much surprise me. But wherever you play it, and whatever the interpretation, one hears it somewhere—from someone on edge, or from one of those you are sure to find among so many thousands, who would laugh still more if the lynching were done on stage.

This, I thought as I walked on with raised arm to summon Pentheus, is the scene our sponsor and his lord have so much looked forward to. We shall see.

This was what the mask of Dion had been made for. Mockery like this is a crucifixion, meant not just to hurt but to kill. Even in comedy it can finish a man; a few score know him, the whole city knows the lie. It was so with Sokrates, they say.

As soon as Pentheus entered, the catcalls and laughter started. One can always tell a claque, they react too soon. Others—democrats, or those who just wanted to hear the play—hissed and shushed them. I had been prepared for all this. Presently they did me the honor of attending.

Much as I had asked from Menekrates, now he gave me more. Whether he read my thoughts, which can happen when the god consents, whether he was making his own answer to what had been put on him, I do not know. Both, I daresay.

Pentheus has refused the god's offered good, and now is given the evil. The god is more wicked now than ever the man dreamed at first, and it is the victim's fate to trust him.

This scene can be done in many ways. One can make Pentheus a loud-mouthed tyrant burlesquing his own pride, with Dionysos all wit and charm. One can direct the sympathy this way or that. This time, Menekrates needed no telling; he could not have matched my purpose better if we had rehearsed for weeks. In the previous scene, he had built up Pentheus' sincerity, his striving for order, and fear of the excess which makes men less than men. Now he showed a man better than his fate, a king in ruins, wrecked through a noble hubris—the belief that man can be as perfect as the gods.

When rehearsing with the chorus, I had arranged in this scene for them to sway forward when I raised my arm, like hounds when the huntsman lifts the quarry. They were intelligent boys; when I heightened my gestures, they worked it up. I heard one or two women scream in front. By this time everyone pitied Pentheus, and felt horror of the mocking, cruel god. But of course the claque kept on; they had been paid to. So at the peak of the action, the pack as it were just closing in, I made one more gesture, wider and higher, bringing in these people, as if they too were my servants. The audience took it, and so did they. There was quite a hush.

"I bring the young man to a great contest," says Dionysos as he goes. But the worst of mine was over. I had given the Messenger's great narration of the death to young Philanthos, to give him his chance, though the protagonist often takes it. He was glad; but not half as glad as I felt now. Pentheus was out of the play; Menekrates now changed masks for the crazed Queen Agave tossing her dead son's head. I left him to dress in peace for this testing role. He was good—though not better, I think, than my father was.

He played the Recognition; the audience groaned and wept; I appeared upon the god-walk dressed up for my epiphany, to pronounce everyone's doom; and the play was done. The chorus sang the famous tag, the flutes receded; we came forward mask in hand to take our bows. When applause is noisy at Syracuse, the echo chamber picks it up, and it goes right through one's head. Mine was aching already.

I lay down (the first man's room there has every luxury) and let my dresser sponge me. He talked away, as they do, and I was glad of it. My mind was filled with darkness. I had done my best, for Dion, and the god, and my own honor; but one can't enact a living man's death without horror, when one cares for him. What he himself must feel, I could only try not to think of. I had borne enough.

Menekrates came in, a towel flung round him, his dark body gleaming with sweat. "Niko. What can I say? That cursed mask came with the call boy. What could I do?"

"Do?" I said. "I never had such support from another artist in all my life. I was coming to say so. Has the sponsor come behind?"

"Not that I know." He dipped his towel in the basin and rubbed it through his hair. "But I've not been out looking."

"I doubt he'll come carrying garlands. But that's the theater."

As I spoke the door opened, and the usual crowd came in, poets and gentlemen and courtesans and merchants and young bloods, with their attendant sycophants, and, nosing among them, like rats when the cargo shifts, government informers and spies of various factions, mentioning the mask and asking clever questions. Menekrates and I kept saying, "Thank you, thank you," and looking stupid. As long as we kept quiet, nothing could be charged against Menekrates. The protagonist directs; they were not to know how we had rehearsed it. As for the choregos, there was still no sign of him.

At last they all went. I was alone, putting on my street clothes, when someone came to the door. It was Speusippos.

There was only one man I had dreaded more to see. He looked worn and ill. I greeted him, and waited to suffer what must be. He was a man who could make his anger bite.

"Niko—I saw the crowd leaving, and thought you would be here." Then he saw my blank face, and said with tired courtesy, "I am sorry to have missed the play. I have been with Plato. I was passing, and stopped to tell you. Dion has been exiled."

No other man, I suppose, is so full of himself as an actor just off stage. For a moment I thought he was blaming me for it. I expect no one to credit this, except another actor.

"Come," said Speusippos, "it could be worse, he is not dead. We shall see him in Athens." He looked about; I told him my dresser had gone. "You know how it's been, like dry brush waiting a spark. It happened through the Carthaginians."

I gaped as if hearing of this race for the first time. I don't know how he kept his patience.

"I told you, he's been in touch with their envoys; he's the only man they are used to treating with, or fear in war. He was sure they would push forward if they knew he was out of power. He wrote to the envoys, men he knew, asking them to let him see their terms first in private. Someone played him false, and gave his letter to Dionysios."

I said nothing. One needed to know no more.

"I imagine his vanity was hurt," Speusippos said impatiently. "But it was Philistos persuaded him that it was treason. We knew nothing of this. On the contrary, Dionysios made Dion a great show of friendship, said he regretted their late estrangement, and persuaded him to an evening stroll by the water stairs, to talk things over. Our authority for the rest is Dionysios himself, who, as you may suppose, has never stopped talking since. He spent hours with Plato, trying to justify himself. I had to leave, it was so disgusting. He wept, laid his head in Plato's lap . . . I thought that I should vomit."

"But where's Dion?"

"Gone. During the seaside walk, it seems Dionysios suddenly pulled out the letter and faced him with it. He says Dion could give no proper explanation. No doubt he gave one which stuck in Dionysios' craw; it's the truth that vexes. In any case, everything was arranged beforehand, the ship at anchor, the boat at hand. I daresay it was done in less time than I've taken to tell you. You can imagine what Plato has been suffering, not knowing what orders had really been given, and whether Dion hadn't in fact been dropped overboard with a stone tied to his feet. But of course he guessed our fears; as soon as he was in Italy, he sent a courier over. He is safe enough. But the cause, Niko—the cause!"

I had no time yet for the cause. I said, "A courier? From Italy? Then how long has he been gone?"

"Since yesterday. Of course it has been kept from the people. That's why he was sent off so quietly."

We talked on, I suppose. He went. I stood in the empty dressing room, hearing the shouts of the cleaners who were sweeping down the benches, calling across the theater. No echo of us, no footfall left. So short a time since I had wrestled with the god, with twenty thousand people, with Dion, with Philistos, with my own soul. Dion had been gone, knowing nothing of it. Philistos had not stayed away in anger; he had serious business. I sat like a grain of sand in a scraped-out bowl, listening to the grasshoppers on the hillside.

Someone coughed hoarsely. An old man stood in the doorway. I thought he had come to clean, and told him I was just going. He paused, and shuffled his feet. I saw he had a basket with him; he had been selling figs, or sesame cakes, or some such thing. He cleared his rusty throat again.

"Pardon me, sir. But when I was a chorus boy, I heard Kallippides in that role. He was the best of my young day, not a doubt of that. But to my mind, you put more into it."

After he too had gone, Menekrates came hurrying. "Niko, I waited, I thought your Athenian friend was with you. What's the matter?"

I should be starting to laugh soon. I answered:

> *In vain man's expectation;*
> *God brings the unthought to be,*
> *As here we see.*

"But never mind. I have had an oracle from Dionysos."

Menekrates looked at the lynx-eyed mask on its stand. "Won't it wait till we feel stronger?"

"No, my dear, it won't wait. Never keep a god waiting. He said, 'Get drunk.'"

# XII

NEXT DAY, PHILISTOS SENT FOR ME TO BE PAID. I
had lain awake half the night, thinking what I would say to
him. I kept improving it, till I wished I had written the best
parts down. Then I slept; and in the morning I saw I could forget all I had thought of. Menekrates' home and kin were in
Syracuse. Dion, in exile, might need a messenger who was not
suspect, and could come or go.

Philistos received me in his business room. His desk was
heaped with state papers, just like Dion's before. His red
pouchy face, with hard little eyes in smiling folds of flesh, made
me queasy, like pork when one is seasick. He greeted me as
someone he had discreetly shared a joke with. As I knew, he
had not been at the play, but he commended my performance.
His Egyptian accountant came at his hand-clap, with a big
heavy leather bag. I waited for it to be opened, but Philistos
just pushed it over. It had the silver talent mark.

In recent years, I have been paid as much for one performance; once, indeed, a rival sponsor offered me even a little more

to go sick and not to play. But in those days it was a sum beyond belief. No actor got such money. I paused, to make sure there was no mistake. I have never been so glad in my life that a fee was big.

"Thank you," I said, "on behalf of the company, and myself."

"My dear Nikeratos," he answered, breezy as a sailor, "your company is provided for. This is your own fee."

This saved me the trouble of doing sums. I pushed the bag back again. "Will you offer it, please, at the temple of Dionysos, for some dedication in my name?"

He went on smiling, but not with his little eyes. "Have you some reason?" he said, and watched me.

"Yes, I have. I was not satisfied with my performance."

"Everyone agrees you performed outstandingly." He did not say it as a compliment, but with hard suspicion. Having pretended he had seen me, he could hardly now go back on it.

"I think not. Conditions were against me. You have a very well-equipped theater here; but I prefer to play where poet and artist are taken seriously."

"What do you mean?" he said, in a voice which did not ask, but threatened.

"Portrait masks are for comedy. In tragedy they distract the audience. To spring such tricks on actors in performance is to treat us like clowns at a fair. What is this money for—my reputation? Thank you, but I'm afraid it is not enough."

He spluttered, then forced a laugh and held forth about the vanity of artists, quite believing, now, that this was all, and, of course, that I would take it in the end. With some trouble I undeceived him, and left him admiring my self-importance. It had never struck me this might impress him, but of course he was just the man. I could see, when I left, that my consequence had been raised with him.

I would have liked to leave at once. Just as when the old Archon died, the streets were full of muttering groups, the citizens in their factions, foreigners with their kind. Now and then soldiers would go past: a great Gaul staring haughtily over people's heads, a swaggering Nubian shouting to another across the street in their unknown tongue; or a group of Romans swinging along in step together, taking everyone's size in the self-sufficient way these people have, as if wondering when they would get orders to clear the street. The mercenaries were making their good spirits known. What the citizens thought, they were not telling.

No man has less taste than I for getting caught in foreign civil wars; yet I had thought that out of all those people I had heard praising Dion's justice, someone would strike a blow for him. But no. I was in Syracuse. They waited to see what would happen to them next; they had forgotten they could themselves make happenings.

Eager as I was to be gone, I lingered, to learn if Plato was leaving. Surely he would go; but if he were delayed, he would need Speusippos with him; and, parted from Dion without a moment's warning, he must have things to write, unfit for the Archon's courier. I knew where he was lodging, at the house of a Pythagorean up on Achradina. But it seemed unwise to be seen there; I was now a caller who would be noticed. So I hung about the wineshops for Speusippos, thinking that if he wanted a word with me he would seek me there.

On the third day of this, I met by chance a most charming person, who came up to commend my performance in the theater. Our talk lasted till bedtime, and one thing led to another; so it was morning when I got back to the house of Menekrates. He greeted me with the news that Plato had been murdered.

"The soldiers did it," he said quite cheerfully. "Everyone knows they've been spoiling for a chance. They said Dion was their best general, before this windbag turned his head. Why, Niko, what's the matter? I thought you couldn't bear the man."

I said, "This news will kill Dion. And I shall have to bring it." This made enough sense for Menekrates. To tell the truth, I was surprised myself at what I felt. I had not understood a word of his lecture on the One; where I did know what he was saying, about the theater, I had thought him dangerous, as men with half a truth can be. Yet, little by little, he had stamped his mark upon my mind, like some great actor beside whom one has played extra. I recalled how his eyes had said to me, What are you? and had seemed to know the answer. He was gone now, and the answer with him.

I was overcome with the guilt men feel, with reason or without, at such a time, because I had spent the night in pleasure. Presently I began to ask Menekrates who had told him, and where the body was; the bones ought to be sent to Athens, and Speusippos might be alive or dead. From the replies I got, I soon realized it was all street talk, nothing first-hand. This gave me some hope, knowing what Syracuse is for rumors. So I went up to the house to see.

There was no sound of mourning. I knocked and asked for Plato, making up some errand. Without going inside, the slave answered at once that I should find him in Ortygia. He was now the Archon's guest.

He must have read my face (this was no doubt a house where people talked freely) for he added that the gentleman had come to no harm so far; I could count on that, for his nephew was here upstairs, packing up his books.

Before I had time to ask for him, Speusippos came running out. If he had looked strained before, he now looked ill. "Niko! I knew that was your voice. Don't stand in the street, come in."

He hurried me through the inner court, and upstairs to Plato's room, now in confusion and full of smoke. The floor was littered with open book-boxes and scrolls. In the middle was a charcoal brazier, where Speusippos had been burning papers. I coughed, and went over to the window. An actor has to be careful of his throat.

"A god sent you," he said. "Are you going back to Athens?"

"Yes or no, according to what help you need."

He clasped my hands, then turned away, wiping his eyes and cursing the smoke. Any small kindness will move a man who is overwrought, but philosophers are not supposed to weep.

"What happened? Where's Plato? In the quarries?"

"God forfend! No, what you heard at the door is true, he's an honored guest—while it lasts, for he's a prisoner too, of course. Dionysios has given him a house in the palace park. No one leaves the inner citadel, by land or sea, without a pass. We were half-packed to go home, when a squad of Gauls brought the invitation. I've just come from there. You should see the place. Bronzes, books, lyre-players, boy-slaves—as full of toys as a jackdaw's cage. It's as if some bandit had captured a chaste lady and were ashamed to rape her, so kept laying his loot at her feet and begging for a word of love. One could laugh. But how will it end?"

"In the end," I said, "he must let him go. Where Plato is, the world is watching—the learned world, at least. Think of the scandal. The second Dionysios is not the first."

"But you know what he wants. He wants Plato to side with him against Dion. Before he will do that, Plato will sit in Ortygia till he dies. And it might come to that. He's past sixty, Niko; this climate doesn't suit him; he's not been well. Besides, Dionysios is as fitful as a woman. It needs only some open quarrel, or public slight; then the soldiers, or Philistos' faction, will take their chance."

"I doubt it. It's not a chance I'd care to take, after seeing them together even once. I told you before, the poor antic is in love. And so vain—he wants to be in the histories as Plato's favorite pupil, not his murderer. Tell me, when did you last eat, or sleep?"

Luckily, soon after, his host sent a tray up with wine and cakes. We got rid of the stinking brazier, and cleared two chairs. Books were piled on everything; Plato must have brought a small library along. Even then, as I remembered, he had written to Archytas asking for more.

Speusippos looked better for the food, and started scrambling about among the litter for things he wanted sent home. The books, to my relief, were going along to Plato; but, muttering to himself or me, Speusippos picked out some notes for a lecture on the nature of the universe which Plato wanted Xenokrates to give for him; a scheme for a future book, which he was afraid of losing in Syracuse; and a rare work of Pythagoras for the Academy library. After looking under everything in sight, he found a pack of paper with dead flowers pressed in it. I supposed it must be some old love-token, till he reminded me he was a botanist. "If you can get them to the Academy uncrushed, I shall be much beholden to you. There is a lad who came to us this year from Stagyra, a promising boy, who helps me with my collection; he will look after them . . . By the dog, I've been so harassed, it's put his name from my mind." He clutched his brow, then remembered and wrote it down, Aristoteles. I promised to see to it.

All this concluded, he went to the door and window before taking from his girdle a little scroll. Softly he said, "This is the thing, Niko. The rest could go by a courier. Not this. That's why I said a god had sent you."

I took it. It had no superscription. He said, "I see you understand."

Now that I was charged with the errand I had come to do, I did not stay much longer, either in that house or in Syracuse: just long enough to give my company a farewell party, and bid adieu to my friend of the night before. I do not name him; he is now the head of a very ancient house, and I have never been one to kiss and brag.

There were two letters in the scroll, the inner one for Dion, the outer for Archytas of Tarentum. I pondered the best hiding place, in case I should be searched. Opening the mask-box, I said, "My lord Apollo, two of your servants want help. If you value this man Plato as much as people say, you will look after his affairs. I leave this in your care."

Just before the ship cast off, some of the Romans came aboard, and searched the ship, as they said, for treasonable matters. They never looked inside the mask, though they stared right at it. The god's face must have overawed them. I concluded therefore that he did take Plato seriously, and it should be borne in mind.

Though we had a fair wind to Tarentum, the rumor of Plato's murder had got there first. Ships cross almost daily between Messene and Rhegium, whence news spreads overland. Sighting a ship with the paintwork of Syracuse, every Pythagorean in Tarentum came to the dock to ask if the tale were true. Some knew me, so came to me first. In their relief they made as much of me as if I had saved his life myself.

I was taken straight to Archytas. Like a good host, and a true philosopher, he offered me refreshment before talking business, and sat quiet as a statue by one of his model machines, though I saw his toes twitch under his robe. I told him all I had heard from Speusippos, and gave him his letter from Plato. Then I asked whether Dion had passed this way, and where he was.

He said, smiling, "Two questions, my friend, with easy answers. Yes to the first. To the second: In the room next door." Then he said with his soldier's dignity, "Where else would Dion go?"

He questioned me a little longer. I was surprised Dion should have stayed outside, till I remembered he had only just heard that Plato was not dead. Philosophers understand each other, as actors do; of course he had to be given time to compose himself.

Just then through the window I saw him pacing in the orchard. He was tired of waiting, and had come out to show he was ready.

I found him on a marble seat under a plum tree bowed with fruit. I remember the limewashed bark, the heavy-sweet scent of windfalls in the long grass, the wasps humming round their juicy caves.

He was haggard, and had lost more weight than one would think possible in so few days; but the good news had pushed his griefs aside, he was calm and smiling.

I told him all I knew, adding that I did not believe the Archon would ever give countenance to Plato's death. Rather, it seemed to me he even had some excuse, and perhaps a fair one, for taking him into the citadel, because of this danger from the troops. "In Ortygia, everyone is accountable. Dionysios may have other motives; he is more devious than he knows himself. But that will be one, I think."

He said, "I wish Plato were in better health," and fell silent, his look of care returning. Presently he said, "You see me, Nikeratos, a man exiled for no crime; fallen from high estate, like the characters you portray." He smiled slightly. "It is said that while Sokrates was awaiting death, his wife lamented that it was the injustice of it she could not bear. He answered, 'Why, my dear, you would not rather I had deserved it?' But if Plato should die in Syracuse, I shall admit that though men have been unjust to me, the gods have not . . . A man more precious than empires, both to us and to men still unborn, with who knows what wisdom yet undistilled in him. He is clear of all misjudgment, except his faith in me. He had not seen Syracuse for twenty years; Dionysios he had known only as a child who rode upon my shoulder. For no living man but me would he have gone again to Sicily. And I sent for him—this is the irony the gods themselves must laugh at—for this very thing which has made and broken all: his charm that can make discourse beautiful and catch the soul through the heart. Was Oidipos himself more blind?"

I said, "You had only seen the son in the father's shadow."

He shook his head, then looked at me. "Nikeratos. Is it true, as I am told, that you refused a talent of silver from Philistos, because of a certain mask?"

"Yes. It was sent without my knowledge; I saw it first on stage."

"Well, it is rightly said that there is good in every state of man. In misfortune, one can count one's friends." Of course he had been new to exile and disgrace when this news had come, so it had touched him. Instead of shutting his door to me for-ever, he had opened even his heart.

I wondered if he was in need, and how one could go about offering help to so proud a man. But he now told me he would be taking a house in Athens. From policy, or decency, or just because he could never have faced Plato otherwise, Dionysios had had clothes and money put in the exile's boat, and not landed him at Rhegium like a castaway. He had been told, too, that his goods and household slaves would be sent him. This would enable him to live like a gentleman, by the standards of Athens; but one can't ship land abroad, and unless his yearly revenues came too, he would not be rich, or not as Sicily under-stands it.

His wife Arete, Dionysios' half-sister, had written confirming that his money and movables would follow; but it was clear, since he said nothing of it, that she was not coming to share his exile. He spoke of her, as it seemed to me, with pity rather than

longing. It was said to be a state alliance, which had never
warmed up in the marriage bed. I recalled his study, so like
Plato's, a man's room well-kept by men.

"Dionysios will not harm her," he said. "But I am most anxious for my brother Megakles. He has never concerned himself
with philosophy; but he is a man of honor, who would revenge
an insult to our house, as Philistos knows very well. If he is
wise, he must be in flight from Syracuse already, before he
meets a knife in the dark. And above all, there is my son."

I said that if Dionysios had been ashamed to offer the father
violence, he would scarcely harm so young a lad, his own kindred too. Dion said, "Not in his body, I daresay. But my wife
will go back to her brother's house, and take him with her. I
would wish him anywhere else on earth. He is restless, easily
led, impatient of correction; he shows no bent to philosophy."

"He must be young," I said, "for that?" I suppose a man of
Dion's life and standards would expect a good deal from his
son.

He was staying on a while, he said, at Tarentum, to await
news of his brother and to enjoy the company of his friends. "I
had forgotten," he said, "that such peace as this existed." His
goods and servants would be shipped here; he would have a
good deal of business; so he accepted my offer to take his letters to Athens. My ship was loading cargo, and would be there
until next day.

I called next morning. He was sitting at his window, which
overlooked the orchard, listening to the chorus of the birds, late
and sleepy with autumn. The air smelled of the turning year, and
in the eaves a dove was cooing. He told me that yesterday,
after I left, he had had good news. His brother Megakles had
been hidden by family friends as soon as they knew of Dion's
exile. He had boarded a ship at Katana, which had just touched
at Tarentum on its way to Corinth. He had sailed straight on
there, where he had friends, but had called to tell Dion he was
safe, and had managed to bring a good deal of money with
him. They would meet again in Athens.

It was the seventh of the month, Apollo's day, and the Tarentines were offering a choral dance to the god. I just had time to

hear it before we sailed. The music was very fine, all strings though, for Pythagoreans think that flutes confuse the cosmic order (or some such matter) and disturb the soul. Young boys dressed in white, and crowned with bay-leaves, circled an altar of honey-colored marble wreathed with a garland of gilded bronze. The lyre answered the kithara; a light breeze blew from the sea. The last sight I had of Dion, he was standing like a marble hero on the steps before the temple porch, tall and straight among tall straight columns, the cool autumn sunshine on his face. It seemed to me that once Plato was safe and free, he could even be happy.

# XIII

ON MY VOYAGE OUT, ARCHYTAS HAD PROMISED
to reward me if I brought useful news from Syracuse. Among
all my concerns this had slipped my mind; but he himself was
not one to forget such things, and he made me a most handsome present, saying it was partly a good-tidings gift, no man
having ever brought him better. What with this, and the profit
from the tour, I might not be as rich as Philistos would have
made me, but I would get along well enough.

Plato was in Syracuse all that winter.

Sometimes I surprised myself by the trouble I took to get
news of him. Once it would just have been for Dion's sake,
or perhaps Axiothea's. Even now, as was natural, I still resented him sometimes, but found I could not indulge it without feeling small. When I had seen him sitting with young
Dionysios, seeing all through him, yet patient as a shepherd
with a sickly lamb, and fearless of the wolves around, I had
known the man was noble. The day stuck in my mind, when
I had brought Dion's letter urging him to go. Actors are vain;

it's true even of the best; but one does not feel one's talent, even when most pleased with it, as a burden one must bear in trust for other men. It was not pride in him; he knew. I thought of it often.

Megakles, Dion's brother, was living in Corinth, a city where Syracusans feel at home; but Dion himself had bought an estate near the Academy, beyond the olive groves. The house was just the proper size for someone of his rank in Athens; his Syracusan one would have looked hubristic. But with his beautiful things set up there, it seemed just the same. He asked me to supper once or twice when he was entertaining poets and their friends, though not, of course, on his philosophic evenings.

Speusippos having stayed with Plato, the Academy was being run by Xenokrates, so, knowing what he thought of actors, I did not intrude. When news of Plato came in, Axiothea would send me a message to meet her in the olive grove, or by some hero-tomb in the Sacred Way. If the news was short, and would have gone into her note, we did not notice it. We had become fond of one another; though she liked the calm spare life of the Academy, she liked, too, to hear of the world outside, from someone who did not disapprove. She was setting into a strange archaic beauty. I have seen such faces in old shrines; there is an Artemis at Aigina very like her.

The Messene strait being so narrow, ships cross all winter in any but the worst of weather, so the Syracusan Pythagoreans could keep their brethren posted. They were in touch with Speusippos, who came and went somehow from Ortygia; no doubt Dionysios, who had always been jealous of him, would have been well pleased if he had slipped off. But he put up with the snubs and slights, which I could well imagine, to be with Plato and to link him with his friends.

At first the news was good; Dionysios was heaping him with honor, entertaining him, deferring to his advice. He had been able to realize Archytas' dearest wish by recommending a peace treaty with the Tarentines, which was already signed.

Archytas' letters were full of this; Speusippos' own were a good deal franker. He made them cryptic with false names, and, for greater safety, addressed them to people outside the Academy, sometimes to me. When he got home, he was at pains to get them back and burn them, in case Plato ever saw them; but I kept this one. The device was his usual one, of someone gossiping about a fashionable hetaira.

Everyone is amazed at the conduct of young Damiskos. When first he courted Heliodora, he vowed no price would be too high. [The price meant accepting Plato's precepts.] Having now drawn back, one would think he might have more pride than to hang about her door and keep sending flowers. Lately she asked him why, if he still desired her friendship, he did not pay up like a man, since he could afford it. And his answer? That his friends had advised him her price would encumber his estate; he wanted to beat her down. How absurd, to someone of her fame and reputation! She is generous in conversing with the youth, whose manners can do with polishing; but that he should presume to be jealous is as vexatious as it is laughable.

The other day there was an absurd but painful scene. She was spending a quiet hour at her music when he rushed in and offered her the direction of his whole inheritance—a gift more to himself than her, for she would do it to his advantage. By now she knows him better than to be transported; she waited to hear more. Can you guess the rest? His condition was that she should shut her door to Dikaios, her friend of twenty years, and proclaim this coxcomb as her favorite. She behaved, as I need not tell you who know her, with the greatest dignity. He left, I think, ashamed. But the folly and the turmoil made her feel ill, and she made no more music that day. I am sorry to say that she is not well, and this did nothing to improve things.

A few days later, the fears this letter had raised were realized. Archytas wrote that Plato was very sick, perhaps to death; for so concerned was Dionysios, he had sent his own wife to nurse him.

Speusippos' code-letters ceased; nothing mattered but Plato's life, and he wrote openly to Xenokrates. Just when things

looked worst, news stopped for nearly half a month, because
the winter storms had cut off Tarentum from Korkyra.

Dion had made many friends in Athens. They called to ex-
press sympathy and ask for news; when he had company I
did not like to trouble him. At first he seemed glad to see me;
I was the only one who had been there, and could picture,
nearly as well as he could, what was going on. He was too
proud to show his feelings among his new acquaintances as
he had to me at Tarentum. After a while he grew withdrawn
even with me, and I left him in peace, asking news from
Axiothea.

At last, a ship got through. Archytas wrote, enclosing back
letters from Speusippos. Plato was on the mend. The Archon's
wife had tended him like a daughter. Perhaps she had been
sent to watch that no one poisoned him, or laid the pillow on
his face. At all events, it did not seem Dionysios himself could
have been better cared for.

It was with an easier mind, therefore, that I went into rehearsal for the Lenaia. I had been chosen early in the draw
and offered the lead in a new play by Aphareus, *Atalanta in
Kalydon.*

I liked the play. It had fine acting roles, both for Atalanta
and Meleager. His part was most tempting, with a lovely scene
where he lies dying, while his stern mother Althaia burns the
magic faggot that holds his life. I could have used in it all
those effects which had made such a hit in *Orpheus.* The fact
was that I could see more in the Atalanta, which had much
subtlety and truth, but did not want to own it. In a female
lead, I would be measured against Theodoros.

He had been chosen at once by the sponsor who drew first
pick, with such alacrity that there must be some perfect role
for him; no knowing what, for new plays are well-kept secrets.
Though still fairly young, he was at the height of his powers;
if women, which the gods forbid, were allowed to play in
tragedy, I am sure the best of them could not have spoken
for her sex more movingly, or with more fire, than he. It would
be wise to take Meleager, and make the best of it.

I was sitting at home with the play in my hands, wondering how to get the most from the death scene, when I felt a pair of eyes staring at my back. Unwillingly I turned, knowing too well what I would see. The sun was westering. The mask stared out into full light, stern, radiant, without pity.

I went over, and looked reproachful. But he only laughed at me, in the dark behind his eyes. So I chose Atalanta, doubling it with Queen Althaia, and asked for Anaxis as Meleager. I was glad to offer him something, for he was then very dejected; he had lately risked half his savings in a trading ship to the Euxine which had gone down. Land prices kept rising, the more he saved; this had been his last chance of buying back his father's land. Now he was almost back where he started. (Things have changed since then. He owns the family estate, and has bought the next-door farm, since he took up politics.)

I enjoyed rehearsals. Once I was played in, I stopped wondering what Theodoros might be doing, and thought only of what I would do. It was a part with plenty of light and shade —complex, spirited, harshly tragic, with a noble close.

At the presentation, Theodoros and his company appeared with golden wreaths, showing they had a rich choregos, and the title of their play was given out: *Ariadne Forsaken.*

Well, I thought, there's the thing settled. He can't miss with that if he tries. The crown will have to have the judges' tears dried off it before he puts it on.

I felt dashed for an hour or two, but it was only what I had expected, and losing to Theodoros, at least one lost to someone good. It was not like being beaten by modish tricks.

It was so-so weather on the day of the performance. We drew second turn to play, and Theodoros was on last. It was blowing, threatening rain, and clearing up by turns all day; I don't think it favored any one play above the others.

Since I knew where the crown was going, I put it out of my mind, and just played for my own enjoyment, and for that of people, like Axiothea, whose judgment I respected. At the end, we were quite pleased with our reception. That's done,

I thought, as I stripped and got dressed; now I'll watch Theodoros, and not give way to jealousy. It keeps one from learning, and one can't see such an artist every day.

As always, he was a pleasure when he only walked across the stage. Moreover, the play had clearly been written for him. If another sponsor had drawn him first, whoever did the part would have had to play Theodoros. But the poet had the real one, and had given him nothing to do but play himself. Every effect he had ever melted the theater with was written in for poor Ariadne. You would have thought he was a juggler in need of five balls and a stool to do his act, not an artist who wanted stimulus. He did his best to give it freshness, but it was like seasoning stale fish. All the same, he was such a delight to hear that I felt sure he must have won, until the herald gave out that I had.

So I had to get my costume on again, and be crowned, and make my bow; then back to the dressing room, with the crowd about me. I was just combing my hair, when a voice behind cried, "My dear! Superb! It killed me to miss the end, I was almost too late to dress."

It was Theodoros. We had met once or twice at parties, but he was always surrounded, and I hardly knew him. He took me by the shoulders and kissed me on both cheeks. No one in the business had a bad word for Theodoros, and now I could see why.

"I sat there, my dear," he said, "quite hating you for having that lovely role and knowing what to do with it. But I had to give in like all the rest."

I knew enough to be honored by this foolery. His dignity could be freezing; he stood no nonsense from the richest of sponsors, nor, I believe, from kings. He kept this kind of thing for equals.

"May I come to your party? A married woman, dear, even though forsaken. A girl from the country needs a chaperone, among all these horrid men."

So began our friendship, which lasted till his death. There was only one shadow on the day, one of those unlucky chances. Dion, while in Athens, attended all the sacred festivals, including those of Dionysos; he would have thought it uncouth to slight the customs of his hosts. But I had never thought for a moment he might come backstage. This, however, he did. The play had not offended his morals or his piety, and he had been struck, it seems, by my performance as old Althaia, when she repents her vengeance after having destroyed her son. What with this and that, he decided to greet me; but by the time he made up his mind to it, the other gentlemen had gone; it was mostly actors and hetairas and old friends; and Theodoros, who had hated his own role, was burlesquing it, kneeling on a table for the Naxian shore, with words of his own invention. When Dion was seen in the doorway, the skeneroom hushed like a class when the headmaster enters. Theodoros changed in a flash from a screaming whore to an ambassador, but still too late. Shocked as he must have been, Dion's courtesy never faltered, and he said his piece. For an instant our eyes met, his saying, "How can you endure this life?" and mine, "You might try to understand." But I don't expect it was worse than his supposings, which had not prevented his former kindness. He soon forgave me, and greeted me as before.

From the Lenaia to the Dionysia never seems very long. I had a good role, but this time so did Theodoros; he won, and well deserved to win; and without him I might still have lost to Philemon. But I had been well received; I was now a leading man sponsors wanted, and felt well enough content. Soon after, a letter came to my house from Dion, speaking gracefully of my performance, then saying, "You will share, I know, our rejoicing at the news of Plato's return. He is already in Tarentum, and will sail for Athens with the first fair wind."

# XIV

IT WAS NOT THE RETURN OF SPRING SAILING
weather which had persuaded Dionysios to part with Plato.
The cause was war.

Dion, from his knowledge of the Carthaginians, had tried
to keep them ignorant of his fall from power; but the upshot
was that they had learned he was an exile who could neither
help nor harm them. Their envoys treated with Dionysios and
Philistos; they distrusted the second, and despised the first.
All winter they prepared for war. They attacked in spring.

Speusippos told me later the tale of those winter months.
While Plato was sick, all Syracuse remarked that the Archon
seemed more concerned than when his own father lay dying.
But the danger past, Plato was barely on his feet again when
once more he was worn out with scenes, always with this
same demand to be first among his friends. Speusippos, who
had had all he could stand and more, said it was like a
young boy at school enamored of another, but owned that the
wretched fellow seemed really to be suffering.

A base man would have flattered him; a man of more common virtues put him quickly out of hope. But for Plato, who was used to young men loving him, this was the first step towards philosophy; he would have thought shame to reject it, just for his own peace of mind. Patiently and selflessly, he used that charm which Dion had remembered for twenty years, to make his jailer captive. Speusippos said it was like a dialogue between bird and fish, each calling from an element the other could not live in. To the one, the crown of love was excellence; to the other it was possession.

"His father has a good deal to answer for," I said. "As long as he lived, the poor wretch was never allowed an hour of self-esteem. Now he comes like a starving man to an elegant symposion, grabbing without manners. Put it down to poverty."

"I don't suppose," said Speusippos impatiently, "he had half the troubles in his youth that Plato did. The war, the siege, the death of friends in battle and by the hands of friends, his kinsmen killed as tyrants, and execrated to this day—and then Sokrates, whom he loved and honored above all men, murdered in form of law . . . But never mind; the man who squeals gets all the pity. At all events, he kept telling Dionysios that the way to his regard led through philosophy; and Dionysios kept replying that Dion must be first disowned, else how should he know he was being advised to his own advantage? Philistos' faction had warned him he was just being softened to make way for Dion's usurpation. He wanted evidence of good faith."

This startled even me. "By the dog! How did Plato swallow such insults?"

"Insults are given by men. One doesn't strike a whining child when it tugs one's clothes."

"Perhaps," I said. "But sometimes he has his wits about him."

"Quite true. That's why Plato struggled all this while. But he is a child in his soul. A stepchild, rather."

Even when the spring brought war, he was very unwilling to let Plato go. Speusippos had been desperate, for the Archon would have to show himself in the field and, left alone in Ortygia among his enemies, Plato would have been lucky to live a week. He knew this, but kept his fortitude, and took care to show no dismay. Urging his long absence from the Academy, and his need for a change of climate, at last he prevailed on Dionysios to part with him, but only in exchange for a pledge that if Dion were recalled from exile, he too would return to Syracuse. Thus for his friend's sake, with both eyes open, for the third time he put his life at risk.

I saw him soon after he got home, at a concert in the Odeion. He stooped more, he was sallow, and had lost a good deal of weight; his wrestler's shoulders looked bony, and deep lines were carved beside his mouth. But a fine head. Leanness showed up its structure. Hagnon said he would like to paint him, though he would be a better subject for bronze.

At the last he, and even Speusippos, had been seen off with a load of guest-gifts and every mark of honor. Plato, if he would have taken it, could have had a fortune in Sicilian gold, either for himself or for the Academy, of which it would have delighted Dionysios to be a patron; but endowments were never taken except from those who had embraced its precepts. Rather than give outsiders the power to interfere, Plato would have taught in the streets like Sokrates before him. Nonetheless, one thing was clear: whereas Plato had left old Dionysios as a wronged man without obligations (except to revenge, if he had not been above it), he was bound now to the son by the sacred ties of guest-friendship, and I wondered what that would lead to later.

I had meant to arrange a tour that year. But I found I had so many offers that engagements kept me busy. I played at Ephesos and Miletos, and while there was asked to Pergamon. And at Delphi, at the Pythian Festival, by Apollo's favor I got the crown. As I bent my head for it, I heard from high up over the Phaidriades the scream of an eagle, maybe the very one who had shouted "Yaah!" at me as I dangled on the crane.

This was my last tour with Anaxis. We still got on pretty well; but he was a disappointed artist now, and the only thing which kept him from growing bitter was the hope of a career in politics. Since this was so, I did not try to dissuade him, and even let him practice orations on me, the sort of exercise they teach in the schools of rhetoric for making, as they so frankly put it, the worse cause sound like the better. This shows, I think, what I will do for my friends.

Once an actor gets known, he does a good deal of traveling; but in the next few years, Dion traveled at least as much as I.

One saw him at all great festivals—at Olympia, Delphi, Epidauros, Delos—always with a crowd about him, always some distinguished person's honored guest. For this reason or that, he was everybody's hero. Most tyrants on seizing power start off by murdering the aristocracy, so conservatives are as tyrannophobe as democrats, and Dion was all that they admired. His political aims had been moderate; his hands were clean; he had never stooped to use spies or knife-men, nor roused mobs to riot; all the gentry of Hellas praised his antique virtues. Even the Spartans gave him the freedom of their city, though they were Dionysios' allies, because of his reverence for law and the sacred bonds of kinship. Yet he was beloved too by all the democrats, having opposed a tyrant and suffered exile. You could not go wrong anywhere if you praised Dion. I grew almost ashamed to do it.

He bore fame as nobly as misfortune. He could wear his honors without fear, being what he seemed, with nothing to hide that could help his enemies. Philosophers dedicated major works to him; poets brought him into heroic odes. His distinguished presence, his great change of fortune greatly endured, his wealth (for his revenues came over every year, a vast sum by Attic reckoning), his links with the Academy, brought credit everywhere to the philosophic life. Living sparely himself, he could open both hands to others. His forecourt was crowded with petitioners; he was a liberal patron of the arts. I think it was the second year of his exile that Plato put on a choral ode in the contest at the Dionysia, making it known that Dion had financed it, as a gesture of thanks for Athenian hospitality. The costumes were splendid, green patterned with vine-sprays worked in gold, with a gold vine-wreath for the flute-player. The music was in the Dorian mode,

Plato and Dion being agreed, like all Pythagoreans, in think-ing the Lydian too emotional. The good breeding with which they shared the public applause was much admired.

This was a good Dionysia for me too. I got the lead in a revival of Euripides' *Chrysippos*, the play it is said he wrote while he was courting Agathon. Doubling Chrysippos' lover Laios and the wicked stepmother, I got the prize, the first I had won at the greater festival. The sponsor gave a splendid party. I did not presume to ask Dion, his friends being all so distinguished now, but he looked in with Speusippos. The two were much in company; Axiothea confided to me that Plato favored it, thinking it would loosen the proud shyness which often caused Dion to be misunderstood. Praise left him at a loss for answers, which made people think him cold, espe-cially the democrats. But now he seemed more at ease than before, smiled oftener, and stayed at the party longer than I had expected. The truth is, I thought, he is an Athenian in his soul. Young Dionysios did him a good turn in the end. He thrives on exile.

One heard little from Sicily; few artists were going, be-cause of the war, which dragged on some years. I could not learn that either side made much out of it. The Greeks lost no major cities, which they owed I think to Philistos; though a bad man, and getting old, he was a soldier and knew his trade.

These were good years for me. I could do the work I wanted. I had worked hard and gone short to make this beginning; for it is that, and not an end. But I had more than my work to live for.

I had bought a house near the Kephissos, just out of town; a pleasant place, not too fashionable, in reach of friends but not in the path of time-wasters. The garden ran to the river; birds sang in the willows, and at night one heard the stream. There were orchards and small vineyards between the houses; the road was quiet, so that passers-by drew a second glance. At sunup, when I did my practice, there would often be some-one loitering. Then it stopped, and I forgot it, till one day as I did change-of-pitch I found that I had an echo. I went on as if I had noticed nothing, and finished with a speech, then slipped quickly out at the back. Against the wall, where its corner had hidden him from my window, a boy was standing, softly running my last speech over, to fix it fresh in his mind. He had every inflection and rise and fall, just so.

When I coughed, he jumped a foot and went white. Reassuring him as best I could, I asked him in. He was a big-boned lad, with high hollow cheekbones and gray eyes, and the auburn hair of the north. Though scarcely past the awkward age, he knew how to manage his big hands and feet, and kept his head up. I invited him to share my breakfast, which my man had just brought in, and asked how long he had wanted to be an actor. As red, now, as if scalded, he answered, "Since first I saw a play." He would not tell me his given name, saying no Athenian could pronounce it. "They call me Thettalos."

"Well," I said, "you speak good Attic, which is right if you want to act." Then, putting in the soft northern *s*'s, "When did you come from Thessaly?"

"That was my father," he answered. "I was born here myself, and we are citizens since last year." But of course, while a metic, he had not been eligible for chorus work at the sacred festivals, so though now eighteen he was quite without experience, and had picked up all he knew from sitting in front, or in ways like this today. His father would do nothing to help; he had come south with little, in flight from one of his country's oppressive local lords, and worked hard till he owned a riding school. He was waiting, none too patiently, for the boy to outgrow his nonsense.

"It seems," I said, "that you chose me to be your teacher. So why not have come to me, and asked for help?"

"I meant to," he said, as if I should have understood. "But I was waiting till I was better."

At these words I refrained from singing a paean, or embracing him, but asked where he went to practice. He just walked, he said, till he found an empty field. "Let me hear something," I told him. "Do what you like."

I thought he would go straight into Electra or Antigone or Ajax, and tear himself to bits. But no. He gave me a speech for the third actor, young Troilos pleading to Achilles for his life. Not only did he know his limits, he turned them to account; he was the youth who would not see his manhood. There was no softness, nothing pretty, but under the pathos a muted terror as he read the doom in Achilles' eyes. I could have sworn I saw the relentless figure standing over him; the placing of his gestures shaped it out of air. He would die with his scream unuttered, because he was a prince of Troy, and had despaired in time. When it was over, he sat back on his heels, a light sweat on his brow, and waited for me to speak.

I forget what I first said. For just then I saw his eyes look up past my shoulder, caught and held. I had no need to turn. I knew where the mask hung in its shrine. It was just as if a look had passed between them, of recognition, or of complicity.

They say that Daidalos, the first artificer, saw his apprentice would surpass him and threw him off the roof. In the soul of every artist the murderer's ghost lives on. Some make an honored guest of him; some chain him, and bolt the door, but know that he is not dead. Well, I could not have been cruel to this boy. That was not in me. There are things, however, one can do and live on with the thought of them. One can say, "You show great promise, but it's useless to start till you have more range. Come back when you are twenty." That would have wasted his time and got him stale, and put back his career five years. But having seen him without the mask as he spoke for Troilos, I knew I could do better for myself than that: "My dear boy, I think you have a future, when you have lived a little. What you need is to feel, to know the passions. Come back at sundown. We will have a little supper, and talk it over . . ." There are more ways of killing a bird than wringing its neck.

Once more he looked past me, and I saw that meeting of silent eyes. Though they only spoke to one another, they spoke to me. No good ever came, I thought, of robbing a god, and this one above all.

"Well, Thettalos," I said, "I think you have learned as much as you will manage from behind a wall. It's time you got up on a stage. Tell me what kind of man your father is, and I will do my best with him. There's not much time; I am taking a company to Epidauros a month from now, and I shall need an extra."

This, then, is how the god acquired his servant Thettalos, an artist seldom surpassed—at his best, unequaled in our day. It was a few years yet, though, before he knew himself, coming to the art so late. He was uncertain, scared often of his own force. It was like training a nervous blood-horse.

Our play for the Epidaurian Festival was *Iphigeneia at Aulis*. From the first I let him understudy the third roles, which include the name part; with only a little more technique, he would have been better than the man I had. At first I took him through the lines once or twice alone. Soon I thought better not. He played it all from the heart, knowing no other way; he was so eager, mulling half the day over everything I taught him; his eyes were flecked with green, and his chestnut brows met in fine down above them; in a word, he was starting to break my rest. But he was using himself so hard, and was stretched so taut, that I dared not disturb him. Besides, he was both proud and honest, and his whole life, as he must see it, was in my power. I waited. Some god said to me that a time would come.

We made a hit at Epidauros. What with the festival, the beauty of the theater, and his first appearance, he was quite drunk with joy; I was relieved that he kept his head. After the performance, I took him sightseeing. Going up to the portico of the Asklepeion, we met Dion coming out. He seldom missed these great occasions. Though men of note were pressing round him, he stopped and greeted me, spoke well of the production, and had a gracious word for Thettalos when I presented him. He, as soon as we were alone, said, "Who was that?" I told him Dion's story, adding, "There goes the best man of our age."

He followed my eyes, then broke out suddenly, "Yes, and how he agrees with you."

"My dear boy!" I said, quite startled, for though frank he was never impudent. "What a thing to say. His modesty is proverbial."

"And he knows that too." He kicked a pebble, and swallowed a curse when it hurt his toe. I could see no cause for this sudden anger, which was quite unlike him, but took it he was overwrought.

"You mistake him," I said. "He is shy by nature; but he is a man of too much pride to own it."

"Why not? Who is he to be proud with you? You're just as great as he is. Why, the first time you spoke to me, I thought I should stifle before I could get my breath to answer you. Even now, if it weren't that I—" He broke off, red to the ears, almost swallowing his tongue backwards, and looking round like a thief for somewhere to run. I just put my hand behind his arm, and quietly walked him on. In silence we said everything.

So the god rewarded us. It may be that when I am dead, if he lives his span, he will hand on, to the young men coming after, small things I taught him. Since memories die with men, that's as near as one gets to immortality.

Success brought his father round; before long, he could leave home without discord, and live with me. Even before that, we were never long parted, and could do as we liked on tour. As I said, those were happy years.

Young as he was, he could manage everything except the heavies. He was, and I think will always be, one of those actors in whom feeling works like intellect, so clearly it forms its concepts. They have it straight from the god; they give reasons if you ask, but those came later. But he was greedy for technique; born knowing why, he had to know how before he could bring it forth; and his reverence for me was touching. He would come to the end of it soon, I thought; what then? Meantime we read *The Myrmidons*, talked half the night, and taught each other; for the thoughts he threw off while we walked, or ate, or lay in bed were full of careless wealth.

At about this time, Speusippos married a young wife, a niece of Plato's. He seemed contented, and praised her to me. I don't know how much she saw of him, between his work and his diversions. As for Dion, I met him often, as I had at Epidauros. I could never think without a smile of Thettalos' betraying jealousy; Dion had come as our god of luck, as the lad himself admitted, adding that no doubt he had been unjust, for what could he know of such a man? To me it seemed that Dion, though a king in exile, was still a king; he might lead no armies, but men would serve him with their minds, for by believing in him they could believe better in themselves.

As I said, the people round him were of many different kinds —gentlemen, soldiers, philosophers, politicians. He joined the best supper clubs; and it was at one of these, I think, that he renewed his friendship with Kallippos, who had been his co-initiate at Eleusis. I myself had known the man rather longer; he was often about the theater. One met him at all the sponsors' parties, and in the skeneroom after the play. He had often paid me compliments, which would have pleased me more if he had not been just as ready with them after a bad performance. It gives me no joy to be praised at the expense of a better artist, by someone who does not know the difference or who thinks me too vain to be aware of it myself. After a while, I used to acknowledge his civility, and leave him, so to speak, hung up with the other masks.

His real interests were political; politics were the first thing he looked for in a play. One that was only true to man's nature, bad and good, he found insipid. He was a sand-colored man, with eyes like shallow sand-pools, which he would fix on one as if to say that he read one's soul. Knowing, as I did at home, what such a gaze is really like, I was hard put to it sometimes not to laugh in his face. I don't know what he read in me; his readings of others were often out, but when this appeared, he put it down to dissimulation, a quality he saw everywhere.

I had a good deal of attention from Kallippos, because I had been in Sicily. Actors and hetairas, in different ways, hear about affairs if they have time to listen, and Kallippos knew it. Charissa the Delian, an old friend of mine, told me he never chose a girl for looks or erotic skill, but according to her clientele, which he took pains to learn beforehand.

Actors and whores, though he found them useful, were passing concerns for him. He had more serious business at the Academy, where he hung on the fringe, attending the lectures and discussions on political theory, but (as Axiothea told me when I asked her) finding no time for those upon philosophy, or the nature of the soul. Such being his interests, he was sure to seek out Dion; and though I was sorry to see him in the company of anyone so much beneath his quality, I could understand it. Kallippos took color from his company, if it sufficiently impressed him. And he was a true hater of tyrants. In this he did not dissemble. He was a hater of many things, beginning I think with himself; but tyrants he had made a study of, and could tell you all their histories, right back to the Peisistratids and Periander. Dion, as I have said, had become for all Hellas the symbol of resistance to all tyranny. He was as a god, therefore, to Kallippos, who showed him a true face, whereas he only made use of men like me. Even fulsomeness, when the heart is in it, does not disgust the just man like sycophancy. I have no doubt, too, that the information Kallippos had picked up in the skeneroom or the stews was believed by gentlemen and philosophers to be the fruit of insight and logic. As for his adulation, Dion was used to that. It met him everywhere.

Meantime, a year as third actor had been enough for Thettalos. Within three years of his joining me, I took him on as second, not just for love, but because I could have done no better. Often I felt like Arion; after the song, after the splendid dolphin swims up at call, comes the breathless sea-ride, feeling the creature's power curbed by its tenderness, yet awaiting the moment when it knows only its own strength and the grace Apollo gave it, and with some great leap or dive is gone into the glassy green, leaving one to swim. He was obedient always. When he had talked me round to his own way of thinking, he would say how wonderful was our harmony, and so I am sure he saw it. When I insisted on my own interpretation, he supported me with all he had. His loyalty was perfect. But there is a curse on him who holds back the messengers of the gods. In the depth of night, the moon at the window would show me his face intent upon a dream. I would think, He will outgrow me and excel me, and leave me to love him still.

In the fifth year of Dion's exile, news came that the war in Sicily was over. It had dragged to a standstill, and ended in a draw. I think the Carthaginians, who are unloved by all their neighbors, had trouble at home in Africa. At all events they got tired, and there was a patched-up peace.

That same year, as soon as sailing weather opened up the sea roads, the Sicilian ambassador called at the Academy. He had a letter from Dionysios, entreating Plato to visit Syracuse.

As you may suppose, Plato asked at once whether Dion, then, had been recalled. The ambassador said that no doubt during Plato's visit there could be fruitful discussions of all such matters. On this Plato declined with thanks, and went back to his studies. As Speusippos said, he detested the very thought of Syracuse. He was now rising seventy, not an age when men lightly go on voyages, with their stale food, bad water, hard beds and the chance of storms. At that time of life a man must take some care of his body, to get the best from his mind.

The peace, though troublesome to Plato, was good news to theater men, and many tours were being planned. For myself, I too had seen enough of Sicily, at least without Dion there. *The Bacchae* had been a bellyful which still lay heavy. So Thettalos and I went east; we played in Ephesos, Lesbos, Samos, Halikarnassos and Miletos, and toured the chief cities of Rhodes.

The old mask-box went with us. I never left it behind. But each time I hung it up on the wall, it seemed that the face within was saying, "Nikeratos, you have something of mine. I have been your friend; but do not tempt me."

The grapes were trodden; winter came; we went by torchlight to bright rooms, then home to lie warm and discuss the party. The Lenaia came, then the Dionysia. It was one of the years I got the crown.

On a warm spring evening, two days after the feast, we sat on the grass by the riverbank, upon one cloak. A thrush swung and sang in the hanging willow. I said, "Do you love me as before?"

He said, "What? Niko, how can you ask me such a thing? What has made you doubt it?" I could not bear to see his look of guilt, so undeserved.

"My dear," I said, "I have never doubted less. You gave good proof at the Dionysia. But there are proofs love dies of giving; it is better to keep hold of love. So you must join another company."

His eyes were like those of a sick man who hears from the doctor what he already knew. He wanted to be angry; it crossed his face and he let it go. When he spoke, it was as if we had been talking of this an hour already. "No, Niko, it's no use; I can't do it. How can I go? We should be forever parting, for half the year. Besides, it's too soon. It's not in reason I can be ready." It was not with me he was contending; I might have known the god had been hounding him as well. "It's you who can get the best from me. Who else would push me on as you've done? Wherever could I do better?"

"Henceforward, anywhere. You know it. Name me one other actor, one, for whom you would have underplayed as you did this time."

"Now you're absurd," he said, pulling up grass by the roots. "In a contest, nobody steals from the protagonist. I should hope I know that. I am sure you never did so."

"Not so as to get pointed at. But one shows what one could do. Come, my dear, you understand me."

"Say I don't wish to. In the name of the god, Niko, what do you want to make of me? From you I have had everything. If at last I've something to give, don't you think I want to give it? Before I can even begin, you start saying no. You make me angry." He made an angry gesture, to show he meant it. I had never loved him more.

"What was yours I have taken gladly. But the time has come, and you have seen it, when you are giving me what is *his*." I had only to move my head towards the room behind us. We had shared that secret from early days. "He will punish it," I said. "There is no escaping him."

"He owes you something. Is he less grateful than a man?"

"He cannot change his nature, which can light or burn. We are scorched already, my dear. You have felt it too. All through rehearsals, through the contest, all through the victory feast, you give and give, you behave perfectly. Then later your oil flask is mislaid, and it enrages you. So it will be; and in two years we shall have nothing. Let us obey the god and keep his blessing. The time is now."

This had come hard to both of us. Having braved it, we were both in pain; but it was the pain of the cautery, not the poison. In our hearts we both knew it would be worth the cost. We disputed a little longer, both knowing the outcome now but offering it as a mark of love, then talked of the past, sharing our memories. But the thing must be finished clean, so presently I said, "Summer tours will be starting soon. You must be looking round." To tease him I added, "What about Theophanes? You'd have the heart to steal from him."

He laughed; we were laughing easily now, as people do after strain. "Theophanes would never let me within a mile of him. He likes his supports made of solid wood."

"To be serious: Miron is getting no younger, and he feels his limits. He is looking for a second who can take more work. Of course all his plays will have some big oldish role, for him, but you will get some very good parts which are past him now. He's a man of the old tradition, but you'll fare no worse in the end from knowing how Kallippides did it in the ninety-third Olympiad or Kleomachos in the hundredth. He is quite well liked, if you can put up with his superstition and eternal omens."

"I don't mind other men's omens," he said. "I watch my own."

"His greatest virtue in my eyes is that he only likes young girls."

"I don't mind his likes. I know my own." He added softly, "I'm not one to go drinking vinegar after wine."

So we talked, and slept, and next day he signed his contract. They were soon rehearsing; he would come home full of talk; we were happy, like autumn grasshoppers, living from day to day. Then Miron fixed up a tour to Delos and the Cyclades. All of a sudden they had sailed, and his absence lay everywhere, like a fall of snow.

I ought to have found a new second before he left. I had known this, but kept putting it off. With every day of missing him, I grew harder to please. I turned down a good offer from Macedon, and drifted, passing the time. It could not go on; I made up a short-term company, and went to Corinth for the Isthmia. Work made me more like myself; when the games were over, I stayed with old friends awhile, and went back to Athens resolved to get my life in order.

Theodoros exclaimed that I was getting dreadfully thin, and gave a party for me at which he produced all the handsome youths he could think of who were free just then. Though they went as free as they came, I was grateful for the kindly thought, and sorry to disappoint him by leaving with Speusippos. But he had let me know he had things to tell me, which would not do in a crowd.

As soon as we were alone, but for his linkboy walking ahead, I asked his news. He said, "The Academy's by the ears. No one knows how it will end. Dionysios has written again for Plato."

"Does it matter? He wrote last year, and Plato told him to go and play with it, or whatever philosophers say instead." I was still rather drunk.

Speusippos, who had sobered quickly, said, "I think this time he may have to go."

"What? You mean Dion's exile is rescinded?" Lately my mind had often turned to him. He was the man, after my father, who had taught me honor. Perhaps, I thought, it was he who had pointed out my way.

"No," said Speusippos, and closed his mouth.

"But that was Plato's condition. So he can stay at home."

"It is not so simple." He looked like a man with warring thoughts. "To begin with, Dionysios has turned back to philosophy."

"My dear Speusippos! It's ten days to Syracuse with a good wind. By then he will have turned on his other side."

"No, he's had a year at it, really studying. He's been writing to Plato and even making sense. So Plato has answered, and at a good deal of trouble too. The mind is there; it's character makes it balk like a half-broken horse. That's what teases Plato —the thought that if the beast could be trained, he'd run."

"Well, but since he got so frisky on the rein, he may study better alone."

"So it began to seem. But it was you, I think, who said he always wants to be crowned before the race?"

"Don't tell me," I cried, "that he's calling himself an Academician?" My laughter stopped when I saw Speusippos was not even smiling. Maybe, I thought, he had drunk himself sad, as some men do.

"That is the least of it. Being a special case, he's got his hands on something no other student of Plato's owns—a written scheme of his oral teaching." He saw my surprise, and said patiently, "Plato believes in the spark that kindles mind from mind. If your brand won't burn, you carry it back to the hearth again. But he had to send it to Dionysios, since he couldn't come and his fire kept smoking. By now it amounts to a thesis, almost. So, instead of using in quiet such disciplines as make the mind's eye to see, he invites a philosophic concourse, and poses as a finished product of the school."

"Plato must be angry. But, surely, not angry enough to get him out to Syracuse?" There was a pause. "Who are these hangers-on?"

"Kyrenians, mostly, from the school of Aristippos. Like him, they equate the good with pleasure, but define their terms less carefully. And he himself wasn't careful enough. He was Plato's fellow guest with old Dionysios; unlike Plato, he did very well out of it."

"Does the son deserve better company? Why can't he leave Plato be? No, I can guess the answer. These are just rivals, flaunted to make the real love jealous. One could laugh, or cry."

"I wish it may end in laughter."

The moon had set, and a watchdog howled in the dark. I thought of the cold bed at home. Whatever bad news he was holding back, I could do without it. But as one always does, I asked.

"Dionysios is resolved to get Plato there. Persuasion having failed, he turns, like every tyrant at the pinch, to power. His last letter invited Plato to confer with him on the settlement of Dion's estates in Sicily. As I suppose you know, the income from them has reached him every year. If Plato goes, everything can be arranged to Dion's liking. If not, not. In other words—confiscation."

"So that's it," I said. "The wretched little blackmailer! He should know better the men he has to deal with." Speusippos was silent. I thought, as we walked on, of Dion's splendid progresses, how he had held court at Delphi, Delos, and Olympia, a beacon to every lover of justice. Of course spies must have brought word of all this to Syracuse, and one could picture Dionysios' jealousy. The wonder was, I thought, that he had not sunk to this meanness sooner.

"Well," I said presently, "it's good that Dion has always lived like a philosopher. With what he has, he'll be as well off I daresay as you or I. His wife and son can't come to harm, being the Archon's kin; and though he'll miss his travels, at the Academy he'll have all he truly values—Plato, his books, his friends."

In the flickering torchlight, I saw Speusippos look at me, then look ahead. Still he said nothing.

"Don't think I make light of it," I said. "Of course it will come harder to a man of rank, especially a Syracusan. But we know the man, and his love of honor. The greater the sacrifice, the higher his tribute to friendship and philosophy. That's how Dion will see it. Depend on it, he will never let Plato go."

When still Speusippos did not answer, I began to be anxious, lest in some way I had offended him; but before I could ask him if this was so, he said drily, "You are mistaken. He has been urging it."

I got him to repeat this. When one sees two moons in the sky, one assumes that it's the wine, not that they are there. Having heard it again, I said, "Why? I don't understand."

"Ask a god why, who can read men's souls."

"But," I said, laboring it over, "even before Dion's exile, Syracuse was not safe for Plato. Philistos' faction hated him; the soldiers openly wanted his blood. Then he was kept there all winter against his will; he was sick; and he was younger then. As it was, he lost a year of work, at an age when every year counts. How *can* Dion ask him to go back there?"

"We must be just," said Speusippos, appealing to himself. "It is not simply the money. Dion hopes Plato will procure his recall."

I asked, "Does Dion himself say this?"

"Certainly. He said it to me."

"How can he hope so for a moment? Dionysios was ready to believe the worst of him without any cause but jealousy. And now, for years, all Greece has been praising the Great Exile, every word of it at Dionysios' expense, every word a stab to his pride. He must detest the very name of Dion. Besides, they couldn't dare have him back; he is the hero of all the democrats in Sicily. Dionysios does not even offer it to get Plato there, for which he would offer nearly anything. Can Dion dream he would be recalled?"

"It is man's nature to believe what he greatly wishes."

"That's true. But is it the nature of philosophy?"

He stopped still in the street. The linkboy paused at the corner, missed us, and came running back to make sure we were still on our feet. Speusippos waved him on. "So, Niko, you were listening all the time. And back it comes, just when I run to you for comfort."

"I am sorry," I said. "What do I know of philosophy? All that sticks in my mind is that Plato is his friend."

Speusippos said, "Yes, you have your own elenchos. I should have feared the logic of your heart."

Now both of us were silent. We walked on through the dark, following the bobbing torch; presently we reached the turn of the road before my house, and the boy ran ahead to light my door. We lingered, both thinking, I suppose, that there must be something cheerful to part upon, if we could lay hold of it in time.

I said, "One thing I can't believe is that Dion would do this only for the money. He has had all the luxuries of Syracuse at call, just for clapping his hands, and has gone without from choice. Look at his style of living."

"I am sure he has no wish to change it. But there is one danger to a rich man in simple tastes: they enable him to be generous. Of course he has asked for no return; he would abhor the thought of buying sycophants. But, the world being what it is, there is a crowd about him—not all disinterested, I'm afraid. It has given him great consequence, without his having anything to be ashamed of. Now he is used to it. As you know, he has his pride."

We had come to the house. For form's sake I asked him in; he thanked me and said he must be at work early tomorrow. We dawdled towards the porch, still seeking the hopeful word.

"I can't forget," I said, "how nobly he used to speak of Plato, the first year of his exile. Of course, you were still in Syracuse . . . There is a book of Plato's I read once—yes, truly, I read the whole of it. It was a supper party where they made speeches in praise of love. I daresay you know it?"

"Yes," said Speusippos. "Yes, I have read *The Symposion* once or twice. I reread it yesterday."

"I just meant that Plato has lived up to it."

"I see. I misunderstood. I thought perhaps you knew for whom it was first written."

Our eyes met. I exclaimed, "This must be a passing mood with Dion. Good actors have days when they can do nothing right; no doubt good men do, too. Now he knows how Plato feels, he will remember himself and think no more of such a thing. I daresay we are troubling ourselves over very little."

Dawn was breaking. Birds sang in the willows, the same that had wakened me when the house was warm within. In the gray light, I saw Speusippos' face creased like a monkey's which has bitten a sour fig. He said, "I see I must tell you everything. As early as last year, Dion wanted Plato to accept the Archon's invitation. Since he refused, nothing has been quite the same between them. Then, when this latest summons came, Dion called to discuss it, walked out in anger, and has not been near Plato since. Plato has written, I know. But there has been no answer."

A cloud had caught the hidden sun, and glowed pink above us. Looking up to the High City, I saw the gilded ornaments on the temple roofs glitter in the first shafts of day. Before the house stood the lad with the torch waiting for leave to quench it. Something stirred in my memory; a shudder like a cold finger rippled up my backbone. I began to speak, and ceased.

"What?" asked Speusippos, roused from his thoughts.

"No, nothing," I answered. "I forgot you missed the play."

# XV

IN EARLY SUMMER, THETTALOS GOT BACK FROM
his tour. I had awaited this with more pain than hope. Days
are long for the young; the past is soon crowded out. But like
a homing kingfisher, he came flashing straight back to his
bough beside the stream.

All the spoils of his voyage, the theaters, cities, triumphs
and troubles, his many scrapes (he was more adventurous
than wild) he flung before me. He talked half the night—
about the plays they had done, how Miron had directed them,
and how he could have done it better. He was just at the age
when one must let out one's new thoughts or burst. Now he
was free to tell them all. When he jumped out of bed at midnight to show me how he would have done an upstage entrance if Miron had let him, I saw beyond the open door the
mask smiling down on us, amused and kind.

We went everywhere together, a joy to those who wished us
well, a grief to the backbiters whose meat is broken friendship,
and who had been busy when he left.

One day, when we were sitting with friends in the scent-shop, I slipped away to Sisyphos the goldsmith's to order a ring for him as an anniversary gift—a sardonyx, carved with Eros on a dolphin. While Sisyphos did his sketches, I idled round the shop, and heard some merchant ask if it was true a ship was in from Syracuse. Someone said yes, but not a trader. This was a state trireme, sent by the Archon to fetch Plato the philosopher.

I had been taken up with my own happiness. This news so shook me that I dropped all my morning business, fetched Thettalos from the scentshop, and told him I must go out to the Academy. Though he knew nothing of Plato but what I had told him, he was quite concerned.

"Yes, do go," he said. "I'll walk with you. It is wicked to treat the poor old man like this. I suppose he'll listen to no one but Dion (whom you know I never took to) and his philosophic friends. But one should at least take notice. We owe him a happy evening." He was remembering a supper for two at home, when we had read *The Symposion* together. I said that Plato would have enough to do without my troubling him, and I would just ask for news.

"I would like some day, Niko, to talk theater with that man. I doubt all his notions are as silly as you think. It's time they stopped turning every play on the gods. Half the modern writers don't believe in them; the rest think like you and me, that they are somewhere or everywhere, but in any case not sitting in gold chairs on Mount Olympos, feuding and meddling like a brood of Macedonian royalty, ready to chop down any virtuous man who forgets to flatter or bribe them."

Though myself not much above thirty, I often found the talk of the new generation standing my hair on end. At his age we whispered such thoughts; in my father's day they were a hemlock matter. Yet Plato had said something not unlike it, and he was seventy.

Among the olives of the Academy we greeted Axiothea, but did not linger, since she was not alone. She seldom was, now that Plato had accepted another girl. Lasthenia of Mantinea wore women's dress, feeling, I suppose, that this suited her soul; she was small and slim, with a kind of serious liveliness. They walked with their heads together, their hands sketching the argument to and fro. It had been a good day for Axiothea that brought her here. For the woman whose mind and body both need men, there is the life of the hetaira; it was not for her. She would have starved and turned sour if Plato had not been above convention. I was glad for her, and wished her joy.

When we reached our destination, Thettalos, who had much delicacy about serious things, said he did not know Speusippos well enough to intrude on him just now, and went to stroll in the gardens.

At Speusippos' door, I could hear a girl inside crying and pummeling her breast, and wailing, for the hundredth time by the sound of it, "I may never see you again!" Not having the face to knock during this scene, I walked off into the grove. I had heard what I came to know, but, longing to know more, persuaded myself I might be of help if I came back later.

Presently I was aware of two men ahead of me on the path between the trees. It was Plato, with Dion. I stopped, meaning to turn back; but just then Plato caught sight of someone beyond (no doubt he was full of business) and went over there, leaving Dion to wait.

He sat down on a shady bench. I could easily have slipped off unseen. But without pausing even to wonder at myself, I walked straight up to him.

It was impossible I could be welcome, and indeed he returned my greeting less coldly than I expected; perhaps I seemed a good omen, a harbinger of Sicily. At any time up till now, I would have walked on without presuming further. But I sat down beside him.

I conversed, I forget of what—of course, nothing to the purpose. I could see Plato deep in talk; he would be some time yet. Dion was quite civil. I could feel him thinking that when Plato came back, I had manners enough to go; meantime, what with one thing and another, it was his duty to put up with me. My awe, I suppose, had first begun to spill away in Syracuse, with the wine from his broken cup. Since then, too, I had advanced in my calling; and, which perhaps made the more difference, also in love.

Awe was gone; yet I had come to recover something. The noble beauty of this face was like a splendid mask I had long been used to live with. I studied it now again. So many men of his age (he must now be rising fifty) have faces getting fat, or loose, or drawn with petty cares, or bitter. But his outlines had kept their shape; if his skin had aged, it was a healthy weathering. A royal face—one of those classic masks made of good hardwood that carves like stone.

I forget how we came to talk of Delphi; but I recalled *The Myrmidons,* and how seldom it was done in Athens. Whichever of us it was who referred to Homer, it was I—as I am not likely to forget—who said, "Aischylos has departed from him here and there. Take Patroklos, for instance. In the *Iliad,* his father reminds him he is the elder of the friends, while Aischylos makes him the youth beloved. But in any case," I went on, following my thought, if you can call it that, "I suppose he would still be a man in the flower of his strength, when Achilles sent him into battle."

It was not till these words were out of my mouth that I perceived what I had been saying. If you ask how such stupidity is possible in a man able to get about and earn his bread, I can only suppose that my soul borrowed my tongue before I knew it. Had it been my own reflection, it was bad enough. But an actor's memory is like a jackdaw's nest; it came from Plato's *Symposion.*

Even before Dion's face went dark and cold as a winter mountain, I knew what I'd done, and had lost the look of innocence. To have begged his pardon would have made it ten times worse; nor indeed did I feel the wish. I can't remember with what form of words he let me know he was not at leisure. He could not have wished me gone more heartily than I did.

One must be prepared sometimes to make an exit when one is upset. Thinking only of what was at my back, I started at running into Thettalos, who made me sit down and tell him what was the matter. At the end he said, "Nonsense. You could have said much more than that. Only wait till you are seventy, and see if I treat you as he does Plato."

Laughing did me good, but it was not till next day that I felt fit to call on Speusippos.

I found him in his garden, talking with the old Persian slave who tended it, and with the young man Aristoteles to whom he had consigned his specimens before. The place was full of small shelters for delicate plants, rock terraces, wind screens and potting sheds. Seeing him busy, I would have withdrawn, but he said he would be glad of a break, and was only fidgeting there from restlessness. "I must remember," he said, "to enfranchise old Oitanes in my will, in case I don't come home. It would break his heart to lose the garden; it would be too much to be sold himself as well."

He called for cooled wine, and conferred a moment with the young Aristoteles, a dapper youth with thin legs and small, keen eyes. Presently he came back to sit with me against the shady wall of the house, under the vine trellis. Sweet herbs stood in pots around. "I can leave it all to him," he said. "He never forgets anything. One of our most gifted men, but not at home with first principles. How, how, how—he will probe into that forever; he can't see that for Plato the use of how is to find the *why*. Why, Niko, is man? And why does man ask why? When we know that, we have all truth in our fingers. Without, a lifetime of *how* leads where? Maybe to designing a catapult like old Dionysios', which can lob a stone two stades from the walls, and kill a man—a mystery of God which we can bring ourselves to destroy because we have never defined it . . . But why run on? What can I do for you, Niko?"

I told him I had heard he was sailing with Plato, and had just come to say goodbye. "You have no notion," he said, tilting his head back against the wall with a sigh, "what has gone on since last we talked—and before that, for I kept things back; you were defining my own thoughts to me faster than I could bear . . . Oh, yes, of course you're wondering how Plato was induced to go. The only wonder is that he held out

so long. He's had barely a day of peace—do you know, Dionysios has written, over the last few months, to every friend of
consequence he has in Athens, urging them to push him on,
saying, as a rule, that when in Syracuse he proposed reforms
which can only be carried out under his direction. He should
know what that's worth; but you can suppose how he's felt,
with half Athens saying he has power to reform the tyranny,
but prefers his ease at home, or is afraid to test his theories.
Besides all that, Dionysios has been pressing the Tarentines,
and has written to Archytas hinting that the treaty may be
denounced if he doesn't get Plato there. Archytas is trusted
like the father of the city; how can he risk the people's safety
for one friend's, when it must seem to him the friend might
even do good by going? Of course the Archon's Kyrenian
guests have written too, praising their host's progress in philosophy, and his devotion to Plato's doctrines—which means
without doubt that he's been expounding half-baked versions
which Plato would die to hear." He paused for breath, while
his servant set up the wine table.

"Poor Plato," I said. "Like a poet when some barnstormer
butchers his best lines."

When the man had gone, he said, "All Dion's friends have
written, too. And there are more of them than all the rest put
together."

I said nothing. He broke off a sprig of basil, and turned it in
his hand, peering into the little flowers.

"Dion is my guest-friend of long standing. In any case one
owes him justice. He has a son growing up in the Archon's
house. There is his wife . . ." He was some time silent before
saying, "There is another threat Dion does not know of. Plato
promised not to tell; those were the only terms on which he
could hope to avert it." Next moment he was distressed at having said even so much, and made me promise to be secret.

I asked when they were sailing. With good weather, he
said, in two days' time. "God knows, Niko, when we shall get
home, if ever. Before my wife I laugh at it; poor girl, she's
pregnant, and hardly more than a child herself. I feel cruel

to go, but it would be worse forsaking Plato. I wonder how long before you and I sit here again." He looked round the garden, his eye dwelling here and there. "Will you be playing in Syracuse? It would be good to see you."

When the ship sailed, I went to see it off, since half Athens was doing the same. It was like a scene in the theater.

Plato and Dion behaved perfectly; no doubt their goodbyes were already said. They exchanged a ceremonial kiss, like two kings in tragedy. I saw Axiothea and her friend shedding open tears, and the eyes of the Academy men were not much drier. They might have been watching Sokrates drink the hemlock. But Dion kept his countenance. His noble bearing so much impressed the audience, I kept expecting applause.

Months passed. It drew near autumn, and no news of Plato's return. I saw Axiothea seldom, both of us having a good deal to fill our time. Thettalos had been doing short tours, coming home between, and it was natural when I had the right offers for me to do the same. These were brief, happy fasts, on which I worked well.

When sailing weather was clearly ending, I went out of my way to ask Axiothea where Plato was. In Syracuse, she said; Dionysios had persuaded him to winter there, and complete the settlement of Dion's property.

"Again?" I said. "No, that's too much!" Little Lasthenia, sharp as a brown bird, added, "I hope he'll get proper thanks for it."

Axiothea looked at us sadly. She had always worshipped Dion; but if she felt a loss, she still had the Cause. It looked simpler to her than to me; she had never been in Sicily.

Winter passed; spring came. At the Dionysia, Philemon, a most distinguished artist, bargained with Miron to release Thettalos for the contest. Their play was *Herakles in Lydia;* Thettalos did Omphale and Iolaos, changing masks with great virtuosity, and most striking in the former role. I could see the pleasure he got from working under an up-to-date pro-tagonist, though old Miron's discipline had done him good. I myself was doing *Theseus in the Underworld,* and would gladly have had him for Pirithoos and Persephone; but one can't have a bird without a broken eggshell. It was one of Theodoros' prize years; we came back from his party tired and happy, not reminding ourselves that roads and seas were opening, and we would soon be parting again.

Presently, after our seeing a good deal of each other in early summer, Miron got an offer to go to Macedon, and then on north to Byzantion. Knowing from the past that I should find it harder when alone to make any plans, I shook myself like a dog and began to stir about.

Only four days later, when they had barely begun rehearsing, Thettalos came home at noon. He had resigned from Miron's company.

"Not another day. I knew I couldn't last out rehearsals, so I played fair by the old monster and gave him time to replace me. Oh, no, Niko, I have to come up for air. O Agamemnon lord of men, boom, boom, ototoi, ototoi, right hand up, left hand out. I feel like some image shut up in a temple strong-room, with the dust settling thicker every day."

"By the dog!" I cried. "I could clip you over the head. You stupid boy, why didn't you tell me you didn't mean to go north? Now I have signed up to go to Sicily."

"Sicily?" He looked up with his mouth full; he was devouring barley cake and raisins and cheese like a schoolboy back from the wrestling class.

"Yes—signed, sealed and witnessed. I shall be two months away, or more."

"Have you got a second?"

"What time have I had? If you had only—"

"Dearest of men! I always longed to see Syracuse."

I started, then subdued my heart, as one covers a cage to stop a bird from singing. "Don't tempt me, my dear. You know as well as I do that you'll never rest, now, till you're creating your own play. It can't be long—two years, or three; meantime you're too sensible not to take direction, but will resent whoever you have to take it from. Don't let me be the one."

"Truly, Niko, I swear, it will be Elysium to work for you. I've been living like someone flat on a frieze. I shall talk my mind out, seeing it's you; that I can't help; but I'll never cross you. All Miron taught me was to know how good you are."

"It would never do," I said, trying to sound resolute.

"Fate intends it. Look how I left him, the very day."

"You've picked up his superstition, if nothing else."

He came and sank down beside my chair. He had filled out his boyish hollows; his stride, like a young lion's, had both weight and grace. He was born to play heroes, though not in Miron's style. He flung his arm across my knees, and went into Patroklos' speech from *The Myrmidons,* putting in all the grace notes. *False to the sacred honor of our bed, O most unthankful for those many kisses* . . . Please, Niko, take me to Sicily!"

"Well," I said, "now, if you grumble, you've put yourself in the wrong beforehand. I was holding out for that."

He called me a monster and embraced me. Within the month we sailed.

Since it would be easy to find third and extra men in Sicily, we sailed alone. Good weather, and showing him the sights, made it a pleasure trip. At Tarentum, I did not omit paying Archytas my respects, in case he had letters for Plato. He thanked me, and said he had just sent a messenger. Though courteous, he was not talkative, and seemed to me an unhappy man. He had sent a leading Pythagorean in Dionysios' trireme, to help persuade Plato; if he had had a hard choice between his people and his friend, and was concerned for the outcome, he had my sympathy, but there was no reason why he should confide in me. He told me Plato and Speusippos were both reported in good health, and in favor with Dionysios. He forgot to ask how Dion was.

The Syracusan consul had of course announced our arrival; but I was amazed to find, when we made port, how many people turned out. Thettalos exclaimed that I must have made the hit of a generation last time I came. But I soon learned the secret. When I had pushed his silver talent back at Philistos, I had supposed it would go straight into his treasury. As I now found out, he had done precisely as I asked. He had commissioned a life-sized bronze of the god, with a gold vine-crown, riding a gilded leopard. Of course, his own name was on the plinth as well as mine; he had the right, as choregos. I don't know if he did it for that, or because with all his vices he was too pious to rob a god. At all events, there it stood, in the sanctuary by the theater; the citizens now supposed I was the richest actor in Greece.

Our informant was Menekrates, who met the ship, sumptuously dressed and looking just what he was, a successful actor-manager who played all the big Sicilian cities, visiting Italy once a year. Last time he stayed with me in Athens, I had seen he was doing well; he must have been rising ever since. He carried us off, not to the lodging in the lower town, but to a great new house above the theater, with a fountain court paved in black and white mosaics, and a carved marble balcony facing the sea. Two pretty gold-skinned children came running out to meet him, from which I guessed, before I saw her, that he had married one of those blond wives so much prized in Sicily.

I had never been there so late in summer; the streets were griddle-hot and dusty, the hills parched brown; but his court-yard, piped from a spring above, was fresh and green, and his thick walls were cool. We supped lying on cushions of Persian stuff, with two men and a boy to wait. Nothing was too good for us. It was his way of saying I had turned his luck, that day at Leontini.

We talked theater at first. A big drama festival was coming on the feast of Arethusa, the local river-goddess. I had been met on the dock with a message from the tragic poet Chairemon, on a visit here from Athens, asking me to see him before I made any plans. In Sicily it's catch-as-catch-can for artists; no draw like ours at home.

It was not till the slaves had cleared and left us with the wine that I mentioned Plato. I had noticed our host had grown more careful in his talk. He had more to lose.

"Plato?" he said. "I've enough to keep me busy without running after sophists, especially when they're as meddlesome as that old man. If we get through to the festival without a riot here, and looting in the streets, we can thank the gods rather than him. I'm thinking of sending Glyke and the children into the country."

Startled by all this, I said it was inconceivable that a man like Plato would be conspiring against his host. "No doubt," he answered. "But with the advice he gives, he'll hardly need to. What the Archon's just done—and everyone blames Plato for it—is to put his veterans on half-pay. Don't go near Ortygia. I tell you, there'll be trouble."

I could believe him. Old Dionysios had had an excellent name with soldiers of fortune everywhere, if with no one else, because he rewarded long service. The country round was full of paid-off men settled on land he had given them, often enough at the citizens' expense. They made a useful reserve, and encouraged recruiting. Menekrates said, "He was one to skin a flayed ox, as the saying is. But everyone knew where the money went; on power. Every few years, when the Carthaginians came, we had the good of that whether he cared or not. But the young one, who's pretty near as greedy, spends on his pleasures. While he's idling, we get twenty extortioners where we had one before. Believe me, he can't afford to stint his garrison. Let's say no more; it's hearsay only, and least known's best. But Plato must know too much, or too little, to give such counsel."

"If he ever gave it. I'd lay a year's takings against. We heard all this last time, put about by Philistos. It was just a tale."

Thettalos, who had maintained a modest quiet but could not forbear supporting me, said all Athens knew that Plato had come out about his friend Dion's property, and to try for his recall.

"Recall?" said Menekrates, staring. "If Dion wants to come home, he'll have to recall himself, not wait to be invited. Then, who knows . . . But that's dangerous talk. We've traveled; we've seen in other cities what comes of *that*." He walked over to the doorway, to make sure the slaves had gone to bed. Coming back, he said, "As for the property, God reward all true friends, but in Plato's case I don't know who else will. Dion's land was all sold up this spring. There was some talk of putting it in trust for his son, young Hipparinos; but where's the odds? It would go the same way as if Dionysios spent it."

I remembered Dion's words at Tarentum. "How old is the boy?"

"I suppose about fourteen. He's a favorite with his uncle the Archon, who's fond of saying he won't grow up a spoilsport like his dad. He comes to all the parties. I was at one myself not long ago, after a *Madness of Herakles* that took well. Plato was there too. A handsome lad, they say, not unlike Dion when he was that age. But the Academy won't see *him;* his education's well in hand. The liveliest of the girls was sent over to his supper couch, but I couldn't see he had much to learn. His hand was down her dress all through the first course, and up it all through the second. Old Plato did try, at the start, to get a word with him, but the boy laughed in his face. Even his uncle had to remind him he was speaking to a guest, though he couldn't keep from smiling."

Thettalos gave me one of his looks when Menekrates' back was turned. He had speaking eyes; sometimes one could see it even through a mask.

"Where is Plato staying?" I asked. "His nephew is a friend of mine, and I'd like to see him."

"Plato himself has that house in the palace garden he had before; it's the Archon's chief guesthouse. But I don't think the nephew's staying there. Maybe he wasn't asked very heartily. I heard he was with religious folk, Pythagoreans. I'll inquire tomorrow. Thettalos, dear boy, your cup—you're drinking nothing. I'll show you our theater, while Niko's hunting sophists. The acoustics are first-class, but you need to know them."

Next morning I went to the house where Speusippos and Plato had stayed before. For fear of missing him, I was there before sunup; when the slave reported him still in bed, I said I would wait till he woke. This was not long; while I sat on the rim of the courtyard fountain, two smiths came in with a great new bolt for the outer door. They said, as they clattered, that they were sorry to rouse the master, but they were pushed with orders like this. One must blame the times.

The din soon woke Speusippos, who looked out to see what it was. A pretty tousled girl, clutching her dress, appeared behind him; he had not counted on early rising today. Having urged her to go home quickly and not loiter in the streets, he turned and saw me. "Niko!" he said, and laughed shortly as he caught my eye. "I heard you were in Syracuse. Have you been waiting long?"

I said I was sorry his night had been cut short so rudely. "No," he said, "it's as well I woke. I must see Plato in Ortygia; it's better to go early, while the streets are quiet. They seem to be expecting trouble. Come in while I finish dressing."

His host greeted us going in, a silver-haired old man shrunk with age, but upright and with a skin like a baby's. In Speusippos' room, with the tumbled bed still warm with the scent of the girl, he said, "I don't think he saw her leave. Not that I've ever deceived him; he knows I follow the philosophy rather than the regimen, which, let us admit, has picked up much superstition since the founder's time. He'd say, I suppose, that I've set myself back two or three rebirths with last night's work. 'The body is the tomb of the soul.' Well, I was on edge, which my soul was taking no good from; besides which, I've learned from her more than she ever set out to teach, as I'll tell you sometime. I must go; will you walk along with me?"

As we headed for Ortygia, I remembered Menekrates warning me not to go near the place. But I was ashamed to be less bold than a philosopher, not to speak of forsaking a friend. So far, only one thing was to be noticed about the streets—that they were empty.

I asked how Plato was, and if his mission had prospered. He made the gesture of a man so weary of his troubles that he can hardly bear to talk of them. "Plato's as well," he said, "as he's likely to be after wasting a year for nothing, or worse than that. I suppose you've heard. All Dion's property has been sold up, a hundred talents' worth or more; and Dionysios has ceased even to pretend that he'll get a drachma."

I exclaimed suitably. There seemed nothing to say.

"You think Plato should have foreseen it. Of course he did. But with all these protestations, appeals and guarantees, he couldn't be certain. Short of that, he didn't think he should hold back."

"When my bad day comes, God send me such a friend."

"He's always been the same. At Sokrates' trial, neither his kin nor his friends could keep him from getting up to testify. When the court laughed him down because of his youth, which I daresay saved his life, he fell so sick with grief, they doubted he'd outlive Sokrates. May he keep his luck. I tell you, I begin to wonder."

"What? But the Archon . . ."

"Every day it's worse. How not, unless the man had really changed? Plato came here for Dion's sake. That was the bait. Merely by taking it, he had Dionysios jealous even before he'd sailed. Every word he's spoken for Dion has been oil on fire. Every friend of Dion's he takes notice of is a mark against him. It can't stretch much more without breaking. Each time I come here, I'm cold with fear of what I'll find."

I don't know what he thought his own life would be worth with Plato gone. He did not speak of it, but strode on, a thin quick harassed man, towards Ortygia. I could hardly keep up.

We got over the causeway and through the gates without any trouble. The reason was simple. No guards were there. They had shut the big gates, but left the posterns open.

At the last of them, Speusippos said, as if we had been strolling from the Agora to the Academy, "Well, Niko, thanks for your company on the way."

"Oh, no," I said. "What do you take me for? Come on."

He was in too much haste to argue, and, with the hill, soon out of breath. Nikeratos, I thought, you are too big a fool to live, and so you may find. At the same time, I am inquisitive; there is no sense in putting up with the hardships of travel unless one looks about.

We had got to the barrack quarter, the street, I think, of the Gauls. It was empty, no men off duty standing about, or dicing on doorsteps. The doors hung open. Soldiers have to be very

overwrought to stop guarding their things from other soldiers.
I was pointing this out to Speusippos, when we heard the yelling.

Someone up ahead had started a kind of paean. Never having
heard any of these barbarians in action, I don't know whose it
was; in any case, all the rest took up their own, in a cacophony
I can't describe. Now and then some howl more piercing than
the rest would catch the general ear, and they would come in
on that with a wordless bellow all together.

I felt a weakness in my knees, like stagefright but worse.
"They're under the walls," I said. "You can hear. The gates must
be shut. No use going further."

There was a soldier coming down the street. I was all for getting out of the way; so I think was Speusippos; then suddenly
he started forward, exclaiming, "Herakleides!"

He was an officer, Sicilian Greek, dark and good-looking,
with the dress and speech of a gentleman and an easy, pleasant
way. He had been so wrapped up in his own concerns as he
came that he had not seen us till he was almost on us; but he
did not look scared or ashamed like a man running away and,
as soon as he saw Speusippos, gave him an open steady look.
Then he said, "I'm off duty."

"In the name of the gods," said Speusippos. "Listen."

He lifted his brows. "What do you mean? I hear nothing."

Speusippos drew breath to speak, then waited. Herakleides
shrugged his shoulders. "Some of my best men are there. Men
who got me off the field with a spearhead in me, when they
might have left me to be cut and trimmed by the Carthaginians. I can't stop them; I can only give them an order they won't
listen to, which won't help discipline tomorrow, and take their
names. No names, no floggings. In their place, I'd be there too."
He went off downhill. I remember thinking what a simple,
decent fellow he was, and how his men must love him.

Up above, the yelling got louder. Across the top of the
street, a troop of Nubians went by towards the palace. They
were stamping as they went, and chanting in time with it; now
and then they would give a whoop, and leap, tossing up their
spears. I pulled Speusippos into a doorway. "Come home," I

said. "What can you do? Those walls there are ten feet thick; they'll never get in."

"Not," he answered, "if the men inside want to keep them out."

"It's with the gods," I said, for want of any other comfort. "Let's be gone from here."

He took a few steps with me, then stopped. "No. I'll wait. If they can get in, then so can I." No doubt my face was an open book. He pressed my shoulder. "My dear Niko, go back, you've come more than far enough. You've no call to stay; I have . . . He would have died with Sokrates, and I've had more of my life than he'd had then. If it's his turn now, I can't leave him to die alone."

One part of me applauded this; the rest was angry with him for catching me up in his choice. I said, "No, I'll come with you to the walls, to see what is going on. If you want to get yourself killed inside, that's another thing." And I turned up the street beside him.

Soon we got to the wide ring-road that circled the palace wall. We could hear the noise further along. As we walked that way, a squad of Romans ran past us shouting to each other. Presently we came to the great main gates, twenty feet high. There was a square before them; below, the Sacred Way cut down towards the causeway, lined with trees, statues and shrines. Filling the square were the soldiers. They had kept together more or less, Iberians with Iberians and so on; beyond this, they were a mob, and the most dangerous sort on earth, being both armed and used to violence. The one comfort was that, since the day was early, they were not drunk.

Now we were near, we could hear that they were shouting in their different uncouth accents, "Dionysios!" When no one came, they threw up stones at the gatehouse. The Nubians were the best shots. There was a sculptured frieze above; they were aiming at the gods' heads, and had knocked half off already. To my surprise, the Gauls were absent.

There were cheers; all heads turned towards the Sacred Way. Here were the Gauls. Stripped naked for battle, with blue war paint flourished all over them, they were hauling up the slope a huge beam, I should think a keel from one of the naval yards. The crowd rushed to help; the beam came up the square as if on wings. They lined up each side, while some expert started a heaving chant. The gate was oak and iron, but I did not see it holding long.

They rammed it two or three times; the tongues of the hinges began to start. Speusippos watched in silence, no doubt composing himself with philosophy. The Gauls plodded back for another run-in.

A trumpet sounded above the gate. The yells died to muttering. The Gauls laid the ram down for a rest. A Greek voice called, "Dionysios!"

An old man in armor appeared on the gate tower. There was almost silence. It was Philistos.

He looked older than I remembered. His florid face had mottled, his eyes had sunk, his nose was sharper and bluer. At sight of him they growled, but listened. He might not be a loved commander; but he was there, standing in javelin-range. He had earned a hearing.

The upshot of his speech was that there had been a great misunderstanding. Ill-disposed persons had falsified the Archon's orders. He had been shocked to learn of their grievance. Not only were veterans' wages being maintained; they would be raised, from today.

There were cheers, of course, triumphant, but ironic. One could hear it in the voice of every race, though the note was different. Even with the Nubians, one could tell.

Philistos gazed down at them. He was a man I detested; but there was not much pleasure in watching an old general shoved out to give his troops this craven lie. He did it, I must own, with what dignity it allowed.

He limped stiffly down to the stair rail. The Greek who had called before shouted again for Dionysios; this time it was an open jeer. But no one came.

The mob broke up, and went off in groups shouting and singing towards the wineshops, leaving the ram in the street. The Gauls shouldered past us either side, but noticed us no more than dogs. The morning was getting warm, and the sweat ran down their war paint. It did not blur; it must have been a kind of tattooing. They smelled like horses.

Speusippos and I were left in the empty square, by the ram with its frayed hammered nose. He did not have to die with Plato, nor I with him. I expected him to be looking as relieved as I. But he was standing with his mouth set in a hard, shrewd look that was new to me, gazing after the soldiers. He said, "Dion should know of this."

Nothing surprised me much by now. I said, "Do you mean what I think?"

"I daresay," he answered. Then: "I was talking to that girl last night. She was twelve years old when some scout of Philistos' saw her and hauled her off from home to amuse Dionysios. Her father objected; he went to the quarries and was never seen again. Dionysios hadn't even decency enough to have her sent home after. She was put out like a stray cat, picked up by some Iberians, and passed around the barracks. Her own story's nothing to some she told me; but sharing a bed seems to bring it home. He can do anything he likes, to anyone, that one man alone. It's hard for the mind to grasp it."

He was right; when one is not bred to it, one doesn't conceive it, it must be smelled and tasted. Like me, he was too young to remember it at home. For that matter, even the Thirty had at least to agree together. "One man," he said again.

"If you call him that. I doubt the troops do, now."

"What was it old Dionysios said on his deathbed, Niko? 'A city in chains of adamant.' The chains are rotting. Dion should know."

# XVI

THE SOLDIERS REJOICED ALL NIGHT, AT THE EX-
pense of anyone they found at hand; then they went back on
duty, and the city breathed again. I was scolded by Menekrates
for going to Ortygia, and by Thettalos for not having taken
him with me. At the mention of Herakleides, our host looked
so nervous that, remembering his past hints, I added two and
two. Though it was hard to think of so frank a soldier conspiring, yet it was certain that the mutiny had tested the troops'
loyalty, and the Archon's strength. I wondered if Speusippos
guessed.

Two days later, all being still calm, I went to call on Chairemon the tragic poet, taking with me Thettalos, whose work he
would certainly know. After asking around (just like a poet, he
had forgotten to say where he was staying) we learned he was
in Ortygia, as a palace guest.

"Good," said Thettalos as we went. "This time you can't leave
me to bite my nails all morning, wondering if you're lying dead
in a gutter. Lead me to the tyrant's lair."

It was with no great delight that I approached Ortygia. If the gates were to be closed again, I had no fancy to be inside. However, I showed our passes for outer Ortygia (these were easily got from the Athenian embassy) and had them endorsed for the palace citadel by the captain of the guard.

I had expected slackness at the guardhouses, after yesterday, but not what met us everywhere—restlessness, rumor, suspicion. At the Iberian gate two men were quarreling. As the first blows were struck, an officer came up cursing; there was a dangerous moment before they obeyed. We went on, not envying him his employment, nor indeed much liking our own. "Never mind," said Thettalos. "It's all in the business. One must study how men behave. Something can happen anywhere— pirates in the islands, satrap wars in Ionia, and in Macedon they're forever assassinating the king."

Our one strict check was the last, into the palace citadel. In the park, we found the groves full of men running about, light-armed Cretans going like beaters through the coverts, calling to one another. Some of them stopped us, but passed us through without saying whom they wanted.

In due course we found our way to the second-class guest-house where Chairemon had a room. All the other inmates— poets, envoys, minor philosophers and so on—were huddled in the courtyard muttering. When Chairemon recognized us they all ran up asking for news. "Of what?" I asked. "If you mean the mutiny, it seems to be over." Someone said, "Then they've not caught him yet?" When I asked whom he meant, he said, "Herakleides."

"I don't think so. The place is full of men searching. Why, what has he done?"

Of a sudden, everyone became careful; Chairemon said one could not be sure, one merely heard he was being searched for; if we would come to his room, he had a play he would like to talk about.

When the door was shut, he wrung our hands and thanked the gods for the sound of Attic speech. I thought he would burst into tears. "Never again! I came with Karkinos; he's been before, and persuaded me to accept—the works of art, banquets, music and so on. Never, never again! Not that I'm concerned in this, not at all." He looked round at the door. "It's knowing that anything can happen—really, anything. It's the thought, just the thought of it."

I answered, "Pythagoras said, 'Accept in your mind that anything which can happen can happen to you.'" I had heard this aphorism at the Academy. He looked at me in appeal, as if I could make it otherwise. I saw Thettalos laughing to himself.

It seemed Herakleides had been accused of causing the mutiny, and had gone missing. His friends, including Plato, had been pleading for him, because he had belonged to Dion's party; and had got a safe-conduct for him from the Archon, to prepare his affairs for exile. Then today, on news that he had been seen, troops had been sent out to catch him. It was now supposed that the safe-conduct had been a trick, to delay his getting away.

"Maybe," I said. "Or Dionysios just changed his mind."

"But, surely, Nikeratos, his honor . . ."

"There's only one judge of honor, in Syracuse."

Chairemon blinked. I said, "Never mind, there's still the theater. If Troy hadn't fallen, where would we be today?" His eyes reproached my frivolity, but he consented to talk business.

He had a choregos for his new play, *Achilles Slays Thersites,* and wanted us to do it for the festival. Although he *would* read it aloud (why do so few poets read well?) it was a good piece of work. It started with the Amazon Penthesilea arriving as a Trojan ally. She challenges the Greeks; Achilles, still mourning for Patroklos, is brought the tale of her victories. Now he has resumed his place as champion of the Greeks, it is for him to meet her. They hail each other, she on the walls and he below, to exchange defiance. Love at first sight. But they are equal in pride and standing; each values honor more than life; they must fight to the death. Achilles wins. He enters from battle walking by the bier on which they bring her breathing her last. There is a lovely speech in which he praises her valor to cheer her parting soul. She's gone. He kneels and weeps for her, bowed upon the bier. Thersites the mocker, who has been longing to hear that the great Achilles has fallen at last by a woman's hand, now has his say. What a mourner! he cries. You've only just done grieving for Patroklos; now it's this Amazon, and both of them died through you. Achilles gets up; Thersites takes fright and runs; off stage sounds his deathcry as Achilles fells him with a blow. After a lively scene with Diomedes, who has to demand satisfaction for the blood because Thersites was his kinsman, Artemis appears to stop the fight and reconcile the heroes. Big choral procession, Penthesilea given to her Amazons for burial, to end the play. It is now well known in Athens, but this was its first performance.

Achilles is for the protagonist, but there is a great deal of fat for the second too. Penthesilea dying is a dummy; he can play both her and Thersites. Chairemon had had the script copied so that we could take it home; we walked off so full of it that we hardly noticed the Cretans still rummaging the boskage. Reading as we went, we missed our way, and found ourselves in a new part of the park, among houses which looked dangerously important. I pushed the script into my robe, saying, "We must go back the way we came."

"By all means," said Thettalos, "if you know which it is."

There were three paths behind us, all much alike. Beyond a grove of pink oleanders one could glimpse the palace roofs. "We had better look through," I said. "If I see which side we are on, I can steer by that."

We pushed into the bushes. As I saw light, I also heard people talking, and stopped dead, gripping Thettalos' arm. One of the voices was Dionysios'.

Thettalos, who read my eyes, stood soundless. It was not a time to be found where one had no business, creeping up on the Archon. I recalled Pythagoras' saying, which I had quoted to Chairemon so lightly.

Thettalos had paled a little, but was already edging softly towards a gap in the leaves. One must study, as he said to me later, how men behave.

At first I could only hear Dionysios' voice, eloquent with self-pity. Now and again one of the men with him, some two or three, would say, "Yes, indeed," or "Everyone can witness that," or "How true!" They were coming towards us; as their words got clearer, fear that they might discover us made me deaf. They paused, however, as they naturally would on coming to a thicket, and I allowed myself to breathe. Dionysios was saying, "But no, a friend of Dion's can't do wrong for him. Anyone, a traitor who eats my salt and corrupts my soldiers, anyone before me." He almost sobbed. He was half-drunk, but quite sincere.

Someone said, "Birds of a feather, sir. You have been too generous to his insolence. The truth is—forgive me for my plain speaking—you don't value yourself enough. It feeds his pride."

"When I think—" Dionysios was beginning; then he broke off. They were now walking away; I crept along to share Thettalos' peephole. There was the Archon with his friends; and crossing the lawn to them came three men, the oldest leading. Thettalos, who was watching entranced, mouthed a name at me with questioning brows. I nodded.

The two younger men stood silent, in attitudes of formal grief. Plato came forward. His shoulders and heavy head were stooping more than I remembered; his beard, which had had some gray in it, was nearly all white, though there was black still in his brows. His eyepits had deepened; from their caves gazed his eyes, piercingly gray. I could almost see Dionysios' gaze shifting, through the back of his head. However, encouraged no doubt by his admirers, he decided to put a face on it. "Yes, Plato?" he said. "What is it?"

"I am here," said Plato, "at the instance of these friends of mine. They are afraid you may be taking some new action against Herakleides, in spite of the promise you made me yesterday. I believe he has been seen hereabouts."

Dionysios' back jerked upright, giving at the same time a kind of wriggle. "Promise?" he said, sounding indignant. He had tried, also, to sound surprised.

At this one of the other two rushed forward, flung himself on his knees before the Archon, and clasped his hand. He made some plea, broken by weeping. Dionysios allowed his hand to be cried on, drawing himself up and looking powerful. Perhaps for once he felt like his father. Plato stood watching this scene with distaste. After a while he stepped forward, and put his hand on the man's bowed shoulder. "Courage, Theodotes," he said. "Dionysios would never dare break our agreement in such a way."

Dionysios' pose collapsed. His hand having been let go before he could snatch it back, he folded his arms furiously. "With you," he said, "I agreed to nothing. Nothing at all."

As I said, Plato had aged. His stoop had settled into his bones; he would never draw himself straight again. Nonetheless, at these words he grew alarming. Once, I remember, in some old country theater, I came to the skeneroom with a torch at night, and found myself face to face with a great old eagle-owl, hunched in his dark corner, his round eyes glaring into mine. I almost dropped the torch and burned down the building.

"By the gods, you did!" He thrust forward his beak; I could almost see the lifted feathers. The sycophants clucked; the friends looked panic-stricken. In case Dionysios had not taken his meaning the first time, he added, "You promised just what this man is begging for." He turned his back on the Archon, and walked off.

There was a silence; then Dionysios told Herakleides' friends to get out of his sight. Next moment he was gone himself, I suppose to urge on the soldiers. The lawn was full of powerful emptiness, like a theater after a play.

We scouted our way back to the public path before either of us spoke. Then Thettalos said, "He called him a liar, in front of all those people."

I said, "And two of them Dion's friends."

"Will he kill him?"

"I don't know." I could feel myself trembling a little. "His father would have done it. I don't suppose he knows himself what he means to do. It's with the gods."

"A terrible old man! Niko, can't we try to get him away? It's like leaving Prometheus to be gnawed by rats. At least he deserves a vulture."

"My dear, he has a dozen devoted friends in the city. The best thing for us is to find Speusippos and warn him. He may need it."

Menekrates, when he heard our news, decided at once to send his wife and children out of town, to her father's place. She could take some valuables with her, in case rioting broke out. The house was in a turmoil of packing.

We called twice at the house where Speusippos was staying, but he was out, they could not say where. The rest of the day we spent going over Chairemon's script; but next morning, resolved that Speusippos should be found without more delay, we called again. The porter, who knew me well, said he and the master were both at the house of Archidemos, the philosopher, where Plato was a guest. We stared. He went on carefully, "I understand, sir, the Archon needed the guesthouse. So he asked him to stay with friends."

We looked at each other with relief. "So Plato is well," I said, "and staying with friends of his own?" He answered yes. "And your master and Speusippos are both there too?"

"That I can't say, sir. But that was where they were going."

No doubt he was keeping things back, but we felt satisfied and walked off in relief, remarking that Plato must be even more glad to go than Dionysios to see the back of him. As Thettalos said, it was the end of a famous friendship, but at least he could go home. I thought of Dion, and how he would take the news.

Our minds now at rest about Plato, we settled down to find a cast and begin rehearsals. There was no chorus, only musical interludes, which would be looked after by a music-master. Chairemon was a very modern author. The third actor I had in mind was free, and brought me a friend to audition for the fourth, who had a few lines; I took him on. The extras were easy. Chairemon had found a reasonable choregos; he was said to be mean by Sicilian standards, and therefore pleased to have Athenian actors, who don't demand bullion trimmings over everything and real gold crowns. I am a little too vain to hide in a heap of ornaments, so we suited well.

We had been rehearsing two or three days when on the way home I said to Thettalos, "My dear, I said nothing before the others, but whatever are you doing with Thersites?"

He met my eye in a way I knew, which meant he was going

to try and talk me round. "Don't you think it would be new, and in the spirit of the times, to play him for sympathy?"

"What times? The play is about the Trojan War."

"Well, but it's true Achilles did kill Patroklos, or cause his death. In Homer, the first thing you hear of Thersites is that he stood up to Agamemnon when he was in the wrong. Who else did?"

"Achilles. Diomedes. Chryses. Odysseus."

"Well, Thersites spoke for the common people."

"No, my dear, just for the mean ones. He is the voice of envy, which hates great good worse than great evil. In this Chairemon has followed Homer. Penthesilea is the part to play for sympathy; Thersites offers you contrast."

"It's in the modern spirit," he said. "It's antioligarchical. Let us show the common man rebelling; they can do with that in Syracuse."

"God help the Syracusans if they recognize themselves in Thersites. They have forgotten greatness; all the more reason to remind them of it. Achilles' anger lasted a few days of his life, but scarcely a dramatist has stepped outside them. It is quite bold of Chairemon to show him at his best; why be afraid of it?"

"O Zeus!" he said. "I believe you think I want to steal the scene. Do you think that?"

"No, indeed. I know you. You want to create what your mind has seen. I could do an Achilles to that Thersites—full of nothing but his own importance, indulging his own grief because it's his, and killing Thersites just for showing him up. It's not in the lines, but one could put it there. Who knows? The audience might eat it."

"Well, then, why not?"

"I suppose because men could be more than they are. Why show them only how to be less?"

"One should show them true to life."

"How not? But whose? Truth is to reckon on Achilles as well as Thersites, and Plato as well as Dionysios. There is truth even in Patroklos, who couldn't pass by a wounded man, and whom the slave-girls wept for because he never spoke them

] 263 [

an unkind word. The world is not Thersites', unless we give it him."

"Dear Niko, I didn't mean to put you out. Don't think of it again. You are directing, and I promised to be good. I just thought it would freshen the theme a little."

As we walked on, I wondered how much of what I'd said I had picked up from the men of the Academy, even while rejecting their views.

Menekrates' house had settled down into a place for men. His wife had never worked, so the steward ran it as well as ever. After a few days, one of the servant-girls looked sleek, and had a new necklace; and Menekrates sang in the bath. His wife, a well-born girl, was inclined to bully him.

We were working hard on the play, but there was something just amiss with it. Thettalos was doing Thersites just as I said; but it was overdone, the character had lost all humanity. I could see he was not doing it on purpose; he was above such pettiness; it was only that the life had gone out of the part for him. I must simply leave him to settle down.

There was a rota for rehearsals in the theater; the rest of the time we hired a room in the usual way. Some days went by before our theater turn. We were still working without masks, so I could see with the tail of my eye; as I did my last exit, someone in front jumped up and made for the parodos. I waited. It was Speusippos.

"My dear friend," I said, "what is it?" He looked unshaven, even unwashed; his robe was dragged about him, and soiled along the border, as if he had trailed it in the dust.

"Niko. Can I speak to you alone?"

"Of course. Not in the dressing room, everyone comes in there. Let us try the shrine of Dionysos." I thought how gladly I had assumed that all was well with him, so that my work should not be disturbed. At least, if he could sit in the theater, he could not be on the run.

The sanctuary was empty, but for an old slave sweeping down. We sat on the plinth of a votive statue; it was my gilt panther bearing the god, bought from Philistos' fee.

"I was here all yesterday," he said, wiping his brow. "Then

I found a man with a list, who told me when you would be coming . . . The guards won't let me into Ortygia any longer. I don't know what to do."

"Ortygia?" I stared in surprise. "I should have thought that would be the last place where you'd want to go. You're both well out of it."

"No. Plato is still there."

"But," I said, as shocked as bewildered, "they said when I called that he was staying with a friend."

"He is the guest of Archidemos, yes. But the house is in Ortygia."

I remembered the porter's reticence. Syracuse, as always, was full of spies.

"A few days ago," Speusippos started to explain, "Plato gave great offense to Dionysios—"

"Yes, yes, I know; never mind how. What happened next?"

"Next day, he sent a message that the ladies of the household needed the guesthouse for retreat and purification, before the Arethusa feast. An open lie, but at least a formal slight, better than a dagger in the dark. Or so we thought. Plato said it showed that the man had not surrendered all his soul to evil. The message said that a mutual friend, Archidemos, would gladly put him up till further notice; owing to the uncertain times, the Archon didn't wish him to leave Ortygia."

"Can this host be trusted?"

"Certainly, for anything he can control. He's kin both to Dion and Dionysios, a Pythagorean, who has never touched politics. He reveres Plato deeply. I've been visiting every day, till now. Oh, yes, Archidemos is safe, but he's been anxious all along. With this feeling among the soldiers, anything can happen. And now they won't let me in." He picked up the dusty border of his robe, and tugged it through his fingers.

"On whose authority?"

"I should think their own. Each day I've been insulted as soon as I was recognized; yesterday a Gaul took my pass to look at, and wouldn't give it back. They were all laughing. I think they hoped I'd lose my temper; I saw it just in time to hold back. I appealed to a Roman officer who was passing—

they're a little less barbarous than the Gauls—but he said that in his opinion I was being done a favor. I daren't think what he meant."

"Are the troops still mutinous, then?"

"No, their demands have all been met. But the long-service men, who led the riot, have revived that old lie about Plato wanting them discharged. They feel sure he advised the pay cut; I am told it's all over Ortygia."

"Philistos," I said. This followed the scene upon the gatehouse as night follows the day. "Well, as we saw, the soldiers can't get into the palace citadel as they choose."

"You fool!" In the impatience of his trouble, he looked as if he could have struck me. "Archidemos' house isn't in the palace citadel. It's in outer Ortygia, where all the soldiers are quartered. The barracks are less than a stade away."

I laid my hand on his knee and cursed Dionysios, neither likely to help much. "At least they can hardly attack the house of the Archon's kinsman."

"Unless there's another mutiny, when anything can be done. Or they can break in after dark, bribe a servant to poison him . . . Niko. Have you a pass for Ortygia?"

"Yes, so has Thettalos. But you can't use a borrowed one; they know you. You would just end in the quarries."

"Of course. It's a great deal to ask, from you especially. I know your feelings about Plato's theory of art; but as a man . . . I've no one else. Do you think you could go in, and see how things are with him?"

I thought, It means canceling a rehearsal, and then, I suppose it will be dangerous. "Certainly," I said. "I'll go tomorrow, one can't get in after dark." Then I said, "Well, I could try." It would save time; and then we could still rehearse.

When I got back, Thettalos was pacing about in his best clothes. "Wherever did you go? Have you forgotten the party at Xenophila's?"

"My dear, that well-named lady must do without me. A subsequent engagement. Give her my regrets."

He had the truth from me within moments, and asked how I had dared think of going alone. I did not withstand him.

Though, as I often told him, he had not sense enough to stay out of trouble, when in it he had great resource.

"Anything that happens," he said, "shall happen to us both. I suppose I must change my clothes . . . No, you must change yours. Why do people like us walk about at night? Of course, to parties."

I had a bath and a scented rubdown, and dressed myself to the teeth. Thettalos went out, coming back with a big straw-lined basket from which poked the necks of wine jars. "I don't think," he said, "we need be above buying popularity."

About sundown we reached the first gatehouse, and showed our pass to the Iberians, saying simply, "We are going to the party." Everyone at once knew which. They added that we should not find the drink run out.

"I told you so," said Thettalos to me. "But you *would* load us up like pack mules. These lads are right. Who'll help us lighten the weight?"

We got in this way through all five gatehouses. Luckily the Gauls were off duty; they can drink like camels, and we would never have finished up with a last jar in hand, which I rightly guessed that we would need.

By the time we were in Ortygia it was almost dark. A linkboy came touting us; we hesitated, then took him on. It would show us up, but looked more natural for party guests. I had been at pains to learn the way to Archidemos' house, to avoid asking, but the boy led us easily; it was his trade to know the streets. We skirted the barrack quarter without mishap; it had been wise to dress well, like the friends of someone important. He had just told us the house was round this corner, when he peered ahead, stopped and drew back. We did the same.

It was a good street; all one saw of the houses was high courtyard walls, broken with thick doors and a lodge or two. Outside one doorway, a little way down, was a knot of soldiers. They were loafing about, keeping rather quiet; a child could see (and this one had done so) that they were up to no good.

"This is serious," I said. "Not like the gatehouses."

The boy, pressed flat to the wall, said quickly that if the gentlemen did not mind the dirt, he could take us round to

] 267 [

the back. We girded our robes, and followed him through alleys just wide enough for a laden donkey, where hens darted squawking from before our feet. Presently he turned and said, "This way, sirs." This alley was cart-width, and fairly clean. Further on a little fire was burning, with five men sitting round it; slaves, I assumed, till we got a little nearer. Then we saw they were soldiers.

The torch wavered; I started to draw back; then Thettalos said softly, "Too late, don't stop." He strode on, pushing the boy impatiently aside, towards the fire. The back gate of a house, no doubt the one we sought, was just beside it. The soldiers stared; a Gaul, a Roman and three Greeks. Even sitting, one could see the Gaul was gigantic. His mustaches almost brushed his chest.

Thettalos said, "Can any of you gentlemen tell us the way to Diotimos' house? This son of fifty fathers swore he knew the street, and now he's lost us." One of the Greeks looked up. Thettalos said swiftly, "Diotimos son of Lykon, the Kyrenian."

"Never heard of *him*." They offered us others of the name, all of whom we rejected. I said it was clear we had been hoaxed; this was what came of wineshop friendships. I was about to add that we were strangers in those parts, when I saw the way they were eyeing our clothes and rings, and noticed that the boy, though still unpaid, had run away. So I told them, with a good deal of self-importance, who we were, adding that the mud had ruined my new robe, which I had meant to wear next day for my audience with the Archon.

They exchanged doubtful looks. My accent had shown I was from Athens. One of the Greeks, who must have been at some time in the theater, peered up. "If you're the actor, let's hear a speech."

"By all means," I said. "But first, since we've lost our party, would you care to help out with this?" I offered the basket with the last of the wine jars. "To Hades with Diotimos, I'd sooner drink with honest men."

This line was well received. It was a big amphora, and of course the wine was neat. No one complained of the lack of water. I thought the Gaul would never stop pouring it down.

When next they demanded a recital, it was merely for diversion. "I will give you," I said, "The Death of Ajax, if someone will lend me a sword."

There was a flash of metal; then the Gaul seemed to jump right at me. The other four grabbed him back; this I could not see well, because Thettalos had thrown himself in between. Bawling with laughter, the Greeks explained that the Gaul, not having followed the dialogue, had thought they were about to cut our throats, and meant to help. It was all over in moments. Thettalos looked like a man who has done the natural thing, and thinks no more about it.

The Gaul begged my pardon, but added that no other man should have his sword. I bore up under this news (the weapon was about three feet long) and took a Greek one. As I walked off to acting distance, it came to me that I had never handled a real sword before. With its greasy handgrip, old blood in the crevice of the tang, hacked blade and razor-bright edge, it was quite unlike a stage prop.

Needless to say, I gave them Polymachos' version of the death, known to all actors as the Barnstormer's Delight. Besides being just their mark, it has that passage where Ajax calls the gods to witness his wounds, and so on, endured in the cause of the Greeks, because of whose ingratitude he is going to run himself through. The soldiers all looked like veterans; the Roman was fairly seamed with war scars. It was, without doubt, the most shameful performance of my life—I dared not look at Thettalos—but I could not complain of the house. They twice stopped the speech with cheering. At the end, since there was nowhere to go off, I had to kill myself on stage; which, having been brought up in the decencies of the theater, I had no notion how to do. I contrived it by turning my back, fearing to the last that I would slice a finger off. As I lay in the dust, loudly acclaimed, I felt myself being lifted in enormous hands. The Gaul thought I had really done it.

I was now everyone's darling. Returning the sword with thanks, and plied with wine, I said they must be guarding some man of high rank, no doubt, to be posted here all night—a love visit, maybe?

This brought me more than I bargained for. It is a kind of wit I can do without. Athenians, used to the good-natured phallic humor we all enjoy at the Lenaia, have no notion how nasty such jokes can be when cruelty informs them. I kept thinking that these were just five men out of thousands in Syracuse alone, all much the same. They were some time accounting for Plato's attachment to Dion's cause, going on to add that it was a pity when they caught him he would have to be finished off quickly, before his rich friends got wind of it. They recounted, like men who sigh for the good old days, how he might have been dealt with in the old Archon's reign. There had been that Phyton, the general who had wasted everyone's time by holding out for months at the siege of Rhegium, till everyone inside was skin and bone, the women not worth having nor the men worth selling. Phyton had been hung all day from the top of a siege tower, where the news was shouted up to him that they had just drowned his son. This he took as good news, which spoiled the joke; but when he was taken down, they whipped him through the streets, where each man could suit his fancy. At this the Roman, who had not said much till now, remarked that he had been there, and had seen no sport in it; the man was a good soldier, and bore it, one could only say, as if he had been a Roman. He himself and his mates had decided to put a stop to it by rushing the punishment squad and getting Phyton away. But they had done too much shouting first, so the squad had settled the matter by throwing him in the sea to find his son. There was some argument about this; but the Roman remained obstinate.

The Gaul, who had been getting a speech ready for some time in what Greek he knew, now said he had once seen Plato with his own eyes. It seemed none of the rest had done palace duty. Pressed to tell more, he brooded awhile, and said, "He looked like an Arch-Druid." The Roman, interpreting, said Druids were a kind of holy warlock among the Gauls; they could call thunder, lightning, mist and wind, wither men away with a curse, and fly at will through the air. The Gaul confirmed all this, and began to look askance at the wall which hid such a person. One of the Greeks, however, pointed out that if Plato could fly through the air at will, by now he would be doing it.

"Sooner or later," another said, "he'll come out upon his feet. We're staying till the midnight watch; then five more of the lads are coming."

I looked at Thettalos, as if I had just made up my mind to something, as indeed I had. "Do you know," I said, "what I think?"

"No?" he answered, on cue.

"We've had a pleasant party. What harm have these lads ever done us, that we should go off without telling them the truth?"

"You're right," said Thettalos. "Just what I was thinking myself. You tell them, Niko."

They all leaned forward. "In my calling," I said, "one hears things. But if it ever gets known that I was the man you had it from . . ." I shuddered. They vowed discretion, slicing their hands across their throats. "Very well, then," I said, playing up the suspense, "I'll take the risk. I don't like to see brave men made cat's-paws of by those they've spilled their blood for."

I now had a breathless audience. All this last week, the army must have been seething with rumor. I went on, "I've had it from someone whose name, by the gods, I dare not tell you, that Plato's lodged where he is to tempt you men into doing just what you plan to do. I was even told, though I don't know the rights of it, that he never advised the pay cut; it was put about to set you on. From what I heard, they want him out of the way on account of Herakleides, but no one wants to answer for the deed. So, if it's done for them, to prove how clean their own hands are they'll make an example of the killers, beside which Phyton's end will look like a pleasure party. I don't know; I'm a stranger here. But when you men struck out for your rights the other day, you seemed to think the wrong man was put up then to be shot at. Well, that's all I heard. We've drunk together; so I give it you for what it's worth."

There followed a gabble of which I understood about one word in three. They discussed it in the idiom of Ortygia, the mixed argot of the foreign troops, thick with the terms of their trade. It seemed I had made sense to them. Indeed, when I thought about it, it made sense even to me. It would be just Dionysios' style.

I had spoken vaguely of Herakleides, not knowing if they favored him. It seemed they did; so I said it was known all over the inner citadel that Plato had quarreled with the Archon on his behalf. I did not say I had witnessed it, which would have made them sure I must be lying.

Presently the Greeks named some friends they thought should hear of this, and got up, followed by the Roman. The Gaul, however, had rolled into the shelter of the wall, with his cloak about him. When called, to my dismay he stayed where he was; he must have decided to watch alone. I could have cried with vexation, after all that work. Then the Roman went and pulled his arm. He turned on his back, and gave a great snore like a boar's grunting. He was dead drunk. The others shrugged, and went off.

We walked the other way till they had turned the corner. We could still hear them going off down the alleys. "And now," said Thettalos, "how are we going to get in?"

"I shall be surprised, with things as they are, if no one is watching this gate inside."

I tapped. There was no answer, but I could hear breathing. I announced my name, adding that we were friends of Speusippos, sent to bring him news of Plato. A stealthy voice was heard, asking me to repeat my name. I did so. It said, "Can you prove who you are, sir?"

"By the dog!" I answered. "Didn't you hear me outside just now? I made noise enough." Thettalos started laughing. I said with what restraint I could, "Fetch your master Archidemos, and I will recite him some Euripides if he insists. But hurry, in the name of Zeus. There may be more soldiers coming soon."

There was an iron-barred squint in the gate; a different eye appeared in it. The fire still gave some light. I heard the bolts being drawn. Archidemos was there beside his porter. He was an elderly man, tall, rather severe (perhaps just from hiding his fear), with the plain good dress of these rich Pythagoreans, and a family look of Dion. He apologized for our being kept outside; the gate was double-barred again. We declined refreshment, pleading our haste, and paused only for a slave to wash our feet, which were filthy, before going in to Plato.

He was sitting at a table, with a writing stand in front of him, working on the wax. I remember noticing he had just rubbed out about half a frame; but the fact that he was trying to work at all showed the man was a professional.

He knew me at once; so I wondered, while I was presenting Thettalos, why his face showed so much dread, till he asked after Speusippos. Then it came to me that when he had failed to pay his daily visit, they had all supposed him murdered. I said he was well, and warned Plato of the danger he was in himself.

He heard me without much change of countenance, his face just setting a little more into its lines. "Thank you," he said when I had done, "for confirming a warning I had yesterday. Some seamen came here, for no reason but that they were fellow Athenians, and, like sailors everywhere, democrats to whom an autarchy is odious. They had heard some tavern talk among the mercenaries, and advised me not to go out. But this guard, I believe, is new. It seems I have God to thank that Speusippos was turned away."

"Sir," I said, "we've rid you of the men out there, or so I hope, at least till midnight. I've been thinking that since actors move about more easily than most men, and with luck one can always appeal to the Delphic Edict, it might be worth your while to take the risk of coming with us now, before things get worse. I don't suppose any of the gatehouse guards would know you by sight." I added, with apology, "I'm afraid, sir, we are supposed to have been to a party, and we would all have to go back as if that were true."

Before the words were even out of my mouth I knew it was no use; but I had never thought he would be amused. I could see his courtesy holding it in. "My dear Nikeratos, you speak like a true friend and fellow citizen; also a brave man. I am not less grateful to you both than if I had taken your offer, and owed you my life; pray believe this. But as you see, I am an old man, set in my ways, and without the skill for which you are so widely honored. I don't think I could sustain the role of an old Pappasilenos, reeling home in a vine-wreath, before so shrewd an audience. I should be unmasked before long, and either end my life in a way not much to the credit of philosophy, or survive to delight the comic poets, and make my friends, both here and in Athens, ashamed to go out of doors. That would be a certain gain for tyranny; my death here, perhaps not."

He had been looking at me; now his glance was caught by Thettalos, who all this while had been sitting, perfectly still, on a cross-legged stool with a woolen cushion, himself forgotten, all ears and eyes.

As I've said, he had never been a pretty boy; nor was he now what people today call handsome. He had the northern face, with strong cheekbones; his nose and chin were too boldly carved to please a modern sculptor. Yet if I could tolerate the notion of any actor playing without a mask, it would be Thettalos. I suppose by now I was in danger of getting used to him. Now, seeing through another's eyes, I thought, That is beauty.

You could not say Plato's face softened; it was more like a lamp touched by the taper, as he turned that way. I felt power flow out, and that charm which, as Dion said, had made and undone his cause.

"Does my choice surprise you? No, I see that you have understood. I must have been about your age, or a little more, when an old friend of mine in Athens was accused of changing the gods' worship, and corrupting the minds of us young men. He was put on trial for his life, the best man, I may say, whom I ever knew. We—all his friends—were present, in the hope of doing something for him."

Thettalos listened with deep attention; I who knew him could see him taking part of the sense from the voice, and storing it away.

"I had hoped to be called in evidence for the defense, since my witness was relevant to the charge; or at least, if we could not get remission, to have the sentence commuted to a fine. But he would not appeal for this. When he saw it meant disowning the truth he lived by, he replied in words something like these: 'It would be strange, Athenians, if I who stood my ground in the line of battle, facing death at my commander's order, should desert the station where God posted me, from fear of death, or any fear. For what death is, we do not know; and no man can tell whether this which is feared as the greatest evil, may not really be the greatest good. But injustice, and disobedience to our betters, of whom God is best of all: these I know to be dishonor. So, if you say to me, *This time we will let you go, on one condition, that you do not ask such questions any more,* then I shall answer, *Men of Athens, I honor you and love you. But I shall obey God, rather than you.*'"

He must have seen me move, for he turned to me, saying, "You have heard these words?"

"Yes," I said, seeing Dion's face above the broken wine cup. "Yes, indeed."

He spoke some while with Thettalos, who told me after that he would remember it all his life. He was amazed my mind could have wandered; but it had concerns of its own. Soon I remembered that time was passing; whether with Plato or without him, we must be away. As I waited for a chance to say this, I recall Thettalos saying (for he had talked as well as listened), "And yet, sir, men's souls put me in mind of scattered seeds, which may fall in cracks of the earth, or at a stream's edge, or where a stone rolls over them, so that each has to find its own path to the light and rain. Can one seed know it for another?"

Plato cast a look of longing at him, not for his body, though he had found that pleasing, but because he had to let him go with their dialogue scarcely begun. "You are standing," he said, "at the very threshold of philosophy. What do we know, and what only guess? We know that without sun the shoot will not grow green, and without water it will die, just as we know that numbers cannot lie to us, but have the constancy of God. These things we can prove. Where proof ends, knowledge ends. Beyond, we must test each step, learning never to love opinion more than truth; never forgetting that men see as much truth as their souls are fit to see; always, till we pass through death and go forth to know ourselves, ready to go back to the start and look at all our premises, and begin again."

I said it was time to be on our way, and asked if there were not some service we could do him. "Indeed there is," he said. "You can tell Speusippos how I am placed, and ask him to send word to Archytas at Tarentum, or go himself if he can. Dionysios guaranteed my safety to Archytas, who can therefore ask formally for my release. If that is refused, Dionysios will have to answer for me to Archytas or anyone else whom it may concern—even to himself, a thing which in his case should never be overlooked. If you will do this, I and my friends will be much beholden to you."

The back-door guard was still absent. On the way to the gatehouses, we picked up some draggled wreaths shed by homebound revelers, and put them on. We were let through, in return for a good account of the party at each gate. When we were past the last and had turned the corner, Thettalos stopped, threw his wreath in the gutter, and dragged the back of his hand across his brows.

"Well," I said to him, "some of them wanted to rescue Phyton. I shall sleep better tonight for knowing that."

"Niko, take those filthy twigs off your head, you don't know what you look like." He removed my wreath, and stroked down my hair with his hand. "Well, you have won, you monster; I shall have to reconsider Thersites."

He was a great success. Whether the troops would have recognized themselves I am not sure, but the audience left them in no doubt. Chairemon, terribly put out, said it would have been as much as any judge's life was worth to give the play a prize; and we thought it better to leave the city before dawn next day.

While finishing our tour in other towns, we heard three pieces of news. The first was that Herakleides had kept ahead of Dionysios' search party and crossed the border into the Carthaginian province, to take ship for Italy; the second, that a state galley had come from Tarentum to ask for Plato, and that the Archon had let him sail. The third was that Dionysios had declared he could endure no longer to have his sister Arete joined in marriage to an exiled traitor who was his open enemy. Without her consent, in his authority as heirophant, he had pronounced her divorce from Dion, and had given her hand to a certain Timokrates, his favorite drinking companion.

# XVII

IT WAS NOW SOME WEEKS PAST MIDSUMMER. WE were in the west, in an Olympic year; it would be stupid to linger in Sicily when we could take in the Games on our home-ward way.

I had had to miss the last festival, and Thettalos had never been at all; his father had believed in attending to business, not jaunting about. I was nearly as eager as he; at my last visit, eight years before, I had been little older than he was now. One's life takes long strides, between Olympics.

I still knew my way about, well enough to buy stores at Elis and hire a pack mule, which costs less than being skinned by the traders on the spot. We bought our own tent; if one sells it later it's as cheap as hiring and much cleaner. There is a bank at Elis where one can leave spare cash before going on. All the great festivals are holy to Hermes the Light-fingered.

Having thus saved time and temper, we got on ahead of the crowds, in time to pitch our tent in a cypress grove with good shade, so that we would not come back tired at evening to lie in a bake-oven. On the best sites near the Altis, which are bespoken by important visitors far ahead, servants were already putting up pavilions, to be ready when their masters came. The athletes who for two months had been training here were still walking about like men with the place to themselves: thick hulking wrestlers, lean runners, broken-nosed boxers, and some most lovely boys, their proportions not yet spoiled, like the men's, with lopsided exercise for one event.

The crowds were coming. Every road had a dust cloud ten feet high for as far as one could see. The first market was opening, for food, cook-pots and oil, blankets and tent ropes, fire grids and knives. Next day, when visitors are settled in, is the time for fairings, such as ribbons, gilt strigils, charms, cheap vases, painted figures of well-known actors in character (the comics sell best, but I found one or two of me). Last appear the costly goods for rich connoisseurs: wine cups with beautiful athletes drawn in the bowls, embroideries, small marbles, inlaid armor, books in fine calligraphy, goldwork from Macedon. There were women answering to all these classes, at prices to match. They had to keep on the far side of the river, but one could see their tents, from straw lean-to's up to silk, skirting the banks, all ready for the athletes when they broke training, and the visitors loose from their wives.

Soon the quiet grove round our tent was a mass of squatters, putting up bivouacs, making cook-fires, or just spreading out the beds they would sleep on in the open. We hired a lad to guard our pitch, and went off sightseeing. In the Altis we met, of all people, Theodoros, without a roof for his head. He had been invited months before by a well-off Athenian sponsor; this man, as appeared later, had been taken suddenly ill, too late to get word to Theodoros, who was then in Corinth, and now looked in vain for his host's pavilion. Of course, once his plight was known he would have had a score of offers, and we were flattered at his choosing to take potluck with us. He was a perfect companion for the feast, knowing who everyone was and what they had all been doing; no city in Greece held many secrets from Theodoros. At bedtime, when we were sitting round our fire, he did us his party tricks; he could imitate any animal or any thing with a sound. When he did his most famous turn, the creaking windlass, all the campers in hearing, who had to fetch water from the river, started up and began looking for the well. To explain would have brought us a crowd of hundreds; we had to smother our laughter and leave them searching.

Next morning was the formal opening of the Games; the air rang with trumpet calls from the heralds' contest; presently the winner, who would give out all the victories, sounded for the dedication. We saluted Zeus and Pelops from a distance; the crowd round the Great Altar was as thick as porridge, and as hot.

By now the sleepy valley was like a city, and all the side shows were on. In the recital hall some political philosopher, from the school of Isokrates, I think, was delivering an endless lecture, instructing the world's leaders on how to conduct their state affairs for their own good and that of Greece. All the envoys, sophists and politicians were there; the hall was packed and they were standing in the stoa, even out in the sun. Theodoros pointed out to us the secret agents, who, indifferent to what the expert insisted should be done, were moving among his auditors to learn what was really happening. We noticed too a knot of bright-haired Macedonians, loaded with massive jewelry (I admit they can wear it and it is exquisitely made) all listening just like Greeks. Though they make wildly enthusiastic theater audiences (every actor has a stock of stories about Pella) this sophistication surprised me. Theodoros, however, said he noticed a change each time he went there; they were getting more and more involved with the southern states; not, he added, that it would come to much until one of their kings could contrive to stay alive for two Olympiads running. It was remarkable, he said, that the role was still so much sought after. He wondered how the lecturer would shape in it.

We walked on, visiting a booth of dancing dwarfs, a concert in the mixolydian mode for double-flute, aulos and kithara;

a diviner who foretold the winner of the stade race by casting
pebbles (the morrow proved him wrong), and even, briefly,
a lawyer's exposition of how he could win his client's case
when justice, law, public opinion and all the evidence were
on the other side. Then we walked back the way we came.
In all this time, the political philosopher had only just stopped
talking. The street crowd had dispersed, and the audience was
coming out, discussing as keenly as if all these words might
engender some real event.

I was saying this to Theodoros, when at the far end of the
street I saw someone coming, whose walk I knew at a glance.
It was Plato. Speusippos was with him, as well as Xenokrates,
and a group of friends and well-wishers. I was glad to see
him back where he belonged, among people fit for him, and
pointed him out to the others. Thettalos remarked that he was
looking better, but that Syracuse had left its mark. Theodoros,
who had been watching intently, said, "From the people greeting him, it seems he has only just arrived."

"Yes," I answered. "He'll have come straight from Tarentum."

"Then, my dears, let us wait where we are, for unless I'm
wrong we shall see a memorable bit of theater. In a moment
he will meet with Dion."

"Are you sure?" For some reason I wished to doubt it.
"There were none of his men working on the pavilions."

"Niko, my dear, you don't suppose Dion has to bring his
own tent like common people? He'll be at the state hostel, the
Leonideion, with the other lions. Look, here he comes now."

He came out into the sunlight, with a train about him,
among them Herakleides and his Athenian friend Kallippos.
They were conversing, and well out in the street before they
noticed anything. Plato saw Dion first. He slowed down; those
with him all fell silent. As he came on, people round them
became aware. He must have felt it; but he had had practice
lately in keeping his thoughts to himself, if he had needed it.
I saw, or fancied, a searching in his face, either of the man
down the street, or the man within.

Now Dion had noticed the stares. He scanned the street, stopped dead, strode forward. Thettalos' hand closed round my wrist.

They met. Dion clasped Plato's hands, took his arm, and drew him aside. The gesture was explicit, dismissing both their retinues; all fell back, and stood looking after them as they walked our way. I saw Kallippos pour out words to Herakleides. I don't know what they were looking for; as for me, I had seen what I had seen: the perfect seemliness with which Dion had greeted Plato and asked after his health, and his impatience showing behind it like fire round a furnace door. It was something to be got through, before he could ask for news.

Of all places on earth, I should think none offers less privacy than Olympia in Games Week. One can't even relieve nature in the presence of fewer than a dozen; one would need walk a mile into the country to find oneself alone. Dion was a Council guest; Plato no doubt was sharing a tent with friends. Neither was one for creeping into a corner. What Plato had to tell Dion, he told him in the Street of Victors, upon the marble seat under the statue of Diagoras the Runner. Standing between two plinths nearby, we saw it all.

No doubt Dion must have heard something about the selling-up of his properties; but I think he must have supposed the capital still intact, if Dionysios could be made to send it. In any case, I could tell the truth had taken him by surprise. One could guess just how it was going: Plato leading in with the loss of the money, as the least of the evils, Dion swallowing that without too wry a face, his calm just setting hard, then asking after his son. I knew that from Plato's pause. He told, I suppose, as much truth as he had to. Dion swallowed, his mouth clenched; this touched him closer. Plato offered some consolation; I don't know how much he heard of it. He was watching Plato's face, which told him something unguessed was still to come. I could tell just the moment when he cut him short to ask.

Plato did not keep him waiting. After that, there was silence.

It seemed to spread from Dion all along the street. It was like one of those great mute build-ups in Aischylos, for Achilles or for Niobe. But no big speech followed. Dion just clenched his fist and brought it quite slowly down upon his knee. His face said all the rest. Looking round, I saw Kallippos grasp Herakleides' arm; Speusippos turned to Xenokrates, triumph in his eyes. Dion saw it too, a man used to living in public, who had said the thing he meant; no going back now. Then, as if pulled against his will, he turned again to Plato.

Plato said something, a handful of words, and slowly shook his head. For a moment he seemed quite alone, like a man watching a ship out of sight. Somewhere she may make port; but not the harbor he faced the storm for. He commends her to heaven, and turns away.

When they had gone, Theodoros, who without knowing what we knew had known well what he was looking for, said, "Did you see their faces? There will be war."

I said that it seemed so to me. We talked; but Thettalos was quiet. At last he turned to me and said, "Did he love his wife? You said not."

"That was my guess. But he would hardly tell me."

"In any case," said Theodoros, "think of the affront. Could there be a greater?"

Looking at me again, Thettalos said, "Well, not to him."

I understood him. I remembered Speusippos' little flute-girl, whose father had died in the quarries, one of thousands in these long years. I had seen, just now, her story and his anger still burning in Speusippos' face. I thought of Plato, thrown to the wolves of Ortygia, barely scraping out with his life. Through all these things, Dion had remembered the maxims of Pythagoras and the teachings of the Academy. But there is a limit to what the just man can bear.

We walked on towards the temple. I lifted my eyes. There on the west gable stood Apollo, stern and beautiful among the Lapiths, shedding victory from his lifted arm.

I thought, Perhaps it is impossible for a philosopher to be a king—at any rate, to be both at once. Perhaps that is only for the god. There at his side stand Theseus and Pirithoos, the heroes who will win his battle. We are weary of ourselves, and have dreamed a king. If now the gods have sent us one, let us not ask him to be more than mortal.

# XVIII

IT WAS A YEAR BEFORE DION WAS READY. THE
talk about Olympia would have died down, but for the rumors that ran underground like the shoots of the aloe, always
coming up somewhere new. Greece was scattered with Syracusan exiles; father and son, the tyranny had lasted nearly half
a century. These people were being sounded; I can confess,
after so long, that I did some of this work myself. Sometimes
I carried a letter to someone of importance, sometimes just
took the feeling of the exiles in the place. I did not often see
Dion; usually Speusippos took my reports. The Academy was
in very deep.

Plato I never saw, except by chance as I came and went.
He would greet me, but never ask my business. He had told
everyone where he stood. Dion had been wronged. He had
the right to claim satisfaction; their friends had the right to
support him. Plato would neither blame nor praise. Himself,
he believed about civil violence what his hard youth had
taught. Besides this, he was Dionysios' guest-friend, with all

its religious duties. When people reminded him of the days in outer Ortygia, he would answer that Dionysios had done nothing to him, though he had had power to take his life and had been angry with him; the sanctities of their bond still stood inviolate. He was old; he could not bear arms, even if he had had the right. Therefore (though often urged to it, I believe) he would not make war with his tongue or pen, which he thought a coward's compromise. If ever the two kinsmen could be reconciled, his duty would be to mediate, being bound to both.

Corinth, the mother-city, had more Syracusan exiles than any other place. It costs a good deal to live there; so it was mostly the exiled aristocrats who had been settling there over the years. With these I did not deal; Dion's brother Megakles did that, being one of themselves. He was Dion-and-water, you might say: good-looking, dignified, soldierly, fairly tall, but everything scaled down. I doubt if the wrongs of Syracuse had ever irked him much while he suffered none himself; but he was a Sicilian noble, well-bred and brave, and eager for revenge. I minded my own business; but from what I knew of the exiles whose children were growing up Corinthians, I did not think they would be rushing to leave this pleasant city and take arms against the greatest power in Hellas.

Thettalos agreed but was less concerned than I. He came and went, trying his hand at whatever he felt he could grow by; he was now wanted as a second by good leading men, and his range was stretching with each new role. We understood each other. I knew pretty well, by now, what kind of actor I was, and how to use it; he was still learning to know himself (I daresay there was more to know); as this or that choice crossed his path he was restless and moody, all ups and downs. Neither of us could have borne for long to work together; owning this frankly, and taking the weather as it came, we escaped shipwreck and found new shores. He came back from Delos, where he had made a hit, swearing nothing had gone right with him, and demanding to work with me, if only for one production. "You taught me how, Niko; now you remind me to ask why. Perhaps it's these philosophers you can't keep away from."

Just now, as I have explained, one could learn a good deal at the Academy besides philosophy—for instance, that Dion was hiring soldiers. With all his Sicilian losses, he was still richer than I had guessed till now. Most of the exiles had failed him; he did not get firm pledges from more than thirty. The rest had suffered too much before they got away, or feared for their kin in Syracuse, or liked their comforts, or simply did not think the venture had any chance. So the landless, banished Dion hired spearmen like a king. They were taken on in the Peloponnese, marched west, and ferried over to Zakynthos, where they were trained by Megakles. Only he and the captains knew what they were to do. Zakynthos is a quiet island, very rustic; I don't think there is even a theater. Not much leaked out from there.

Nonetheless, by next year's sailing weather, something was known in Syracuse. No doubt the exiles had talked. Greece was as full as ever of Dionysios' agents—which meant Philistos'. The latest fugitives, friends of Herakleides, went straight to him and Dion, and said that the old man now ruled Syracuse in all but name. They added that he could have had that too if he had tried; he had at least the virtue of loyalty. Since Plato left, Dionysios had thrown himself back into dissipation, and was seldom sober enough for any serious business. As the drink gained on him he grew grosser in his pleasures; Philemon, who had lately appeared at the theater there, assured me that the very hetairas, when the Archon asked them to supper, drew for the short straw because no one wanted to go. His son Apollokrates, now a growing youth, despised him openly, preferring the company of the mercenary captains. But young Hipparinos was still to be seen at every party, his uncle's favorite, very much at home.

Speusippos supported the war without reserve. The little flute-girl, whose sleepy face I remembered, had kept him awake to some purpose. Afterwards he had met some of her friends; and, in the end, people had talked to him who, be-

cause he had been received by the Archon, had fought shy
of him before. The more he heard, the angrier he grew—but
also the more hopeful. Dion's exile had made him a legend
among the people. He would come again, like some ancient
hero-king, to lead them all to freedom. If no one would sail
with him, let him come alone, and he would have an army
from the moment his foot touched land.

Some of the younger men of the Academy were already
setting their affairs in order, to be ready for the call. Axiothea
confided to me her grief that she could not be one of them.
"I must have done wrong," she said, "in my last life on earth,
and this is the punishment I chose when my eyes were opened.
So I ought to bear it patiently, and hope for better next time.
But oh, it is hard."

Speusippos himself would not be going. Plato, now trying
to make good a lost year of work, could not have spared him;
besides, he too had been, even if uneasily, the Archon's guest;
he ranked next to Plato at the Academy, and it would have
been almost like Plato going himself. But some of their most
distinguished men were putting their books aside and polishing
their armor. One of them, Miltas of Thessaly, came from a
long line of seers in Apollo's service; it was he who chose the
day when Dion sailed, just after the god's feast day. Dion
arrived at Zakynthos in time to perform a sacrifice of dedication.

He reviewed his troops the day before, and told them what
the war was. They were shocked; they were professionals, and
knew the defenses of Syracuse. They started to shout; but
Dion had not commanded troops all those years for nothing.
He got them quiet, told them the prospects of success, with
no words wasted, and had them cheering for him at the end.

On Apollo's day, he arranged a splendid ceremony, every
vessel made of gold; then he feasted his men, all eight hundred, at the race track. Such wealth he had left, after hiring,
keeping and training them. The display did its work; they were
certain he could not spend like this unless he were sure of
support in Sicily.

Word of all this came back to Athens, then and later, as the

Academy men sent news. To tell it whole, however: on the very night before they sailed, when everyone was happy, singing by moonlight round the fires, the full moon started to wane and to change her color, and presently was in eclipse. The men were appalled. No omen, they said, could be worse for an army; this very same sign had come to the Athenians before Syracuse in the Great War. The whole force had perished off the earth, and even that had been only the beginning of evils.

Here Dion, who could have explained the matter by its rational laws, showed himself a shrewd commander. He called on Miltas to read the signs. That wise man proclaimed that the moon must stand for the brightest and biggest power on earth, as in the heavens; here was the empire of Dionysios being quenched before their eyes to give them heart. No omen could be better.

The men were cheered. One thing Dion and his brother took care to keep from them: Herakleides, who had promised to raise a fleet of ships with men to sail and fight it, had not arrived at Zakynthos.

During the year of preparation, a coolness had begun between him and Dion. As exiles working together they had had to see more of each other than at home. Herakleides had an offhand hail-fellow way, which was part both of himself and of his politics; he made it a touchstone of good will to be met on his own terms. This Dion would not do, at first because it went against his grain, later because he grew to distrust the man. Now Herakleides sent excuses, whether good or not I don't know—nor, I daresay, did Dion either. At all events, he put his faith in the god, and set sail with what he had.

There were three good-sized freighters in the little fleet, with two war triremes for escort. As well as his men's own arms, he carried shields and weapons for two thousand men. At the heel of Italy, the fleet of Syracuse, under Philistos, was waiting to cut him off.

He got word of this in time; and now truly he threw all into Apollo's hand. Instead of hanging back in the hope of Philistos' going away, he left the coastal route which every sane shipmaster follows and struck out across open sea. I turn queasy even to think of it.

Apollo blessed him. They made Sicily in twelve days with a fair wind all the way. Their landfall was the South Cape, which was a bare thirty miles from Syracuse; this seemed tempting the god a little far. They stood out again; and as if to punish their doubt, ran into a storm which blew them across to Africa, and nearly ran them aground. They labored with oars off a lee shore, were becalmed off Great Syrtis Heads, and said their prayers. A breeze from the forgiving god cradled them back to Sicily; they landed at Minoa, in the Carthaginian province.

The troops of the guard-post all turned out, thinking the war with Syracuse had started up again. For this Dion was prepared. He had warned his men that their lives would depend on their steadiness; they had the advantage of numbers, and must push back these men without bloodshed; then he could treat with the commander. They locked shields, and took the strong point without killing a man. Dion sounded for a parley. Up came the captain, and turned out to be a man he knew. Dion had accepted his surrender in some old campaign and treated him with honor. As soon as he was assured they were not marching against the power of Carthage, he came to terms. Dion gave up the strong point; Synalos quartered his soldiers and gave them stores. Anywhere in Sicily Dion's word was good. If he threw out Philistos and his master, no Carthaginian would complain; if, as rumor had it, he meant to disarm Ortygia and disperse her mercenaries, they would object still less.

Dion's men were in camp at Minoa when news came to them of the god's greatest favor yet, a bounty almost past belief. Not only was Philistos still away watching the door of the empty stable; Dionysios himself had sailed from Syracuse with eighty of the ships that were left, all filled with troops.

Don't ask me why. Perhaps he thought Dion would put in at Tarentum, and he could kill two birds with one stone; I don't suppose he had forgiven Archytas for demanding Plato. Or maybe he just wanted to be in at the death. Whichever it was, I am sure he did it on impulse after being left to his own devices. I should think Philistos could have killed him.

Dion's men were so struck with this run of luck that they declined the rest he offered them to get over the sea trip and begged him to push on while the stars were good. I don't know what they would have said if they had known the whole story of Apollo's care for Dion. He had just worked him a miracle.

Dionysios, when he sailed, had left as regent his favorite, Timokrates, the husband of Dion's wife. This man, at the news of the landing, sent a fast courier to Italy with letters to him and to Philistos. The courier landed at Rhegium, and took the quick inland road towards Kaulonia, where the Archon had his ships. There he met someone he knew who had been at a sacrifice and had brought back a gift of meat. Since the courier could not stay to share it, the friend gave him a cut to eat when he had time. Knowing the business urgent, he pushed on long after dark; when he had to rest, the hills were desolate, with no shelter but a wood beside the road. Too tired to cook, he supped on a crust, and slept with his letter bag by his head. He awoke to find it gone, along with the meat which had been tied to it. His panic search showed him no trace of human thieves, only the marks of wolf pads, and a dragging trail between. All morning he searched the wild country round about, hoping that when the wolf had eaten, it would have dropped the bag; but it must have taken it to its lair for its young to chew on. No one, it seems, had told him what the message said; he was there to do as he was told. He could only confess, with you may suppose what result. So he did just what I would have done in his shoes—ran away up to Italy and changed his name. Long after, he told the story. The wolf, as everyone knows, is a creature of Apollo.

Meantime Dion set out for Syracuse with his eight hundred, leaving his spare arms with Synalos, who agreed to send them on.

They were needed soon. They were hardly across the river Halys into Greek lands when men started coming in: cavalry from Akragas, hoplites from Gela (which old Dionysios had let the Carthaginians sack when it served his turn), more from Kamarina. As soon as they got to the country around Syracuse, the peasants came down from the hills: serfs of the great landowners, the little russet Sikels who were there before the Hellenes; poor Greek smallholders, ruined by the taxes which had bought old Dionysios' catapults and young Dionysios' girls. Load after load the spare arms were issued. It was as if a god had come down to lead them.

All who were there are in agreement that Dion never sank, in all this time, below his role. It was as if he had been rehearsing for it all his life. He was now at an age when he might have sat for a sculptor as Zeus rather than as Apollo. In the years at the Academy he had grown his beard; now it had a short soldier's trim. He was a hard-muscled, noble Zeus, fit to throw thunderbolts, a Zeus for Pheidias; the grizzle in his hair only gave him dignity. He was savior, hero, father; if he kept his distance, it was only fitting.

Timokrates, his dispatches bringing no help, was trying to put Syracuse upon defense with the few men left him, and had to call in reservists to man the walls. These were mostly land-pensioned veterans of the old Archon's wars, from Leontini. He put these on the city ramparts, keeping his regulars to hold Ortygia. Dion, whose last recruits had come from inside Syracuse itself, heard of these dispositions, and staged a feint advance on Leontini, now stripped of all its men. Young boys came racing up to the Syracusan walls to warn their fathers, who opened the gates and quick-marched for home, not reckoning they owed young Dionysios anything. After dark Dion marched straight on to Syracuse. Daybreak found him at the river Anopos, a mile away.

Before he went on, he sacrificed to Apollo Helios. He now had five thousand men behind him. He looked so godlike to them, bay-crowned, lifting his hands to the sun, that they all broke sprays from the trees and wreathed themselves for victory. Nor was their overconfidence punished; let us call it prophecy.

When the Leontinians deserted, Timokrates sent orders to

close all the gates into Ortygia. But before he could get back there himself, the Syracusans were rushing out through the city to welcome Dion. If Timokrates showed himself he would be lynched; and outside was the man to whom he had done that wrong which demands the extremest vengeance everywhere. He grabbed the first horse he could find, wrapped his cloak round his face, and got away. To justify himself, he galloped about describing the vast might of Dion's forces and making him sound invincible, so that those who from prudence had held back before, now flocked to join Dion. All the veterans of Leontini, finding their homes and women safe, joined to a man.

Syracuse was free. Before Dion had set foot inside, the tyranny was broken. Every man could speak his mind and do as he chose. They chose first of all to hunt down Philistos' band of informers. All over the streets, these people, and people who looked rather like them or were their kin or whom someone denounced for private vengeance, were chased or run down at home or dragged from the temples they had fled to, and battered to death by the crowd.

Dion marched up to the walls, and they opened the great gates for him. He had put on his parade armor, inlaid with gold. On his right marched his brother, on his left Kallippos the Athenian. Herakleides and his ships had still not arrived.

The chief men of the city came out clothed in white. As they went up the Sacred Way, flowers and wreaths and ribbons showered on them from the house roofs. People set up altars and sacrificed in thanksgiving as Dion passed by. Treading in laurel and myrtle, rose wreaths and blood, he went on to the great sundial of Dionysios which stands opposite Ortygia, and from its dial addressed the citizens. With the favor of the gods, he said, he had brought them liberty. It was theirs, if they would only help him to defend it.

At once they wanted to give him and Megakles the office of military dictator the Archons had held before. He thanked them, would not take advantage of men so unused to freedom, and proposed a council of twenty from the returned exiles and such loyal friends as Kallippos. This being carried with ac-

claim, he marched on the last strong point that still held out—
the great fortress of Euryalos. Its garrison had barred themselves in for safety rather than offense; they surrendered, on
condition they either joined Dion or left the city. The garrison
of Ortygia could do nothing but watch all this from the gatehouses, and be thankful for the gates. In the captain's lodging
of Euryalos were the great bronze keys of the quarries. Among
cheers that must have been audible on the slopes of Etna,
Dion turned the locks to free the captives.

Now only Ortygia still held out. That was impregnable; but
Dion had a siege wall built on the land side of its neck to seal
it fast. He got his new recruits armed and drilled, and set up
his command in the Euryalos. Seven days later, Dionysios,
who had had the news at last, sailed up with his ships into
Ortygia dockyard.

If Herakleides and the promised fleet had come, they might
have stopped him. As it was, Dion's men could do nothing
but look on. Dionysios could bring in everything he needed;
soon Philistos came too, with a second fleet. Ortygia would be
a long business. But meantime, Syracuse was free.

With the forces he had, Dionysios could have landed along
the coast and attacked by land; but he stayed in Ortygia,
hoping, as it turned out later, to agree with Dion privately,
as one gentleman with another. As the Archon saw it, the
rabble had just been the engine of Dion's private war, and
need not be considered. Having known Plato, he should have
known Dion better than this. He sent back the envoys, saying
he would read nothing that could not be laid before the people. Public proposals came, for remission of taxes, talks, and
so forth. The Syracusans laughed, and Dion sent word that if
Dionysios would abdicate, he would treat with him for his
safe-conduct. Short of that, he could save his breath.

After a while, Dionysios offered to consider this, on terms
to be agreed, and asked for envoys. Some leading citizens
went; the gatehouse guards were seen idling, calling out to
the people that they would soon be out of work. At sunset
the talks were still going on; the envoys would stay overnight.
However, all seemed settled; the troops on the Syracusan

siege wall took a lazy watch, as the enemy was doing. Work on the wall, a rough makeshift meant to be reinforced, had stopped. At midnight the five gates of Ortygia opened; the garrison rushed out upon the siege wall and its sleepy men.

The yelling Nubians, their faces daubed like white skulls; the naked, painted, seven-foot Gauls, drunk on raw wine; the steady iron-hard Romans, rushed on citizens unused to fend for themselves, new to arms and half-awake. They broke and fled screaming. That would have been the end but for Dion's regulars, who did not wait for the trumpet but got to the wall as soon as he. His voice drowned by the din, he just showed himself in the vanguard and led them on. A fine thundering Zeus, with a javelin like a lightning bolt, he rallied the line till his shield was stuck full of broken points and his corselet dented all over. Even when a spear went through his right hand, he got on a horse and rode about to encourage the Syracusans, getting some back to fight. By now he had brought up the men from the Achradina; the enemy was contained in the streets nearest the causeway; under this new onslaught they broke and fled, many being trapped below the wall. On Dion's side only seventy-five were killed, partly because his regulars fought so well, partly because the Syracusans had not stayed to fight at all. They were very grateful, and voted the troops extra pay of a hundred minas; the men spent part of it on a golden wreath for Dion.

Next day the envoys were sent home. Dionysios, though he broken the truce, had not sunk to killing them; perhaps after all Plato's visit had not been for nothing.

The next embassy from Ortygia was addressed to Dion in person. He received it publicly and was handed letters from his wife and mother. These he read aloud to the people in a steady voice; they were sad, but innocent of intrigue. At the end, one more letter came out; this he was begged to read in private, since it was from his son. He must have been tempted for many reasons, but he broke the seal. The letter inside was not from Hipparinos at all, but from the Archon. It is in the archives of the Academy; I read it once. People say now it was a clever bit of policy, but to me it reads just like the man—

all feeling, petulance, self-pity and unreasonable hopes. It dwelt on Dion's years of faithful service to both the Archons, reproached him with unjust resentment, swore his kindred, wife and mother should suffer for it if he kept it up, begged him not to throw holy Syracuse to a senseless mob, who would bring her down in chaos and then blame him for it; and, as a flourish at the end, offered to accept him as the Archon, if he would maintain autarchic rule. I daresay Philistos added that.

Dion disdained to write back, and sent a short soldier's answer. But the letter had not been in vain. The people knew he had had these offers; surely they must tempt him? It was argued in the wineshops; Dion's men just laughed, or hit out if they were fighting-drunk. By now they loved him like a father.

It was now that at last Herakleides arrived in Syracuse, with twenty triremes and fifteen thousand men.

He had held back a long time. If his heart had been in helping, he would have come, like Dion, with what he had. The triremes alone, without the troop freighters, might have kept Dionysios out of Ortygia. One can hardly doubt he meant to find Dion in trouble, rescue the enterprise and take command. What he wanted after that, whether it was for the people or himself, he is not here to tell us.

In any case, he found Dion an honored victor, adored by his troops and respected by the citizens. Something had to be done, if Herakleides was not to be just the slow-belly who gets there after the feast. He still had much in his favor; his exile spoke for his stand against the tyrant, and he had his cheery, hearty way. No one could miss the contrast. If Dion at fifty had not learned ease with people yet, I suppose he showed a kind of sense in not straining at it, like an actor forcing his limits.

All these parleys with Ortygia having ended nowhere, the land war was getting static; but some of Dionysios' war triremes decided to join the Syracusans, so that Herakleides now commanded sixty ships. One day he got word that Philistos was sailing up towards the straits. Now was his chance of glory. The fleets engaged; Philistos was hemmed in. When they took his galley, the old man was lying on the poop, with his sword stuck into his belly. Being nearly eighty, he had not had strength enough to do a clean job, and was still alive. Herakleides, who always knew how to please the people, gave him to them to play with.

You may say he knew what he deserved, which was why he had tried to kill himself. He had been the right arm of the tyranny, father and son, since it began. But you could say of him too that he remained faithful to the son, from whom he could have taken everything, though the father had had him exiled on mere suspicion. That he should have put on arms at all at his age, when he could have sailed off with a sack of gold to die in bed at ease, might have earned him some grudging honor. No matter; it was the death of Phyton all over again, though there was no tyrant now to order it, just the free citizens of Syracuse. A siege tower they lacked; in any case, they were too impatient to wait a day. He was stripped naked, and haltered. Because of his wound he could not be made to walk about the streets, but he was dragged along, and every man did what pleased him. At last, when it could be seen he was senseless and would give no more sport, they hacked his head off, and gave his trunk to the boys for what it was worth. They tied it by one leg, lamed in battle fifty years before, and pulled it about till they got tired, when they threw it on a dung-heap. By the time Dion got the news, the man was dead.

I have been told, by Timonides of the Academy, who sailed with him, that Dion shut himself up alone till night. It had always been his faith that honor begets honor. He had sweated and bled to free these people; they had had a share of his soul. Small wonder if while Herakleides went drinking with the captains, everyone's hero, he did not join the feast. Long ago at Delphi, when they killed Meidias, I had seen he did not understand. He did not know a crowd. He had not learned, even yet, what most men are who have had to eat dirt for two generations. He was not content to pity them, and be angry with those who had debased them; he had wanted to persuade himself that freedom would ennoble them. When they had forsaken him in battle, he had forgiven them; he was a soldier, and did not expect too much from half-trained men. I think it was this killing that first seared his mind. Such people, he began to think, could not know their own good; if left to fend for themselves, they would suffer worse than under the tyranny, and sink even lower: for he believed what Sokrates had taught Plato, and Plato him, that it is better to suffer evil than to do it.

Autumn was closing the open seaways, though ships still crossed the straits to Italy, as they do in good weather all the year. There were no more sea fights; but Herakleides now equaled Dion in public esteem. He was pleasant to everyone, and made no secret of his belief that Syracuse should be governed just like Athens, by popular assembly and the general vote. As long, however, as Dionysios still sat in Ortygia, the need of a commander was clear to everyone. Herakleides was content at present to intrigue for an equal share in the command.

I don't know what Dionysios did when he learned of Philistos' death, and knew he now had to conduct the war himself; I suppose he got drunk. What's certain is that before long he sent to Dion, offering the surrender of Ortygia: the palace, the castle, the ships, his standing army and five months' full pay for it, in exchange for his own safe-conduct into Italy, and a yearly revenue from his private estates.

Dion must have been tempted by now to make his own terms out of hand. However, he had pledged his honor to lay all tenders before the people, and for him this settled the matter. With one voice the people said no. They had tasted blood with Philistos; how much sweeter would his master's be! Dionysios must be at his last gasp, to make this offer; they were resolved to have him alive. In vain Dion told them that all they had been fighting for was theirs to take if they chose. They only thought (and said), "There is a man who has not suffered." Sicily is a land where revenge is prized. Some said he must have had a better offer than before, to let the tyrant off scot-free; but then the man was his kin. None of these rumors was opposed by Herakleides. Perhaps he believed them; it is easy to think the worst of a man one hates. The envoys were sent home empty; the siege went on. Herakleides spent more and more time ashore, busy with his politics. And one misty dawn in early autumn, when the lookouts of the fleet were taking it easy, Dionysios boarded a ship, cast off with a little squadron that carried all his treasures, and sailed away. By the time the news broke, he was in Italy.

When this reached Athens, nothing else was talked of all over the city. The greatest tyranny in Hellas had been broken, and by a man trained in Athens—almost an Athenian, you might say. At the Academy, gray-haired philosophers ran about like schoolboys. Axiothea and her friend both kissed me in the olive grove. They told me what was not yet known in the streets—that Ortygia still held out without its lord, who had left the young Apollokrates in command. This passed even my notion of the man; if his son was like him, the war was as good as won, and we agreed we might as well rejoice now as later. We recalled that not very long ago a shooting star had crossed the heavens, so brilliant that it had been seen from a dozen cities and had turned the night into day.

A number of people gave parties in honor of the event, among them Thettalos and I. Theodoros told us a splendid story. He had lately played in Macedon before the new king, Philip, a man he predicted would be harder to kill than those before. It seemed that when the bright star appeared, this hill-king thought it had been sent in his own honor, because he had won some battle and a chariot race, and then his wife had had a son. He and his whole court had drunk all through the night upon it. Then, only a few weeks later, had come the great news from Syracuse. So having laughed at the barbarian's pretenses we thought no more of him, and drank to the freedom of all Greeks.

# XIX

"OH, NIKERATOS!" SAID AXIOTHEA, WHO WAS THE
first I told. "Are you really going to Sicily? Dear friend that
you are, I could almost hate you. Where will you be playing?
Not, surely, in Syracuse, with the siege still on?"

"Nowhere, that I know. For once I'm traveling for pleasure.
Why not, while I've got my strength?"

"Strength? After that lionlike Diomedes? I am ashamed of
you. Is Thettalos going too?"

"No, he's in Ionia. He's a partner now, and won't be free
for some weeks. This I am doing just for myself. I saw this
enterprise begin; I'd like to be there when it is crowned."

These words, once spoken, displeased me. When a tragic
actor talks of crowns—especially when he has just won one—
he talks of tragedy. I had only just dodged the bad-luck word;
I am careful of such things, and it was unlike me.

I asked her what fresh news there was. Timonides still wrote
to Speusippos; but he, between his research, his Academy business, and keeping up the archives of the campaign, was too

busy now to get about much, and I seldom met him. She answered that he had had a letter last week and there seemed no great change. Then she added, "But we don't see all the dispatches now. They used to be read aloud. Of course, there must be less to tell. It seems the man Herakleides—you know, he was never one of *ours*—is still giving trouble. Did you ever meet him?"

"For a moment, once. I thought him a good simple soldier, which he is not. He should have been an actor. But I wouldn't want him in my company. He'd hide your mask and do a brilliant impromptu while you looked for it."

"Did you hear what he did to get back in the citizens' favor, after he let Dionysios get away? He proposed at the Assembly that all Syracusan land should be divided equally."

"What, now?" I said. "With the war still on? I don't believe it."

"It's true. I saw that part of the letter."

"In Sicily! No one would give up a yard of onion patch without a fight. There would have been a riot, then a sortie from Ortygia, and Dionysios back at home."

"Herakleides must have known that, I suppose, as well as Dion. But it was Dion who had to say no."

We were sitting on a marble seat, by the statue of the hero Akademos. His shadow fell far beyond us in the evening sunlight, a long thin helmet crest, a spear stretching ten cubits over the grass.

After a while she said, "We always heard all the letters . . . They say Dion has changed."

"I doubt it. Stopped trying to change, more likely."

"Plato has changed," she said.

"Yes; there I can believe you."

"When he was young, you know, he traveled, like Solon and Herodotos. He studied in Egypt. He doesn't see barbarism everywhere outside Hellas, as most men do. Not even always in Macedon. But he's always taught that one must legislate for any polis according to how many of its men can think. Once he believed there would be a good many, if they could be chosen out freely from rich and poor alike, and trained together. He still prefers merit to birth; but now he thinks such men are fewer, not enough to bring it about, or keep it working. That is all."

"All? It seems a good deal to me."

She sighed. "He has been there, I've not. Well, you are going, Nikeratos. How I envy you."

I had arranged to sail in about half a month. Speusippos gave me a pile of letters for Dion. He said that Herakleides and Theodotes (that very kinsman who had entreated Plato to beard Dionysios for him) were writing to all kinds of leading people in Greece, making mischief about Dion, and he must be warned.

Plato wrote too. Long after, when it was in the archives, I learned what a troubled letter I had carried. It started with good wishes and good hopes; reminded Dion that the eyes of the world were on Syracuse, on him, and through him on the Academy; warned him that rumor was running everywhere about strife between him and Herakleides, which was endangering the cause; and added that hearsay was all he knew, it was so long since Dion had written to him. The end, as near as I remember, went like this: "Take care; it is going about that you are not as gracious as you might be. Don't forget that to achieve anything you must conciliate people. Intolerance keeps a lonely house."

I had the roughest sea crossing to Tarentum since the one when I was wrecked there. With a first-rate pilot and good crew, we just weathered it. I was deathly frightened; but there were people on board who knew who I was. If I had ever doubted how much vanity there is in most men's courage, I knew it then.

I crossed the straits at Rhegium and went on by road, not wanting to run through the war fleets off Ortygia. Most of the city's traffic was going the same way. I hired a good riding mule, for the look of it, since I was known thereabouts; it was a long ride, and I was tired by the time I got to Leontini. The city seemed empty of its men, who I was told had all gone to fight for Dion. When I asked the boys about my old host, the Roman captain Aulus Rupilius, they said he was here, burying his father. I called to pay my respects and make an offering. They pressed me to stay the night, and although I would not intrude on a house of mourning, a friend put me up instead; Rupilius saying he would be glad of my company next day when he rode back to Syracuse.

We set out early together. He was in no deep distress (the old man had long been failing and witless) and seemed fretting to get on, concerned more for the future than the past. When I asked what the matter was, he would only say he had heard everything was not what it ought to be in Syracuse. I noticed he was in armor and wore his sword. He jogged along, a broad gray-bearded man with a boxer's nose, red-faced and sweating as the sun warmed up his corselet, brooding, with half an ear for what I said.

I wondered if he had been turned against Dion by Herakleides' faction. It was lucky I kept this to myself. As soon as Dion's name came up, he shamed me with an encomium that took us over several stades of road. Ah, there was a man with the ancient virtues! Nothing for himself, everything for the common weal. Courage and strategy in war; the endurance of a man twenty years younger; a general who never slept softer or drier than his men, nor ate while they were hungry; a man with *gravitas* (a Roman word, which I think means dignity of soul); incorruptible in office, flawless in personal honor. He might lack the arts by which base men flatter foolish ones; but he was never at a loss for the right order in a tight place, or a cheerful word to the men. In a word (it slipped out in spite of him, civil man as he was), Dion was wasted on Greeks. He should have been a Roman.

Plainly, this was the praise of indignation. But I could not learn the cause, so resolved was the man that only good should be spread through him.

Wherever there was a sea view it showed us warships. I asked how the siege went, and found him hopeful. Apollokrates, a lad of about sixteen, could hardly be more than a token leader, a hostage to the garrison for their flitted lord. The blockade was tight and they must be pinched for most things. "Everything," he said, "favors the Syracusans, except themselves. They remind me of the people in that play you did here, resolved to drive out the gods."

"You are making me anxious. How long before we reach the city?"

"It depends on whether we can get remounts. Nowadays one can't be sure. If not, we shall hardly do it by nightfall."

"Never mind," I answered. "It's a pleasant ride up here. A pretty road. This next rise should show us the sea."

"Be quiet," he said.

Romans, like Spartans, don't see the need for wasting words. He held up his hand, and reined in. I heard, as he had done, the battle noises from on ahead.

"What can it be?" I asked. "That's nearer than Syracuse."

"It's at the river crossing down there. Dionysios may have landed troops. Keep in cover, till we see."

We rode up the nearest hill, tied up our mounts below the skyline, and finished on foot. All the while the sound got nearer: two fighting forces, one lot quite out of hand, yelling catcalls and abuse (the sound told that, even from here), the other strangely silent, except sometimes for the sharp sound of an order.

We were just below the crest; Rupilius, panting and grunting in his armor, had paused to breathe. Suddenly he grabbed my arm so that I nearly cried out. Then I too knew the commander's voice.

Clambering so fast we grazed ourselves, we made the summit. Then we forgot to take cover, just stood backed to a rock, and stared.

Below was the river, widening in the flat land between hills and sea. A regiment had started to ford it, in good order, going north towards Leontini: a file of men plodding through the rocks and thigh-high water, keeping their equipment dry, while the main body covered their rear. The other army, if one could use the word for what looked more like a mob, was trying to harry them. Some of these were armed like soldiers, some with whatever people snatch up in a brawl; others were hurling stones. There were also a few light horse skirmishing about and waving spears, as if getting ready to attack the column, if they could make up their minds to it. No one seemed to be leading them, unless it was from behind. The other leader, however, was clear in sight, encouraging the rear guard. I could hear the crack of a stone against his shield. It was Dion.

Rupilius clutched my arm, hitting the bruise he had made before. "Ours!" he said. "I must go. I must go down."

"Wait," I begged, "till you tell me what is happening." I could not think why trained soldiers should fall back before such a force, Dion above all.

Rupilius craned forward. Dion had now formed up his men, of whom only a few were yet in the river, in six-rank line of battle. The enemy, at once less eager, milled awhile; however, someone yelled out a paean, and they made a ragged charge. Dion's men stood firm. At first they just shouted and clashed their arms. This daunted some of the attackers, but most came on. The foremost of these Dion's troops struck down with blows of their shields or spear butts; when they fell stunned, the rest backed into a huddle. There was no pursuit; the line just waited on the defense, while Dion signaled for the crossing of the river to continue.

About another fifty had forded it, when the stunned men started to stir and help each other up. At this the others took heart again, and shouted war cries. Somewhere I even heard an order.

Dion halted the crossing, and again dressed his line. But this time (I could tell from his loud shout), he gave the word to charge.

His men ran forward, keeping a steady, solid shield line. They hit the others like a wave that breaks hard and heavy in one piece. Now men were really falling, most of them the enemy's. It was soon over; they ran like rabbits; those who were caught could be seen making the ritual gestures of surrender, kneeling before the soldiers to touch their beards or knees. Some of Dion's men, whose blood was up, started off in pursuit, but he called them off and they came back like good hunting dogs, lugging a few more captives with them.

All this while, Rupilius had been rooted where he stood, knowing he could not be in time to join the action. Now he started scrambling about again and saying he must go. "Get your horse, then," I said, "which you will surely need, and I'll come with you."

He just stopped himself from telling me I would only be in the way. As we climbed down to our mounts I could hear him, when he thought I was out of earshot, calling down curses upon treacherous, envious, cowardly, thankless Greeks.

When we reached the ford, Dion's men had finished crossing; they were looking after each other's wounds, and pushing the prisoners into the center. Dion had ridden up to these, and was sitting his horse in silence, looking down at them.

I said to Rupilius, "By the dog! Those look like Syracusans."

Rupilius just leaned over and spat in the dust; then he kicked his horse's flank. I followed him.

As he came near, his mates in the column started calling. I could make nothing of it but abuse of the Syracusans, as if this would speak for itself; and that they were marching to Leontini. At this Rupilius, without waiting for more, dashed over to Dion, threw himself from his horse before him, and, looking like a dog that has swum from Piraeus to Salamis and found its master, said, "Sir, Aulus Rupilius, back for duty."

"You are welcome, Rupilius," Dion answered. "Though it seems neither of us has any more duties here."

Before I could hear more, I was surrounded by soldiers asking me if I were Syracusan, as they might have asked some snake if it was the poisonous kind. I told them who I was; soldiers are friendly to actors, unless there is some good reason not to be, and when they knew I was not even a Sicilian, they all started to talk at once. Piecing it out as best I could, I gathered that Herakleides (whose name no one uttered without a curse) had again brought up at Assembly the share-out of the land. Dion had again opposed it as inopportune; the people, worked up beforehand, had then voted him out of his office as commander in chief. This angered his troops, who cheered for him and booed the new generals chosen instead. At this, Herakleides had moved that the men were a private army kept at the city's expense to further Dion's aims and set him up as a tyrant; he proposed that their pay (which was five months overdue) should not be met from the treasury. This was carried by acclamation.

"And so," said someone, "we told them what they and their Archon were welcome to do with each other, and took the general away out of the muck. And lucky to get him."

Others broke in, saying Herakleides' faction had offered to make them citizens—what a gift!—and even pay them, if they would leave Dion's service. Those rats could keep their filthy silver. They themselves would go anywhere—Egypt, Persia, Gaul or Babylon—to fight under Dion. They would go to North Africa and found a colony. And so on. They were half out of their minds with anger.

"But," I said, "you had left; so why this battle?"

Curses followed, of which it was hard to make sense. "The general took it too cool, they must have thought he was soft." "The demagogues meant to get him." ". . . snapping at our heels like pi-dogs after a beggar." ". . . before we were out of the city. We just turned and rattled our spears against our shields, and they all fell down and wet themselves." "Dion wouldn't let us lay a hand on them." ". . . driving him like a scapegoat into the hills, the sons of whores." "I suppose their mothers laughed at them, so they came out to try again." "Stay and watch what we do to those we've got." They jerked thumbs at the captives, who were wailing and stretching out their hands. The soldiers shouted at them, promising them horrors.

Dion was still there, looking down at them, a tall man on a tall horse. He looked no older than when I'd seen him in Athens —younger, I think—tanned, lean and active, with the quickness of a man long at war. Bronze man, bronze horse, like a victory statue. Like a statue, too, he was there to be looked at if one wished, not to reply. His face told me he had ceased to put himself out for anyone; no sense in it, nothing gained; he would tell his thoughts when and where he chose, if he chose at all. He saw me, and moved his head in greeting, without asking why I was there. He had business of his own to mind.

Rupilius was still up by his bridle, fidgeting for another word with him. "Sir, as long as you're in Leontini, my house is yours. My guestroom is nice and cool, Nikeratos here will tell you . . ."

Another officer said, "You're late in the day, Aulus. Do you suppose no one's thought yet of bidding the general to his hearth? He's promised me that honor."

The Greeks, who made up the greater part of the army, grunted their approval. They could not compete, being from the mainland: Argives chiefly, the stocky men who win the wrestling at so many games, with a sprinkling of Corinthians, and tough Arcadian mountaineers.

"Thank you, Rupilius," said Dion. "Silence in the ranks. I will see those envoys."

Two men were coming from the distant rout of Syracusans, waving green branches. Dion sent no one to conduct them, just sat his horse and let them come up. The soldiers leaned on their spears, silent as ordered, like dogs called back from a cat chase. You could almost see them twitch.

The envoys sidled up, while the troops did all they could, by scowling and slyly fingering their swords, to keep them scared. With glum servility, they asked leave to remove their dead, thus conceding, by the law of arms, the mastery of the field.

"Take them," said Dion.

They waited; but that was all. Dion's horse shifted impatiently; its rider ceased to attend. They coughed, and asked if he would graciously declare the captives' ransom.

There was another pause, while the soldiers growled in undertones, and Dion looked the envoys over, as he had done the prisoners. Presently he pointed to a pile of shields which his men had collected from those dropped in flight. "I have heard," he said, "that not long before Dionysios was expelled from the outer city, he stripped the citizens of their arms, for fear of their rising against him. But you came armed, I see. Who armed you?"

They shuffled with their feet. I looked at the shields. They were Corinth work; one knows it anywhere. The soldiers gave a roar of anger. Then I understood him.

"Silence," he said again; then, "Go, and take those men with you." He pointed to the prisoners, who had been craning in anguish to hear the outcome. "I am a Syracusan. I do not hold fellow countrymen to ransom. And I have no other use for them. Take them away."

It was not till envoys and freed men were wading back through the river, and I saw him at leisure, that I ventured up with my bag of letters. He thanked me, courteously but shortly, and gave it to one of his officers to look after. I said, "Here is one more, sir, which I thought you would want by itself." And I gave him Plato's.

He took it, thanking me. As I saw, he was on the point of putting it with the others; then he noticed me looking, and perhaps it brought things back. At all events, he opened it and read it. It was short, as I had known from its thickness. There was no change in his face.

"Thank you, Nikeratos," he said. "I am obliged to you. There is no answer."

# XX

I NEARLY RODE STRAIGHT BACK TO MESSENE, TO take ship for home. Leontini would be crowded three to a bed; and I sickened at the thought of Syracuse. However, I had come a long way. Everyone in Athens would ask for news, and I should look a fool to have run off. Besides, I had written to Menekrates that I was coming; he could be trusted at least to have minded his own business, and I would not need to break bread with one of Dion's enemies.

At his door, however, the porter told me he was on tour in Italy; my letter had missed him and lay unread on his table; his wife and sons were at her father's. Wishing once more I had not come, and now travel-weary, I walked round the New Town to find an inn. The porter had expected him home shortly; I would stay awhile in the hope of seeing him. It was windy weather, and I had had enough of the sea.

The city was fuller than ever of party warfare, the leaders chosen in Dion's place each having his faction; they had united briefly in an interest common to them all. I was told that Dion, while they were stoning him out of the city, had pointed towards Ortygia, whose ramparts were crowded with watching men. But no one heeded him.

Having found a quiet clean inn, I went to bed early. But I had had enough to keep me wakeful and, when almost off, was disturbed by someone in the next room weeping. I listened for some time to see if anyone came to comfort her, but she seemed quite alone. It was no affair of mine, whether she was some woman of the house or a hetaira; she must be one or the other, to be by herself here. If she had been noisy, I might have thought less about it; but the way she smothered the sound disturbed me, and I could not rest. People were still about; I found a servant and asked who had the room. A young man, he replied, from Athens.

I went back upstairs. I could have sworn it was a woman—a man's weeping is harsher as a rule—but it explained the wish to hide it. I hesitated no longer, but took my lamp and scratched at the door. The sobbing went on, unheedingly. I tried the latch, and finding it give went quietly in.

All I could see upon the bed was dark hair and a cradling arm. Disturbed by the light, however, my neighbor started up with a gasp, clutching the sheet. Disheveled, with drenched eyes and features blotched by many tears, the face made me stare, it was so like one I knew. "Forgive me," I said, "but I am an Athenian, Nikeratos the tragic actor. They say you come from my city. You are in trouble. Can I help?"

"Niko! Oh, Niko!"

I walked over to the bed. I could scarcely believe my eyes; but they were right.

"Axiothea! In the name of all the gods, what are you doing here?"

She looked as glad to see me as a friendless child its mother; and, more like that than anything else, I sat down and took her in my arms. I had guessed the truth already, before she poured it out. All her men friends were with Dion; she had thought how the world was being changed while she sat at home like a housewife, had quarreled with Lasthenia, who had thought it madness, and slipped away. The voyage had been wretched for her; though often taken for a youth she had never tried to sustain the role, or thought what it would be like on shipboard. Nobody shaves at sea; they had taken her for a eunuch, which she had had to confirm and bear the sailors' jokes. Then, when at last after a bad crossing she got to Syracuse, it had been just in time to see Dion driven out like a dog.

Shaken already by the voyage, she found everything scared her: the soldiers, the beggars, the young drunks coming from the wineshops, the agents who canvassed her for their factions, the pimps offering her girls or boys. Every moment she expected to be caught out and stoned by the crowd. She had meant to join her Academy friends who were with Dion, hoping they would admire her boldness; in this wilderness beyond the olive groves they seemed just men among men, who would despise her folly and find her a burden they were ashamed of. Now in any case they had left for Leontini. She was quite alone.

I told her what I had seen, and that Dion was safe. "I saw him at Assembly," she said. "He has changed, Niko. But who can wonder, among such people?"

"He was born among them. I suppose, in Syracuse, it is hardly his fault he did not know them. If he had, he might have done no better, just given up beforehand. As it is, he and the people are like figures in a tragedy, who come together meaning well, but are born to work each other's ruin. Neither is without good; but they are fated never to find it in one another. Dion has more virtue; but he has suffered less. Only a god could judge justly here."

"Is there justice," she said, "anywhere under the sun?"

"Come, dry your eyes," I said. "You've read too much, my dear, before looking about you. You can take the word of a man who has been poor: goodness is there, and with the world what it is, that's proof enough to my mind that the gods exist; I don't see how else you can account for it. But goodness is like money —a city only has so much; you have to start small and build up the capital. It's no use to overspend the assets, then when the bank goes broke to get bitter and believe in nothing."

"Now you are here, dear Niko," she said, smiling, "I can believe."

"That's better. You never called me that before. Smile again! Here we both are in Syracuse, with time on our hands, and who knows when you'll travel so far again? You can't hide in a hole till you sail home. So wash your face in cold water, get some rest; I want my boy friend to do me credit; and tomorrow we'll see the town. Knock on my wall if anyone tries that door; why didn't you lock it?"

"The bolt is warped; I was afraid to complain, in case the landlord looked too hard."

"Well, now you can leave such things to me. Sleep well."

Next morning I got her out of doors, and we spent some days seeing Syracuse. She had always been a slender girl, without much bosom; the journey had left her far too thin for her sex, but quite interesting for a youth, as some of our acquaintance showed us. If she blushed, I explained that she had been reared by a pro-Spartan father in the strictest decorum. She never spoke before her elders. When we were alone again, neither could help laughing. To keep up the joke, I bought her the latest fashion in keepsakes, a brooch with a flying Eros, and we went everywhere hand in hand, to warn off rivals. Apollodoros was the name she went under.

I showed her the theater and its machines (the caretaker was most obliging) and my gold leopard in the shrine. Then we went down to the waterfront, whence we viewed Ortygia and its catapults, a use for mathematics which surprised her, as it would have done Pythagoras, I daresay. Dion's siege wall was still unfinished; they had not touched it since he left. One end was still rough piles, brush and timber. The garrison inside had raised the flanking walls of the first gatehouse to overlook it. I showed her, under the water-stairs of Ortygia, where the spring of Arethusa comes up fresh into the sea. "They'll never lack water," I said, "but it seems certain they're short of food. It can't last much longer."

"And Herakleides will take the credit. Is that his fleet coming in?"

We watched awhile. "What are they about," I said, "sailing so close in to Ortygia? They must be in catapult range." Just then they struck sail and started rowing. I said, "Those are the enemy's."

A patrol ship in the harbor was making for shore like a scalded cat. People started shouting and running and crowding to the waterfront. I put my arm round Axiothea in case we were pushed apart. "Don't be afraid," I said. "They've no time for us. Herakleides has blundered again. That's a supply fleet for the garrison."

Cheers sounded across the water as the ships moored by the water-stairs. Unloading started at once. The garrison would eat well for some time to come.

As this thought got home to the crowd, there was a furious rush towards the galley slips. After much noise and milling, prows thrust out into the harbor, and oars were seen.

"What use is that?" I said. "Except to save Herakleides' face."

The ships rowed full-speed across the harbor. The freighters kept on off-loading cargo, but the escort triremes came smartly about. It was a brisk engagement, in which the catapults could not be fired for fear of hitting their own side. The end of it was that the Syracusans sank two or three of the warships, and captured four which (without their men, who dived off in time) were towed home in triumph. The freighters, all safe, went on unloading.

It could be seen that not only supplies were going ashore, but soldiers. Before long the guard of the outer gatehouse yelled across to the Syracusans on their wall that the great Campanian captain, Nypsios of Neapolis, had brought his troops; they had better rejoice while they still could. These men were silenced rather sharply by an officer; but in any case, the Syracusans were taking their advice.

I never saw such another public orgy. They were dancing in all the streets, to the piping of flute-girls from the brothels, while they still had legs to dance; the wine flowed like streams in spring. Herakleides was carried about the city like the image of a god; the very oarsmen were feted from house to house until they dropped dead drunk where they were. One would have thought Dionysios and his whole navy had been sunk, and Ortygia stormed. By my guess, they were ashamed in their souls of the way they had treated Dion, and scared, too, to be without him. Now they could love themselves again, and it went to their heads.

I soon took Axiothea back to the inn, after two roaring-drunk men had tried to grab her from me. As we took to our heels, they bawled out, asking who I was to keep all the pretty boys to myself—an oligarch? One of Dion's set?

If it had looked ugly in the streets, it looked worse from the inn roof at nightfall. They now had bonfires to light the revel. The sentries up on the siege wall could be seen with a wineskin big enough for a satyr play; between swigs, they bawled abuse at the enemy on their rampart; who stood listening, quiet as judges in a theater.

Downstairs, the din nearly burst one's ears, the women louder than the men. No one had mended Axiothea's door, so I made her come in with me. She was worn out by now; we seemed like old companions, and when I got her settled on my bed, saying (which was true) that I would not sleep in any case, she made nothing of it. She lay decorously, wrapped in her robe; as by degrees the people drank themselves quiet, she grew drowsy and closed her eyes.

I was getting tired myself, and wondered whether she would notice if I lay down beside her, when suddenly the night was split by a most frightful yelling. I nearly swallowed my heart. I don't think I doubted for a moment what it was. Flinging open the window shutters, I leaned out. The night sky was clear, showing me the top of the siege wall swarming with men. Bodies were falling, ladders waved about as the storming party lowered them over. From the sound, they must have all been over the wall before the sentries woke.

It is the nightmare of every touring actor that he may be caught in some town during a sack. All through my career, by using my head, I had managed to avoid it. Now, without even the excuse of a good role or big contest, here I was. If I had had my wits about me, I should have taken the road before sunset with Axiothea. Never, in my worst dreams, had I seen myself with a woman on my hands at such a time.

She had been slow to stir, having heard so much noise all day; but now she was sitting up and asking, "What it it?" I said, "A sortie from Ortygia. I'm afraid they have forced the siege wall, and you know what that means. My dear, you and I will have to look out for ourselves. Go and get your traveling shoes. Is that your money bag? Tie it round your middle; don't bring anything else. We'll try the roofs. One can get trapped in a place like this."

She was quickly back. The noise was getting closer at a speed that frightened me, but should hardly have surprised me after what I'd seen all evening. Suddenly a great sheet of flame roared up from the crosswall; the Syracusans had fired the timber end. As usual they were too late; the enemy were through and the blaze just lit them on their way.

The roof stairs were outside. We ran down through the inn, where the half-sobered were stumbling about over drunken bodies. The floors were slimy with vomit, and in the clean night air outside the stink clung to our shoes. But it was soon overpowered by the smell of burning. Caught from floating sparks, or started by the raiders, fires were breaking out on house roofs, and showed us the Ortygians pouring through the streets. Already women were shrieking. Axiothea's fingers, icy cold, closed round my wrist.

"We must keep ahead of the crowds," I said, "or we'll be trampled on. The roofs stretch a good way. Gird up your robe, you can't run like that." Seeing her fumble, I did it for her. We clambered along the rooftops, hearing behind us the panic roar of the Syracusans and the Campanian battle yells. Their officers were no longer troubling to keep them in hand. It was plain the town was theirs. Axiothea was behaving very well, keeping up without fuss. I remembered the girls' race at Olympia. When we paused for breath, she said, "Where are we going?"

I had not known myself, but now answered at once, "To the theater." There was a climb to the next roof. When we had hauled each other up, and seen the red glow getting brighter in the sky, I said, "It's as good as anything—full of places to hide in. I can think better there what to do next."

Our line of roofs running out, we had to take to the streets and were caught up in a flying crowd making for the city gates, but we were still ahead of the thickest press. Wherever one could glimpse the outer walls above the houses, they were being overrun by the Ortygians. As we turned off into a side street, I heard a frenzied din from the gate; we had been right not to think of trying it. Here was the theater, just ahead, its tall gilt thyrsos catching the firelight. "Come," I said, "we'll entrust ourselves to Dionysos. I gave him a splendid present, apart from all the work I've done for him. Now he can do something for me."

There was a temple of Apollo near the theater, crowded to the doors with people taking sanctuary. Inside, the god's golden hair glittered by lamplight; I lifted my hand and invoked his blessing. But the temple was full of treasure and of women; I feared it might strain the Campanians' piety. Men don't dread the gods of the conquered like their own. It was Dionysos or nothing.

The theater was quite empty. Like a sounding-bowl, its hollow curve magnified the roar and screeching of the sack. Backstage, it seemed pitch-dark at first, but soon we found the windows gave light enough. In the caretakers' room I poked about and found some food; there was even a wine jar. We took them into the protagonist's dressing room. Neither of us was hungry, but we were glad of the wine. We must have been the only people in all Syracuse who needed any. I said, "Stay here, don't wander about; I am going up on the god-walk, to see what is going on."

I saw nothing, however, the high tiers of the theater cutting off the view; there was just the din, and the glare. I lay down (an actor can't be on the god-walk without feeling twenty thousand eyes on him) to think awhile. I had forgotten, as we came, the splendors of the theater, given by the elder Dionysios for the glory of his plays. There were bronzes and gilded swags wherever you looked; it might not be the first place they thought of looting, but once inside, they would go through it end to end before they put a torch to it. Dionysos, I thought, won't you help your servant? And I remembered the last time I had been up here; it was in *The Bacchae*, appearing as the god to close the play.

I suppose one thought leads to another; but it was just as if he lit up my mind with a flash of lightning. I clambered down and groped my way over to Axiothea, my eyes unused to the dark again. Her hand reached out from the couch; I got up beside her. "I have been thinking," I said, "what to do if they come here." I felt her stiffen like wood, but she did not let out a sound. She was trying hard, poor girl, to follow Plato's precept, Be what you wish to seem.

"Remember," I said, "that these men are Campanians, upcountry peasants from Italy. I don't suppose any of them has been in a real theater; they've only just arrived. It is for us to put them in a proper fear of the god. Come with me, and I'll show you how."

I led her out, among the levers and tackle and big wheels. I have never yet been in a play with special effects without finding out how they work. In Syracuse especially, the machines are so famous it would have been unprofessional not to study them. I knew them all.

"This big one," I said, "is for the thunder. It is heavy, but you must pull it somehow, and keep pulling till you get the thunder-drum to turn; then pull twice more. Then wait till you hear me shout, and do the same again. After that count up to ten and pull this one here. This is for the earthquake."

We went over this several times; then I looked about for the pulley of the sounding board. It must be somewhere up in the dark. I tried this or that, in dread of releasing something that would get us noticed. At last it came down, and I got it fixed. "We mustn't stir from here till morning," I said "so as to be ready. How cold you are. Wait while I look for something warm." There was an old door-curtain among the skene-flats. I pulled it round both our shoulders, and rubbed her hands in case they should be too numb to work. When some shriek more dreadful than the rest, and getting nearer, rose above the din, she crept closer and I took her in my arms. Her thin shoulders were touching, felt like this in the dark.

The sky was covered with fiery smoke which hid the stars; I lost count of how the night was passing. I thought of Thettalos, whom I might have to leave without farewell; she, of Lasthenia, who had begged her not to go. We talked of our lovers, for comfort, holding each other's hands. I kept to myself the thought that if the Campanians were coming here, it had better be before daybreak. It would be long odds against our fooling them in the light.

The night was rent by an outcry that made what had come before seem like a hush. A thousand women seemed to be shrieking at once, amid the death cries of as many men. A child screamed on and on, shriller than a bird. They had found the temple of Apollo. I wrapped the curtain round Axiothea's ears; she pushed out her head to say, "Shall we try the thunder?" I answered, "No. The acoustics only work inside. Poor souls; may the god avenge them."

It took them a good while to go through the temple. After a time, we heard the wails of the women left alive, being dragged off to Ortygia. The child screamed on one note until, I suppose, it died. I looked over Axiothea's head at the sky beyond the window, fancying every moment the first gray of dawn.

Then they came. I could hear their uncouth shouts as they went through the top entrance and found themselves on the upper tiers; bewildered at the strange-shaped precinct, then baying at the loot below. "Let them come down further," I whispered to Axiothea. "Get them all well in, don't play to half a house. I'll make you a sign." By now we could see in the night like cats. I gave her a kiss for luck.

The board at Syracuse has a secret, which you don't learn unless you are in the right play, one like *The Bacchae*, or one with a ghost. Turn it a little to the right, and it catches a shaft to the echo chamber. The noise is dreadful; it is hard to believe a human mouth has made it, even though it's one's own. I waited, getting it placed just right. They were coming down the center steps and scrambling over the seats, a hundred or so; by now looters straggled as they chose. When I saw no more were coming, I gave them still a little longer, to feel the space and quiet. Then I filled my chest, and yelled, "Iakchos! Iakchos!" praying the god in my heart for his gift of terror. He did not fail me. The sounding board was unearthly; but when it came back from the echo chamber, it was like all the Furies in full cry.

All the shouts ceased. I waited, it seemed forever, wondering if the lever had stuck or she had pulled the wrong one. Then came the first peal of thunder, the great drum turning its stones. That sounds too into the echo cave. It is loud enough by day, with a full house to tone it down. In the empty theater, by night, it was beyond belief. Feet started scrambling. I yelled, holding it longer this time. Again the thunder. In the pause before the next effect, I heard them all clattering off like madmen. I doubt if even one stayed on for the earthquake.

I ran back to Axiothea, who stood clutching the earthquake lever as if frozen there, and picked her up in my arms. I remember carrying her over to our heap of curtain, hollowed like a dog's bed. We fell down clinging together, laughing silently, and kissing. I can't, though I have often tried, remember just how it happened; all I know is that we surprised ourselves and one another, yet there seemed nothing strange in it, and it did us good. All was still in the theater; in a little while, as if the god had told us we were in his care, we slept, and did not wake till daybreak. When I had watched in dread for dawn, it cannot have been more than an hour past midnight; such are the illusions of fear.

Doves were cooing in the trees outside; there was still noise from the city, but broken now and further off. Axiothea stirred, and looked at me dazedly, wondering, as I could see, how much she had dreamed of it all; but having been a virgin in respect of men she could not be in doubt for long. I pushed back the hair from her brow and stroked her head, saying, "Well, dear friend, we gave ourselves into the hand of Dionysos, and you know the sort of god he is. After all he did for us, we can't grudge him his little offering. Come, it's another day, and you are Apollodoros once again. You know, nothing that happens at a Dionysia needs to be remembered after."

She shook her head a little, as if to clear it, then kissed me quickly, and started putting her clothes to rights. I went off to find the water tap; her mouth had been as dry as mine.

We found the streets round about all quiet now. The Achradina still held out, and the soldiers had been called back to their work. We picked our way through smoke, ashes and blood. Of what we saw on our way, I have forgotten as much as I am able to—but not the temple of Apollo. It would have been better not to look in. An old priest, with a bandage round his head instead of a bay wreath, wandered round among the corpses, crying like a child with his hands pressed over his mouth, the whole shrine one vast defilement and only he to cleanse it. Somewhere the dying moaned in corners. And on its plinth stood the statue of Apollo, the gold bow wrested from his hand, his head bald as an egg. The gold hair had been made like a wig, just fixed with pins. I don't know why this should have seemed the crown of horror; yet if ever to this day I see a bald young man in the street, my stomach turns.

A dead girl was lying on the threshold in a pool of her blood. My eye was caught by her hair, which I felt I had seen disheveled like this before. So I had. She was Speusippos' little flute-girl, whose wrongs had made up his mind to war. Much good it had brought her.

Axiothea stood beside me in the porch. I tried to pull her away, but she stood her ground. "No. I have been concerned with making laws for men, and have only known the best of them. I've no right to hide from the worst." She went forward, and took a long look. "Now come," I said, "that's enough," and dragged her to the steps by force. In the street she said, "Plato and Dion have both been soldiers. I suppose they knew."

"I'm told it is worse with Carthaginians. This will be just a common sack. Now let's talk of something else, before we fall into despair. Let's talk of the good men we have known; they are real too."

Not to make a long tale of a tedious business, we got out of the city by the northern gate of the New Town, and started walking along the road to Leontini. We had what was left of the caretaker's food to keep us from hunger on the way. The road was not crowded. I suppose few citizens wanted to take refuge in a city filled with Dion's soldiers.

A man stood shouting by the road, a seaman, making his profit as someone does from every disaster, offering at a high price a passage along the coast to Rhegium. Though it was certain the boat would be overloaded, we closed with him at once. Both of us longed for Athens like the babe for the breast.

We were just walking the last stretch of highway before the turnoff to the shore, when the clatter of hooves sent everyone scattering. We looked after the six flying horsemen, wondering what news they carried. One had stared at me as he passed; I heard him call my name to another. Then they all pulled up and rode back.

They were Syracusans, so I waited. A man dismounted; he looked like a gentleman through the dirt and dust. "I am Hellanikos," he said, and told me who the others were. "You are known to Dion. I beg you, in the name of Zeus the Merciful, ride with us to Leontini, and join us when we throw ourselves at his feet. The Achradina has fallen. He is our only hope."

I could hardly credit my ears, even in Syracuse. Not wishing to insult men in misery, I just said, "You cannot suppose he will come. If he would, his men would not. My friend and I have just taken our sea passages for home. I am sorry."

"Niko," said Axiothea, "don't be a fool. Do as they ask. I'll see you in Athens."

She had forced a boy's voice so well, it quite startled me. She pulled me aside. "Go to him. If he is still Dion, he will come."

"Impossible! What man upon earth . . ."

"He despises vengeance; he says it is sharing in the evil. Isn't that what he told you at Delphi?"

"Nikeratos!" someone shouted. "I beg of you. Time presses."

"No, by Zeus! To leave you on the road like a stray dog . . ."

"I came for the cause. Since I could not help, at least don't let me remember that I hindered it. I've learned how to manage on the ship; it will be nothing, after all this. Goodbye, Niko. You have made me a truer philosopher. Go with God."

The men coughed and fidgeted, hiding, since they needed me, their contempt for the silly actor who could not set out without kissing his fancy boy. One of them, who had agreed to stand down because Dion did not know him, gave me his steaming horse. From the bend of the road I looked back at her; but she did not turn, walking with her thin shoulders held straight, down the path to the sea.

# XXI

WE GOT TO LEONTINI AT EVENFALL, WHEN THE
men were strolling in the cool and sitting outside the taverns
under the trees. At our noisy entrance they all came crowding.
When we asked for Dion his own voice answered: he had been
taking the air with Kallippos and his other friends.

We all dismounted and ran to him. While the onlookers stood
on tables or climbed trees to see, we knelt in the pose of sup-
plication. It is a thing one needs training to do with grace. One
man almost fell over.

Hellanikos told the hideous tale without excuses; an old-time,
decent small squire, eating dirt for what he had had no part in
—a clever choice, for an envoy to Dion. Then each of us said
something. His eyes moved from face to face in a kind of wonder; one could not tell what he thought. Not being a Syracusan,
I spoke last. "Sir," I said, "we come before a man more deeply
wronged than Achilles, asking far more than Priam did. But the
city is Syracuse, and the man is Dion."

He gazed down, his face held stiff, swallowing and biting his lip. Then a hard sound came from his throat. I saw that he wept.

When he had mastered his voice, he said, "This does not rest with me alone. The men must judge for themselves. Is the crier here?"

The Assembly met in the theater, as it does at Leontini. Last time I was in it, I had played lead. Now I was an extra; but there is no protagonist I have felt so honored to support. Gladly I would have swept the stage for him.

Hellanikos did his speech again, this time to the soldiers, and we ad-libbed as best we could. Then Dion addressed them. "I have called you here so that you can decide what you think best for you. For me, there is no choice. This is my country. I must go; and if I cannot save her, her ruins shall be my grave. But if you can find it in your hearts to help us, foolish and wretched as we are, you may to your eternal honor still save this unhappy city. If that is too much to ask, then farewell, and all my thanks. May the gods bless you for your past courage, and the kindness you have shown to me. If you speak of me after, say I did not stand by to see you wronged, nor forsake my fellow citizens in disaster."

I don't think he could have gone on, but the cheering drowned his voice. They yelled his name like a war cry, then shouted, "To Syracuse!" I suppose Hellanikos made a speech of thanks; I think he embraced Dion. I could scarcely see for tears.

They stayed only to eat and get their kit; that same night we saw them off on the thirty-mile march to Syracuse. As for me, having served Dionysos all my life, I never bore arms except upon a stage; and this was work for professionals, not walkers-on. But though the boatmen were still hawking passages to Italy, I did not sail. I had witnessed an act of magnanimity it would not be impious to call godlike; I felt a need to know the outcome. Great evil, or great good, seem the concern of every man; they touch our destiny.

This is what happened, as I heard it later from Rupilius. All day in Syracuse the raiders had been plundering, or storming the few street barricades that held out. Herakleides and his officers dashed hither and thither, trying to order their scattered forces; but they could not overtake the wasted hours of drunkenness and panic. At nightfall, like wolves gorged with prey, the men of Ortygia went back over the causeway, to the women they had taken.

The Syracusans crept forth, and spent the night searching for kindred, or patching some shelter from the ruins. Daylight showed the city still their own. They shored up the crosswall with half-charred timbers, and got it manned again. By noon, a rider brought news that Dion was on the way. Are you supposing they flocked to the temples to give thanks? This was Syracuse.

Herakleides took the news as his own death warrant. As it was, the people were blaming him for the debauch rather than themselves; for his petty triumph he had lost the city. If Dion, whom he had driven out, marched in as savior, what could he expect? Perhaps he thought of Philistos. Such men see in others what they know about themselves.

He and his friends rode among the distracted people, crying out that the danger from Ortygia was over; they would be mad to let in a tyrant they had expelled, with his own army, every man hot for vengeance. Fear was the air they breathed; tyranny they had grown up with; it all made sense to them. They dispatched envoys to tell Dion he was not needed, and could go back.

The small gentry, whose forebears had fought the elder Dionysios and paid dear, witnessed in helpless horror the loss of their only hope, together with the rags of their self-respect. They knew why Dion had marched. Since the tyrant crushed their fathers they had kept themselves to themselves; the great estates went to his friends; but a little piece of land, a few rents coming in, had bought them schooling from mainland teachers; they had learned to wrestle by the rules, to sing the old skolions, even to remember honor.

They sent their own envoys, begging Dion's pardon for this last disgrace to Syracuse, praising his greatness of heart, and imploring him not to repent of it. It was madness to suppose that Nypsios' troops were sated yet, or could be contained again. Without Dion all would perish.

Both messages reached him nearly together, and he heeded both. He now ceased to force-march his men; but he still came on. I suppose by now nothing much could surprise him.

At sunset, to keep him out, Herakleides posted troops at the northern gate. But they were called to other business. With the fall of dark, Nypsios' men burst out from Ortygia and poured over the crosswall like a river in spate. This time they had come to destroy the city.

By now, I suppose, Dionysios valued nothing but Ortygia. The city had rejected him; let it perish with its rabble, and if he got back he could repeople it more to his mind. Nypsios and his army must have brought dispatches with them; their leader must have had orders. Perhaps Dionysios now saw himself in the role of Herakles translated; except of course that the pyre was not for him.

Everything worth having had been looted; there was nothing left but to kill. They went through the city not like men but like Gorgons or unpitying Furies, cutting up the women, spitting children on spears or hurling them into burning houses; they brought fire wherever they went, and shot flame arrows at the roofs too high to reach. In that night died Glyke, the wife of Menekrates, and his young sons with their golden skins. It seems she had come back to the city just before Herakleides' victory feast, to prepare for her man's return. I have heard how they died, but have always denied to him that I knew anything, and as far as I know he has not learned it. May the gods keep him ignorant.

The roar of the fires, the incessant screams, like a single cry of the dying city, the crash of falling houses sounded as if the gods had sent Death himself to end mankind. Into this Tartaros came Dion and his men, and were received like rescuing gods. How not? He was brave, generous and noble—true as gold. No one remembered, that night, that it was he who had begun the war.

All night they fought among the smoke and flame and cinders and charred corpses, keeping discipline, holding their lines of communication open, threatened not only by the enemy but by falling walls and beams. Before morning the raiders were driven back. Those who were trapped under the cross-wall were killed where they were found. After that, there were the fires to be put out.

All this Rupilius told me, when he was carted back with the wounded to Leontini. After fighting all night with a burned arm, he had taken a leg wound which went half through the tendon; the doctor forbade him to walk or stand. I repaid a little of his kindness by doing such business for him as was beyond the servants, or reading Greek to him; he only knew it by ear. Dion, he said, had been wounded too, but had fought on, bandaged with a rag torn from the clothes of a corpse, the usual dressing that night. As for Herakleides and his friends, they had gone like ghosts by cockcrow; seeing the temper of the people, they had been wise.

News came in daily to Leontini. When victory was certain, the City Council came to me, offering me a chorus to put on *The Persians,* as a thank-offering to Apollo. I accepted, provided I could find some supporting players alive in Syracuse. I went on this business sooner than I had meant, when we got the news that Herakleides had come and given himself up to Dion, throwing himself upon his mercy.

Rupilius frankly disbelieved it; the teller was offended, and said he would demand an apology in three days' time, when Herakleides and Theodotes were to be tried by the Assembly. I calmed Rupilius by undertaking to be there.

I rode, therefore, from the cool of the hills across the hot dusty plain with its cactuses and aloes, down to Syracuse. Roofs had been patched, corpses and wreckage cleared away; but the place still stank of burning, fear and death. I wondered if they had destroyed the theater in the second raid, but it was unharmed. There was a rumor that it was haunted at night by the vengeful god. At present it was full, since they were using it for Assembly. I was just in time to get a tenth-row seat.

Entering through the orchestra to roars of applause, Dion went up on stage with his brother and Kallippos. Then Herakleides and Theodotes were brought in under guard, with a cordon of soldiers round, to keep the crowd from lynching them. Theodotes had given up and looked like a corpse already; but Herakleides was still giving a performance. He stood upright, brave without defiance, a man whom fate had tricked into folly, who, if he must, would accept his doom without repining. More than ever I could imagine him an actor: talented, but making mischief everywhere and stealing from other artists, till no company would have him.

When the charge had been read, they were given leave to speak in their own defense. Herakleides came forward; I saw his mouth open, but the sound was lost in the howls of anger and shouts of "Death!"

After some while of this, Dion stepped forward; the curses changed to cheers. He held up his hand for silence; they offered it like a garland. Instead of speaking, he led Herakleides forward.

Thus sponsored, he was listened to. He had got the feel of the house; it was his greatest gift. Wisely, he kept it short. Pointing towards Dion, he said this man's virtue had conquered all his former enmity; nothing was left to him, but to appeal to a generosity he had not deserved. In future, if there should be such a thing for him, he hoped he might learn to do so.

The audience jeered. Unlike Dion, they had heard Herakleides on Dion in the past, and guessed what this was worth. Hellanikos, or some old-style squire just like him, jumped up and begged that the city might be delivered from this double-tongued snake. One or two others followed, pointing out that the man had harmed Syracuse more than Dionysios ever did. The shouts for his death redoubled. It was now clear that Dion was about to speak. At once the theater was as quiet as at a tragedy.

"Fellow citizens," he began, "I am a soldier." (Loud applause.) "While I was young here, I trained like other officers in the use of arms, in strategy, and in the care of my troops." (Cheers from the soldiers.) "Then I was sent away; and rather than waste my life in idleness, I took up other studies. I went to the Academy of Athens, which teaches men to be truly men. Instead of Carthaginians, I learned to conquer anger and the lust for vengeance, not to lay down my arms before them or drop the shield of self-command. If we do good to those who have done us favors, where is the merit? The true contest is to do good for evil. Triumph in war is a passing thing; time changes every fortune; but to excel in mercy and in justice is to gain an unfading crown. This is the only victory I wish for over these men; and I believe that if you grant it me, it will enrich us all; for I think no human heart is so lost to the memory of that good our souls were born from long ago, that it cannot be reminded, and its eyes washed clear. Men sin from ignorance of the good; once shown it, they know their happiness. Let us show it now to these men, and I believe they will return it to us, many times over, in the coming years. If I have deserved any kindness from you, men of Syracuse, do not involve me in wrong, but let me go home free of it. Vengeance is for the gods alone."

There was a long, murmuring hush. I thought how if this had been a play, the applause would have stopped the show. It was magnificent, spoken with a whole heart by a man whose voice and presence were equal to every word. And yet I sat here, dry-eyed, in the tenth row, bearing my part in the troubled silence. It had not been so when he spoke at Leontini. Was the fault in me? I still did not know, when next day I sat down by Rupilius to tell my story.

He listened at first with exclamations, then in silence, just like the Syracusans. At last he said, "And they gave the pardon?"

"They did it for Dion. The men went off with their friends. Of course there were speeches first. I left before the end."

He gave a long sigh. "What is it?" I asked. I was asking myself as well, as I suppose he saw. "Do you believe, Nikeratos," he said, "that Herakleides will keep his word?" I shook my head. "Well? Then what's your question?"

"Perhaps Dion was right, even so. He was the victor in virtue."

He leaned over, grunting from a twinge in his wounded leg, and patted my knee. "Don't take offense," he said, "at my plain speaking. A friend to a friend. Dion is the best man I know. I'd die for him, and not wait to ask why. But at bottom, when all's said, he's a Greek. If he had been a Roman, he'd have known why he couldn't pardon Herakleides. In Rome, you'd not be asking yourself."

All Romans are vain of their home customs, even if they can't make a living there and have to hire out their swords. I had become fond of Rupilius. When he saw I was not angry, he went on, "You Greeks, I know, excel us Romans in all the gifts of Apollo. But in the gifts of Jupiter—Zeus, I mean—you sometimes seem like children. It's each man for himself before the city, and each city for itself before Greece. You've come to harm from it often, and you will again. Dion I thought was different. He's never looked out for his life or anything he owned, if the people needed it. But now see what he's done. Because this man was his personal enemy, whom he wants to excel in virtue, he lets him loose on the Syracusans, as if it weren't through him their streets were like a shambles the other day. If he doesn't mend his ways, which Dion, being a man and not a god, can't guarantee, mayn't it be so again? By Hercules, he could at least have insisted on exile! To a Roman's way of looking, he's helped himself to public property, as surely as if he'd put his hand in the treasury. Not that I hold it against him. He's a Greek, he thinks like a Greek; that's all. He's still the best general I ever served under. Perfection is for the gods alone. But the truth's the truth."

I suppose it was knowing we both loved him still that made us able to talk. I said, "He has been like a god, Rupilius. It must be hard to come down. Our greatest sculptors leave some little bit unfinished, or rough, so as not to challenge the gods. Once one has been a god, one must be perfect, and seen to be perfect. I don't know how that seems to you, as a Roman. I'm a Greek. And it frightens me."

# XXII

AT THE NEXT ASSEMBLY, WHEN THE DEAD WERE
scarcely buried and the prisoners just ransomed from Ortygia,
Herakleides proposed that Dion should be offered the title of
supreme commander with full powers. It was the old office
of the Archons. Dion neither agreed nor refused, but left it
to the people. The gentry and middle citizens were for it; the
commons, led by his friends, cheered Herakleides' bigness of
heart, and voted him back into his rank of admiral, with equal
status.

I was rehearsing for *The Persians*, but getting this news in
the agora of Leontini, I brought it straight to Rupilius. "Thundering Jupiter!" he groaned. "The man's not fit to take a grain
fleet across the straits. How did Dion stop it?"

"How could he? He has forgiven Herakleides solemnly, in
public; he has refused supreme power on principle. If he'd
opposed it, he'd have looked suspect both ways."

"And Herakleides knew it. Dion shouldn't have let him live."

"He once said to me that a state is the sum of its citizens; if they have all renounced their private virtue, how can they build a public good? Surely it's true."

"Well? What then?" He felt about for his stick; I put it in his hand.

"I don't know," I said. "Even Plato has gone home to think again. But he's old. He hasn't much time left."

"Plato! Don't name that man to me." He leaned politely over, to spit on the far side of the couch.

At the next Assembly, Herakleides brought up again the redivision of the land, reminding the people it had already been passed once, but not mentioning what had followed. It got a majority vote. Those against were the landowners, large and small, who were also the citizens trained in arms, bearing the brunt of the war. Dion, without wasting words on a formal speech, vetoed it as supreme commander of the land forces. The people went off grumbling, as poor men would anywhere on earth, and Herakleides' faction went among them murmuring, "Tyranny!"

Shortly after this I put on *The Persians*, sharing the leads with Menekrates, who had said that he must work or lose his mind. He had dashed home from Italy, but happily too late to find the bodies of his family. So I paid off the man I had engaged, who did not like it but understood; it was little enough to do for an old friend. I played the Messenger and the Ghost; he did Queen Atossa and Xerxes. It was a bad production. I had not given my mind to it, and was off form myself; the chorus was a scratch one; Menekrates, though I think he saved his reason by purging his grief through this tale of old disasters, gave a poor performance, as actors do when playing from raw emotion instead of considered art. However, as always at these times, the audience was sure that, feeling what he portrayed, he must be superb, and received the play accordingly. He was in tears by the end—no matter, the action called for it—but from then on he could eat and sleep again.

He left Syracuse soon after for Ionia, which was new to him, trying to forget. His house had been burned to the ground, but his money was still buried there in a place he had shown to nobody. I don't suppose the knowledge would have saved his wife, after she had told the soldiers; but they might have killed her more quickly. Since he knew nothing about this, he could find some relief in not being destitute. I myself stayed on a little longer, teaching Rupilius to write Greek. He would soon be on his feet again, but had come to count on me meanwhile; his daughters were married, and he had no sons living. It was a reason to give myself for staying on. I don't know if it was hope or fear that really held me.

Dionysios had settled down in Lokri, his mother's city, up the coast north of Rhegium. It was said he was rarely sober much after sunup. But his captains were, and his fleet was troublesome. So Herakleides' navy sailed north to sweep the straits, and anchored at Messene.

The ships' fighting men were soldiers serving under their own officers in the usual way. They had scarcely made camp when their commander sent dispatches back to warn Dion that Herakleides was working up the fleet to mutiny.

Its men had always served under him; he had won their favor by slack discipline; they did not know Dion like the troops. In Syracuse as elsewhere, the seamen are poorer than the citizen soldiers, who have their own panoplies to find. All sailors are democrats; but ours in Athens are used to public business, and have heard promises from too many demagogues to take them all on trust. These men had had less practice. Herakleides was telling them that whereas their old tyrant had been too sottish to do worse than neglect them, their new one was cold sober, and would never let them be.

The soldiers being loyal one and all to Dion, the whole expedition was almost in a state of war. Soldiers and sailors would wreck any wineshop where they met. The officers meantime were watching Herakleides like dogs around a foxhole. A doubtful messenger was pounced on; it turned out he was treating with Dionysios.

On this, they faced him with it, threatening to march their men back and accuse him if he would not sail home. This he was forced to do, just at the time when Dionysios sent a mercenary army, Spartan-officered, across to Sicily. They met no trouble from Herakleides' ships, and got ashore near Akragas.

Rupilius was hobbling about by now, but could not have marched across his garden. I thought he would kill himself when this news came in, trying to drill himself into fighting shape. I felt a fool running about after him, trying to make him rest, while he held himself back from asking what I knew about such things. The wound started to look angry, the doctor angrier still. He had put himself back instead of forward, and would have wept, I think, if Romans ever did.

Leontini is the sort of small town in which an Athenian feels mewed up; I soon found business to take me into Syracuse. The city looked dreadful, full of rat-ridden rubble with people squatting under wattles, hurdles or hides. The theater tavern, in order to keep open, was selling raw wine to anyone who came by; there was not an actor to be seen. Still, it was where Dion was and things were happening. He was never seen, he just sent out orders; but the factions from Messene had come back here to breed. Street fights were three a day. There were always soldiers marching about to clear the streets; often the sailors met them, stoning them or trying to hold them up.

I met in the street Timonides of the Academy, that same man who wrote the history later, and who was now keeping Plato posted with the news. Though I hardly knew him, our being Athenians, here, made us greet like friends. He was a small wiry man, with a high bald head now covered by a helmet. He told me the force of Dionysios was digging in, and Herakleides kept urging that the army should march to meet it, though a child could see it would be madness as things were. As with the land division, it was left to Dion to say no. Herakleides then accused him of dragging out the war, to prolong his time in power.

"But," I said, edging him out from under a stoa with three broken columns, which looked about to fall down, "why isn't this man brought to trial? Not only has he broken solemn pledges made in public; he is now a traitor to the city three times over."

"Not unless the citizens say so. If not, who can try him?"

Timonides was yellow from a recent fever, as thin as a wasp, and as tetchy. "I have told Dion," he burst out. "All of us have told him, he put himself in this dilemma when he pardoned the man at first. Moral logic, statesmanship, the common sense of a country housewife—show me even one of them in it, I said to him, even one. But no, he freezes and taps the table. He is Dion and won't be less; and there's an end . . . Law, the assent of the citizens, justice—after the sack, when the man was tried, he had them all behind him. And now what's left for him? Only to say like old Dionysios, 'To the quarries, because I so command.' Can you see it? He'd as soon tumble a whore in public. He's tied hand and foot. We all know it. He knows it. Even more to the purpose, Herakleides knows it. What can we do? Just pray the fellow gets killed in battle. My dear Nikeratos, I pray it daily, to every god I think will listen."

"What battle? Since you can't set out because of this?"

"Oh, we shall set out. Dion won't endure the imputations of cowardice and of tyranny."

"*Cowardice?*" I said.

"Oh, yes, yes. People forget. Don't you find in your calling that the crowd forgets?"

"It's a cold world you show me, Timonides," I said.

"Well, that's nothing new. We must all do the thing we can . . . 'Know yourself.' 'Nothing too much.' There's truth in these old saws." He had taken leave of me when he turned back to say, "He's a good man. One of the best of our time. If he could only question it, like Sokrates, then he would be great."

Sure enough the expedition set out against Dionysios' troops, the fleet coastwise, the troops inland. They were gone some weeks, with nothing settled either way. Rupilius began walking again, telling everyone, though it was now clear he would be lame for life, that he would soon be in the field. Then came word that Dion, with all the cavalry, had come galloping back to the city on almost foundered horses. He shut the gates and manned the walls; the man who brought us the news had been kept inside till morning. Word had come to Dion just in time that Herakleides was sailing back with the fleet to seize Syracuse. Finding himself forestalled, he made a peaceful entry, pretending he had heard Dionysios' fleet was sighted. Every one knew the truth, but no one could prove it.

The trouble was now bruited all over Greece. The Spartans in fact, with their ancient insolence, just as if they were still the masters of Hellas, sent over a general to take charge of Syracuse because its leaders could not agree. Herakleides got to him first with a pack of lies, but though a Spartan he had sense enough to look about for himself. Having done so, he declared for Dion. Herakleides had made so sure of the man, he had publicly welcomed his arbitration. So at the Spartan's instance, he now had to go into a temple and vow to mend his ways. This contented the Spartan, who went home. They are a simple, pious folk.

Soon after this I heard from Thettalos, asking if I had gone mad to linger on in a cauldron of trouble like Sicily, by my- self and without work. Had I found a new lover, as he was starting to suppose? His letter was full of theater news, neatly planned to make my feet itch for home. What indeed was I doing here, putting on plays at local festivals (I had just done *Niobe* at Katana) and watching great hopes withering? I wrote back that I was sailing as soon as I could, with un- changed heart. This was true; there had been a curly-haired, Roman-Greek lad for a while in Leontini, but nothing seri- ous.

I had now been so long from Athens, I knew I must take care to come back on a good ship, looking like someone. So I let go the first I might have caught, because it carried hides. Some god must have guided me. It was wrecked off Lokri, with half its people drowned. And, just after I would have gone, Ortygia surrendered.

Since Herakleides had been brought to heel, the blockade had been kept tight. The gatehouse guards had stopped sing- ing. A deserter who had swum across by night revealed that they had eaten the elephant, though it was at least forty years old. Even then no one dared voice his hopes till the envoy came from Apollokrates. He agreed to give up Ortygia, with its standing army, navy, war engines and all, in exchange for a safe-conduct covering five triremes, to take away his mother and sisters with their things. It seems Dionysios had left these ladies behind when he ran away. To do him justice, he may have feared being attacked at sea.

Anyone in Syracuse who had friends within reach of the city sent them word to be there on the great day. Rupilius and I got early news, and went in overnight to be sure of good places near the sea. All at once the half-ruined city seemed to burst out with life. Porches hanging askew and propped with logs were now adorned with garlands; skinny children stuck flowers in their hair and danced in lines down the streets. All the hetairas put on their thinnest silk dresses, like naked-ness but prettier, and drove shoreward in painted carriages, singing to the lyre. Boys hung on the palm trees as thick as date clusters. At every altar the priests were offering libations and wreathing the statues of the gods.

It was a bright day with fair wind; light gleamed on the unfurling sails and flashed from the dripping oar blades. Dion boarded the escort ship which saw off the last of the tyrants' line. The trumpets sounded from the walls, and the cheers rolled like surf along the shore. Old men stood weeping; young men danced, and threw each other in the air. The gates of Ortygia stood wide and unguarded, after fifty years.

Timonides, whom I saw before I sailed, told me that as Dion reached the palace, his mother came out to meet him, leading his son by the hand. Behind them his wife, a woman with graying hair who must have seemed like a stranger, walked in tears. Since her second husband had fled before Dion, she had lived on in Ortygia, the wife of two men and of none. His mother, a noble old woman with the family's fine bones, and little more of her left, led forth this poor soul by the hand, asking if Dion wished to receive her as his kinswoman, which she was by right of birth, or as his wife, which in her heart she had always been. Dion behaved superbly. If one were writing a play to show him at his best, one might con-trive some such scene. He embraced and kissed her tenderly, committed the boy into her care, and had her led to his house with honor. Timonides, wiping his nose when he recalled it, said there was not a dry eye as far as you could look.

"How did young Hipparinos take it?"

"He looked frightened, and sullen. But he may simply have been overwhelmed by the occasion. He is only sixteen or so; plenty of time to correct his upbringing."

"Of course," I said. For the play must close here, with the victory procession, the wife restored, the hero at the height of honor, the chorus singing praises, the happy audience going home. I could sail back to Athens, the first with the good news. A long piece of my life, which sometimes had caught up my very soul, was ending in a paean of joy.

Next day, or the day after, I went to pay my respects to Dion, as everyone of consequence was doing. He saw us a dozen at a time; I had expected nothing else, so great was the press; my only wish was to wish him joy. He met us in a plain white robe, simple even for him. In the time of the factions, he had lost weight; but it just showed up the splendid bones of his face, now lit with his fulfillment. He was the savior of his people, had avenged his exile and his wife's wrongs, conquered a base enemy without once sinking into baseness. He was Dion, and never had been less.

He singled me out for a greeting, saying he had given me short thanks on the Leontini road. His kindness touched me; he had forgiven me my calling, in the fullness of his heart. The plain room was brimmed with happiness and triumph, like a beautiful krater filled with wine.

Some close friends stood round, who would stay when the rest had gone: Timonides, longing, I expect, to be off and write up his history, and Kallippos of Athens, the tyrant-hater, who had long been Dion's right-hand man. I wondered how he felt when he saw Ortygia empty. His pale eyes wandered, as if looking for something he had lost.

It was time to go. I took a last look at Dion, smiling among his friends, and there came into my mind the story of the old Olympic victor who saw both of his sons crowned in one year. "Die now!" the people cried to him, meaning that no moment of his life to come could equal this. I stood in the doorway, though my exit was already made, looking at his stern happy face, and a voice in my soul, which I could not silence, said, Die now, Dion. Die!

I brushed it from my mind—one must avoid words of ill omen—and went off to take my ship.

# XXIII

I WAS BUSY THAT YEAR. I CAME BACK TO HEAR
what everyone else had been doing while I was out of the way.
Thettalos, as he confessed, had had an affair with a youth in
Corinth. Nonetheless we met again with joy, forgave each
other, and talked two days without stopping. It is always so
when we've been apart, and time does not change it.

Rumor had it that I had been on secret missions in Sicily, to
keep me there so long. I held my peace and was praised for
discretion. While I was away, Thettalos had been put on the
protagonists' list, and at the Dionysia for the first time we
were in rival plays, he as Troilos, I as Ulysses. Each knew he
would do his best and there would be no repining; we had
outgrown such follies. I won, on a divided vote; his turn would
be soon. At the feast, we got so taken up with talking about
technique (he could at last direct, and it had been a striking
production) that our friends had to drag us apart. I had nearly
forgotten whose the party was.

We decided to tour as partners for a while, and went to

Ephesos. Once every few years it is a joy to tour with Thettalos; after that, one needs a year or two to get one's breath. Between his work and his escapades, the days are full and there is not much left of the nights. In his art he pleases himself; in his adventures he always asks my advice, and is as grateful as if he took it.

Here and there we heard news of Sicily: that Dion was still in power; that Dionysios had not tried to return, though much detested in Lokri for his beastly drunkenness and debauching of the local girls. Both armies still served in Syracuse; Dion had packed off Nypsios' men but kept the rest. The city had never been so well defended since old Dionysios' day. Dion himself still lived by Pythagoras' chaste and simple rule.

I heard no more than this; perhaps because I did not ask. The play was over. The hero lives on in honor; the audience knows it; but the theater is empty, and the sweepers have moved in. It is the time for memory.

Returning by way of Delos, we stayed for the feast of Apollo, and put on *The Hyperboreans,* the setting of which is the island. It was during rehearsals, on one of those dazzling, scorching Delian days, that walking on the Lion Terrace by the lake to get the breeze, we met Chairemon the poet. He had taken care never to go back to Syracuse since he had been Dionysios' guest, but having spent a whole month there at that time, was reckoned an authority on its affairs. We now heard once more the tale of his adventures, which everyone in Athens knew by heart, except for the touching-up added each time to prove his hatred of tyranny. At the end he said, "Unhappy people! Ever since their cruelty to Nikias' men in our fathers' day, they seem under a curse."

"But now," I said, "the Erinyes have relented."

"Do tell us," said Thettalos, breaking in, "is your new play ready?"

Chairemon never liked being interrupted, even with flattery. He turned back to me. "That we wait to see. It seems that, but for the palace orgies, everything goes on much the same."

"Come," I said, "they are living now under law."

"There is a constitutional council sitting. One can't expect

a statute book overnight, of course. Meantime, military government still continues."

"That could hardly be helped. Well, the people no longer
have to pay for Dionysios' parties."

"Taxes are still heavy, I hear. There are the troops to be
maintained. *They* have nothing to complain of—strict discipline, but looked after—none of young Dionysios' meanness.
And then, of course, all who helped Dion to power have been
treated well. He was always generous, even in exile; but it's
grown beyond what anyone could meet from a private purse.
Well, he's supreme commander, he can do what he chooses.
No one accuses him of spending on himself."

"Herakleides has really kept those vows, then?"

"Herakleides!" He looked surprised, and pleased to be better
informed. "He can't choose, where he is now."

"Niko," said Thettalos, "the flute-player will be there waiting.
You wanted that bit of recitative gone over."

"What!" I cried, "Herakleides dead? A blessing to everyone.
The gods owed Dion that."

Chairemon lifted his brows. "The gods help him who helps
himself. In that sense, you may be right."

"Very true," said Thettalos. "You will have to excuse us,
Chairemon. We—"

"No," I said. "Wait. Chairemon—how did he die?"

"He was stabbed to death in his house, by some gentlemen
of ancient lineage who had been waiting a year for leave to
do it. This was withheld, till he moved at Assembly that Ortygia be dismantled and its walls pulled down, as a den of tyranny fortified against the people. They, it seems, had expected
this from the time it was surrendered; and Herakleides was
getting increased support. It was thought unwise to try him
publicly . . . Appalling, dreadful. But that is Sicily. One has
ceased to expect Greek ethics there. One might as well be in
Macedon."

Thettalos, who had been drawing me off, stood quiet, with
his hand on my arm. It is a mistake to think, as some people
do, that he has no discretion.

"My dear Chairemon!" I said. "The deed doesn't surprise

me; but I'll believe that Dion gave it countenance when I see water run uphill."

"I assure you, I had it from Damon the banker, who was there on business, a very sober man. Dion as good as owned to it in the funeral oration, but said it was necessary for the sake of the city."

"What funeral oration?" I heard my own voice, sounding stupid. "Who spoke it?"

"Dion, as I said. He gave him a state funeral, because of his past services, and made the speech himself . . . You are feeling the heat, Nikeratos. This is the fiercest sun in Greece. Let's go under the stoa."

"We must get on," said Thettalos, shoving me. "A rehearsal call." Chairemon said he would walk with us to the theater. The streets were hotter than the terrace. Thettalos walked in the middle, to give me quiet. I heard Chairemon say to him, "I daresay this self-sufficiency has grown on Dion since his son died. He has no other."

I woke from my daze. "Has he lost his son?"

"Say rather he never regained him. He had acquired all the tastes of his uncle, and did not like correction. It must have been a trial to Dion, both as a father and a public man. They say he was somewhat severe. One can't believe all one hears; it may not be true the boy threw himself off his father's roof. Very likely he was drunk, and stumbled."

The skeneroom seemed dark after the brilliant light outside. Thettalos had packed off Chairemon at the door. "My dear," he said, "I wish I'd told you in Samos. But it was the night before the performance when I heard; there was no sense in upsetting you; and then I kept thinking some better news would overtake it."

"He did it for the city," I said. "Or so he saw it. How he must have suffered! But the oration, the state funeral . . . Who could conceive such a thing?"

Thettalos said in his lovely voice, *"The god for his presumption struck him down, But then, relenting, raised him to the stars.* That's how I think he conceived it. Come, Niko, let's work, or you'll get no sleep tonight."

I had been back in Athens some weeks when I heard from Speusippos, asking me to see him at the Academy.

I had been keeping away, mostly because Axiothea was still so shy of me. The memory of our Dionysia confused her, and brought back too much else of that night. The look into the temple had been more than her soul could bear, and she had thrown herself into philosophy, trying to understand why the gods allowed it. She said it was better than the peace of ignorance, and no doubt she knew best. But it was a good while after this before we had our old ease together. Meantime, after having made sure I had not got her with child, I did not intrude. Lately, too, I had been afraid of hearing any more news from Syracuse. This summons disturbed me, for Speusippos did not entertain at the Academy, and there was only one sort of business in which I would be of use.

"Niko," he said as soon as we were alone, "have you any engagements in Sicily?"

Once I would have answered yes, whether it was true or not. But I shook my head, and waited.

"Then," he said, "I can only beg you, if you are my friend, if you love Dion, to make some pretext for going. None of us is expected there; a sudden visit would look strange, and might hasten the very thing we fear." He picked up a letter from his table. Still I did not say that I would take it, but looked at him and waited. When he saw he would have to tell me more, he said, "Plato asked me to keep it as secret as I could. This man, you understand, has been at the Academy; never really one of ourselves, but the world doesn't make such distinctions. The truth is, we have fears for Dion, even for his life. Not from known enemies, whom he can well deal with, but from a trusted friend."

"Kallippos?"

"What?" he cried, almost jumping up in his chair. "You knew?"

"Only now. I should have known. He is a man in love with hatred. He has lost Dionysios; where else can he look? I saw it in his face, if I had only understood it."

"We have heard from friends at Tarentum. Someone who

had been sounded came to warn them. He said he had first warned Dion himself; but Dion would not believe him. Now you see what I ask of you, and why."

"Yes," I said. "I'll go. Dion deserves that much of his fellow men."

He looked at me with sadness; as I suppose I had looked at him. "You have heard, then. Try, Niko, to think of him as a man trapped not by any baseness in his soul, but by its magnanimity."

"I do. It comes easily to an actor. Tragedy is full of it."

"He is accused of prolonging his own authority. This I am sure is unjust. Plato and I have sent out a draft constitution, the best that the city as it is will bear; Corinth has sent advisers too. But where there's justice, no one gets all he wants to everyone else's loss. Such things take time to agree on; there has been faction and distrust; Herakleides left his legacy."

"What will Dion be, in the end?"

"A constitutional king."

Even now the word sang in my ears like a great line in a play. I said, "Surely it was ordained by heaven."

"A king under law. He will have no powers of punishment; those are vested in the judges. There will be a senate, and some form of consultation with the people, not yet determined."

"That's where it rubs?"

"How not? Don't tell anyone in Syracuse, except Dion, that you come from us—for your own sake, as well as his."

"I will take good care. I have known Kallippos a long time."

"There is a great freight of human good," he said, "almost safe in harbor. You may yet save it for the world, Niko. Go with God."

The year was turning mildly. The ship labored through calm seas under oars. At evening the sky was pale red above a pale blue horizon; the ruddy hair of the Thracian rowers smoldered like embers. Their chantyman sang endlessly, an air like a breaking wave, mounting in a wail, crashing with the oar stroke. We were three days late at Syracuse, but I lost the sense of passing time in the space and quiet of the sea. At night I would look at the low stars turning, not knowing if I fell asleep late or soon. For the first time since boyhood, I had no wish to end the voyage.

Syracuse had been cleared of rubble and almost rebuilt. Everything seemed quiet. The same thin-legged, swag-bellied children were scavenging among the pi-dogs. Now, though, when a carriage passed they would sometimes chuck a stone after it. They would not have dared before.

I went to the theater tavern, to account for my presence with the story I had prepared: I had been told that now things were settled down here, the theater was not getting as much encouragement as it should. Athenian actors were concerned about it, and I had come to see, before any of us risked capital on the journey. I talked vaguely of looking out for talent. This brought the answers I needed. There were still plays at the greater festivals; but as the Commander never went, those who liked to stand well with him also stayed away. In Athens, choregos duties are a tax levy on rich men; in Syracuse they had just done it for the glory, or to please the Archons. Some could afford it no longer; others would not, without hope of gaining by it. Theater was as good as dead, except that Kallippos the Athenian had lately sponsored *The Offering Bearers*, which had pleased the people and given a few artists work.

I thought it was just the play for him, all hate and vengeance. Then I was approached by a group of young actors, all eager to get out of Syracuse, and was busy till it was time to find an inn. My former one was still standing. They gave me the room that had been Axiothea's.

I had refused evening invitations, meaning to be up early, and was going to bed when my host announced a visitor. It was Kallippos.

He was now a man of importance here; it would have been natural, if he wanted to see me, to invite me to wait on him at his house. With some men, I should have thought this unassuming; with him I thought that he would take more care, if it were not near the time.

He was just as I had remembered him at home, when he came sniffing about backstage, except for a certain tautness which he was trying to hide. He asked after my career, and I thought as usual that he was waiting for me to relate some harm that had been done me, so that he could be angry, and that for having no grievance he liked me less. However, this time he did not much care; he was hurrying through the civilities. To help him on, I told him how sorry I was for the artists of Syracuse in their hard times. It was sad, I said, to think they had done better under a tyranny than now with enlightened rule.

At once he began to feel his way with me. It was the only time I have been approached with such a purpose, and I hope the last. It was like some suitor who disgusts one, starting to stroke one on the supper couch, beginning as if by chance. There however one can move aside, whereas I had to pretend to like it. He began with faint praise of Dion, going on to disappointment and faint excuses. I replied that all this confirmed what I'd heard; I did not say of whom. Then, casting off all disguise, he said it was certain Dion had brought war to the city only to take the tyranny for himself. "We of the Academy" —I could picture Speusippos white with anger—"have been most bitterly deceived."

I said this was terrible news; that if he wished, I could see Speusippos in Athens and tell him; or would he like me to carry a letter? I was anxious to see if this frightened him; if it did, his plans might not be too far advanced.

"I should welcome it," he said. "You, with your knowledge of Syracuse, would be believed. You have watched this man's career; you have seen the tyrant within the egg tap on the shell and crack it, and start to look about for food. You have seen the beginning . . . are you staying with us long?"

He did not ask idly. I felt my hands grow cold and damp, for he had meant me to understand. His pale eyes waited. I knew, as if I saw through his clothes, that he had a knife on him, in case I showed he had said too much. Why did he think he could kill in the city and not answer for it? That told more than all.

I now had to act for my life; to seem well disposed without seeing his purpose. He wanted me to justify him to the Academy. If I seemed to consent, he would be encouraged. I could think of nothing a man like me could say to him which might persuade him to delay.

So I became full of my own affairs, which surprises no one in an actor. I told him about a play I had just read, how I would direct it unless I changed my mind, what Syracusan actors I might take on, consulting him about each. I told him I had meant to call on Dion on behalf of us artists, asking him for his patronage, but now could not make up my mind to it after what I'd heard; I must sleep on it and think again. He soon had enough of this, and got ready to go. To see him off smoothly, I commended his reviving that fine old play, *The Offering Bearers*. He paused at the door with a meaning smile. "It was a comfort, I think, to those who mourned for Herakleides. And it reminded them that the mourners for Agamemnon did more than weep."

I scarcely closed my eyes all night. Knowing Dion always rose at dawn, I got up in the dark so as to lose no time. He had gone back, as I knew already, to his old house in Ortygia.

The gatehouses were still manned. The guards were civil, though, and only asked my business; one did not need a pass. No one had followed me there. I must have persuaded Kallippos he need not trouble.

Dion's house looked the same as ever, well kept, simple and clean. This time no lively boy came peeping. I looked at the roof; on the side where the slope fell away, it was a long way down.

At the door the porter told me I had just missed the master. He had gone up to the palace, to start the business of the day.

In the porch, between the red lions of Samian marble, a sturdy Argive with polished armor saluted and took my name. He led me in, though I had no need of it. I knew the way so well my feet could have taken me by themselves.

The clothes racks were gone from the searching room. It was just an antechamber, with a few people waiting already, early though it was. I remembered the faces one had seen hereabouts in the old days: frightened, or insolent, or cunning; faces that watched each other, eager faces of flatterers. They were gone; but the new ones were not those of happy men. Worry, resentment, impatience, long-suffering duty, all these I saw. I did not see hope or dedication. I did not see a smile, or love.

However, I had not long to look; almost at once a clerk came out to say the Commander would see me. I went in, hearing angry mutters from those who had come first. The gilt bronze grille stood open. I entered the room I had not seen for a dozen years.

All the gaudy trimmings had gone. It was almost bare; there was only one bit of furniture that I remembered. Dionysios couldn't take that off to Lokri; it would have sunk the ship. It stood in its place, on its bronze winged sphinxes, solid as a tomb, just where it had been when its first owner sat at it to write *Hector's Ransom*. Behind it, in a good plain chair of polished wood, was the master of Ortygia.

I would hardly have known him. His hair was almost white. He had never carried spare flesh, but his body had had the athlete's hard smoothness. He was lean now; the loose skin on his arms dragged about his battle-scars. He might have been sixty; but he had shaved his beard, perhaps to try and look younger, as aging leaders must if they can. Between his strong cheekbones and the fine arched brow above, the skin of the eyelids looked brown and creased, with blue shadows under; the inner ends of his eyebrows were drawn together in a fixed frown he no longer seemed to feel. His dark eyes looked at me with a kind of hunger—for what? For old years, for some simple comfort of man to man, for a message of good tidings? I don't know; he put the need aside, whatever it was, with an air of habit. He had been weak in sending for me first, and was angry with himself, but too just to turn it on me.

He stood up. I was from Athens, where citizens are not kept standing before seated men. It was the courtesy of a king to one who had been his host in exile. We were going, I suppose, through the formalities of greeting. I remember only his face. A king, I had said; he will be king at last; the gods ordained it. Well, now I looked on it; the name was nothing, here was the thing. Always, when I had pictured it, I had seen him as on that day in Delphi long ago, when he came into the skeneroom like the statue of a victor. I had seen his face like the antique masks of Apollo, which stamp on youth the wisdom and strength of manhood. Now I stood before a king—an old king weary of the burden, stained by the sins that power forces men's hands to when they dare not lay it down, bearing their shame with his other cares in a stubborn fortitude, the familiar of loneliness, forgotten by hope.

The godlike mask was off; as with the lover of my boyhood, it was I who had put it on him for my own need. Who does not dream of clear water when the springs are brack? But I had only dreamed; he had tried to bring the dream to pass. Now he had all which if he had sunk his soul to evil could have made him glad. Old Dionysios had had it and died content. He suffered because he had loved the good, and still longed after it. And I thought, I too am marked with my trade. Next time I play Theseus in the Underworld, I shall remember him.

"Sir," I said, "I've a letter here from Speusippos; may I beg you to read it soon? Since I came here myself, I've learned that the warning in it is true. The man it names has approached me. He is planning an armed revolt, which is almost ready. He intends your death."

He heard me steadily, without change of color, nodded, and held out his hand for it. I think he would have asked me to sit while he read it, then remembered there was no other chair and went on standing himself. It was a fairly long letter, but he skimmed it quickly, looking for something; when he had found that, he laid it aside.

"It seems," he said, "that Speusippos told you what he had heard. It was only Kallippos you were warned of? No one else?"

"Only him. I knew him in Athens. He took less care with me than I expect he did at the Academy. He is a dangerous man."

"Subtle, let us say, and capable." He smiled at me, the smile of a king to a simple fellow who means well. "Set your mind at rest, Nikeratos. If Kallippos is dangerous, it is only to my enemies. I shall give you a letter for Speusippos, if you will be good enough to carry it, which will reassure him."

I was alarmed, rather than surprised by this. Men expect of others what they know of themselves, I thought. So I described to him all last night's talk, leaving nothing out, even what might insult or wound him. The thing had gone beyond delicacy.

"Yes, yes." He sounded indulgent. I could hardly believe my ears. "As I told you, he is a subtle man. For some time he has made it his business to test people in the city whose loyalty he feels doubt of. Of course he asked my leave; someone he tested might, as you and others have done, loyally report to me. I am sorry he so mistook you, Nikeratos. But now you understand and I hope are satisfied. Thank you nonetheless for your good will."

I said something. I believe I even apologized. My whole body seemed one grief. All was gone—the bronze-hard honor, the pride of Achilles, pure as fire. There was just an old king, fallen to the sad needs of sick power, who had learned to use a man like Kallippos as a spy.

I said whatever I said, and waited for leave to go. Yet he kept me back, asking things about Athens, with that hunger in his face again. I had never known him to talk for the sake of talking. He was alone, and would always be; perhaps even the memory of other days was something.

"You may assure Speusippos," he said, "that his fears are groundless. Even my own wife and mother were deceived, and I could not reassure them. Kallippos did so, however, by taking the holy oath of Demeter in the sacred grove. You must understand, Nikeratos, that Syracuse is not Athens."

I thought of the road to Leontini and answered, "No."

"These people are my charge. Fickle, foolish, cowardly, abject as they are, my forebears helped to make them so. I must save them in spite of themselves, and give them time to grow before the Carthaginians make them slaves forever. You do not know, Nikeratos, you who show kings and rulers at a simple crux of fate, the base means men require of those who would rescue them from their baseness. Do you know they have wanted me to pull down the monument of the elder Dionysios, the father of my wife, the man who for all his faults loved me more than his own son, for he trusted his life to me alone? Can they think I would buy their love so sordidly?"

"We must respect the dead," I answered. "They are helpless, as one day we shall be."

"Helpless?" he said, staring at me out of his sunken eyes. "You think so? You hold with Pythagoras that they sleep in Limbo, till they are brought before the Judges to choose their own expiation? You don't believe in dead men's vengeance, the stuff of all your tragedies?"

"I don't know, sir," I said. "All actors are superstitious. But I think I would rather leave it to the gods. They know more of the truth."

"You are right," he said. "That is the answer of philosophy . . . I had a strange dream yesterday, if one can say one dreams when one is waking. I was reading in my study, when my eye was caught by some movement. I looked up; at the end of the room was an old woman with a broom, sweeping the floor. No servant would do so in my presence; as I looked in surprise, she turned towards me. She had a face, Nikeratos, like the masks of the Furies in *The Eumenides*, more dreadful than I can describe. The mask was alive, with eyes like green-burning embers; and the snakes moved in her hair."

I saw sweat on his brow. With almost any man I knew, I would have gone up and laid my arm across his shoulders; but of course I knew I could not. "Sir," I said, "you have been spending yourself night and day for the city, without getting much thanks for it to ease your heart. You dozed, I expect, as you read, and dreamed of some fright in childhood. When those masks come on, I've heard of women miscarrying in the theater. In my opinion, no young child should see the play at all."

He smiled, chiefly from pride, but I saw in it too a certain kindness. He was about to dismiss me. Suddenly—I suppose

it was his words of ill omen—I was possessed by the thought
that I should never see him more. Like a fool I exclaimed,
"Sir—remember how happy you were at Athens. Everyone
there honors your name. Why don't you come back to the
Academy? Think what joy it would give to Plato."

He drew himself up, if that was possible for a man who still
held himself straight as a spear. His brows lifted; for a moment
in the old worn face I saw the imperious youth I had glimpsed
at Delphi. "To Plato? To come running like a coward, with
nothing achieved save to have changed tyranny for chaos—
back to Plato, who three times risked his life here for my cause
and me? I had rather have died unborn, than return from
battle a man who threw away his shield."

"You speak like Dion, and I see it must be so. Forgive me,
sir; but since Kallippos thinks you are in danger, don't people
see you too easily? I had not much trouble in getting in—not
like the old days."

"The old days?" he said. "I hope not, or why am I here?
Better death before this day's sunset, than such a life."

He said a few words more, promising me the letter for
Speusippos if I would come back tomorrow, then wished me
goodbye. I went away thinking, Well, then, after all I am sure
of seeing him again.

I went about the town, saw one or two friends, and was told
that a certain young actor, who I had been told had promise,
had been seeking me. It seemed a pity not to see him, so in
the evening I went to the theater wineshop.

Through lack of custom, they were still serving all kinds of
people; it was not the pleasant place it used to be. The long
table at the bottom end was full of soldiers, young Greeks
with their heads together, talking quietly. They looked strong
young louts; when such men are quiet, one always suspects
mischief. Just as I had been served my wine, a man got up
from among them and went out. I recognized Kallippos. If
the wretched fellows had been foolish, then, they would soon
be sorry.

They went on talking in a huddle; they were in street dress, without their arms, so I supposed could not be up to much harm just now; yet they were neighbors I did not like, and I decided I would wait no longer. I had almost stood up, when a man of about fifty, who had been sitting alone in a corner, crossed to my table. "Nikeratos," he said, "I have been making up my mind whether to greet you, or if you would remember me after so long."

He had a kind, gentle, failed-looking face, which must once have been handsome. I could not recall if we had met, but liking the look of him, I murmured something. He went on, "No, of course you could not; you were just a boy, walking on in your father's plays. But I would have known you anywhere . . . Once, long ago, we met to read *The Myrmidons.*"

"Ariston!" I said, and grasped his hands. It was like meeting a stranger; I had forgotten our love like a dream; but all through these years I had cherished gratitude. It was his kindness I had remembered.

He told me he had been touring each time I came before. I don't think it was true; I think he had been out of work, and was afraid of seeming to trade upon the past. Never having heard his name in Syracuse, I had thought he must be dead; but it was just that he was not a very good actor. His robe was darned; he looked hungry, but had bought his own drink before he spoke to me. I suppose that now, when no one had work in the city, it had come easier.

I resolved at once that I would take care of him, get him to Athens, and find him something; but that must come later, for he was a man with self-respect. So we talked of the past, and so on, while at the long table the young soldiers muttered together, or laughed sharply like boys up to something bad which frightens them, but not enough to make them cry off.

Once I heard something, some phrase I can't bring back, which caught at my mind, so that for a moment I tried to listen. I think it was, "He'll have gone to his house," which might have meant anyone in the city. I don't know why I noticed it. Yet I did, and my attention wandered from Ariston, just long enough for him to feel it, and for me to know he did.

This I could not bear. I was too well dressed to afford it. I would not have hurt him for the world. It is true, too, that I would not think of myself as such a man. To each his own shape of pride.

So I turned my mind to him, and talked, and listened, and got him to take a good meal with me; and before we had finished, the young Greeks left all together.

We parted, arranging to meet again (I knew better than to ask where he was living), and I walked towards my inn in the dying sunset. In the south night falls quickly; red turns to purple as you look. Whether it was this brooding light, or words heard and not heeded stirring in my head, or whether some new note reached me through the city's noise, I cannot tell, but of a sudden my heart jumped, and I understood. I had heard the truth from Kallippos. It was to Dion he had lied.

I began to run through the streets towards Ortygia. People stared at me; I ran as a child does from some bugbear he knows that only he can see. As the fading day sank to a murk in the west like blood, I knew I was running from the knowledge in my soul that it was too late.

Already shouts came from Ortygia, passed along from gate-house to gatehouse. On the palace roof stood a man with two torches, signaling his news against the darkening sky.

I did not run on, in the hope that my fears were folly, that the tumult had some other cause. I knew; and now fear was over, I did not even grieve. It was all that was left him, to die like a king in tragedy, treading upon purple to the axe behind the door. He was freed from his prison in Ortygia, in the only way he could be freed, before it closed on him forever. I had no need to be told he had died with courage, fighting like a soldier against them all. I hoped, for as long as it was possible to hope in vain, that he had not fought alone.

I had no wish to stay on in Syracuse and speak his epitaph. There was no one here to write it; that was for the old man in Athens, who had written it, I suppose, already in his heart. As for me, Kallippos would not take time to look for me, a vain actor with a head for nothing but his roles. I would sail with Ariston, who had been kind when kindness or cruelty had power to shape my soul, and see he did not die hungry, or alone. That, I thought, is as much as most men can hope to bring away from the march of history, when all is said.

# XXIV

A DOZEN YEARS HAVE PASSED SINCE THEN. I HAVE never been back to Syracuse. They say grass grows in the streets there, and it has fewer people now than a country town in Attica. Tyranny has followed tyranny (that of Kallippos was so hateful that it only lasted a year) and for a time even Dionysios himself came back to rule over the desolation. At last Corinth, the mother city, taking pity on her wretched child, sent them a general, a good man it seems. He has driven Dionysios out again; whether he can get rid of the Carthaginians, only God knows. Meantime, he has had faith enough in men to disarm Ortygia; the walls of that lair are rubble now.

Dionysios got off just with his life. He is no one any more; he keeps a boys' school in Corinth, and goes shopping in the market for his own dinner. Last time I played there, he came behind to commend me. The gods did him a backhand favor, for he can't afford to drink himself into the grave, and is merely getting fat. He still thinks himself a good judge of the drama, and held forth for some time, till some more important citizen interrupted him.

Except in Corinth, which has an interest of its own, no one thinks much about Syracuse. It is a place where things happened once. Too much is going on now in Greece, with Philip of Macedon pushing south and meddling everywhere. No one has time for a backward island, full of squabbling bandits, with all its glories in the past. I suppose now and then there are a few hundred folk in that great theater. All the good actors left years ago.

Greece has plenty of work for us. It is said that technique has never been so advanced, though it's long since I read a good new play. The great successes are all revivals, which we try to shed some new light on, or at least to present with a splendor worthy of the mighty dead.

Thettalos and I still share the house by the river, and tour as partners every few years. We have our own ways and our disagreements, but neither of us can conceive of being without the other. It is lucky I am the elder. There is a life in him which will demand its own span to work in, when I am gone, whether he likes or not.

We were together through most of this year's spring. He was crowned at the Dionysia, and gave a party which, like all his others, will be talked of through the year. Then he went touring north, to Pella. Nobody nowadays who wishes to be considered at all in theater can leave Pella out for long. Actors are so esteemed there, we even send them on embassies.

Thettalos enjoyed his tour, and came back with some handsome presents as well as his fee. He told me he felt startled when, being presented to Queen Olympias, he found her wreathed with tame snakes, which stood up and hissed at him; she seemed to have stepped straight out of *The Bacchae,* but then Pella was never dull. "Besides," he said, sighing and shaking his head, "I am in love. I have lost my heart forever. I shall never be the same again."

I was used to this declaration, and to pulling him out of whatever scrape it meant, and said I hoped this time she was not the wife of a general. I was quite relieved when he told me it was a boy, and asked if he had brought the fair one to Athens. He laughed immoderately, and said when he could get it out, "No, I was afraid of his father."

Macedon being as full as it is of powerful brigands, I praised his wisdom. He added, "And still more of his mother, and more than all of him." I raised my brows and waited. "No," he said. "You'll be at Pella next month, and can see him for yourself."

"Excellent. Tell me his name."

"You will know when you see him. He will be there. He never misses a play."

He would tell me no more, but said a little later, "When you go up to Pella, why don't you put on *The Myrmidons?*"

"My dear," I said, "I think it is time I hung up the mask of Achilles. I've left fifty behind, though it is kind of you to forget."

"Nonsense. You wear a young mask as well as ever. You know if you were making a fool of yourself I'd be the first to tell you. Do it while you can; you are a beautiful Achilles. Give them something to remember."

I was touched, and pleased, for it was true he could not have lied about it. Then I said, "But why *The Myrmidons?*"

"Well, it has not been done there for something like ten years; the young generation has never seen it."

"Thettalos!" I said. "I believe you are asking me to put on this whole production simply to oblige your boy friend."

"My . . . ?" He stared, laughed, then said, "Alas, you flatter my hopes. But it is true he is anxious to see it. I would have done it myself, if I could have raised a script in Pella."

"Couldn't he lend you his?"

"He's never had one. It is only that he has heard it follows the *Iliad,* most of which he knows by heart."

"Well," I said, "that's something. Your last flame could not read. I might really do it, if it's so long since they had it there; I should enjoy it myself."

"Good. I promise you won't regret it. But let your third man fly on as Apollo. I can't spare you, dearest Niko. The crane-man drinks."

"I've never done it, except that once in Delphi as an offering to the god." I fell silent, thinking of the war there, the
very sanctuary plundered of its gold. Nothing is sacred to our
age.

In due course I took my company to Pella, which gave us
its usual eager welcome. By now, however, they are used to
actors going to bed early before the play instead of drinking
till dawn. The noise downstairs is something one must put up
with.

King Philip has adorned King Archelaos' theater; everything
of the best. The crane-man was sober. Just before I went on, I
touched, as I always do, the antique mask of Apollo. I no
longer wear it; no one would understand it now; but I take
it everywhere, thinking, like Lamprias' old friend, that it brings
me luck. The god looked stern but serene. I thought he said
to me, "You must be good today; there are reasons. But don't
fret; I will look after you." I had been doubting myself before,
but it left me as I went on, and I don't think I was ever better.
At the end I thought, I must never do it again, for fear of
tempting the gods.

There was a crowd in the dressing room. I was still in costume, with the dresser combing my mask, when there was a
stir about the door, and the people parted, just like extras for
a big upstage entrance.

A boy was standing there, about fourteen or so, with fire-
gold hair lying loose on his brow and down his neck. All
Macedonians have blue eyes, but not of a blue like that. Half
a dozen other lads, about his age or somewhat older, were
standing behind him. When I saw that none of them pushed in
front, I guessed who he was.

He came in, sweeping his gaze about the room, and said,
"Where is Achilles?"

It is a big theater; even from the front row, one is a good
way off when one takes one's bow. I said, "Here, my lord."

He stood still, looking. His eyes were big, which made them
look even bluer. I was sorry that so beautiful a boy should be
disappointed; at his age, they always half expect the face to
match the mask. I supposed him at a loss for words, till he

came nearer and said quietly, "That is most wonderful. There must be a god in your soul."

I did not spoil it by telling him I was lucky to have kept my teeth. I said, "I had a good father, sir, to start me off young, and I keep up my practice."

"Then you've been an actor always, all your life?" When I assented, he nodded his head as if this answer satisfied him, and said, "And you always knew." He asked me one or two questions about technique, which were far from foolish; I could see that he had talked with Thettalos. Presently he looked at the people standing round and said, "You have leave to go."

They bowed out. When the lads behind him started to follow, he reached out and caught one by the arm, saying, "No, you stay, Hephaistion." The tall boy came back with a lightening of all his face, and stood close beside him. He said to me, "The others are the Companions of the Prince; but we two are just Hephaistion and Alexander."

"So it was," I said, smiling at them, "in the tent of Achilles."

He nodded; it was a thought he was used to. He came up and touched my flimsy stage armor to see how it was made. On his arm, half covered by his big gold bracelet, was a thick scar one would have thought had been done in battle if he had not been so young. His face was a little longer than the sculptors' canon, just enough to make the canon look insipid. His skin was clear, with a ruddy, even tan; he was fresh, yet warm. A sweetness came from him; not bath oil, but something of himself, like the scent of a summer meadow. I would have liked to draw him nearer, to feel the glow from him; but I would as soon have touched a flame, or a lion.

He noted that we had the place to ourselves, and said, "I have something to tell you. You shall be the first to hear. One day, I shall make a sacrifice at Achilles' tomb. Hephaistion will do it for Patroklos. It is a vow we have made."

Good news, I thought, if King Philip means to turn eastward. I said, "That's in Persia, my lord."

"Yes." He looked serene, like Apollo among the Lapiths.

"When we are there, you shall come out and play *The Myrmidons.*"

I shook my head, saying, "Even though it is soon, I shall be too old."

He looked at me with his head a little sideways, as if reckoning the time. "Perhaps," he said. "But I want to hear your voice on the plain of Troy. No one else will be the same, now. So if I ask you, you will come?"

As if he had bidden me to supper across the street, I answered, "Yes, my lord. I will come."

"I knew that you would. You understand these things. There is a question I have to ask you."

Someone coughed in the doorway. A small, dapper, thin-legged man came in, with the beard of a philosopher. He looked at the boy with dissatisfaction, like a hen that has hatched an eagle chick. The boy looked back, and then at me, as if saying, One must take men as they are, no sense in making a fuss. "Nikeratos," he said, "let me present my tutor, Aristoteles. Or perhaps you have met in Athens?"

It was plain he did not recall it, and plainer still that he didn't like being presented to an actor. One could hardly blame him. I smoothed it over as best I could. He had left the Academy, so someone had told me, in displeasure when Speusippos became its head. I had not known he was here.

Setting this business briskly aside, the boy said to me, "There is one thing in the *Iliad* I have never understood; I was hoping the play might explain it. Why didn't Achilles kill Agamemnon in the very beginning? Then Patroklos and the other heroes need not have died. Have *you* heard why it was?"

"Well, Athene counseled prudence. Agamemnon was the greater king. And he was supreme commander."

"But what a general! He wasted his men's lives. He never really led them. He robbed his best officer, to cover a debt he owed himself, and had to beg his pardon. He started a rout with a stupid order, and then couldn't even get them in hand; he had to let Odysseus do it. Can you think of anything more disgraceful? Supreme commander! He couldn't have stopped

] 363 [

a Thracian cattle raid. I can't think why Achilles didn't kill him. He owed it to the Greeks. They knew him. They'd all have followed him, and finished off the war. No one but Agamemnon could have made it last ten years. They should have taken Troy between two winters."

Aristoteles fidgeted, trying, I perceived, to get the prince away without telling him to come, in case he might say no and authority be lost. I could see the boy taking it in, not as boys do, but like a man measuring men. I think it amused him, too, but not enough to keep him long from his thought.

"If Achilles had taken Troy, I doubt he'd have sacked it, not if Patroklos was alive. (If they'd killed him—yes, then!) It was such a waste. The Trojans were fine, brave people. They could have made a great kingdom together. Think where Troy was! And all those ships, never used at all. He could have married one of Priam's daughters. *He* would never have stooped to enslave the royal ladies. I am sure of that." He gazed out past me, seeing it all. The shine from him almost scorched me. He said, speaking the verse well, "*Sing, Goddess, the destroying anger of Achilles, Peleus' son, which brought great sorrows to the Greeks. Many the brave man's soul it sent to Hades, and flung the flesh of heroes for the gorging of dogs and kites . . .* But it wasn't his anger. It was his not seeing at first what he had to do."

With his long hair, cut as they show it in the archaic statues (Macedon is full of these old customs) and his ardent eyes bluer even than theirs, he was like some kouros in ancient legend, listening for the voice of a lover who is also a god. Aristoteles coughed, and the boy withdrew himself calmly from his vision. He said, "But Achilles must have had some reason. It was so long ago—twelve generations of men, they say. I suppose the real reason has been forgotten."

Aristoteles reached out discreetly and plucked Hephaistion's tunic. The young prince looked round, as if by chance, just in time to catch him at it. "We must be going," he said, like someone rewarding a dog that has done its trick. He remained, however, standing by me. I thought it was just to tease the man. Then he said, "I have always tried, when I read the

*Iliad,* to give a voice to Achilles, and have only heard my own. He will have your voice now. This is a great gift you have given me."

As I was seeking some answer fit for this, he tugged off his arm his great heavy bracelet of Macedonian goldwork, a thrice-coiled snake with ruby eyes and delicately graven scales. He took my hand, and slid it up into place. There was a life in his touch that seemed to kindle all up my arm, with the warmed gold. "This for remembrance," he said. I thought he spoke of the gift, till he took me by both shoulders and kissed my mouth. Then he put his arm round Hephaistion's waist, and they went out together, the philosopher following behind.

This morning, having got back to Athens, I went out to the Academy. No one was about; I chose the quiet time, when everyone is working. The myrtle they planted on Plato's grave is getting thick and tall, and the marble begins to mellow.

The grove was green. But I saw in my mind the white slopes of Etna, the titan lava-rocks black on fields of snow, and the snowlight on those blue eyes, enrapt and listening.

He will wander through the world, like a flame, like a lion, seeking, never finding, never knowing (for he will look always forward, never back) that while he was still a child the thing he seeks slipped from the world, worn out and spent. Like a lion he will hunt for his proper food, and, fasting, make do with what he finds; like a lion he will be sometimes angry. Always he will be loved, never knowing the love he missed.

No one would fight for Dion, when he gave, as his own soul saw it, his very life for justice. But for this boy they will die, whether he is right or wrong; he need only gaze at them with that blue fire and say, "My friends, I believe in you." How many of us, like Thettalos, I suppose, and me, will follow this golden daimon, wherever he calls us to show him gods and heroes, kindling our art at his dreams and his dreams at our art, to Troy, to Babylon or the world's end, to leave our bones in barbarian cities? He need only call.

I thought how, before I went on at Pella, I had touched the mask for luck, and it seemed that the god had said to me,

"Speak for me, Nikeratos. Someone's soul is listening." Some-one's always is, I suppose, if one only knew. Plato never for-got it.

Sitting by the tomb, I took from my arm the golden bracelet. It seldom leaves me; most people put it down to conceit, but not Thettalos, though he laughs at me. The marble was warm with sun and dappled with shade. I laid the gold on it, as if it could speak, as if I laid a hand in a hand.

All tragedies deal with fated meetings; how else could there be a play? Fate deals its stroke; sorrow is purged, or turned to rejoicing; there is death, or triumph; there has been a meet-ing, and a change. No one will ever make a tragedy—and that is as well, for one could not bear it—whose grief is that the principals never met.

# AUTHOR'S NOTE

Nikeratos is an invented character. The inscriptions which listed the victors in the Athenian dramatic festivals survive only in fragments, few of which relate to the years covered by the story; the name of the leading man in *The Ransoming of Hector* has not come down to us. Nor is it known who the actors were, or what they did, when the exiled oligarchs of Phigeleia stormed the theater. Both events are related by Diodorus Siculus; so is the story of the chorus-man who brought Dionysios the news of his fatal victory in 368 B.C.

Thettalos and Theodoros are both named in the victors' lists, and there are literary references to their gifts and fame. I have inferred the character of Thettalos from a highly dangerous adventure he undertook on behalf of the young Alexander in 338 B.C., four years after this story closes. During one of the recurrent Macedonian family feuds, Alexander, on purpose to foil his father's dynastic plans, wanted to arrange a marriage contract between himself and the daughter of the satrap of Karia. Thettalos went on this secret mission, in which he was succeeding until Philip found out. The King's arm was by then a long one, and he had Thettalos brought to him from Corinth in chains, apparently reprieving him later. It seems unlikely that Thettalos could have expected, in the circumstances, payment from the eighteen-year-old prince in proportion to the risks involved. That he took them is informative about both parties.

Theodoros was one of the Greek theater's greatest stars. Like all other actors of the day he must have had to satisfy his audiences in male roles; but his fame rested on his tragic heroines. When he was playing Merope before Alexander of Pherai, that bloodthirsty brigand had to leave the theater, ashamed to be seen in tears.

It is important to remember that the grimacing, flat-faced masks of Tragedy and Comedy which are a cliché of today's commercial art bear no relation to anything worn on the Greek stage. Masks covered the whole head and included a wig mounted upon cloth, only the front being of rigid material. In Graeco-Roman times, as theaters grew more enormous and taste declined, tragic masks were grotesquely enlarged and stylized, while the actor was padded and raised on high pattens to give size and height. Since his neck could not be extended in proportion, the total effect became progressively uglier and more conventional. But in the fifth and fourth centuries masks followed the trend of sculpture, idealizing or enhancing nature; from the few representations that survive, they seem to have had great subtlety, variety and often beauty. The mouths were not, as with late examples, opened in a vast dolorous gape, but parted as if in natural speech.

No part of Greek life has aroused more scholarly debate than the techniques of the theater. Literary accounts are late and conflicting, contemporary references casual. In a novel one has to choose between rival theories on such matters as the use and form of the machines, and the height of the stage above the orchestra. (I have listed some books for those who would like to examine the evidence for themselves.) It is certain however that three men sustained all the speaking roles in every tragedy, the extra, if there was one, being almost or wholly mute, and that the actors somehow achieved the amazing versatility required. There is an anecdote about one who became so absorbed in doing his voice exercises that he missed his cue to go on.

By the start of the third century, actors were highly organized in guilds centered in large cities, through which their tours were arranged. The fourth century must have been a period of transition, with a good deal more left to private enterprise; I have had to conjecture what arrangements actormanagers of the time may have made for themselves. Their use in diplomacy is well attested.

Throughout the whole classical period, actors, though often dissolute in private life, were held in their work to be performing a religious rite in the service of Dionysos, or any god to whom the performance was dedicated. (For this reason they were exempt from military service.) Plato's concern about the content of plays should, in fairness, be seen not as a mere censorship of ideas, but more like the wish of an enlightened Christian to drop from the liturgy passages about the wicked gnashing their teeth in flames of eternal torment.

The deep political disillusion of the time expressed itself intellectually in a search for ideal systems, and historically in the phenomenon of Alexander. To understand it one has only to recall the long miseries of the Peloponnesian War, and to read the speeches of fourth-century politicians. The mean-minded, snobbish and dishonest personalities to which even Demosthenes sank in public controversy have to be read to be believed; and these were not published by enemies, but by the author himself after careful polishing.

For the story of Dion I have relied mainly on Plutarch, who had access to many sources now lost to us, including the accounts of Timonides and the History of Philistos. On Plato's second and third visits to Syracuse we have Plato himself. Nearly all scholars today now accept as authentic the important Seventh and Third Letters; the personal voice which sounds in both is highly persuasive.

Axiothea and Lasthenia are listed among Plato's pupils by Diogenes Laertius. He tells us nothing of their lives or personalities except that they continued at the Academy under

Speusippos after Plato's death, and that Axiothea "is said to have worn men's clothes."

Ten years after Dion's death in 354 B.C., the Syracusans appealed for help to Corinth against the renewed tyranny of Dionysios and the impending threat from Carthage. Timoleon was sent with a small force. Gifted with astuteness and luck as well as solid integrity, he was successful within a few years. Under his fatherly guidance the city enjoyed two decades of peace and prosperity before the cycle of demagogy and tyranny began again. The constitution of Timoleon seems to have been a limited democracy with a qualified franchise; in view of the grateful honors paid him during his life and after, it must have satisfied the citizens. In justice to Dion's failure one must remember that Timoleon was dealing with a different population. So decimated had the Syracusans become through war, privation and flight that one of his first measures was to invite, with their consent, new settlers to strengthen the city. He got about sixty thousand (a figure for men only, not including their families), of whom many thousands came from Corinth and other stable polities. If the Syracusan lands could support so many, there can have been very few native Syracusans left.

No true parallel exists between this passage in Syracusan history and the affairs of any present-day state. Christianity and Islam have changed irrevocably the moral reflexes of the world. The philosopher Herakleitos said with profound truth that you cannot step twice into the same river. The perpetual stream of human nature is formed into ever-changing shallows, eddies, falls and pools by the land over which it passes. Perhaps the only real value of history lies in considering this endlessly varied play between the essence and the accidents.

## AUTHOR'S NOTE

The short book list below is not a bibliography, but gives the most important sources and works of reference for anyone interested in following up the subjects concerned.

### HISTORY

Plutarch: *Lives of Dion and Timoleon.*
Plato: *Letters; Republic; Symposium.*
Diodorus Siculus: *History,* Books XV and XVI.
George Grote: *History of Greece*

### THE THEATER

Margarete Bieber: *The History of the Greek and Roman Theater.*
A. Pickard-Cambridge: *The Dramatic Festivals of Athens.*
T. B. L. Webster: *Greek Theatre Production.*
Demosthenes: Oration against Aeschines; *On the Embassy.*
Aeschines: *Orations; On the Embassy;* Reply to Demosthenes.
   (Aeschines was an ex-actor who took up a career in politics.)

Aeschylus' *The Myrmidons* has been lost to us, except for a few passages preserved as quotations in the works of other authors, some of which I have used. Out of a very large output by the three great tragic poets, only a small fraction remains. Other authors, sufficiently valued in their day to have defeated these masters in dramatic contests, are now known only by name, their entire body of work having disappeared. Plays mentioned in the story are therefore often fictional.